Fenton was grinning like a gargoyle. "The Pope never made it."

Vickers blinked. "What the hell are you talking about?"

"Wasn't the Pope supposed to have a place down here when the war came?"

"Yeah, right. I heard that."

"So he didn't make it."

Vickers shook his head. On top of everything else, Fenton was the final straw.

"You're a sick man."

Fenton continued to grin.

"Maybe, but I ain't out frying cities."

MICK FARREN

Author of the acclaimed *Phaid the Gambler* and *Citizen Phaid*:

"One of the most fully realized and realistic decadent future Earths depicted in science fiction!"
— Norman Spinrad, author of *Child of Fortune*

"Reads like a prototype for the hot, hip movement known as 'cyberpunk.'"
— New York *Daily News*

"Buy volume one first, but by all means buy them both. The fact that it took this long to reprint such a fine novel in this country ought to be a crime."
— *Science Fiction Chronicle*

Ace Books by Mick Farren

VICKERS

The Song of Phaid the Gambler

PHAID THE GAMBLER
CITIZEN PHAID

MICK FARREN
VICKERS

ACE BOOKS, NEW YORK

This book was previously published
in Great Britain (August 1986) by
the New English Library, under
the title *Corpse*.

VICKERS

An Ace Book / published by arrangement with
the author

PRINTING HISTORY
Ace edition / July 1988

ISBN: 0-441-86290-X

Ace Books are published by The Berkley Publishing Group,
200 Madison Avenue, New York, New York 10016.
The name "ACE" and the "A" logo
are trademarks belonging to Charter Communications, Inc.
PRINTED IN THE UNITED STATES OF AMERICA

10 9 8 7 6 5 4 3 2 1

ONE

IT WAS ONE of the second generation of shuttles, the kind that were already being called "Roman candles" by the media. Two of them had roman candled inside of eighteen months. Vickers' pessimism did its best to convince him that he was riding on number three. He imagined that burning up in the atmosphere would be fast. A streak of fire when the heatshield ruptured and good-bye. Would you char-broil or would the smoke get you first?

Vickers remained doggedly in his cocoon like the kid who gets to the beach and won't take off his jacket. He'd removed neither the H-bar nor the straps. He glared out balefully at the banks of electronics. LEDs rippled and twitched back at him. The cabin was filled with pulse, whistle and rumble. Vickers also glared at the crew as they moved fluidly around, reaching with their slippered feet for the velcro anchor pads. He didn't want to hear that freefall was fun. Also, he had thrown up when the shuttle started to decelerate. The contents of his stomach were still spread around the cabin in a fine floating fog of tiny droplets that tended to cluster around the larger pieces of more solid material. Vickers saw it as a microcosm of the universe. The crew hated him. On the ride out, he had thrown up three times. That crew had hated him even more.

From the very first moment, Vickers had decided that freefall was one of the nastiest things he had ever encountered. He couldn't remember many things that remained so consistently unpleasant. It was like a continuous bad dream, one of the falling kind. It went against all the lessons his ancestors had learned while they were still furry and living in a tree. His instincts told him that the conclusion of freefall was splat! No amount of logic could dispel that yawning anxiety.

The crew tended to stay as far away from Vickers as was possible in the extremely confining cabin. It wasn't just the vomit. The community of those who ventured beyond the atmosphere was small and not much could be hidden. The crew undoubtedly knew why he'd been sent from earth and what he had done. To Vickers' knowledge, he was the first man to kill in space. It had to be worth a dubious something even if it was only a measure of privacy.

The target had been short and balding with a gut and a goatee. His name was Wilson Theodore Dewhurst, age 35, chemist. Vickers usually didn't ask why. The information was never volunteered although there was always rumor. Rumor had it that Dewhurst had developed some wild theory that the continuously recycled water on the big donuts contained contaminants that would have everyone who drank it down with liver cancer in five to seven years. A story like that can run through a donut crew with potentially disastrous results. Dewhurst had had to go.

As Dewhurst was a Contec employee and working on the Contec donut, it was therefore down to a Contec corpse to put him to sleep. Since Vickers was generally acknowledged as the best of the Contec corpses, it had fallen to him to do the deed.

There were four of the big donuts, each one owned and operated by one of the Big Four. The smaller corporations had to make do with drones and robots. The satellites of the Big Four contained men. They hung in their geosynchronous orbits some forty thousand klicks out with human creatures inside them going about their weird business. Originally the agency had wanted to call the donuts RWs—rotating wheels—but ABC News had called the first one a donut and the name had stuck.

All corporations constantly generated their own words and

expressions. Some were euphemistic, others were just bizarre. The designation Corpse was an example of the sickness of corporate humor. CORPorate Security Exec. Corpse. Get it? A killer for the corporation. There was an ambiguous saying among corpses and those who dealt with them. "The best killers have already died." It probably started with the Japanese. Their lives are run by that kind of thing.

In theory, the hit had been a simple one. Vickers thought that it was a particularly stupid decision. Killing the sucker would only validate his theory. As usual, though, he bit down on his opinion and scrolled through the program. As the computer told it, the round trip on the shuttle was the dangerous part. All he had to do was to walk in and garrote Dewhurst in his sleep. It is, of course, a very foolish and dangerous act to fire a gun in a spacestation.

According to the data, Dewhurst slept alone. This wasn't true. At the time in question, Dewhurst had, in fact, been in bed with a physicist five years his junior, called George. From the way they were breathing, it sounded like they were both drunk. Vickers had raised a silent eyebrow. The computer had told him that Dewhurst was heterosexual and a non-drinker. Maybe the strain was getting to him.

Vickers had raised Dewhurst's head by the back of his hair. He had deftly flicked the length of thin stainless steel wire around his neck and jerked outwards on the black plastic handles. Dewhurst didn't know a thing. George was something of a problem. The request had called for a single termination. It had not called for a witness. Dewhurst and George were pressed together in a narrow bunk, buttoned in by a safety web. Dewhurst had spasmed briefly before he died. George grunted and moved his hand. He seemed to be attempting to caress Dewhurst's shoulder. Vickers had held his breath and readied the garrote. George sighed. He slumped and inhaled with a loud snore. In that instant he'd saved his life. Vickers slipped out of the cubical. George's certain hysteria when he woke with a hangover and a strangled lover could cause some useful confusion.

As always, the soulsickness began immediately after the deed. Disgust gnawed at him. Inner voices, thick with contempt, reproached and berated him. There was nothing he could do to fight it. The sickness followed a kill as surely as the tension preceded it and the brief flash of exultation accompanied it. He was unclean. He hated himself and the huge, devious, slithering mass of the corporation that owned him. The voices told him that it was a vicious dog world, corrupt with creeping life. He was the one that did their dirty work. Perhaps the Japanese were right. "The best killers have already died." When you're dead inside you don't feel the sickness. Vickers' only consolation was that the sickness would pass.

The station execs who escorted him to the shuttle looked like they wanted to handle him with long tongs. It was as though they thought that he was leaving a trail of slime in their bright, white, sterile corridors. Okay suckers, you want to put your hands on your hearts and say that you don't have anything ugly or dangerous brewing in your labs? As they walked, it appeared they were permanently in the bottom of a concave dip. It was an illusion of the centrifugal force that passed as gravity on the donuts.

He caught one of the station execs looking at him out of the corner of his eye. It was a look that he'd seen a hundred times after a kill. They all wanted to know how it felt. How did it feel to kill another of your species? They were fascinated by the idea of being able to inflict death. Vickers could remember one time when he himself had looked with that look. He had been about thirteen. The checkout clerk in the corner store had been shot dead in a robbery. He had been standing on the sidewalk watching when the killer was brought out in handcuffs. The young Vickers had wondered how it felt.

The trouble with squares was that they equated death with sex. These fools were looking at him like small boys in the schoolyard who know that one of their number has gone all the way with a girl.

As Vickers crawled from the umbilical and into the cabin of the shuttle, the execs' contempt was echoed in the faces of the crew. At that point Vickers had resolved to remain buttoned up in his bunk until the wheels touched. He wanted out of this little world in space. It was too clean and too innocent.

The shuttle started to vibrate; it shuddered and bucked. Vickers was leaking sweat from every pore. It sounded like it was tearing itself apart. A terrible metallic clanging echoed through the ship. Vickers was unashamedly terrified. At any moment he expected to see white-hot gas fountaining through a hole in the hull. A voice crackled in his headset.

"Nothing to get twisted about, my friend. We're just hitting the atmosphere. If you look forward through the ports you can see the glow of the heatshield."

Vickers muttered under his breath. "I'm not a tourist. What happens if there's a tile missing?"

If anybody heard him they didn't acknowledge. Someone shut off the interior lights. All that remained was the red glare of the heatshield, blazing as it absorbed the first contact with the atmosphere. The cold green, amber and red of the electronics was punctuated by the occasional small patch of cathode blue. Vickers tugged off the headset, tightened his grip on the cocoon's grabholds and resolutely shut his eyes.

The violent motion of the shuttle became more controlled and regular. The random whomps and shudders organized themselves into a series of measured, heavy bounces, like a rock that's been skimmed across the surface of a lake. Vickers tentatively opened one eye. The glow increased just before each bounce and faded a little afterwards. Vickers closed his eyes again. He wanted as little as possible to do with the mechanics of what he was still convinced would be his death.

The bouncing went on for quite a long time. Vickers was almost getting used to it. Despite himself, he had started to ride the rhythm. Then there was a bounce that was nothing like those that had gone before. The shuttle wallowed. It seemed to slide sideways. The grabholds were slick under his palms. The ship was dropping away. He was convinced that it was falling. He hated any situation in which he was powerless. He knew it. The damn thing was falling away to the side. Something was pulling him down into the cocoon. They'd lost it. The crew had screwed up and lost it.

And then the shuttle was behaving like a plane. It was flying. He opened his eyes. Sunlight flooded through the forward windshield. Freefall had gone and reliable gravity was back. His arms and legs felt impossibly heavy. He didn't think that he could lift his head. The crew were heaving themselves out of their cocoons. One of them was leaning over him, standing on the cabin floor like a real person. She pointed to the headset, indicating that he should put it on. Vickers scowled and did as he was told. He noted in passing that she was really quite pretty. Even in space, she wore eyeshadow. She was probably Korean. Koreans seemed driven to excel. A male voice grunted out of the headset.

"We'll be down within the hour. You might as well climb

out of some of that webbing. You'll only need a lapstrap, just like on a regular scheduled flight."

Vickers sniffed and flexed his fingers. He hadn't realized how tightly he'd been squeezing the grabholds.

"I think I'll stay as I am."

"It's up to you, friend, but if you do, you're a damned fool. If we have any problem on landing, you'll never get out of all that stuff."

Vickers made a low growling sound deep in his throat but he touched the cocoon's attitude control and returned it to a sitting position. He swung up the rubber-padded H-bar and started unhooking the webbing. A man had to know the difference between stubbornness and stupidity. A couple of the crew were grinning at him. He ignored them. He went right on ignoring them until the wheels touched. At the very last moment, the shuttle popped a wheelie. It was like a final insult, a final tweak at his nerves.

Vickers took a limousine into Manhattan from Kennedy. Originally, he had intended to take a taxi, even a train or a bus, as anonymous as his blue jeans and his white lightweight jacket. On the commercial flight up from New Mexico, he had cleanslated himself. At thirty thousand feet, the few credentials of Hamilton Dryden, the identity who had gone into space and killed, had been carefully cut into plastic slivers and flushed down the lavatory and into the septic tank of the 921.

In that moment, he was Mort Vickers again. When a man changed identities as often as he did, it was hard to stay in touch with who you really were. It took an act of faith to believe that he had always been Mort Vickers. He had stared at himself in the mirror of the 921's lavatory. He was tall, he was slim and, at the moment, his hair was dark. The problem was his face. He could swear that it was starting to blur into something like one of those composite photographs that are supposed to be a picture of Mister Average, the kind that has no discernable features and no discernable character. He reminded the mirror who he was. Mort Vickers, thirty-four and the best executioner that Contec had ever had. How could it be otherwise? His past was little more than a series of bloody traumas of which he was usually the sole survivor. How was it that none of the deaths and none of the pain showed in his face?

In the beginning, he'd had no choice. He'd been drafted and

he'd been too macho dumb to weasel out of it. Six months later, he had been in Yemen. After what had gone down there, there was no possibility of turning back. He had re-upped and volunteered for the debacle in Panama. After that, there had been the freelance jobs and finally the invitation to the corporation. Neither the slaughter nor the horror ever stopped. It only ebbed and flowed. The best killers are already dead.

The desire to travel by limo was clearly a product of a need to be someone other than Mort Vickers as fast as possible. He reflected on this as he picked up the courtesy phone under the Laverne Continental sign. If he was going to fall straight away into a new ID, it might as well be an affluent one. He hated assignments where he had to shuffle around as a wino. Pride dictated that he do them, but he didn't have to like poverty.

Once inside the womblike back of the stretch Lincoln, he poured himself a drink, turned on the TV and selected a new identity from the small collection in his case. Joseph Pope. He half smiled. Pope was the richest of the collection. He could live very handsomely as Joseph Pope for the few days before he was plugged back in. Joseph Pope would be a man who knew how to unwind. He told the driver to take him to the Plaza.

The driver was a strange combination of black and blond in a severely jackbooted uniform. The blonde came from a bottle but the black was natural. As he'd climbed into the car, she'd snapped off a flashy salute. He'd forgotten that Laverne Continental was strictly a showtime operation. The competition between limo lines was intense. They'd never really recovered from the Millennium Fair. She spent most of the ride sizing him up. Vickers pretended not to notice, and stared, stonefaced, at the TV. All you could get in the car was the networks. On ABC, *Grab* was in its second hour. The contestants were on the floor howling and fighting for money. Vickers turned the sound up and waited. It took until almost the Midtown Tunnel before the intercom flashed. Vickers killed off *Grab*.

"Hello."

"We'll be in Manhattan in a few minutes. Is there anything I can do for you before we reach the Plaza?"

"Do?"

"Anything you might want but not know how to get."

Vickers shrugged.

"I can always use a few pills."

"What sort of pills?"

"Greenies, Marvols . . ."

"You'll have to get those from the bellhop at the Plaza. I can sell you twenty eighty-eights."

Vickers grinned.

"They'll do."

"Let down the security glass."

Vickers hesitated for an instant before he touched the button. It could be an elaborate trap but it was unlikely. If they'd been meaning to hit him they'd have done it way back in Queens. A hand reached through with a small baggie in it. Twenty eighty-eights. Vickers went to take it but the hand held back. "Fifty."

"Can I charge it on the bill?"

"Fuck no, this is free enterprise."

There were two schools of thought about Manhattan. Some said that you cleanslated it so nobody noticed you. Others claimed that you took on the strongest ID and hoped that if anybody did notice you they'd be convinced that you were somebody else. The one thing that everyone agreed on, on the few anxious occasions that corpses got together to agree on anything, was that Manhattan was lousy with bounts.

Bounts were what stopped the occupation of corpse from being a very attractive one. Bount was corpse talk for bounty hunter. They were a product of corporation policy. Bounts had a twisted Darwinism about them. Involuntarily, they policed the ranks of corpses. They picked off the stragglers. They preyed upon the weak and unwary. Each corporation had a price on the head of every known corpse of every other corporation. Bounts came out of the woodwork to claim the money. You could get the information from a terminal in any bank, hotel or train station, descriptions, pictures, all known ID that a particular corpse might be using. ID departments were constantly being penetrated and each time any corpse so much as used a credit card, there was a flash of fear.

The real trouble was that anyone could be a bount. Anyone could get a bunch of descriptions and start going after corpses. It was legalized murder. Nothing would happen to you if you killed a corpse as long as you didn't do it right in front of a cop. On the other side of the coin, though, nothing would happen to the corpse if he killed you. Such was the power and also the nature of the corporations. Bounts were invariably the worst.

They were psychos and short-spans, and terrorists without a cause, the drug wreckage of five continents and those who just liked to ultimately do it to others.

The corpses had fought the system for as long as it had been in existence. Their argument was simple. A corpse's life was hard enough. Why complicate matters with a lot of homicidal amateurs lurking around each corner waiting to ventilate you. The end result was that highly trained operatives went nuts from anxiety long before their natural time. It was needless and inefficient. Naturally, the argument cut no ice with the corporate execs. Something like the bounty system was a way for them to get their kicks. They saw it as a bolder, more absolute version of the way they perceived their own lives. It was competition brought to a razor's edge, and wasn't competition what fueled the free enterprise system?

There were times when the corporations went completely too far and even exceeded their own slight standards of decency. When McKinney was all-time hot at D&C, Soji had come out with a television commercial on him, an actual prime-time commercial with a half-dozen clips of McKinney: McKinney walking on the street, McKinney in a bar, McKinney at an airport, some shots of McKinney at home that only indicated, at least half the time, that they were using a look-alike. The sound track had been blatant. "Have you seen this man? This man is a killer. This man is worth $100 thousand—dead!" The music was like something from a snuff flick. In fact, according to market research, more than two-thirds of the people who saw the first airing assumed that it was a teaser campaign for a movie.

In the following week enough people caught on in the markets where the Soji corporation had run the commercials to cause the violent deaths of twenty-seven people who looked a little like McKinney. Ironically, McKinney himself was un-scathed. The protests followed thick and fast. Rival corporations used their media subsidiaries to set up a ringing scream of outrage. D&C, McKinney and the relatives of the slain all filed suits against Soji in the courts of a dozen countries. Even some national governments tried to get in on the act but, even back then, their power had been so eroded and they were so enfeebled by their own corruption that there was no real chance that they could stand up to the corporations.

At first, Soji was intransigent. They didn't want to compromise. McKinney had wasted the five-man design team that was masterminding their most precious of secret projects. They were about as crazy mad as a predominently Oriental corporation could get. They only relented when everyone else started gearing up for a consumer boycott. They issued a somewhat stilted apology and paid off the relatives. In a way, Soji actually won. McKinney never worked again. After all the publicity, he knew that he had to hang it up.

About the only positive thing that came out of the entire debacle was a kind of ad hoc agreement that pros didn't go after pros except in the line of duty. The only time a corpse went after bounty was when he was perilously on the skids. Bounty meant it was the end.

The desk clerk at the Plaza seemed a little distressed by Vickers' blue jeans, his lightweight jacket and his singular lack of luggage. The distress faded a little when Vickers proffered gilt-edged plastic. It didn't fade completely, though. Here and there in the world, there were still places like the Plaza that tried to maintain the pretense that money wasn't everything.

For a corpse, a hotel was a mixed blessing. It was a place off the street and out of the rain but there was no true security. Maids and bellhops came and went, phone and computer lines went through central switch gear. Too many people going in and out, too many people listening, no locks that didn't have a spare key. The only real way to stay safe was to remain random. The clerk smiled and handed Vickers a key. Vickers scowled and asked for a different room.

Once inside, he took a four-way detector from his case and scanned the suite. The detector showed nothing except the smoke alarms and the simple tamper sensors on the door. This didn't actually mean very much. Surveillance technology had become a matter of gizmo and countergizmo. No sooner was a new spy toy developed than someone invented one that could negate its usefulness. Life at the top of the line for a bugging device was little more than three months. His detector was last year's model. If there was anything at all sophisticated in the room, it would know nothing about it. He threw the detector onto the bed and turned his attention to the other equipment in his case.

He picked up the Yasha 7 and thumbed both the ammunition and battery checks. LEDs obediently glowed green. Vickers handled the compact, plastic machine pistol almost lovingly.

The Yasha was anything but last year's model. It was state of the art for sideautos. He looked around for somewhere to stash it. The refrigerator was as good a place as any. He went back into the bedroom, took his second gun, a Walther 9mm, from the case and slipped it under the pillow. Now there was a gun at either end of the suite. All he had left were shirt, socks, underwear, his remaining four identities and the bag of eighty-eights. The shirt, etc., went into a drawer, the identities were hidden under the carpet. With a strange meticulousness, the eighty-eights were placed on a glass shelf in the bathroom. He could consider his next move.

He needed a drink. In fact, he needed several. According to the book, he was in a situation where he should go out to an anonymous bar or, better still, not drink at all. To hell with it, hadn't he helped write the book? He called room service. He was exhausted. While he waited for the three double scotches and the quart of milk, he decided to make a start on building an image for Joseph Pope. He reached for the TV remote, flipped for Shopex and ordered several thousand dollars' worth of clothes from Barney's. It was a wordrobe suitable for the self-obsessed rich boy who had never done a real day's work in his life that Vickers was conjuring in his imagination.

Despite his previous bravado, Vickers jerked when the knock on the door came. He flashed the scene in the corridor outside. It looked like a perfectly normal waiter with a perfectly normal tray. Even the order was correct. Vickers forced himself to act like a perfectly normal guest and opened the door.

All went according to plan. The drinks were set on the table and the bill was signed, the tip accepted. With the door closed behind the waiter, Vickers sighed into a chair and started his first scotch. He was suddenly very aware that he was in the Plaza. He stood up and walked over to the window. The sinister velvet gloom of Central Park was spread out below him. He turned and surveyed the room. The real secret of the Plaza was that everything was a little larger than you expected. It was as though their fittings and their fixtures and their furniture, even the rooms themselves, continued to be designed for the original weighty robber barons, the Morgans and the Astors and the Vanderbilts who had built the city and built it large.

Through the second scotch and milk he slightly mellowed. He began to feel just a little human. He wondered if he should do something outgoing. That would be the style of Joseph Pope. He'd call a woman, eat at a restaurant, go to a nightclub or, at the very least, take a cab downtown and get drunk. Unfortunately, he couldn't be Joseph Pope yet. Joseph Pope's clothes had still to arrive. He was still Mort Vickers who had been to space to kill and was weary as hell. He sank deeper into his chair with something close to relief. He flipped around the TV dial. He paused for a few seconds at an old Jamie Lee Curtis movie and then flipped on.

During the third scotch he decided to call Myra. In his heart, he knew it was a stupid idea and by the third ring he was hoping that she was out.

"Hello."

"It's me."

"What the hell are you calling me for?"

"I don't know. I just wanted to speak to you."

"What are you trying to pull? Are you trying to con me that you can feel anything?"

"Myra, listen . . ."

"I don't want to talk to you. I told you after the last time, I can't take you, Mort. There's too much wrong with you. I can't deal with it and there's too much to ignore."

"Myra, I'm telling you . . ."

"Are you drunk?"

"A little."

"I don't want to talk to you, Mort."

"But I want to talk to you."

"Have you just killed someone?"

"Why don't you turn me in for the bounty? I'm up to sixty-five thou."

"Get off my phone, Mort."

"Myra, I need to talk to someone."

"Not to me, Mort."

"Myra!"

"Good night, Mort."

"Myra!"

"Good night, Mort."

She hung up. Vickers had an urge to redial her number and start yelling abuse. Instinct restrained him. If he pushed her too far, she might turn him in. In that moment, he felt wrenchingly lonely.

When the order from Barney's arrived, he wasn't as casual

as he'd been with the waiter. His instructions to the desk clerk were precise and clear.

"I want your people to bring up packages. I don't want Barney's' delivery people coming up here. Do you understand me? I don't want them up here."

The desk clerk assured Vickers that it would be Plaza employees who would bring up the considerable quantity of packages.

"First, however, sir, we have to settle payment. Would you please place your card in the slot on top of the television set—magnetic side down, please."

Carrying the phone with him, Vickers did as he was asked.

"Thank you, sir. Four thousand, six hundred and thirty-seven dollars and nineteen cents have been deducted from your account."

Vickers grinned. Contec could afford it. He dialed room service and ordered more drinks.

When the captain and five bellhops paraded in with his purchases, it was like the opulence of a lost age. The single advantage of permanent unemployment is that there were a lot of surplus people only too willing to fetch and carry for those with money. When the packages were neatly stacked, Vickers beckoned to the captain. He handed him a twenty.

"What channel have you got the hooker commercials buried on this week?"

The captain smiled and winked. "J7, sir."

"Thank you."

When they were gone, he flipped to the channel. Some of the whores used a soft sophisticated come on, fuzzy focus, big soulful eyes, red lips and risqué patter. It was, after all, the Plaza. Others preferred a more basic approach. They displayed their tricks for the tricks. Vicker's eye was caught by a pair of supposed twins. In the brief video clip, they were performing an act that, if not cruel, was certainly unusual. The recipient was a sallow, Hispanic teenager who seemed less than overjoyed by their attentions. Vickers decided that they were the kind for whom Joseph Pope would go. He tapped the displayed number into the phone.

A voice answered that might conceivably have belonged to one of the twins in the commercial. He gave his location and a brief outline of his preferences. Once again he slipped his card into the slot for a credit check. On the spur of the moment, he asked a final question.

"Do you have a video tape of the two of you fucking?"

While he waited for them to arrive, he took a swift shower, swallowed two eighty-eights and opened the packages. For Vickers, it was almost like Christmas. Most of his Christmases were a solitary vice. Finally he slipped into a yellow kimono with some sort of Oriental bird on the back. He inspected himself in a full-length mirror. Sure, he was Joseph Pope. He'd pass as a rich idiot.

When the two women arrived—separately and about four minutes apart, the Plaza still having its standards—they proved to be less than identical. The resemblance was mainly a result of common makeup and matching wigs. Vickers wasn't particularly disappointed. At best, hookers were a tacky illusion that matched his own make believe. In the care of a pair of well-paid professionals, he had at least a passing chance of pretending that he was enjoying himself. It was little wonder that Myra refused to speak to him.

"Did you bring the video tape?"

Late the following morning, Vickers called his control. He had been putting it off since the previous day. There was something lightheaded about the short periods when he was beyond their reach. He was free to be irresponsible. There was nothing he needed to think about except indulging himself. The only threatening thought was that, sooner or later, he had to plug himself back in. He noted the time as he punched up the special number. It was 11:57, almost high noon. Do not forsake me, oh my darling. The voice that answered could have been any receptionist.

"Designated Projections."

Vickers didn't recognize the voice.

"Victoria Morgenstern, please."

"May I say who's calling?"

"Tell her that Joseph Pope is calling."

"Does Ms. Morgenstern know you, Mr. Pope? Will she know what this is about?"

"She will when I tell her."

"I have my instructions, Mr. Pope."

Vickers found himself on hold. Rinky-dink idiot music came down the line. He hoped that the receptionist would know enough to check Joseph Pope against the phony ID directory. Victoria had a weakness for pretty but idiot bimbos fronting her office. The receptionist came back on the line.

"I'm afraid Ms. Morgenstern has no recollection of ever speaking to you. Perhaps if you wrote . . ."

Another bimbo. An earlier lapse of Victoria's had all but gotten him killed during a messy little incident in Milan.

"Sweetheart, did you ever hear of a code seven?"

There was an audible intake of breath. "Oh."

Victoria was instantly on the line.

"Where the hell have you been?"

"I took the night off, any objections?"

"There wasn't supposed to be a witness."

"You're damn right there wasn't supposed to be a witness. There was nothing in the profile about him being a gay drunk, either."

"Why didn't you kill the other one as well?"

"I was only asked for one victim. Besides, he didn't wake up. Do we have to talk about this on an open line?"

"Where are you?"

"I'm not going to tell you that. I'll come to you."

"This isn't some weird attempt to jerk me around, is it Mort?"

"Would I do anything like that? If anyone's complaining about what went down on the donut, they can complain to someone else but me. I was incorrectly briefed."

Victoria Morgenstern was someone whom Vickers would never jerk around. Victoria Morgenstern was an exceedingly determined and ruthless woman. Only the exceedingly determined and ruthless rose to head a corporate death squad. Victoria had enjoyed what used to be called a checkered career. At seventeen, she had been the mistress of Ruggy Toliver, who had invented the concept of retroactive foreclosure and made himself fabulously rich in the process. Ruggy had been 67 at the time with a set of sexual tastes that had become severely baroque. Before he finally died in harness, Ruggy had introduced Victoria to the fact that a substantial section of the power elite had a devilish need to physically ease their most deep-seated guilts.

Even before Ruggy was suitably buried, the family settled an undisclosed sum on Victoria with the understanding that she should depart quietly and never darken their self-image again.

She and her finely honed services were eagerly snapped up by the venerable C.J. Caulfield. In his late seventies, C.J. was known in the media as the friend of Presidents. If anything, he was richer than even Ruggy, but he was also eaten up by cancer. Despite that, C.J. was a good deal more outgoing than Ruggy. He was no longer able to participate but liked to watch. Victoria discovered that her main duties with C.J. were that of hostess, organizer and sexual stage manager at his regular but distinctly bizarre soirées. It wasn't on just one level that C.J. was the friend of Presidents. When he finally terminated, she managed to hold onto her position as queen of the Washington dungeons. She arranged the parties, hired the boys and girls and saved the video tapes. It wasn't long before it dawned on even that particularly self-obsessed group that the young woman had a quite unreasonable hold over them. It was decided that she either had to be killed or co-opted.

Victoria had no desire to die and readily went along with the new life plan that had been devised by a worried consortium of lover/clients. She abandoned her whips and all but the most crucial of her files and allowed herself to be enfolded by a corporation. At about the same time, she abandoned men. Vickers didn't know who had offered her the introduction to corporate homicide but it had been an inspired guess. Victoria had risen rapidly through the control division until she commanded Contec operations in the United States from the clandestine center in Manhattan.

"When are you going to come in?"

"I don't know. I figured I'd take a few days off. Just as long as some bount doesn't make me."

"I can't spare you that long. There's a panic brewing. I want you available."

Vickers started to protest. "I'm not ready to plug in. I don't want to be available. I've been to space and back. I'm stressed out. I need rest."

"I can't spare you."

"You have four hundred operatives. You can get by without me."

"Do I have to have you brought in?"

Vickers was angry. The damned woman was asking too much.

"You'd have to find me first."

She sounded out of patience. "We'd find you."

Vickers knew that this was true.

"Okay, okay, I'll come over but I'm damned if I'm going straight out on another assignment."

"I'll expect you in an hour."

Vickers slammed down the phone. Who the hell do they think I am? I'm no fucking superman. I need rest. I need relaxation. I am not a machine. He fumed as he dressed himself in one of Joseph Pope's daytime suits. He continued to fume as he removed the 9mm from beneath the debris of the bed and dropped it into a clip-on holster in back of the waistband of his pants. The fact that he was still fuming when he closed the door of the suite behind him and started down the corridor was almost certainly what made him careless.

The blast of pressure noise knocked him off his feet. He clutched groggily for the wall. Hands grabbed him. They were going through his pockets. They had his keys. They also found his gun. His vision was blurry. He swung out with both fists and feet, but he was roughly slammed back against the wall. The sonic blast had left him weak as a kitten. He was bundled back to the door of his suite. The door was unlocked and he was pushed inside.

It turned out that there was only one of them. She was, however, enormous, without a doubt some steriod beef job in an orange sweatsuit. Her hair was greased back, she had a five o'clock shadow and there was thick hair on her massive arms. The blast of pressure noise was starting to wear off. Vickers tried to struggle to his feet. She slapped him open-handed and he was sent staggering. Had she been an athlete or was she just a leftover from the muscle craze? The noise generator was in her pocket. She was pointing his own gun at him. She juggled it from hand to hand as she pulled the plugs from her ears. She was laughing at him.

"So how does it feel to be on the receiving end?"

Vickers shook his head. He couldn't speak. He finally managed to get onto his feet. The woman slowly walked around him.

"You sure don't look like no sixty-five grand."

Even a steriod beef could hunt bounty. Vickers was disgusted with himself for being caught so easily. He blustered without conviction.

"I don't know what you're talking about. If it's money you want . . ."

"You can cut the crap. I've checked you out. You're a Contec corpse called Mort Vickers and you're worth sixty-five thou—dead."

"My name is Joseph Pope, and if it's money you want . . ."

"Save your breath, Vickers, you're going to die."

Vickers shrugged.

"Why don't you get it over with, then?"

The woman shook her head.

"Oh, no, nothing as easy as that. Strip."

She wasn't only steriod beef. She was also a sadist. What were steriods supposed to do to the personality?

"Strip?"

"I said strip. What's the matter with you? Shy or something? I want to see more of what they're paying sixty-five grand for."

"And what will you do if I don't? Shoot me?"

The woman grinned. "I could hurt you plenty without using this gun. Nothing you could do to stop me."

Vickers didn't bother to resist any more. As he took off Joseph Pope's daytime suit, the huge woman lowered herself into a chair as though expecting a show.

"You're a sorry specimen." Her voice was an approximation of a bullfrog.

"At least I'm natural."

For one so big she was amazingly fast. He hardly saw the punch coming before his head exploded.

"Wipe that stupid expression off your face and get down on your hands and knees."

How weird was this going to get? The woman mountain settled herself back in the chair.

"You don't look much like the big bad killer."

Vickers didn't say anything. He stared resolutely at the pile of the carpet. He didn't want to show that he was sick with fear. This, however, didn't satisfy the woman.

"Hey! I'm talking to you. Look at me while I'm talking to you or I'll break your kidneys."

Vickers looked up. She was clearly getting her kicks from watching him grovel. He didn't want to guess what might be next on the menu. She started to answer the question he was hoping to avoid.

"This is going to take a long time. I've got plans for you."

Vickers wondered what would happen if he simply began

screaming. He didn't really want to find out. Then the steriod woman stopped his train of thought dead on the tracks.

"You got any booze?"

Vickers was so stunned that he almost said no. He caught himself in the nick of time.

"Yes . . . there's some vodka. It's . . . in the refrigerator."

He could feel sweat running down the inside of his arms. Her bloated, meaty cheeks dimpled nastily. She gestured with the 9mm.

Vickers got to his feet. He walked slowly to the fridge, doing his best to look totally humilated. He opened the fridge. The woman's chair creaked. Was she getting up, coming up behind him? He didn't want to look back. The Yasha was on the top shelf. He put his hand on it. The black plastic grip was cold to his touch. The fingers of his right hand curled around it. With his thumb he moved the control to full auto. Red LEDs came to life. His left hand folded around the barrel.

"What's keeping you?"

Vickers turned, firing. The Yasha blared its high-speed snake hiss. His teeth were bared and he was snarling. He savored the instant of complete atavism and then he became coldly practical. The steriod woman had been blown across the room. She was a mess. There was blood on three walls. He stood perfectly still and listened. There were no running feet. No one was beating on the door. Perhaps he hadn't been heard. His next move was clothes. Joseph Pope's daytime suit wouldn't do. He was on the run until further notice. He selected a leather space jacket with built-up shoulders that was of ample enough cut to hide the Yasha. He pulled his spare IDs from under the carpet and stuffed them into his coat. The case and the detector could stay where they were. So could the 9mm. It had no serial number and the steriod woman's fingerprints were all over it. It would add a token confusion. At the door, he hesitated and hurried back to the bathroom. He grabbed the bag of eighty-eights, swallowed two and dropped the rest into his pocket.

He eased carefully into the corridor. It was always possible that the steriod woman had brought some backup. Nothing happened. There was no alarmed Plaza security or lurking bounty hunters. Vickers quietly closed the door and started toward the elevators. He turned a corner and was startled by a maid with her pushcart of mops, brooms, cleaning materials and fresh stationery. She looked at him with complete indifference. It seemed impossible but apparently she'd heard nothing.

Once inside the elevator, he felt safe enough to take his hand off the Yasha under his coat. Three floors down, a pair of middle-aged women filled the car with Chanel No. 5. They glanced at him briefly but again the looks were indifferent. Every time that he killed, he expected the first people he encountered to smell the death on him but they never did.

He walked swiftly through the muted sparkle of the cut-glass lobby, whirled through the revolving doors and started down the steps. On the nearside of the street, yellow cabs were coming and going, on the far side, chauffeurs lounged against a line of limos. Beyond them, tourists sat on the steps of the fountain. A couple was feeding the pigeons. One of the Plaza doormen was looking enquiringly at him. Did he want a cab? Vickers realized that he had no plan. He hadn't thought ahead. He started toward the first available cab. It was a yellow Mercedes. There seemed to be more of them each time he came to New York. As he reached for the door handle, he spotted a face among the tourists by the fountain. Recognition was a shock. It was one of the whores from the night before. In the same instant, she spotted him.

She nudged a companion, a man in nondescript overalls. They were both looking at him. It all fell into place. The hooker must have made him for a corpse. She, the man and the steriod woman had decided to go after the sixty-five thou. They'd been confident. Steriod woman had thought she could handle him on her own. Vickers twisted away from the cab. The world went into slow motion as his reflexes took over. The doorman looked confused. The whore's companion was holding some kind of gift-wrapped package. He was desperately ripping it open. He was shaking the wrapping from a squat military-green object. It was a gun, one of those Brazilian frag guns that fired exploding .50 caliber plastic bullets.

Vickers was on his knees. The man had to be mad. A frag gun was a ludicrous weapon to use in a crowd unless you wanted to kill the whole crowd. They were wildly inaccurate and slaughtered en masse. The hooker's companion had laid it across the roof of a limo. A chauffeur turned to protest and caught the first bullet. The second hit the Mercedes cab. The third exploded somewhere behind Vickers as he hit the ground and rolled.

Would anyone notice that he had started for cover before the shooting began?

The main entrance to the Plaza was instantly turned into a scene from a nightmare. One of the revolving doors had been blow apart. Five people were dead and at least twice that number injured. Art Nouveau glass cascaded down from the big decorative awning. The hooker, her companion and three innocent tourists were cut down in a crossfire from Plaza rent-a-cops and regular NYPD. The companion's final shots had gone wild.

When the gas tank of the Mercedes exploded, Vickers was blown against the wall. He began to crawl. The sidewalk was made of blood and glass. A blown-apart suitcase had strewn a weird top layer of stockings and lingerie. He reached 58th Street. He got to his feet and fled, heading west at a desperate trot. There was sufficient panic for him not to be conspicuous. At Sixth Avenue, he slowed to a walk. The air was filled with sirens shrieking and whooping like every emergency unit in New York was running to the carnage at the Plaza.

He turned down Seventh. His mind was numb. He just kept walking. The air was steamy and the sidewalks were choked with people. He noticed that they were starting to step out of his way as though he was a psycho or a crazy drunk. At 49th Street he ducked into a bar. The bathroom stank of the battle between urine and industrial strength disinfectant, the walls were caked with graffiti but at least there was a functioning sink and a cracked mirror. He looked bad. His face was filthy and beaded with sweat. The patrons in the bar probably thought he was a junkie. There was a tear in the shoulder of his leather coat.

After washing up, he looked a little better. He swallowed two straight scotches and another eighty-eight and he hit the street again. On the big screen that floated at the southern end of Times Square there were already pictures of the bloody front of the Plaza. A giant microphone was thrust into the face of an equally giant cop. The cop shrugged. There was too much background din to hear the audio but the caption read ". . . but, did the bounty hunter's victim die in the massacre?"

Vickers halted. This was all getting far too close. It came

frighteningly closer. The screen was filled with an enormous blotchy photograph of himself. It was almost certainly taken by a security camera. It was followed by a gruesome shot of the interior of his room and the dead steroid woman. Then the screen lost interest in his problems and switched to a story about Tomoyo Nakamora, the Japanese porno star who had contracted to fuck with a mountain gorilla on live television. Vickers felt himself hemmed in. All around him were the disorganized mobs of slowly shuffling gawkers. The sharks that preyed on them darted and briefly flashed. Vickers knew that he had to get away. He had to get off the streets. He had to put himself on ice until the incident at the Plaza had become old news. He pushed his way to a pay phone and deposited a dollar. He tapped out the number from memory. It rang four times before anyone answered.

"Yeah?"

"Joe?"

"Yeah, I think so. Who is this?"

"It's Mort."

"Mort? Where are you? Are you in New York? I'm groggy. The phone woke me."

"Yeah, I'm in New York. Can I come over?"

"Now?"

Vickers glanced around. A tall, skinny black man in dreadlocks and a lot of gold was staring at him intently. Had he recognized him or did he just want the phone?

"Yes, now."

"Are you in trouble?"

"Turn on the TV news."

"What?"

"Turn on the TV and I'll see you in as long as it takes."

Vickers could almost hear him shrug.

"Okay."

Joe Stalin was the closest thing that Vickers had to a friend. The name wasn't real. He'd adopted it years ago in the days when he'd been a bright young cultural rebel. It had stuck. The black man in the dreadlocks and gold was moving in his direction. Vickers ducked through the crowd, scanning the street for an available cab that would actually brave the area's reputation to make a pick-up.

Down the block someone started screaming. Another head-case had popped. Vickers could feel the anxiety that spread like a wave through the crowd. You never really knew who might be next. It might be the guy next to you. A couple of local merchants' association goons with kamakazi headbands pushed past him heading for the source of the disturbance. They carried short black billy clubs. Therapy was rough in this area.

An empty cab was headed down Seventh. A city bus turning out of 42nd Street cut across it and brought it to a halt. Vickers sprinted. He skipped through the traffic and reached for the handle of the rear door. He wrenched it open. It wasn't locked, an oversight on the part of the driver. As Vickers scrambled inside, the driver turned and snarled. "I don't pick nobody up 'round here."

Vickers just stared at him. The driver saw something in Vickers' eyes with which he just wasn't prepared to argue.

"Okay, sure. Where to?"

TWO

"WHEN DEMOCRACY GOES down the tubes, murder, by necessity, becomes an instrument of policy. If you can't vote 'em out you gotta kill them."

"Don't ride me, Joe."

"You suckers with your intrigues and killings are turning public life into the court of the Borgias."

"Me? I'm usually the one that's being shot at. I just do what I'm told."

"That's what they always say. You're as much a part of it as anyone. You labor in the deepest pits of the corporate fantasy."

"I asked you not to ride me, Joe."

It had just taken twenty minutes for Vickers to feel confident enough to let go his grip on the Yasha, but Joe Stalin didn't seem willing to indulge him. He was greatly upset by the reports of the carnage in front of the Plaza.

"I'm not riding you, damn it. I'm just hoping that you'll eventually get wise. I thought you were supposed to be good at the shit you do. How the fuck could you be mixed up in a mess like that?"

"Amateurs."

"Is that all you can say?"

Joe Stalin turned back to his stove and removed a pan of kippers from under the grill. He inspected them as though daring them to be anything but perfect. Joe Stalin was a mass of contradictions. Despite his anger at the massacre, he had, between the time of Vickers' call and his arrival, organized a gourmet breakfast, Norweigan kippers, Oxford marmalade, coffee and Jack Daniels, which he now placed truculently in front of Vickers.

"Eat."

Vickers hung his head.

"I swear to God, Joe, I'm in no condition."

Joe Stalin brooked no argument.

"Sure you are. Booze, caffeine, sugar, protein, salt. All the right stuff for a homicidal maniac in shock."

Vickers had to admit that the smell was appealing. He jabbed at the kippers with an experimental fork. Joe Stalin grinned. Vickers ate a little. It was good. He ate some more. He sipped his coffee. He sipped his drink. He realized that he was ravenous. He slid his fork under another section of kipper. Joe Stalin grunted like a man who's been proved right and started on his own food.

"You only pretend that your stomach's knotted with guilt. It's a corporate trait to observe the niceties. Suffer as you kill. It's like putting a Henry Moore in the executive parking lot the same time as poisoning the air, right? The truth is that you're a feral animal. You just killed and now you want to eat. Civilization, like beauty, is only skin deep."

Joe Stalin poured himself some more coffee. He spent a lot of time on his own, so whenever he had company he tended to expound. He was such a fine fellow in so many other ways, he felt that he had the right. At the root of his charm was the fact that he was someone who didn't have to worry about money. Back in the early nineties, he had written a piece for *Playboy* on the Ghoul Children, which had been turned first into a TV documentary and then into a monstrously successful and degenerately violent movie. From that point on, the checks came faster than he could spend them and he had devoted the rest of his life and energies to a singular self-indulgence that had cost him three wives and all but the most irrational of his friends.

As far as Vickers could tell, he was in his mid-to-late fifties. He was seriously overweight and his liver had little excuse for continuing to function. On that particular day, his full head of gray hair was shaggy and uncombed. He had been living in the same filthy sweatsuit for at least a week and appeared not to have shaved during the same period.

The loft, which he rarely left, was more like a natural formation than part of a building. It was like a long, low cavern, dark and encrusted from floor to ceiling with his million-or-so possessions, the gadgets and toys and the random junk. One long wall was filled with a huge accumulation of books and tapes that had long exhausted the shelf space and spilled over onto floor and furniture. A personal robot attempted unsuccessfully to deal with the tide of dust and made soft electronic whimpers. The windows had long ago been sheeted over with steel and the only light came from within. It seemed to gather in isolated pools. Five TV sets were playing as well as two computer displays and the four tiny monitors of the security system. In one strange, homemade construction, organic cultures, like brown stains, were growing on glass plates under a battery of blue-white floods. In the last five years, Joe Stalin's narcosis had spread into outlandish territory. A magnificent antique jukebox pulsed red and amber. It was stocked with genuine 45s from the rock era. Vickers had heard they were worth many thousands of dollars.

The focus of the whole cave was the bright corner area that, with the stove, the sink, the refrigerator and the larger of the computers, served Stalin as a combination of kitchen and study. It wasn't only that Stalin rarely went out. He stayed mainly in this one spot, leaving most of the rest of the loft to the four prowling cats and the robot. In fact, it wasn't too surprising that Stalin didn't leave the loft except when it was totally necessary. It was the top floor of an abandoned factory in a twilight zone that had been promised a half-dozen renaissances but had been let down each time. All had foundered on private graft, public corruption and politics. The nighborhood had fallen slowly but surely to winos, weirdos, shot-spans and gangs of vicious children. The cab driver had been even more unhappy bringing Vickers to the area than he had been at picking him up.

As a counter to the menace of outside, the loft was nothing short of a fortress. Cameras watched all the possible ap-proaches; traps and alarms lurked in the dark of stairwells and hallways. Steel doors and state of the art locks provided

Stalin's final redoubt against the ghoulies, A-boys and gutter-jumpers who would just love to get him and loot his home.

Three of the five TV sets were tuned to the Natcom Non-Stop News. The top stories were still the deaths at the Plaza, Tomoyo Nakamora's upcoming bout with the mountain gorilla and the opening by the Tyrell Corporation of a brand new free hospital in Quito, Ecuador.

Reporters had dug up some background on the steroid woman. She had indeed been an athlete. Her name was Jessica McKenzie and she had tried out for the Canadian shotput team in the 1996 Olympics. She had failed. After that, she'd wrestled on local TV in West Texas under the name Diamond Head. Conservation groups were searching Japanese law for a way to stop Ms. Nakamora from being fucked by an endangered species. Tyrell were proving their generosity and compassion in concrete and steel. There was footage of Norman Tyrell with crippled children. Joe Stalin found this part particularly vexatious.

"Will you listen to that bullshit? Will you look at that crap? They liquidated the last viable government, they directly caused the deaths of one-seventh of the population and then they give a lousy hospital and everyone weeps tears of gratitude. Shit, Ecuador isn't even a country anymore. It doesn't even have a puppet government. It's quite literally a Tyrell satrapy."

"Nobody cares. The motherfucker will probably fall down in five years."

Vickers poured his Jack Daniels into his coffee. He knew there was no way to stop Joe once he got going.

"You get what you deserve. Ain't that the heart of freedom?"

"I can't argue with that. We got what we deserved. We built working models of competition and greed. It was deliberate. We took the worst side of our collective personality and designed global systems to accomodate it. Maybe that's why communism failed. It believed that human beings could learn to freely cooperate. The system knew our weaknesses and it turned 'round and seduced us with them. Now they've got us by the balls. Hell, we didn't even need seducing. We were like a bitch in heat."

Despite himself, Vickers smiled at Stalin's willingness to mix genders.

"We laid down and spread 'em. We handed it to them. We begged them to take us and all we had. First it was the environment, the air, water and the land. Then it was medical care and the space program, communications and law enforcement. In the end we gave them national defense and finally the real function of government. We sold ourselves out like a whore on a holiday."

Vickers sighed. "You got to admit, Joe, the corporations work. That's it. There's nothing more to say. You can huff and puff but you know I'm right. The system's dog eat dog, but it's a dog eat dog world."

"That's the only way the corporations can deal with the world. That's their sole principle. The human being will always react in the worst possible way. The human being is greedy, treacherous and venal and always will be. That's the only way they can operate."

"For all the corporate evil you talk about, we ain't had a nuclear war."

"We still may, if the Russians decide to go down in a blaze of glory."

"We've had fewer regular wars."

"Of course we have. When the only principle is that the world is rotten, you don't defend it to the last man. You defend it just as long as defense is viable."

Vickers shook his head. "I don't know what the hell I'm doing standing up for the corporations. Contec's never done anything but screw me."

Joe spread a half-inch layer of marmalade on a slice of wheat toast.

"I'm not really attacking the corporations. Any half-bright executive would agree with me. They might object to the way I framed the argument but that's only more of the damned niceties."

A huge blue Persian cat hopped onto Stalin's lap. He automatically petted it.

"The only time that anyone takes any notice of what's going on is when the niceties break down. That's what happened with that mess in front of the Plaza. The veneer wore thin and we had a look at particularly savage reality."

Vickers grunted. "If they let us run the business our way, things like that would never happen. The way the rules stand now, they let the fucking amateurs climb all over us."

"What's all this us and them talk? You're all part of the same thing. Uh-oh, what do we have here?"

Something had caught his eye on one of the security monitors. It was the one that covered the street door. Three people were approaching, two men and a woman. They were anything but neighborhood. They were dressed for the Upper East Side. The men wore wide-brimmed hats and expensive overcoats cut in the current voluminous A-line fashion. The woman was exactly the opposite. She was an inverted triangle. Tailored pinstripes with wide padded shoulders and a narrow slit skirt. Her hair was swept up into a service-style pillbox. The men's outfits were totally unsuitable for the heavy, swampy weather.

"What *do* we have here."

Some of the local juveniles were slinking along some yards behind, trailing the trio like jackals that are too confused to actually attack. Stalin reached for a remote. He brought up the magnification.

"You know these people? I almost never have visitors, particularly visitors who dress like that."

Vickers sighed. "Yes, I know them. They're for me."

"Who are they?"

"Two ballerinas and a corpse. The ballerinas have been sent to fetch me. The corpse is to make sure I come."

"What the hell are ballerinas?"

"Ballerinas? Internal Security. Corporation secret police. In this case they're the flunkies of the person I work for. They're the two guys in the hats and coats. They're even starting to look like the Gestapo."

"And the woman?"

"She's the corpse. Ilsa van Doren. Nasty Ilsa, our very own she-wolf. She once put a target away by substituting nitric acid for his Visine."

"She's come to kill you?"

Joe Stalin seemed a little anxious. Vickers shook his head.

"No, just to remind me not to play hookey."

By this time the trio had reached the street door and were inspecting its defenses. One of them was looking straight into the camera.

"What do I do with them?"

Vickers smiled. The smile was nasty.

"You can let them inside the first door."

Joe Stalin pushed a button on the remote. The trio looked surprised as the door clicked open. They gingerly eased into the hallway. The Internals drew their weapons. Both had Yashas. They started up the first flight of steps with the woman hanging some way back. Vickers snorted in djsgust.

"Will you look at those ballerinas? Under those coats they're weighted down with body armor. Damnfool incompetents."

"She's a high stepper, though."

"Oh sure, Ilsa's a real high stepper."

The three were moving up the building at a steady rate. Vickers glanced at Stalin.

"Can you hold them up any?"

"Not until they reach the main door on this floor."

"How about annoying them some?"

"Without bodily harm?"

"Something like that."

"I've got a string of pressure horns. I could douse them with noise."

Vickers grinned.

"That would be ideal."

"Say when."

The three were cautiously climbing the final flight of stairs. At the halfway point, Vickers nodded. Stalin thumbed another button. They could hear the scream of the horns through the steel door. On the monitors, the two corporation cops clapped their hands over their ears and dropped to their knees. The woman, however, stood calmly waiting, four or five stairs behind them.

"The bitch is smart. She came with ear filters." Vickers gestured to Stalin. "Ease up on them a bit."

The two Internals were fumbling in their pockets and stuffing plugs into their ears. Vickers shook his head.

"Cut it off." He stood up. "I'll meet them at the door. You better stay out of the way."

"I don't want any of my stuff damaged."

"I don't want *me* damaged. Just stand back. Nothing's going to happen."

Vickers faced the door. He had left his Yasha on the table in among the remains of the breakfast. He signaled to Stalin to turn off the locks. He reached forward and snapped back the

manual bolts, then hastily retreated a couple of paces. The two
ballerinas came in taking Tiger Mountain. They were all over
Vickers like a pair of cheap suits. One stuffed his Yasha hard
under his chin. They seemed bitter about the blast of pressure
noise. Vickers stood perfectly still with a resigned expression
on his face. When Ilsa came through the door, he addressed
himself exclusively to her.

"Will you call off these idiots before they kill me by
accident?"

Ilsa van Doren's lipstick was a contemptuous scarlet,
flawlessly applied.

"Accidental death seems to be today's special around you."

Once in the back of the official car, Ilsa revealed a need to
maintain brittle, non-stop conversation.

"Do you ever push yourself, Mort?"

Vickers was suddenly very tired. He wasn't actually under
arrest, but there was the release of tension. He was no longer
responsible for what was going on around him. He hardly had
the energy to understand what she was saying. He found
himself staring at her legs. Her stockings were patterned with
tiny stars.

"You know what I mean?"

Despite the perfect makeup and tailoring, she still chewed
gum when she talked.

"Don't you play games? Try and beat your own record, so to
speak? You know what I mean, do a hit the hard way to prove
something to yourself?"

"I usually find that the easy way's hard enough for me."

"There are times when I just want to do something different,
just to see how it would be. Don't get me wrong, I don't want
to cause the target any unnecessary pain. I just like to vary the
routine so I stay sharp."

Vickers couldn't stand any more of this killer to killer
conversation. He locked his fingers like he was handcuffed,
bowed his shoulders and pushed his hands down between his
knees.

"Honey, you're sicker than I am."

"You'd better sit down, Mort."

Victoria Morgenstern's office had one large window that
overlooked East 58th Street and the enormous air conditioner

on top of the multiple parking lot opposite. Steam rose from it constantly, adding its own contribution to the soup that passed for air in the city. In the far distance, he could see passenger aircraft coming and going to and from La Guardia. Vickers stood with his hands in his pockets, looking out at the view. Behind him, Victoria tapped impatiently on the glass top of her desk with long purple fingernails.

"Sit down, damn you."

Vickers turned. His expression was one of cold, exhausted non-cooperation.

"I want to know what I'm doing here. You didn't need to send those three assholes for me. I'd have come in my own good time."

"I needed you."

"To throw to the wolves?"

"Don't be ridiculous."

"I'm not. I'm thinking ahead. Everybody's getting so twisted about what happened at the Plaza, I figure someone's going to be sacrificed."

"It'll blow over."

"Yeah? It'll blow over quicker if there's a scapegoat. Am I the scapegoat, Victoria?"

"Sit down, Vickers."

"Well, am I?"

"Of course you're not. You're much too valuable to be thrown to the wolves. It has, however, cost the department an arm and a leg in both finance and favors to keep the wolves confused about you. If anything's to be salvaged from this total loss, we are going to have to put you straight back to work."

"I'm not going back to work. I'm not ready. I need to rest up."

Control occupied a single floor in a perfectly normal midtown tower. From the outside, it could have been any low profile business, personnel movement, data shuffling, something non-dramatic. The sign on the door read "Designated Projections—A Contec Enterprise." Nobody would look twice at it. There was another office in the subbasement. This could only be reached by a private elevator from the underground parking lot. It was the S&I Department. Screening and Interrogation. It was where the real spite came out. Vickers had gone down there once and refused to ever go again.

"Sit, Vickers."

Vickers finally sat. The pattern of their relationship was such that he always wound up obeying her in the end. Victoria Morgenstern was certainly the most forceful woman he had ever met. She was also an extrememly beautiful woman just starting on the journey into middle age. Perhaps her nose and her chin were a little too pointed, but these only served to reinforce the first impression that here was someone with whom it would be foolish to mess. The tailoring of her lilac suit was almost military in its severity. Her only possible concession to femininity was the way she wore her jet-black hair unfashionably loose and long.

"I'm not going back to work. I'm not emotionally capable. I'm not accepting another assignment minutes after the last one."

Vickers' voice was icy. Victoria pretended not to have even heard him.

"On one level, all this could be looked on as something of a gift. There's a situation that's been building for some time. It could be that you've inadvertently provided us with a solution. Or, to be more precise, you have provided the basis of a cover that will enable you to solve the problem for us."

"You're not listening to me, are you."

"No."

"If I go out on a job right now, I'll screw up. I'll probably be killed."

"If you look at it another way, you're lucky to be alive." She touched the intercom on her desk. "Rebecca, dear, please bring in the disk in the red sleeve."

Vickers assumed that Rebecca was the one that he'd spoken to on the phone. It was a quirk of the Morgenstern style. She always had a dopey sex object in the front office. This one was blonde and had big tits. She indulged the current vogue for toreador pants and those halo haircuts. Vickers first reaction had been bimbo and he saw no cause to revise it. Victoria didn't do anything with the disk. She placed her clasped hands on top of it and regarded Vickers with a look as cold as his own.

"Have you finished sulking?"

"I'm not going out on an immediate assignment and that's that."

Victoria appeared not to have heard him.

"Do you remember the bunker craze?"

"Of course I remember the bunker craze. How could anyone forget it? Billions were pissed away."

Billions had indeed been pissed away. Some dozen or so years earlier, it had finally dawned on the military-industrial complex that there were, in fact, finite limits to a continuous arms build-up. They had already moved into the realm of the absurd with stuff like the Hidey-Seekey "minisile" system and the J20. Their next-best answer was to move into space. At this point, the corporations themselves had dug in and resisted. The Big Four had just come into their full power. They were moving aggressively into space. There was serious money to be made beyond the atmosphere and they didn't want the military in the way. They didn't need random nuclear fireworks, EMPs or stray hunter-killers interrupting their highly profitable work. The military had no option but to accept the area bounded by the moon's orbit as a practical DMZ. They really had no counter-argument. The Russians, the eternal bogeymen, were now so close to bankrupt that they hardly could maintain even a token space program. The Chinese had been so infiltrated by corporate economics that only the most rabid could consider them a threat.

One problem remained, however. Limiting the toys available to the military was one thing. Drastically cutting the profits of the toymakers was quite another. This could turn one division of a corporation against another. This could not be countenanced. All of the Big Four and most of the smaller outfits enjoyed fat arms contracts. Something had to replace them. The solution was to burrow. The sad symbolism of this was not missed.

Before you can burrow, you have to convince someone to pick up the tab. As with all the other truly huge and truly worthless projects, it was the hapless population that would be billed for the insanity. The first move had to be to soften them up. For this, a brand new fear had to be created. Red Armageddon was the phrase. Even the Pope was pulled in on that one. The fantasy was the Last Twilight of communism. The scenario went thus: As the Soviet system fell to pieces, as the famines raged and the vast, hungry and totally disorganized Red Army couldn't put down the dozens of local uprisings, a gang of ruthless, bloody-handed Commissars would decide that everything would go out in a blaze of glory. They would let off the entire nuclear arsenal. In this refined nightmare, the old fashioned idea of deterrence, of MAD, no longer signified. The only solution was protection. As the Pope put it, "Our most sacred duty is to ensure the survival of both our culture and our species."

To perform this sacred duty a consortium was formed between the largest corporations and the national governments of the West. The corporations would build ten very large underground bunkers that could withstand nuclear attack and maybe even a square-on asteroid hit. They would house the art, science and philosophy and enough representatives of the human race to repopulate the planet when the dust settled. The Pope was promised a place in the one under the Atlas Mountains provided he could wing it in from the Vatican in time. All that the governments had to provide was the money of their citizens. It was one of their last acts before they slipped into powerless limbo and the corporations assumed all of their functions.

It took five years to complete the ten bunkers. Their creation produced the final, spluttering surge of old style full employment. When they were finished, the Big Four simply took them over. They were manned, they were stocked and, from that point on, they were publicized as little as possible. They waited quietly for any available apocalypse.

"There were billions pissed away."

Morgenstern slipped the disk into her desk unit. Two pictures appeared on the worktop screen. She rolled them around so they were facing Vickers.

"You know these men?"

Vickers stared from beneath raised eyebrows.

"You want me to kill these two? Have you gone crazy?"

"I asked you if you knew them."

"Of course I know them. The old one's Doctor Kurt Lutesinger, the main architect of the bunker plan. The other one is Anthony Lloyd-Ransom."

"Lloyd-Ransom now commands our bunker under the desert in Nevada."

"I didn't know that."

"Few people do. There isn't much about the bunkers that's for public consumption."

"I'm hardly the public."

"You are where the bunkers are concerned."

"Why are you showing me these pictures?"

"It appears that they may be on the way to creating a problem."

Vickers shook his head. "No."

Victoria's eyes narrowed.

"What do you mean, 'no.' Is this more of the I'm-too-sensitive-for-another-assignment garbage?"

"I'm not ready for another assignment but this is something different. If you're sending me after these two, you're up to something that's in no way kosher. Lutesinger is the biggest of the big and now you tell me that Lloyd-Ransom has got himself pretty damned elevated. They're not only biggies, they're Contec biggies. Anything that involves people like that isn't normal corpse work."

"You've taken out our own people plenty of times. That damned bigmouth chemist on the donut was Contec."

"I'm not talking about some lower-echelon troublemaker who has to go. I'm talking major league. When it's heavyweights like this it's called taking a side. I don't do corporation vendettas or wars between divisions. The whole corpse unit has always worked that way. We've never been compromised. I don't know what you're involved in, Vicky, but I'm not going with you."

She hated to be called Vicky but she didn't react to the goad. She reached into the top righthand drawer of her desk and took out a pack of unfiltered Camels. She put one in her mouth and lit it. Vickers had never seen her smoke before. She inhaled and coughed.

"This isn't a vendetta. This is an operation that has the full sanction of the corporation—the *whole* corporation."

"What operation?"

"We have lately had a suspicion that Lloyd-Ransom, and possibly Lutesinger, too, have crossed a line beyond which their behavior is no longer acceptable."

"Suspicion? Possibly? Not acceptable? This is double-talk. What are you really saying?"

Morgenstern looked uncomfortable.

"It looks like Lloyd-Ransom is turning the bunker into his own private kingdom. Lutesinger may be in it with him. Have you ever met Lutesinger?"

Vickers shrugged. "I was once in the same room as him at some kind of reception. I wouldn't say I'd met him."

"How about Lloyd-Ransom?"

Vickers scowled. "I know him."

There was a long pause. Vickers waited. Morgenstern seemed unwilling to go on. Finally she took a deep breath.

"The board itself has decided that, for the moment, we have to work on the premise that Lloyd-Ransom and Lutesinger are attempting to put a major corporate facility to unauthorized use."

"A whole bunker?"

"A whole bunker."

"That beats stealing the pencils. What am I to do?"

"We want you to infiltrate the bunker, observe and ascertain if there is any foundation for what's suspected."

Vickers couldn't quite believe what he was hearing.

"Me? Observe? I don't observe, I kill."

"We don't yet know if killing will be necessary."

Vickers' eyes narrowed. "You don't know? If you're sending me into the bunker to find out what's going on, it's sure as hell others have been sent in before me. What happened to them?"

"There were two previous agents."

Vickers' expression was grim. "I asked what happened to them."

Morgenstern toyed with the pack of Camels. "We don't know."

Vickers started to lose his temper.

"What do you mean you don't know?"

"Remember who you're talking to."

Vickers pursed his lips. "I want an answer."

"There isn't one. For all practical purposes, the bunker is a sealed enclave. Lately there has been no communication."

"People come in and out, don't they? Crews are rotated, aren't they?"

"The ones we've questioned claim everything's normal."

"So what about your agents?"

"They weren't my agents. They were from the intelligence group."

"Don't split hairs."

"They didn't come back. They may have been killed or just co-opted."

Vickers slumped in his chair.

"Fucking great."

"You asked."

"And you want me to be number three."

Morgenstern nodded. It was as if she didn't actually want to say it. A long silence settled on the room. Steam from the giant air conditioner gusted past the window in unravelling swirls. Vickers slowly shook his head.

"How come nobody foresaw this? Megalomania is hardly an obscure disease. How come some kind of control body wasn't set up to guard against a particular group taking over a bunker? It's kind of an obvious move."

Vickers had only seen Morgenstern look uncomfortable on three previous occasions.

"Of course there was. There's always a regulating body. Just like any other regulating body, though, it was a compromise between the heartbleeds and the freebooters. A committee was set up but it was filled with incompetents and crazies. It was powerless. Lutesinger walked all over them."

Vickers leaned back in his chair and treated Victoria to the long, hard stare of the bitter professional. Her continuing discomfort afforded him a certain measure of twisted satisfaction.

"So what you're telling me is that Contec has lost a bunker."

Morgenstern nodded. "It's a slight exaggeration, but yes, that's pretty much the case."

"And you want me to go in and get it back for you."

Victoria allowed herself the slightest sigh of resignation.

"At least find out how we could get it back for ourselves."

Vickers knew that he had her. On a much more basic level, though, she had him. There was no way that he could pass up this job. He began to raise difficulties.

"Lloyd-Ransom knows me. He knows what I am. It won't be a case of just walking up to the door and knocking."

"We hadn't expected it to be."

"I imagine that you've formulated some kind of a plan."

Victoria smiled. "Indeed we have."

They had gone to the larger briefing room, just Vickers and Morgenstern. There had been no escort, no secretaries, no aides or flunkying subordinates. The details of the plan were for his eyes only. At the start of the session, Victoria had asked him to neither interrupt nor lose his temper. As the session

progressed, this had proved not to be easy. The plan, as it was
progressively unveiled, had proved to be a monster.

At the start, it had all been fairly innocuous. Victoria had
been softening him up with a lot of background basics, profiles
of the individuals involved and the layout and capacity of the
bunker itself. He hadn't realized that they were quite as vast as
they were, but it was hardly eye-opening stuff. He would have
printouts of all that material and he would be able to study it at
his leisure. He began to make small gestures of boredom. They
stopped, however, when Victoria moved on to the actual
details.

Someone had devoted a great deal of time and thought to
wringing the last drop from the incident at the Plaza. Someone
deep in the security think-tanks had made the connection and
seized the opportunity. From their point of view, the massacre
was the starting point of an ideal cover. From where Vickers
sat, it was humiliating and dangerous. The first move was for
Contec to publicly acknowledge that one of their security
people was the target of the attack. Without admitting any
measure of liability and promising to stand by their man, the
corporation would express their distress at the terrible tragedy.

Of course, the signals they were giving out were quite the
reverse. The implication that lurked just below the surface,
plain to those in the know, was that they were embarrassed by
the killings and fearful that the involvement of one of their
employees would stink up the corporate image. Thus they were
beating their detractors to the punch by making the admission
themselves. Since the world was clearly looking for a live
scapegoat, the security exec in question would be dropped
down the long chute.

Vickers would be held, under guard, at a fairly anonymous
New York hotel pending a final dispatch of the problem. The
Holiday Inn at Kennedy Airport had been chosen for the
purpose. There'd be sufficient leakage of the supposedly secret
action to again let the cognisenti know what was being done.
At the appropriate moment, however, Vickers would escape.
Behaving like a revenging corpse on the run, he'd take a flight
to Las Vegas. In Vegas, he'd hide out among the tourists and
wait to be contacted by one of Lloyd-Ransom's agents.

"What maniac thought up this scheme?"

"You don't need to know that."

"It won't work. It's insane. How do we even know that Lloyd-Ransom has agents in Las Vegas?"

"We know."

"And even if he does, why should they come anywhere near me? What the hell would someone who's got his own bunker want with a newly dumped corpse?"

"It would appear that Lloyd-Ransom is recruiting himself a smart, heavy goon squad. You'd be ideal."

"Thanks."

"We don't quite understand why and we don't know the details, but it appears that Herbie Mossman is somehow helping him in this endeavor."

Vickers was genuinely surprised.

"Herbie Mossman? *The* Herbie Mossman? Herbie Mossman of Global Leisure? He's involved in all this?"

"Global Leisure is a much more exotic corporation than ours. They still take pride in a sordid past, and they still enjoy the semblance of an adventure. We will make sure that he knows of your situation. You'll be the bait and we're confident he'll rise to it."

"Bait frequently gets eaten."

"If you don't have any more questions . . ."

"Sure, I've got a whole lot more questions. For a start, what about this escape?"

"What about it?"

"Do the people doing the guarding know what's going on?"

"No."

"Who does know what's really happening?"

"You, me and five other people whom you'll probably never meet."

"That's just great. Nobody will be pulling any punches."

Victoria smiled. "No one."

"So how much force do I use when I go through my chaperones at the Holiday Inn?"

"Anything that's necessary. It has to look good."

"The easiest way is usually the most extreme."

Victoria didn't say a word. Vickers' eyes narrowed.

"Who *is* guarding me?"

"Van Doren and the two Internals who picked you up. You think you can get by them?"

"Of course I can get by them. Particularly if you don't care whether I waste Ilsa or not."

"Naturally, we'd rather you didn't."

"But you don't care either way? Is dumping Nasty Ilsa policy or personal?"

"That's something else that's none of your damn business."

In the back of the car, Ilsa was pawing through a red folder. It was the same red as the disk sleeve. It was full of printouts. The two ballerinas were in the front. One was driving and the other was staring back at Vickers with his hand under his coat clutching his Yasha. The men were as skittish as Ilsa was cool. As they turned into the Midtown Tunnel, she glanced up from the folder and grinned at him.

"You know what this is?"

"Some poor bastard's file?"

"It's yours, sucker."

She held up a color eight by ten that had been taken some eighteen months earlier. Vickers grunted.

"Does it make interesting reading?"

"You're a loser, Vickers. If you get much worse, you'll be scarcely human."

"I get by."

"Barely."

"Are you going to ride me all the way to the end of the line?"

"Sure, why not. Isn't it all part of the fun?"

An NYPD cruiser cut in front of them with its lights flashing and sirens howling. Vickers scrunched lower in his seat. He was becoming increasingly certain that not only did Ilsa not know what the real deal was but that she'd also been given the impression that she'd be the one to kill him when the time came. The bitch was a sadist. She liked to talk her targets into the ground before she greased them. She was leafing through the folder again looking for more ammunition.

"You were married."

"It didn't work out."

"She took an overdose."

"She found out how I made a living. Before that she'd been convinced I was a bucket salesman."

"How did you feel when she died?"

"I had a lot on my mind at the time. There's been plenty of other bodies since."

"Is that why you've got this thing about hookers and video tapes?"

"Doesn't it say anything about hair dryers and ten volt batteries?"

For an instant, van Doren was totally taken in. She scanned down the page as if searching for the relevant item. Then she realized and caught herself. Her eyes slitted, promising Vickers that he'd pay for the lapse. While she was still off balance, he shot the question.

"Are you having an affair with Victoria?"

To his complete surprise, she actually colored. Was this a hang-up that hadn't been crash-therapied out of her?

"That's none of your goddamned business, Vickers."

Vickers settled back in his seat to enjoy the rest of the ride. Some kind of orange smoke drifted across the highway. Despite his overall sense of doom and betrayal, he had to admit that life was at least taking a turn for the interesting.

Vickers glared blearily at the nearest ballerina.

"Why don't you make yourself useful and call room service. The scotch is almost gone again. Get some food while you're at it."

He was pretending to be much drunker than he really was. Red, late afternoon sun streamed through the half-open curtains. He was slumped in a deep armchair with his back to the light. The suite on the top floor of the Holiday Inn was starting to turn funky. Nobody had been allowed in to clean for the three days that they'd been there. Only room service with hotel booze and hotel food. Beyond the windows, the planes thundered in and thundered out again. The television played constantly and boredom was closing its grip. Control called three times a day but the lengthy instructions amounted to little more than that they should stay put and do nothing. There was also nothing to indicate to Vickers that he should make the break that was dictated by the master plan.

While he waited for a sign, he did his best to make Ilsa and the two Internals believe that he was practically harmless. He behaved like a man who truly believed that he was going to die and had given up. He drank a lot, stared out of the window and watched a lot of TV, impatiently flicking from channel to channel. He didn't shave, he didn't bathe and he didn't change his clothes. The two Internals started to behave like they were his private deathwatch. Their names were Malmud and Klauswitz. Out of their trademark hats and armored coats, they were almost human. They came on cheerfully sympathetic and kept offering to play cards with him.

Klauswitz shrugged as if he personally believed that Vickers had drunk enough but wasn't going to say so. Ilsa, who was standing watching the planes come and go, glanced at him with contempt.

"Soaking it up to the bitter end, Mort?"

"It stops me having to think."

"You're a loser, Mort."

Ilsa didn't exactly look like a winner herself right at that moment. She had started out bandbox fresh, going to extremes to keep her seams straight and each hair in place. Two days into the waiting, though, she had been hit by the general boredom and lowering of standards. She had taken to wearing her hair like she'd just gotten out of bed, walking around in a silk slip and chain smoking. When this had started, Vickers had wondered if she was going to go all the way and actually sleep with her target.

It didn't happen. The only outbreak of that kind of activity was when Ilsa and Malmud had ordered a mess of cream cakes and locked themselves into one of the bedrooms. The whole thing was done with such slickness it was plain to Vickers that this wasn't the first such interlude.

Ilsa managed to generate a level of tension that only evaporated when she took her turns to sleep. When Ilsa was away, the men let out a collective sigh and relaxed. They were developing the strained camaraderie of a condemned man and his jailers.

Ilsa turned in early on that third afternoon. She retired for a few hours of sack time just after sunset. The three men started a game of five card stud. About an hour into the game, the phone rang. Klauswitz picked it up.

"Yeah?" He looked a little surprised. "Are you sure about this?"

He held out the phone to Vickers. "It's for you."

Vickers was equally surprised.

"Who is this?"

"It's Victoria. Shut up and listen. It's time for you to get out of there. There's an Amjet leaving for Las Vegas in two hours. Be on it. A car and driver will be waiting outside the hotel in one hour. It's a beat-up Ford Fabian. It'll take you to the right terminal. Everything has been seen to. That's all. You can hang up now."

Vickers had a dozen questions but he couldn't voice them in front of Malmud and Klauswitz. He placed the phone carefully back in its cradle. Klauswitz looked at him curiously.

"What did Morgenstern want?"

"Basically she was telling me not to panic."

"She was probably talking about the TV statement."

"Probably."

The previous day, Contec had made its electronic confession. Anton Fellful himself had appeared on all the major channels expressing the regret of the corporation. It had been the first tangible sign that anything was happening on the outside.

The poker game was resumed. On paper, Klauswitz and Malmud owed Vickers some fourteen thousand dollars. There was much strained laughter about who would live to collect it. This game didn't, however, last for very long. It quickly started to deteriorate as Vickers appeared to grow drunker and drunker. Finally it broke up. Vickers went on drinking, Malmud stared at the TV and Klauswitz stripped down his Yasha and started to clean it.

At the peaks of his drunk act, Vickers would launch into long disjointed stories of his past exploits. The two Internals humored him by pretending interest. After all, how much longer did he have. One of his favorites was the tale of when he and Mad Jack Cardew were in Cameroon together. He reached the slurring climax of the story just as Klauswitz was reassembling his gun.

"By the time we reached Yaounde, the second biggest city, it was pretty damn clear that although we'd toppled the government, the bunch we'd put in their place was ten times worse. M'Tubo had given his troops their head, and let me tell you that their head went a long way beyond ordinary barbarism. They were going feral all over the town while M'Tubo himself was sitting in the town hall or whatever, blind drunk and yelling bloody murder at the head of some local biggie. He'd got it set up on a table. Did I tell you that the head had been cut off a few hours earlier? Anyway, Cardew, who's past caring by that point, was almost as roaring drunk as M'Tubo, walks in and starts calling M'Tubo sixteen kinds of asshole."

Klauswitz snapped the clip back into the reassembled Yasha. All the green LEDs were alight.

"M'Tubo didn't seem to mind too much and he tells Cardew to fuck himself an' points out that he was now so powerful that he could shit where he liked."

Klauswitz put down the Yasha on the coffee table on which they'd been playing poker. Vickers grinned briefly and went on.

"So Cardew starts laughing at him. M'Tubo's got this nickel-plated machine gun laying on the table beside the head. It went everywhere with him. He'd damn nearly started to think of it as his symbol of office. Cardew points at the machine gun and tells M'Tubo that he wouldn't be able to shit at all if he, Cardew, simply picked up the gun and blew him away. Cardew and M'Tubo both have a good laugh about this and then Cardew does exactly that. He picks up the machine gun and blows the bastard clean across the room."

As if by magic, the Yasha was in Vickers' hands. He was no longer drunk. Without a moment's hesitation, he shot Klauswitz in the head. The next instant he had it pointed at Malmud.

"If you don't want to end up like M'Tubo and your pal, you'd better not move a muscle, kidlet."

Malmud raised his hands. "I'm not arguing."

"Do you have a set of handcuffs?"

"Of course."

"Cuff your hands behind your back and get down on the floor."

The bedroom door opened. Ilsa was silhouetted against the light. She was naked. Her voice was sleepy.

"What the hell's going on out here?"

Vickers covered her with the Yasha.

"Put your hands on your head or I'll cut you in half."

"Fuck you, Vickers."

"Just put your hands on your head."

Mad as she might be, she knew enough to do only what she was told. As she raised her arms, he couldn't help noticing what nice breasts she had.

"I believe that I'm expected to kill you but, instead, I'm going to give you a break. If I was you, I'd take the matter up with your boss—or your girl friend—whichever way you think of her."

THREE

THE BEAT UP Ford was waiting as promised. The driver was a heavyset black man with a 'fro combed out past his shoulders. He was wearing anonymous mechanic's overalls.

"I want to go to the Amjet terminal."

"I know."

The driver pulled quickly away from the front of the Holiday Inn. Once they were on the airport connector road, he picked up a plastic folder from beside him on the front seat and tossed it back to Vickers.

"I was told to give you this."

Vickers broke the seal. The folder contained four thousand in cash and a one-way plane ticket to Las Vegas.

"Is this all? No ID? No credit cards?"

"Don't ask me. I'm just doing what I'm told. I did hear, though, that Vegas is one of the last places they really welcome old fashioned cash money."

Vickers grunted. He felt like he'd been screwed again. Without ID, he'd never get his gun onto the plane. He'd arrive in Las Vegas completely unarmed. He would have to dump Klauswitz's Yasha that was right then nestling under his coat. He was suddenly rather glad he'd let Ilsa live. It was never too soon to start deviating from the program. With any luck, Ilsa would go crazy and have a crack at Victoria.

The black man dropped him at Amjet departures and drove away. Vickers watched the Ford disappear down the ramp. He suddenly felt very alone. He fought down the feeling and headed for the check-in desk. With the formalities completed, there were still some forty-five minutes before the plane left. He needed something to do that would preferably keep him largely out of sight. On the next level up, there was a row of therapy booths. For a deposit of ten dollars, you could talk to a computer that was programmed in basic psychology. The booths in airports were mainly concerned with the fear of flying.

Vickers normally hated the damn things. He considered them as so much shuck and jive. The benefits were minimal and he was certain that confessions made in these booths were taped and filed for future use. In his current situation, a booth, with its spherical, dark-blue plastic bubble, would be an ideal place to keep out of sight until the plane left. The bubble was almost opaque when a customer was inside and the lights were down. He ducked into the nearest one and slid the door closed. The door catch activated the computer.

"How would you like to pay?"

"Cash."

Vickers could have sworn that the flat, synthetic voice sounded disgusted.

"I have no facility for handling cash. The only machines capable of handling cash in this location are at the far end of the line, nearest to the book stall."

Vickers hurried down the row of blue spheres. Fortunately, the one at the end was empty. He fed a ten dollar bill into a slot and stretched out on the plastic recliner. The lights dimmed and the computer became electronically soothing.

"Why don't you describe the anxieties that you are experiencing."

"Every time I get into one of these things I have an overwhelming urge to blow up the machine and myself with it. The only thing that's consistently saved me is that I've never had any explosives with me."

"How long have you been experiencing these hostilities?"

"Since I was weaned."

"Go on."

"Listen, would you please just leave me alone? I ducked in here to stay out of the way until my plane boards."

"Why are you so fearful? Why don't you tell me about the things that scare you."

Vickers sat up straight, aware that he was getting mad with a machine. The knowledge only made him madder.

"I'm a professional assassin with a price on my head and my picture's been splashed all over TV. I've got a right to be scared."

The only advantage of a cash-operated machine was that, if there really was someone recording the session, without a credit card there was no record of his identity.

The 1009 eased its bulk into level flight, and the warning lights went out. The passengers started to relax. Back in smoking they were turning the air blue. Vickers flicked on the tiny TV screen in the back panel on the seat in front of him. The cabin attendants were breaking out the booze carts. The woman next to him was looking around as though she needed a drink. He read her as an out-of-towner who thought that she was cute and slick but had altogether overdone it. The elaborate ringlet coif was draped too heavily onto her right shoulder. The neckline of the black, tailored exec suit plunged just a little too deep. The skirt was fractionally too tight and the slit up the side was fractionally too long, or maybe she just intended to have a good time in Las Vegas. Vickers had given her a look of polite interest when she'd first sat down but there'd been no response and from then on he'd minded his own business.

Amjet prided itself on being a sensible airline. Apart from cramming its cabin attendants, man and women alike, into ludicrously brief shorts and halters, it had resisted the trend toward increasing the in-flight fun. It had no swing flights with people fucking in every toilet, no dip movies, no lasers and no audio pressure. All you got on Amjet was food, booze and seat television. Vickers flicked channels on the TV until he got to what looked like newsreel tape of ragged, wild-eyed soldiers ravaging some bleak, snowbound steppe village. It was undoubtedly supposed to be Russia. He slipped on the headphones. Sure enough, a smug commentary was describing how breakaway units of the disintegrating and half-starved Red Army were preying on the civilian population of the eastern Soviet Union but all the time moving west toward richer

European picking. The commentator's concern over the human suffering involved was thoroughly swamped by his obvious glee at how this was final proof of the failure of the Marxist system. The woman next to him was pointing her index finger at the screen. The nail polish was black with a tiny red dragon decal on each finger. Vickers hadn't seen such attention to detail in a long time. Maybe she really did want to have a good time in Las Vegas. He pulled off the headphones.

"I'm sorry, were you speaking to me?"

"They mass produce those things in northern Canada. All that Russian atrocity stuff. I work for KJHJY back in Trenton. We buy it by the mile."

"Should you be telling me this?"

"Sure, why not? Nobody believes what they see on TV. They know anything goes. All the news shows use simufilm. The corps are too cheap to send crews all over the world. Mind you, I doubt you'd be able to find a cameraman willing to point a lens at the Red Army. I figure we're probably doing the Reds a favor. The real thing's probably ten times worse."

"You sound cynical."

"Sure I'm cynical, I'm going for a weekend in Vegas on my own."

Vickers took another look at her. She was running just a tad toward overblown but there was somthing quite attractive about the severe way she kept it in check. Vickers smiled despite the fact that he didn't feel in any condition for conversation. The arrival of the booze cart gave him a little more time to put off the effort. The woman ordered a martini and Vickers asked for a scotch. She half raised her glass.

"Are you on vacation?"

Vickers shook his head. "Just looking for a change of scene." He realized that he'd delayed too long in the matter of assuming an identity. He didn't know who he was and what he did. He could see that, at any moment, she'd be asking him exactly those questions. Already she had halfway confided in him and was certainly looking for some kind of reciprocation. He got in with the first question.

"Why Vegas, though?"

"Isn't that what it's there for?" She took a swift hit from a plastic PAM puffer. This could be the reason why she was so talkative. He pretended not to have noticed. "It's nice to be in among a lot of people who appear to make a profession out of being lucky."

"They run out of luck and they move on."

"So what? I'm only going for the weekend. I can pretend."

The woman looked around for the cabin attendant to give her another martini. The carts had all returned to the galley. Vickers swallowed the last of his scotch. "Maybe I should go and get us two more."

The woman shook her head. "No, no, I'll go. I'm on the outside."

As she slid out of the seat, the slit in her tapered skirt allowed Vickers a fast glimpse of an expanse of thigh topped with black lace. He doubted that it was an accident. While the woman was gone, he did some swift thinking. In the normal run of things, he would have rebuffed her. A lady TV exec on a desperate spree was the kind of relationship that could end, if not in disaster, at least in a mess of resentment well before her weekend was out. Not that he wasn't tempted; there was a part of him that could think of nothing better than spending seventy-two hours wallowing in bed and booze. It was just that he'd been down this same road too many times before. On the other hand, though, his brain had started ticking. Nobody looked twice at a guy flying into Las Vegas with a good looking woman. They also had a ready made excuse for why he didn't use a credit card or produce major ID. Husband and bimbo on a classic weekend. She might well be the best cover he could come up with on the spur of the moment.

She returned, juggling a couple of miniature scotches for him, two readymixed martinis in those plastic bulb containers, disposable glasses and some ice. She deftly slid into her seat without using her hands, which, on reflection, Vickers decided was quite a feat. She put Vickers' scotch in front of him, cracked the neck on the first readymix, poured it and raised her plastic cocktail glass in semi-toast.

"Viva Las Vegas!"

Vickers hadn't opened his scotch yet. The old fashioned metal cap was fighting back. He swirled his ice.

"Yeah . . . right."

"My name's Lavern Brisk."

It was that moment. He extended a hand.

"Mort . . . Mort Vickers."

She squeezed it.

"Well, hi, Mort."

"Hi Lavern."

It wasn't as crazy as it seemed at first. He had no choice but to go into Las Vegas and wait for someone to contact him. If he had to be a sitting duck, he might as well use his own name. It would at least hasten the process. He finally wrestled the cap off the scotch. He sipped it and smiled. The TV screen had given up on the Russians. Stanley Frog was doing something offensive in a polkadot suit. Lavern again pointed at the screen.

"You mind if I shut this off?"

"Not one bit."

He was fascinated by the dragon decals. He'd made a decision and he might as well get into the spirit of it. Lavern seemed to be doing the same. She cracked her second readymix, eased over into the corner of her seat, kicked her shoes off and tucked her feet up under her.

"I can't handle Stanley Frog. He's got to be an all-time slime."

Vickers began to ponder on just how soft and pink she might be beneath the suit. He found that, despite himself, he was actually starting to relax. The scotch helped, easing his imagination as far as wondering just how shockable she might be, in just how much experimentation she'd be happy to engage.

"I travel a lot. I manage to avoid him."

"I didn't think there was anywhere on the planet that didn't get Stanley Frog. He's on every fucking satellite."

Her propensity to talk might prove to be a problem.

"Or do you work off-planet?"

Vickers blinked. He'd known that he would have to concoct some story sooner or later. He'd been so busy speculating about Lavern that he'd been hoping it would be later. The question was sufficiently close to home to prevent anything coming trippingly to his tongue. The best he could do was mysterious.

"Not quite."

There was something watchful in Lavern's eyes. This woman might be horny but she wasn't stupid.

"What's that supposed to mean? You work in midair?"

"That's where I am now."

The language of her body became a good deal less inviting.

"You can be pretty oblique when you want to."

"I'm sorry. There are times when I tend to fall into it. What I was going to say is that I did once make the jump up to one of the donuts."

Once again the truth was as good as anything else. Certainly Lavern's eyebrows shot up. She even clutched at his arm.

"You really went into space? Oh, I'd love to do that. It must have been so exciting."

"Actually, I hated every minute. I was sick as a dog from liftoff to touchdown. I sincerely hope I never have to do it again."

The clutch relaxed. Lavern drew her hand away, she was no longer impressed. Vickers smiled and attempted to regain ground.

"A lot of things aren't as wonderful as they appear."

"That's not a very romantic view of the world."

"It's not a very romantic world. The best we can do is take our pleasures where we find them."

Lavern made a wry grimace and swallowed the last of her third martini. "That's true enough." She beckoned to a cabin attendent. He seemed to be forgiven for not liking space travel. Vickers stretched out in his seat.

"Where will you be staying when we land?"

Lavern turned from ordering. A half-smile played around the corners of her mouth.

"I have a reservation at the Pyramid. How about you?"

Eye contact was direct. Vickers' smile turned into a grin. He half shrugged.

"I hadn't really made any plans. This trip was kind of spur of the moment. I'd been thinking that I might check into one of the older joints on the strip, but I should go to the Pyramid too."

The pause was long and the eye contact total. Then Lavern produced a lipstick and a tiny mirror from her bag. She checked her reflection.

"That could be nice. Maybe we'll have the chance to get to know each other better."

The desk clerk was beckoning him back. Lavern, with a bellhop in tow with her luggage, was almost at the elevator. She turned and called to him.

"What's wrong?"

"Nothing, go on ahead. I'll catch up with you."

She nodded and was swallowed up by the crowd around the banks of elevators. Vickers went back to the desk.

"I didn't want to say anything in front of the lady but . . ."

Vickers scowled. "I don't understand."

"The Intercontinental Pyramid can't accept you as a guest under the present circumstances."

"What are you talking about? I just registered and paid for three days in advance."

"I'm sorry, Mr. Donne. We have to think of the security of the other guests."

Vickers had registered under the name of John Donne. There was no way, in the time, that they could have found out who he was.

"What's the matter with me?"

"Nothing, sir. It's just that you don't have any credit cards or any backup identification. You could be anybody."

Vickers jerked his head in the direction that he'd last seen Lavern.

"I just don't want this visit to be on the record. It might prove embarrassing."

"I can understand that, sir, but there are a lot of strange people on the wander these days."

"I'm not on the wander, damn it. I'm a respectable citizen."

"The trouble is that you have no way of proving that, sir."

"So what am I supposed to do? Stay in some fleabag motel full of roamers and structurals?"

"We might possibly reach an accommodation."

Vickers raised an eyebrow. "Oh yeah?"

"If you felt like leaving a further sum on deposit, we could issue you with a temporary hotel credit card. It'd make for greater convenience for you and give us a greater sense of security."

"I bet it would."

"I don't see any other way around it."

"In other words, I have to put up a bond to stay in your damned hotel."

"It's for your greater safety and pleasure."

"So how much do you want?"

"That would be up to you, sir."

Vickers was resigned. "Would two thousand make Intercontinental Hotels feel any more secure?"

The desk clerk smiled one of those bland, computerized, cream-of-wheat smiles that they teach at low echelon corporate seminars with names like The Human Interface.

"I'm sure that would be adequate."

The clerk prepared the temporary card. It was one of the fancy new clear-plastic kind that are almost impossible to read. He extended it to Vickers on a small silver tray.

"If you'd just validate it by placing your thumb on the blue area."

Vickers silently cursed. The damn card was printcoded. In half an hour everyone with access to the hotel computers would know who he was. There seemed to be no way around it. Both the right and wrong people would find out who he was eventually. With a sense of plunging off the deep end, he pressed down on the small blue panel on the card. Finally he counted out two thousand dollars for the impassively pleasant clerk. As he walked away from the desk he wondered exactly what they'd find. Presumably Victoria had continued with the makebelieve that he was an employee who'd been terminated in high disgrace. He could easily be listed as having no job, no corporate line and, in fact, no visible means of support. The only redeeming feature of all this was that, if fired, no bounty would be payable on him. Of course, there still could be amateurs with old information.

The main elevators were lavish affairs of Art Nouveax glass that ran up and down the sloping sides of the huge entertainment complex. For twelve years the Intercontinental Pyramid had been the single landmark by which the city of Las Vegas was recognized across the world. By sheer volume, it was the world's largest solid structure. Unlike its ancient cousins in the Egyptian desert, its four faces were more than just bare areas of stepped stone. The surface of this modern extravaganza was textured with terraces, glass canopies, solar reflectors and the tracks of its dozens of elevators. Of course, the Las Vegas dome would have eclipsed the Pyramid if the dome had ever been built. The dome, which had been intended to enclose a whole section of the city like an air-conditioned moon colony, occupied another place in history as, so far unchallenged, the world's greatest development swindle. All that was left was a couple of abandoned sections of block-wide base ring.

Once the elevators cleared the thirtieth floor they offered a panoramic view out across the city. The desert sunset was sufficiently majestic to slow even Vickers' racing thoughts. It was a deep, brooding and slightly preposterous red that completely matched his mood. The lights of the city were starting to come on and the skysigns were just faintly beginning to show. As the day faded further, the holograms would ghost in the darkness. Formless afternoon was turning into the manic, driven night. Down on the street they'd be getting restless pretty soon. So much to want before sleeping. Lights were the hallmark of this city whose only industry was raw fun. They were so imporant that they actually usurped the solid architecture of the skyline with dazzling structures of light and air that soared up and out, at times seemingly reaching for space. A billboard blimp drifted in close to the pyramid, glowing with a Teshko commercial that alternated Japanese text with the regular English and Spanish. The Japanese came to Las Vegas in the millions, spending their welfare money while the robots worked the Nissan and the Shogi factories. They were not only gambling-happy but also perversely excited by the ethos of the place. They'd also spend hours taking pictures of the statues of Elvis and Ann-Margret in Wayne Newton Plaza.

The elevator stopped at the fifty-fourth floor. Vickers crossed to the moving walkway that took him closer to his room. He and Lavern had decided to take two separate but adjoining rooms. That way they were acknowledging the possibilities but also not making any commitment. The two rooms could be opened up into a single suite or the doors could be locked on the two units. It was the seemly way to do things. It was, after all, the Age of Appearances. After the discovery of the ephracine treatment, debauchery was once again the norm, except one was expected to close the doors first. They'd even paid top dollar and taken rooms on the outside of the building. This got them a small, shared terrace as a bonus.

All the way there, Vickers kept turning his situation over and over. If, indeed, he had been officially fired from Contec, how many people knew that he was really still working for them? The chances were that Victoria Morgenstern was the only one. That put him in an extremely precarious position. The moment anything went wrong, she'd just let him fall. The termination would become real and his lack of support would be breathtaking. Another not too pleasant thought occurred to him. If, as his cover suggested, he'd been terminated, held pending an inquiry and then escaped, it would be a matter of course for Victoria to send a team after him, either to kill him or to bring him back. If she didn't, someone would be bound to smell a rat. As if his problems weren't varied and complex enough, he would have to constantly be on the alert for a Contec murder squad dropping on him. It was possible that Victoria might have mitigated the threat by sending a team of dummies, but he couldn't count on that. For all practical purposes, he'd have to behave as though there's never been any conversation with Victoria and that the bunker mission didn't exist. He was an ex-corpse on the run from his former employers. That was as much as anyone could be expected to handle. The cover was too damn tight and too damn convincing. The worst part was that he had to absolutely trust Victoria Morgenstern. It was this single fact that made him the most uncomfortable.

The walkway was bringing him up to the drop-off point for his room. He wanted a shower, a scotch and then a long, dreamless sleep. He was in no mood for a bout of strenuous romance with a hyperactive TV exec from New Jersey who puffed PAM, talked incessantly and probably had all kinds of odd ideas about him. He walked down the short corridor and slid his card into the lock to let himself into his own room. The connecting doors were closed. There was something very wrong with moving into a hotel room with absolutely nothing. There was a refrigerator in the bathroom. Inside, he found a selection of miniatures. There was only one scotch. He drank it straight from the plastic. It didn't make him feel much better. He crossed the room and pulled open the glass doors that led to the terrace. As he stepped out of the air conditioning, the heat sandbagged him. The outside air reeked of dry, overheated city.

The sunset had faded to a final, deep purple. The holograms were now clear and ghostly among the first shimmering desert stars. A dozen blocks away, a twenty-story cartoon cowboy leered and beckoned, pointing down at the neon slab of the New Gold Nugget at his feet. Immediately outside, on the forecourt of the Pyramid, a hologram showgirl, maybe twice as tall as the cowboy, bumped and ground. Why the hell did they have to send him to Las Vegas? It was a city with nothing to do with reality. Behind him, the doors to Lavern's room were also open. Vickers leaned on the balustrade and watched the cars fifty stories below. He turned and looked at the open doors. What was she doing in there? He faintly hoped she might have passed out. She'd had enough martinis on the plane. Then a voice came from within.

"Is that you out there, Mort?"

He sighed. "It sure is."

"You sound tired."

"Maybe I am."

He was going to go in to her, but then she was there, framed in the doorway with soft, yellow light behind her. She was holding a bottle of champagne and two glasses.

"We'll have to see what we can do about that, won't we?"

She was wearing the same red shoes that she had worn on the plane. Vickers hadn't noticed before quite how high the heels were. The stockings were a matching red as was the corselette with the straps and the intricate lacing. It was an exact recreation of the costume Vespa Matins had worn for the chapel scene in *The Penal Colony*; it was indeed the Age of Appearances. The red fox fur was a whimsical and slightly improvisational touch, as were the blinking red LEDS that she's twined into her piled hair. It was a full-scale show.

"You look magnificent."

Vickers wasn't sure for how long he'd dozed. It was still bright Las Vegas night on the other side of the terrace. He could just see one giant undulating thigh of the huge, hologram showgirl. Lavern was asleep on her back. Her mouth was slightly open, allowing small, ladylike snores to escape. Just one red stocking still remained. The floor was littered with the debris of her somewhat over-energetic lovemaking. The discarded corselette with the straps and buckles was directly in his line of sight. There was also broken glass. He seemed to remember something about a tray of glasses going over. He hadn't been in a position to care at the time. He pushed himself up on the pillows and massaged his right wrist with his left hand. He felt ragged. Lavern had proved to be not only enthusiastic but also Girlscout-prepared for all eventualities. Later she'd probably want to run the tapes with him and, after they'd watched them, she'd want to do it all over again with variations. Over on the other side of the room the TV was playing some kind of multiple pornography with the sound shut off. The light on the ceiling camera had gone out. Vickers sighed. For the first time in years, he wanted a cigarette. Lavern's PAM puffer was down between the pillows. He hated the stuff but he took a puff anyway. The room spun and he knew that it'd been a mistake. Lavern muttered something in her sleep but didn't wake.

The phone rang in the next room, his room. It shrilled through the open connecting door. Vickers looked balefully toward the source of the sound. It could only mean trouble. He decided not to answer it. He didn't see how he could learn anything to his advantage. It rang seven times and stopped. He relaxed and closed his eyes, only to have them jerked open again when the phone shrilled right beside him in Lavern's room. This was too much of an invasion of privacy to ignore. He reached for it but stopped in mid-reach. Las Vegas was the only city in the world to have installed video phones. It had been around the same time as the dome scheme had been in full swing. They had proved to be almost as much of a white elephant. Although they were a fine idea in theory, in practice nobody wanted them. Nobody wanted other people peering into their homes. Everyone kept the lens covered except hookers on call, exhibitionists and a couple of obscure religious groups who believed they had nothing to hide and constantly called each other to make sure. He grabbed his shirt, draped it over the lens and picked up the handset.

"Yes?"

The screen glowed. It had a pretty blue graphic on it. There was a message: This Is A Call From Eisenwoe Associates. The voice on the other end sounded like an associate.

"Mr. Vickers, my name is George Revlon."

"I think you have the wrong peron."

"I don't think so."

"So much for privacy."

The voice sounded singularly uninterested. "We all have to make sacrifices in this life."

"I seem to be making more than my fair share. What do you want?"

"I represent Eisenwoe Associates, Mr. Vickers."

"I've read that much already."

"We handle intercorporate liaison."

"A dip outfit?"

"We prefer the word liaison to diplomacy. Diplomacy has too many connotations."

"What do you want with me?"

"One of our accounts is to handle relations between Intercontinental and Global Leisure."

"Global Leisure?"

"That's right."

Vickers wished that he hadn't taken the toot of PAM. Victoria Morgenstern's plan seemed to be coming together with alarming swiftness.

"I realize that I'm staying in Intercontinental's Pyramid but I can't see for the life of me what interest Global Leisure might have in me."

"You underestimate yourself. When anyone with your background arrives in the city, Mr. Mossman likes to know about it."

"So we're not just talking Global Leisure? We're actually talking Herbie Mossman himself."

"Indeed we are."

"Are you sure you're not doing some sort of liaison for Contec?"

"I understand that you terminated your relationship with Contec."

"They terminated it, Mr. Revlon. I'm not altogether certain that they don't still intend to terminate me. Since you seem so particularly well informed, you probably already know that up until yesterday they were holding me under house arrest."

"The management of the Pyramid also knows about it. They're a little distressed. They fear an incident."

"What time is it?"

Revlon sounded puzzled. "Five thirty in the morning, why?"

"Couldn't this have waited until a more civilized hour?"

"The management is quite agitated and Mr. Mossman wants to talk with you as soon as possible. I was instructed to call you straight away."

"Mossman wants to see me at five thirty AM?"

"Mr. Mossman keeps unconventional hours."

"There's no bounty on me."

"I'm not a bounty hunter, Mr. Vickers."

"I still have the feeling that I'm being set up."

Lavern moved. She was awake. Her voice was slurred. "Setting you up for what?"

"Sshh."

"Huh?"

"Is there someone there with you?"

Revlon's voice was suddenly guarded. Vickers was impatient.

"You know there is. Tell me what you want me to do."

"I want you to come to see Mr. Mossman as quickly as you can."

"And if I don't?"

"At this moment, the Pyramid is intent on ejecting you as a security risk. How long do you think you could survive as a tagged security risk without a single corporate line, Mr. Vickers? You'd be better off a non-person."

"I feel fucking terrible; I ache all over."

Lavern was out of bed, stumbling for the fridge. Vickers didn't even glance around.

"I can't just take a cab to the Global tower and ask for Herbie Mossman."

Lavern had found herself a container of orange juice and was peering at the TV with a puzzled expression. At Mossman's name her head snapped around.

"What the fuck are you taking about?"

Vickers ignored her. He was listening to Revlon.

"I'll send an escort for you."

"The hell you will."

"Why not?"

"I still think it's a setup."

"So you tell me."

"Will somebody tell me what's going on in here?"

Lavern was struggling into a silk robe.

"I'll leave here. I'll walk around for a couple hours, maybe have breakfast and then, when I feel enough time has passed, I'll call the main switchboard at Global. You'd better make sure by that time they can connect me with a George Revlon. That's when we'll talk about my meeting with Mossman."

"Mr. Mossman could be doing you a favor."

"I doubt it."

"Then all I can say is that I'll be waiting for your call."

Vickers nodded and slowly put the phone down. Lavern no longer looked bleary. She was staring at Vickers as though she didn't quite believe what she saw.

"What are you, Mort? *Nobody* meets Herbie Mossman, for God's sake. *Nobody*. Even I know that."

Vickers was searching around for his clothes. "It's best that you don't know anything about it."

"What are you doing?"

In fact, he was pulling on his pants, but he suspected that she wanted a little more background information.

"I have to go out."

"Where? You're making me crazy."

She seemed to be looking for something in the bed. Vickers was pulling on his jacket.

"You heard me on the phone. I have to see Herbie Mossman."

She'd found the PAM puffer.

"There you go again. How can you do this to me?"

Vickers shrugged and headed for the door. Lavern's face dissolved.

"After last night? Just like that? Don't you have any finesse at all?"

Vickers turned; he walked over and put a hand on her shoulder.

"I'm in more trouble than you could ever want to know about. I'll try and get back."

He kissed her. She grabbed and pressed against him. Her voice was angry.

"You make me crazy."

Vickers selected himself a strategically placed corner table. It was about the best he could get. He could see three of the five entrances and had adequate warning of people coming through the other two. He was in the restaurant of the Pharaoh Room on the Pyramid's thirty-sixth floor. He'd chosen the floor at random. He hadn't even pressed a button in the elevator, just stepped out when someone else had. He figured that if the hotel's security was already tracking him, he might as well make it as hard as possible for them. Picking a floor was an easy bet. They all had roughly the same facilities. On any one, he knew that he'd be able to find a public room in which he could vanish for a couple of hours.

The restaurant was separated from the main gambling room by a long glass wall. Its lights were a little more dim than those in the main room and the diners were treated to a panoramic view of the crowds around the flashing Mirage machine, the old fashioned slots, the crap and blackjack tables, the roulette wheels and the fan tan games. All along the wall behind him, giant hieroglyphics, cartoon versions of Isis, Anubis and Ra followed each other across a huge fiber-optic display with the angular jerkiness of sand dancers.

"You want something?"

The waitress looked like she was just about to go off shift. She was the usual statuesque, leggy, Las Vegas type. They didn't seem to employ any other kind for jobs that involved handling the public. There were so many unemployed they could ultimately pick and choose. This one was definitely five hours frayed and starting to wilt a little. Her extremely short tunic and overdone eye makeup was some cheap Hollywood mogul's idea of an ancient Egyptian slavegirl right down to the incongruous platform sandals. The look she gave Vickers owed its lack of enthusiasm to something more than her weary feet. He realized that he must have started to look noticeably disreputable.

"What time is it?"

"Just after six."

"I guess I might as well have breakfast."

"You can have what you want. We serve all things at all times."

"Breakfast will do. It'll help get me on to real time."

Without a word, she handed him a breakfast menu.

"A large scotch, a glass of milk, eggs benedict and coffee."

"How do you want your salad?"

"I don't."

"Any particular scotch?"

"Johnnie Walker Black."

"Cash or plastic?"

"Cash."

It was a protective impulse. Using the card would instantly give his location. He watched the waitress walk away and then stared up at the mirrored ceiling. If he wasn't being scanned right then he certainly soon would be. There was little doubt that she would tap in a report that someone who didn't look quite right was sitting at one of her tables paying cash. In a world of infinite data, everyone spies for the computers. He wasn't all that worried. If Mossman wanted to see him, it was unlikely that the Pyramid security would make a move to eject him or anything of the kind, but it didn't hurt to protect himself. Protection was more a matter of carefully cultivated unconscious habits than any considered design. All too often, there wasn't time for a plan.

Even at six in the morning the gambling room still did a roaring business. The rule in the casinos was no windows and no clocks. They were a world of gaudy hope and equally gaudy despair. It seemed to Vickers that there were a disproportionately large number of Japanese in the room, or maybe they were Koreans. Lines of them were bent over Mydak machines, concentrating on the concave screens and mechanically palming the rollers, hanging in like obsessives as the machines nibbled away at their credit. They seemed as fixated by the glowing, interlocking patterns of color on the screen as with the occasional credit leaps that showed on the win counter.

"I can bring a baby Mydak to your table if you like."

The waitress had returned with his food. He shook his head. Casino gambling was a vice in which he never indulged. He had no desire to become addicted to trying to beat out a Mydac machine, baby or full-sized.

"No thanks, I prefer just to eat and watch."

She set his food down with a look of deepening suspicion. If she hadn't reported in on him already, she undoubtedly would now. As she departed, he raised his scotch to the mirrored ceiling and then poured it into the milk. Beyond the glass, out in the gambling room, a crowd was gathering around one particular table. Vickers guessed someone was having a big win. Those who hadn't been suckered into a machine were homing in on the lucky streak, probably hoping that some of it might rub off on them. It was rumored that the casinos staged regular, spectacular winning streaks just to encourage the others. Up in a high, vaulted section of the room's ceiling, a show had started among the intersecting, triangular beams. Holographic dancers swivelled in midair while human trapeze artists flew through and around them. After a short while, Vickers had to stop watching. There was something about the spectacle that made him non-specifically uneasy. There was a hypnotic quality to the way the solid bodies arced in and out of completely insubstantial ones. He distrusted anything that seemed hypnotic. It usually meant that it was. Even the corner store was stacked with little subliminal mindfucks to make you spend or consume or not steal the merchandise. He concentrated on his eggs.

After he'd lingered in the restaurant as long as he could, even listening for a while to a drunk in a cowboy hat recount tearfully how he'd lost all his money and his girl friend without even leaving the hotel, Vickers paid his check and went looking for a clothing store, a washroom with a shower and a barber shop. Part of the reason people were giving him strange looks was that he'd been in the same clothes for four days, or maybe it was five. Inside of forty-five minutes, he felt at least partway to being a new man. Normally he wouldn't have been seen dead in a tan jungle suit, but it did blend him with his surroundings. He'd had to use his card to pay for the suit. He no longer had enough cash. Hotel security would know where he was but it didn't really matter, he was about to leave the Pyramid. It was almost time to make his call.

As he hit the street, the noise and heat hit him. He'd been inside the Pyramid for long enough to have forgotten what protected environments the Las Vegas hotels really were. There was a pale blue desert dawn beyond the lights and already the air smelled like burnt metal. A doorman dressed as an ancient Egyptian soldier waved up a cab with his spear. Vickers ducked into its haven of air conditioning.

"Just head down toward the old part of the Strip."

Even in the dawn the sidewalks in front of the older casinos, with their threadbare, gum-trodden carpeting had a complement of aimlessly wandering crowds. Mostly they were guaranteed structurals in gaudy trylon slowly shuffling and trying to make sense out of an endless holiday. Vickers reminded himself that, as far as all the world, with sole exception of Victoria Morgenstern was concerned, he was also terminally unemployed. In fact, he was worse off than the hordes on the sidewalk with their matador pants and Hawaiian shirts. He hadn't been bought out of his life with the promise of a pension. He'd simply been fired.

Las Vegas had to be one of the most thoroughly policed cities in the world. They stopped the vags and bums and homeless roamers at the city limits while, inside, it seemed like every block had its squad of uniformed cops, private security or rubberroom squads of parapsychs to deal with flips, screamers and the silently berserk. When the major industry is supplying the fantasies of greed to tourists, it was important to make sure that all the tourists had the price of admission.

He had the cab pull up by the Xanadu's watercade. He climbed out and crossed the street, away from the complex of lasers and fountains and kept going for two blocks until he was fairly confident that no one was following, then he looked for a phone booth. He called information for the main number for

Global Leisure and, after a final look 'round, he tapped it in.
The voice was simulated feminine, programmed mildly sexy.

"Global. Can I help you?"

George Revlon, please."

"One moment."

A human voice came on the line. The computer on the board
had clearly been alerted.

"Can I help you?"

"I'd like to speak to George Revlon."

"Your name, sir?"

"Vickers."

"Will you please hold, Mr. Vickers? I'll try and locate Mr.
Revlon."

This was going as well as could be expected. After a short
wait, Revlon came on the line.

"Vickers?"

"So, does Mossman still want to see me?"

"Indeed he does. In fact . . ."

"Don't worry about it. I'm coming straight in."

He hung up. There was no point in waiting any longer. He'd
proved that Revlon was connected with Global. Now he had to
take his chances.

"You don't mind if I call you Mort, do you?"

Vickers shook his head. Herbie Mossman could call him
anything his heart desired. When you're that powerful, you
tend to get your way whether anyone minds or not. Where
other corporations had tense little oligarchies at the top of their
towers, Global Leisure was an absolute, magnificent dictator-
ship. For fifteen years, Herbie Mossman had balanced his
warring factions one against the other and made himself indis-
pensable to all. The concept of a single overlord, a boss of
bosses went deep into the roots of the Global's corporate
tradition. There was little shame at Global Leisure that they
were descended from an organization that, sixty years earlier,
was known as the Mob.

"I have a problem with you, Mort?"

"I hope nothing that can't be worked out, sir."

Mossman formed his two index fingers into the approximation of a steeple. He didn't tell Vickers to call him Herbie. His
pudgy fingers were encrusted with gold. He was about the
fattest man that Vickers had ever seen, an emotional baby with

a mind like a vise who had long ago abandoned all ideas except
power and gluttony. He suspected that Mossman was actually
too fat to walk. His rolls of flesh, that could scarcely be
contained by a dark-blue bell tent of a funsuit, sagged and
flowed and sweated into a monster of a chair, a creation of
chrome and black leather that contained him like a vat. The
whole thing was mounted on a rugged set of servotracks, the
kind that they use on guard robots.

"I have to decide whether to accept you on face value or
whether you are something much deeper and dangerous. I have
to entertain the possibility that Victoria Morgenstern is using
you under the deepest of deep cover."

"Victoria Morgenstern was holding me under house arrest
and might well have had me executed if I'd stayed around."

"You are still alive, though, aren't you?"

"I hope you won't hold that against me."

Vickers could feel sweat under his right armpit. Mossman
wasted no time in conversational detours.

"I don't hold anything against you, Mort. This is pure
business. It may even be that Morgenstern is using you without
you knowing it. I have to satisfy myself as to what you are and
how you will affect me. Bit by bit, the process reduces it to a
single question for me: should I let you run or do I need to
neutralize you?"

"I'm a little confused. Why should I be of any concern to
you at all? I'm an out of work corpse. I'm in enough trouble
already."

Mossman's voice came out like slow gravel.

"But you are a corpse, Mort. You're a corpse and you're in
this town. This is my town, Mort, and any kind of corpse
causes me concern. I wonder who you might be here to kill,
Mort." He made a dismissive gesture that might have been a
shrug in a man who wasn't too heavy to raise his shoulders.
"You might have come here to kill me."

There was silence in the room. George Revlon was standing
a little behind Vickers on his right. Mossman's personal
attendant, a world-class muscle builder called Chuck, stood
further back on his left. Both seemed to be waiting for an
answer. All Vickers could do was look pointedly around the
penthouse. The top of the Global tower was a cluster of
transparent domes of four-inch blown plexiglass. They all
belonged to Herbie Mossman. They were his private domain

from which he could personally watch the sweep of his desert empire. One dome was his vast office, a second housed an equally vast dining room, another his pool and the one that was a constant opaque black hid his legendary bedroom. In the office, as the sun rose higher, light sensitive pigments progressively filtered it through a screen of deep gold. It was like being dipped in maple syrup. Vickers' chair had been set at sufficient distance from Mossman's huge desk and huge chair to make it feel like an inquisition.

"I think you know that I haven't come here to kill you, sir."

On the way up to the penthouse, he'd been scanned and body-searched no less than four times. The room itself showed all the symptoms of being equipped with a Gee Ten Thousand, which was about as far as it currently went in automated defense systems. By the way the decor was arranged, he suspected that, in any emergency, an armored steel shield would drop around Mossman while the rest of the room could be pumped full of high velocity metal fragments. Mossman caught his look and smiled a smile that was completely lacking in humor.

"Perhaps not a frontal assault, but who knows what might be contemplated in the dark schemes of Victoria Morgenstern."

It was Vickers' turn to shrug. "She cut me loose. There's nothing else that I can tell you."

A white-coated butler appeared at the other end of the room and came silently across the acre or so of deep pile carpet. He held a silver tray in his right hand. On the tray was an extremely generous slice of banana cream pie, a large glass of chocolate milk and a large Coke. Mossman postively beamed.

"Flanders."

"Sir."

Mossman patted the left arm of his chair. "Just set it down here, Flanders."

The chair arm was quite large enough to accomodate the tray. The righthand arm had a small computer terminal built into it.

"Will that be all?"

"All for now."

"Thank you, sir."

There was silence in the room while Mossman ate. All conversation was put on hold as he shovelled pie into himself with a silver fork. His eyes were half-closed and he was clearly in ecstacy. Vickers couldn't remember seeing anyone so absorbed in their food. When he'd finished he wiped his mouth with a linen napkin. His eyes flicked to Vickers and it was back to business.

"Suppose I offered you a job, Mort. What would you do?"

"I'd jump at it."

"Without knowing what it might be?"

"I'd assume you'd want me as a corpse, but I'd take anything that'd get me out of the storm."

"From my point of view, having you on the payroll at least puts you where I can keep an eye on you."

"Then you are offering me a job?"

"Provisionally. You have a good reputation. If you're not pulling something, you'd be a valuable asset."

"I'll take it."

"I rather thought you would."

Mossman glanced down at the computer terminal. "Note to Pattel in Legal. Vickers is to put on a standard corpse indenture with the rider added to cover the special project."

Vickers raised an eyebrow. "Special project?"

"You didn't ask what the job was."

"That's right, I didn't. But now I have."

"I'm putting together an elite team for a very special project. You'll be a part of that team, Mort. That's all you need to know at the moment, except that you'll initially be based at a place in the desert just out of town. You and the others will be isolated there. You can look on it as refresher training."

Vickers tried to picture Mossman dragging his lard around a strip of blistering desert doing "refresher training." He hadn't forgotten that the man mixed chocolate milk and Coca-Cola. Something flashed on Mossman's terminal. He tapped the keyboard.

"This is very interesting." He regarded Vickers with an amused expression. "I wonder how you'd react if I told you that a Contec hit team has installed itself in your room at the Pyramid."

Vickers didn't even try to disguise his concern.

"You're not serious."

"Indeed I am. According to our tap into the Pyramid's computer, they've made a prisoner of your girl friend and are, at this moment, watching the tapes that you and she made last night."

Vickers stood up. "I have to get over there."

Revlon quickly interjected. "The woman didn't mean anything to you, did she? If you take on a hit squad actually inside the Pyramid while you're registered in the employ of Global Leisure, it could cause major intercorporation problems. I seriously advise you to accept Mr. Mossman's offer and simply leave town."

Vickers shook his head. He was tired of running; the point had come where he had to settle the situation.

"I owe Lavern that much. I'm going back over there." He glanced at Mossman. "We haven't inked anything yet. If there's trouble, you can always disown me. Everybody else does. I'd appreciate it, though, if someone could supply me with a gun."

"Quite the little knight errant, aren't you, Mort? I wouldn't have expected it."

To be truthful, Vickers himself wouldn't have expected it, either.

"I'm getting tired of being bounced around."

In the back of his mind there was also an image of a trio of ballerinas sitting around laughing at the video tapes of his antics in bed. His pride gritted its teeth and wanted to hurt someone.

"You'd be a fool to go against three of them on your own."

Vickers was surly. "I can handle it."

Mossman shook his head. "You won't have to. I'll give you the backup that you need. You can go and rescue your girl-friend as a Global corpse."

Revlon's mouth opened and closed like the beak of a chicken in shock.

"It would have serious repercussions, sir. I insist."

"Don't insist to me, Revlon. Just warn the Pyramid as to what we intend and have them make the arrangements. There'll be no repercussions. They don't want to fuck with me."

Vickers' eyes narrowed. "What if they warn the Contec team that we're coming?"

Mossman dismissed the idea.

"This is hometown boy against outsiders. We have to coexist fifty-two weeks in the year. They won't warn them." Mossman's look of amusement returned. "This is a great test of loyalty, Mort. On your very first job for me, you're going up against your old employers."

* * *

Vickers gave a final tug on the blue nylon climbing rope. He
hated to work either on cliffs or on the outside of buildings, but
in this case there seemed to be no other way. Mossman had
supplied him with two companions, an Australian surfer with
an extra Y chromosome and the unoriginal name Bruce, and
Frank Lang, a wiry Oriental stress freak in a black track suit
who probably believed that he was the descendant of ninja.
The three of them were poised on the edge of a fifty-fifth floor
terrace, one floor above the suite where the Contec team were
holding Lavern. Bruce seemed totally unmoved at the idea of
rappeling down the side of one of the world's biggest
buildings. Personal danger and the chance to hurt people
seemed a natural break from beer and sun. Frank Lang, on the
other hand, was a pocket package of compressed tension who
might well go off like an uncoiling spring once they were
inside the place.

They stood, leaning back against the anchored ropes,
angling out into a fifty-story void. Inside the hotel, Pyramid
security had sealed off the suite. All that remained was for the
Global team to go in. They were all waiting for Vickers to give
the signal.

He nodded and they jumped out and down into nothing.
Only skill beat down the fear. Down and swing in, playing out
rope all the time. Their feet hit the terrace. Bruce stumbled
slightly but the other two moved forward like a textbook
example. Both sets of French windows were closed. Bruce
swung the M90 off his back and started for the glass, swinging
the heavy weapon like a club. Vickers allowed him to get
ahead. If he fancied himself as Conan, let him go. The
windows crashed into diamond smoke. Bruce was going
straight through them. Subjective time had slowed. Vickers
suddenly was above his fear. There was only the breathlessness
and the taste of anxiety in his mouth. He was in control. It was
all going to be easy. He and Frank Lang went through the glass
together, exactly in Bruce's wake. Already it was carnage.
Bruce had sprayed the room with the twin-barreled machine
gun. The three-man hit team were dead on the floor. Walls and
ceiling was riddled with bullet holes and spattered with blood.
Vickers lowered his Yasha and thumbed on the safe. For a
moment he thought that Lavern had been killed along with the
Contec people. Then he saw Frank Lang helping her to her

feet. She appeared to have had the presence of mind to roll down behind the bed when Bruce came crashing through the windows. In this, she'd been faster than the three supposed professionals. It didn't look as though the Contec team had been exactly easy with her. There was a bruise on her cheek, her robe was torn and she was secured with her own handcuffs. Her mouth moved in wordless shock as Lang started to search for the keys.

Vickers inspected the bodies. They were three men, all extremely young. It was little wonder that they'd been taken so completely by surprise. They could scarcely be long out of training school. Why had Victoria sent such babies? It would be a near miracle if Mossman didn't smell a rat. Bruce was also moving around the room inspecting his handiwork. He bent down and came up with a video tape in his hand. He grinned at Vickers.

"Maybe we ought to take a look at this."

Vickers scowled. "You can get on the phone and tell hotel security that it's safe to come home. Tell them to bring a doctor for her and bodybags for the other three."

Bruce was still holding the tape. Vickers extended a hand.

"I'll take that."

"Prude or something?"

"Maybe. Or maybe I just don't want to give away trade secrets."

The Pyramid security came in with a seemingly endless supply of grim hostility. There must have been two dozen of them, with discrete dark suits and hard, bleak expressions. Contec and Global had fought a battle on their territory and they'd been forced to stand by and watch. They were madder than hell and they icily eyeballed the Contec trio while the bodies were bagged and Lavern was examined by a medic. Once she'd been shot up with tranquilizers, it was suggested that she be admitted to the hotel infirmary and given a thorough checkup. Lavern, who'd recovered a little of her composure, nodded mutely. She had to pass Vickers as she was helped to the door. She hesitated in front of him. Her face was slack with the exhaustion of prolonged fear and her eyes were wide as a child's.

"What the hell are you, Mort? What the hell are you?"

Vickers had no answer, but before he could even invent

something the phone shrilled. He snapped around. Bruce was reaching for it.

"Don't touch that! Let me get it."

He moved and grabbed while holding up a hand for quiet in the room; he made his voice neutral before he answered.

"Yeah."

"Vickers still hasn't come back?"

The voice was instantly recognizable. He hardly needed the face on the uncovered screen.

"Sure, Ilsa. I'm back. I'm afraid we had to grease your boys."

So Ilsa van Doren had been sent in to get him. She, in her turn, had delegated the job to the kids. It was all getting a bit messy. Ilsa made what, transmitted through the phone, sounded like a viper hiss.

"Damn you, Vickers. You're making this matter very personal."

"Then perhaps you'd better come in person."

"I will next time."

"Next time?"

"Trust me."

"You'd better tell Victoria I'm working for Global now. You may find that she doesn't want anyone to fuck with the property of Herbie Mossman."

"I promise you there'll be a next time. You can count on that."

Vickers wondered if he'd made a rather foolish error in not killing her back when he'd had the chance.

FOUR

IT WAS DECIDED that Vickers should leave the city. He should be straight away transferred to the mysterious training camp in the desert. Even though he protested that he didn't feel any need to run from Ilsa van Doren, Mossman had been adamant. Vickers had become valuable. He was to be placed beyond the reach of Contec. Vickers wasn't clear what it was about him that was considered so valuable but he accepted it as a great deal better than being considered worthless. Mossman appeared to have completely bought the charade at the Pyramid, if indeed it had been a charade at all. Vickers still had his reservations. If Mossman had noticed the youth and inexperience of the Contec squad he hadn't seen fit to mention it. The fact that Ilsa was in the city and apparently directing them seemed to confirm that Vickers was a genuine target for a genuinely vengeful former employer.

Vickers had been given a line of credit and allowed out on a brief shopping trip to equip himself with an assortment of combat clothes, three pairs of boots, a flak vest, a bunch of toilet articles, some books, a tape player and a couple of bags in which to carry it all. The last stop was a gun store. With formalities smoothed by the mention of Herbie Mossman, he had bought himself the usual Yasha 7 plus the backup of a nine millimeter automatic and, as an afterthought, a shoulder holster. By the time he had all that he felt he needed, the sun was once again going down on Las Vegas. He was informed that a car would collect him at midnight. They were seemingly leaving the city under cover of darkness. This left him enough time to go back to the hotel for a shower, an early supper and then four hours' sleep.

It was Bruce who wakened him from an anxious and depressing dream in which naked people roamed a chill blue-gray desert and fought each other with long chrome spears like giant needles. At first he was disoriented and didn't recognize the room. He'd been temporarily housed in a small, faceless motel in back of the Strip. When he realized where he was, he profoundly wished that he was someplace else.

"Damn."

He needed a holiday.

"Time to move now."

"I feel terrible."

"Let's get going, shall we mate?"

Vickers had slept in his clothes, so all he had to do was to splash water on his face and gather up his belongings. On the way out the door, Bruce reached for the case that contained Vickers' brand new guns.

"I'll take that for you."

Vickers halted. "Yeah?"

"It'd be better."

It seemed tactful not to make an issue of it.

"Whatever you say."

Bruce took the case and started toward the parking lot. On the way, they passed a line of vending machines.

"You mind if I get some coffee?"

"You'll find everything you need in the car."

When Vickers had been told a car would collect him, he'd expected nothing more than that. He was surprised to discover a minor motorcade. A black stretch limo was preceding and followed by a matched pair of lime green Jeep Comanches with inch-thick plexiglass and wire-mesh screens on the windows and windshield. To say the least, he was confused. One moment they were buying him guns and the next they were taking him away; one moment a cracker box motel, the next the red carpet. What did they want with him? What did they want him to do? He was even more confused to discover a nurse waiting for him in the limo. He assumed she was a nurse because she wore a nurse's uniform. She was so totally Vegas that she could just as easily have been a hooker on special assignment. Whichever one, she seemed almost unnaturally calm as she sat with her long legs neatly crossed and the reading light burning in the far corner of the dark-blue leather interior.

"This has to be a joke."

"Something wrong, Mort? Why don't you get in?"

Vickers hesitated and then sat down beside her. Bruce also got in. Vickers was very aware that they were on either side of him.

"I wasn't aware that we were going to a costume party. I was told I was on my way to the desert."

The car was moving.

"You are."

Vickers looked at the woman.

"So why the nurse suit?"

"I'll be administering the medication."

"Medication?"

"You'll be out for part of the trip."

"Out so I don't know where I am?"

"Exactly."

"I'm starting to feel like a prisoner."

"You could look at it like this, sport: you don't have the option of changing your mind anywhere in the near future."

Outside, the night glare of Las Vegas was whipping past. Vickers didn't know the city sufficiently well to be able to work out what direction they were taking. Soon, however, the liquid glare of the opticals was replaced by old fashioned neon. This was only to be expected. They were headed out of town. Vickers explained to himself that there was no percentage in speculating. Somewhere along the line they'd shoot him full of dope and then he'd wake up someplace. He'd be disoriented and the place would undoubtedly be weird. That was assuming he woke at all. The thought had crossed his mind that he might be the subject of a Herbie Mossman merciful execution. He couldn't work out a reason for that, though. It was all too elaborate. So elaborate, in fact, that he did his best to concentrate on the moment. He remembered the coffee. The limo came with a bar, a TV and an Eldo simulator. He helped himself to coffee from the Mr. Coffee built into the bar and then he hesitated. The booze was in plain sight in cut-glass decanters.

"Is there any reason why I shouldn't have a drink? We're not headed into any kind of emergency, are we?"

Bruce shook his head. "Not that I know of."

As Vickers poured himself a scotch, Bruce leaned forward and turned on the TV. He flipped through the channels until he found one that was showing reruns of *Rogan's Vengeance*. Bruce had the manner of someone who made the trip regularly and Vickers wondered how many others had been ferried out to this place in the desert before him. The limo was now running through dark, edge-of-town streets. There was nothing to look at and Vickers' attention was drawn to the TV screen. He discovered with a little consternation that Bruce tended to bare his teeth in a faint but unholy grin during sequences of physical brutality. Even this, though, didn't stop his being sucked in by the flicker of mindless sex and violence. In fact, he was so sucked in that he only looked away when the car slowed to a stop. They were at a city limit checkpoint. Beyond it were the *barrancas*, the unlit, unpoliced and completely unwanted twilight zones of shanty towns and bum jungles that surround almost all of the sunbelt cities but, in the case of Las Vegas, weren't even acknowledged to exist.

This was something of a puzzle. To drive out of the city through the *barrancas* meant that you were going somewhere obscure along a rarely used route. As they pulled away from the checkpoint, it was like entering another world. Tin shacks sagged against decaying tract homes. Dead cars, rusted down to their skeletons, formed the basis of even cruder homes. Narrow, rat-run alleys and trenches that were open sewers snaked and zigzagged between the shanties, shacks and hoochies, tightly packed as more and more desperate wanderers daily arrived at a city that didn't want them. Vickers noticed a large plastic freight pod, white in the night. It was the kind they used on the C400 shuttles. It had been dragged from God knows where to house what looked like an entire extended family.

The original road was cracked and overgrown but comparatively clear of obstacles. Neither the limo nor the pair of jeeps showed any inclination to slow down. The limo's deluxe ride gave it a tendency to yaw and wallow on the uneven surface.

Vickers got a firm grip on a handhold and continued to lean forward and peer out of the window. Here and there, it was possible to see the yellow-white glow of what had to be stolen electricity but, for the most part, the only real light was from the fires that had been lit all over. Each one was surrounded by its own circle of figures with their dull brown faces. There were more faces lining the sidewalk. They looked at the limo with an implacable, angry hate. It was the kind of hate that can only be known by those who, in a world that knows it has too many people, have been declared by the rest to be surplus. Fists were raised and some of the faces seemed to be shouting. Urchins ran alongside the car also yelling.

"They'd drag us out and tear us to pieces if they got half the chance."

The nurse didn't seem particularly concerned. "They won't get the chance."

Vickers shook his head. There was just too much fury waiting to erupt. He experienced a brief twinge of shame to be riding in the limousine. It was so much of an affluent, ruling class affront to these people's poverty. If anything, the jeeps were the targets of even more glowering hate. They constituted an even deeper arrogance and more of a sneering threat. Jeep Commanches with protective screens, security glass and garish paint jobs were favorites with all the rabid groups who made a practice of venting their angry fear on the structurals—the Klan, the Red Squads, the Aryan League, the Sons of Davy Crockett and all the other quasi-legal vigilantes who liked to roar into the *barrancas* to murder and terrorize.

The brake lights of the leading jeep came on and the limo also slammed on its own brakes. The last of Vickers' scotch leaped out of the glass. Bruce and the nurse both grabbed for handholds.

"What the fuck!"

The Australian rolled down the window and stuck his head out.

"What the fuck's the hold up?"

At an intersection up ahead, a jalopy had broadsided an equally beat-up pickup and both were now burning. A crowd had gathered, black silhouettes against the red, gasoline fire glare. At first they were too concerned with the collision and fire to notice the jeeps and the limo. Then Bruce quickly pulled in his head and rolled up the window.

"Some of those bastards have spotted us; it could get ugly."

As if to emphasize the point, the lead jeep jammed its gears into reverse and pulled back beside the limo. On the other side, the rear one drew up level. The maneuver had an instant effect on the crowd around the burning wrecks. The knot that had wandered away from the fire simply to check on the vehicles were suddenly halted. Some ran, fearing an attack, but others stood their ground and even kept on coming. There were shouts. A rock hit the roof of the limo. The crowd was growing in size. The bulk of them kept their distance but every few seconds someone, usually a kid or a teenager, would dart forward, yell abuse and hurl something. The little motorcade was rapidly creating its own riot. In the front seat the driver was talking into a microphone, presumably coordinating action with the jeep drivers. A bunch of youths dashed out of the crowd dragging a chunk of blazing debris from the fire. They launched it into the air. As it flew, it disintegrated and one chunk landed on the hood of the limo.

"That's fucked up the paint."

The driver threw the limo into screaming reverse. At the same time, the two jeeps rocketed forward, straight for the crowd. The crowd broke, howling. Vickers couldn't see but he thought the jeeps had actually hit some of them. He, Bruce and the nurse were tossed back into their seats as the limo breaked and then took off after the jeeps. Bruce was cursing but the nurse, save for a strand of blonde hair that had fallen out from under her cap, maintained her absolute calm even when the car seemed to be accelerating straight for the burning wreckage. The limo was laying smoke as the driver stamped down on the special overdrive designed to save millionaires from kidnappers. At the last minute, he threw it into a shrieking, drifting turn. They bounced across a section of sidewalk and then were racing down clear road. A jeep had stopped and was waiting for them to catch up. Someone was putting down covering fire with a heavy riot gun. As soon as the limo had passed it, the jeep spun its wheels and accelerated to maintain the rear position. Somewhere nearby there was the sound of helicopters. Bruce was still cursing.

"That'll be the Stress Squad. I hope they gas the bastards. I fucking hate structurals."

Vickers looked at Bruce with a raised eyebrow. "How can you hate them? It isn't their fault they got the bad breaks."

"I hate them because I got out and I don't like to be reminded how it was. They had camps for structurals outside Melbourne. I spent five years being shuffled around those fucking hellholes until I volunteered for New Guinea. Even that was a lottery. Can you imagine that? Hoping that you can win a chance to get your head blown off in some stinking jungle?"

Vickers said nothing. Bruce abruptly turned up the sound of the TV. The subject had clearly been dropped. They drove in silence for another twenty minutes. By that time they were in open country. A bright moon made the scrub desert landscape look like the surface of Mars. On TV, the episode of *Rogan's Vengeance* had reached its bloody finale. The nurse seemed to treat this as a signal. She took out a small zippered wallet and opened it. Inside was a loaded syringe. She smiled.

"I think it's time for your shot, Mort."

The room contained exactly three pieces of furniture, an iron hospital-style bed, a metal locker and a chair. His luggage had been dumped in a corner. Another cool, leggy nurse was sitting on the chair watching him.

"How long have I been out?"

"Twenty-seven hours."

"Unh?"

"They kept you under while they ran some tests and stuff."

"Oh shit."

"Worried that you might have missed something?"

"Worried *what* I might have missed."

Vickers had woken on his back. He turned over on his side, wrapping the blankets protectively around him. He stared at the wall. It was painted a drab, duck's egg green. The paint was brand new with a fresh turpentine smell. The effect was someplace between a hospital and a prison. He realized that someone had removed his clothes. He glanced around. They were folded on top of his bags.

"Where am I?"

"Do you know that's the very first time I've ever heard someone use that line in real life?"

Vickers slowly sat up. Whatever drugs they'd used on him had left him dizzy and his stomach kept threatening to heave. He was also profoundly depressed by a rapidly fading dream. It was like the drugs had taken him to some wondrous place where all the secrets of the universe had been revealed to him. As consciousness came back it had melted away like the morning mist, leaving him with a gaping, empty sadness.

"I guess it's just the drugs."

"I'll try and get you something."

"Am I allowed to get up?"

"You can do pretty much whatever you like . . . except leave, of course."

He wrapped the blanket around himself and swung his legs over the side of the bed.

"What do I call you?"

"You could try 'hey nurse.'"

"You don't give much away."

"I'm not paid to."

"What *are* you paid for?"

"To sit here and make sure you don't vomit or choke or anything."

"It sounds boring."

"It was." She held up a book, *The New Celibacy* by Wilma Deering.

He wasn't sure that he could stand but he tried anyway. He swayed dangerously. Hey Nurse was quickly beside him.

"Jesus Christ!"

"I think you'd better sit down.'

He sat. Sweat was running down his face. "I feel like I've been poisoned."

"They really did keep you under for a very long time."

"What were they looking for?"

"Ah, come on, you know I can't tell you that."

He waited a few minutes and then tried to stand again. This time he was more successful and Hey Nurse didn't have to help him.

"Can I take a shower?"

There were two doors in the room. Hey Nurse opened one of them; a small hotel-style bathroom was behind it.

"I'll fix the water for you."

"Do I have to leave the door open?"

"Don't do me any favors."

He closed the door behind him, dropped his blanket and stepped into the warm spray. Gradually the water worked on his locked muscles until he no longer felt like he was mummified. His brain also started working again. If he'd been out for twenty-seven hours, he could be just about anywhere in the world. He could assume nothing and he'd be well advised to get past Hey Nurse and on to someone who was a little more informative. So far, it had been a bit too close to brainwashing. Part of his wish had already come true when he came out of the shower. A tall, broad-shouldered man in military fatigues was flirting with Hey Nurse. He turned and extended a hand.

"Mort Vickers, my name's Streicher. I'll be in charge of you while you're here."

Vickers felt a little awkward accepting introductions wrapped in only a towel.

"I'm glad to meet you. Do you mind if I get dressed?"

Hey Nurse made her excuses. "I'll leave you two alone."

After she'd gone, Streicher grinned at Vickers.

"Isn't she a peach? Don't you just love nurses? It's all that starched cotton and those white stockings . . ."

Vickers was pulling on his pants.

"Where, exactly, is here?"

Streicher looked a little disappointed that Vickers didn't want to share his appreciation of nurses.

"Just like you were told, a desert location about sixty clicks outside Vegas."

"I've been out so long I could be anywhere."

"That's true, but you ain't."

Vicker unzipped one of his bags, looking for a clean shirt. He was surprised to see that both his weapons were right there on top. The ammunition he'd bought had, however, vanished. Streicher didn't have to be asked.

"You'll get ammunition when you need it."

"Are you going to tell me what I'm here for?"

"You look like you could use some breakfast."

Vickers had met a lot of men like Streicher. They were the perpetual NCOs. They hung securely in the middle levels of authoritarian violence. Having raised themselves from the drudgery of the common soldier, they somehow lacked the wit, the intelligence, the courage or the contacts to scale the lonely peaks of real command. Instead, they carved out miniature empires based on a capacity for unquestioning loyalty and a talent for keeping things extremely simple and, on occasion, also extremely brutal. Sometimes they were sadists, sometimes they were closet homosexuals. Almost all had problems with relationships that weren't based on regulations and orders. This was the basic Military model. Other variations were Gangster and Law Enforcement. The differences were mainly ones of style. Streicher seemed to have learned his mannerisms from watching old John Wayne movies. He also seemed to have something of a body fetish. In what Vickers estimated to be his leathery late forties, Streicher was in perfect condition except for a slight beer belly. He was tanned and his visible muscles, on his forearms and neck, stood out like ropes. His eyes were blue and calculating, his hair was cropped to little more than a suede scalp and his jaw was polished by a lifetime of close shaves. Vickers knew there was just one way of dealing with people like Streicher. If you made it very clear, very quickly, that you were the boss you could have them kissing your ass. If you didn't, they would undoubtedly force you to kiss theirs. The first rule was not to give an inch.

"Breakfast sounds good; is it that time of day?"

"It's around dawn."

"So, an early breakfast."

"You can bring your stuff. You won't be living down here."

Vickers picked up one of his bags and nodded down at the other.

"You want to give me a hand with some of it?"

Streicher's gruff-but-genial mask slipped for an instant but he quickly gathered it up along with the bag and ushered Vickers out of the door. The small empty room and four others like it were part of an ultra-utilitarian basement that in no way prepared him for what he would confront when he reached the top of the flight of cast iron steps that seemed to be the only exit. Streicher laughed at his obvious surprise.

"Step back and take a good look. You don't see many places like this."

It was what had come to be known as western sci-fi, the Martian ranch, a flamboyant creation of curved glass, angled steel beams and flat, kidney-shaped slabs of floating concrete. Somewhere, back around the middle of the twentieth century, an architect who must normally have worked on ice cream parlors had had a vision of the future.

"Like something the Jetsons would live in. It was built by some Hollywood sex goddess in the early sixties. It was supposed to be her desert retreat but she took an overdose before she could even move in. Her estate sold it to a rock star and then a dozen or so years later he had to give it to his cocaine dealer when his band hit the skids. The dealer went crazy and let this cult move in. From there it went through a procession of weirdos and hoods on the lam until, somehow, the titles became the property of the corporation. When the project came up, one bright boy in real estate suggests we make use of it. We've got a heart-shaped pool out back. If we stay here long enough we'll get it filled."

"You seem very proud of the place."

"I am. I've been here four months."

"Working on the project?"

"Right."

"The project that no one will tell me about?"

Streicher grinned. "That's the one."

They'd come into a big ranch-style living room with a sunken conversation pit and a futuristic chimney in black and baby-pink marble. Blue morning light was leaking through the not quite drawn drapes on an enormous picture window. A couple of hunched figures lay asleep among the cushions in the pit. One seemed to be clutching a whiskey bottle. The air in the room was heavy with booze and cigar smoke.

"Keep things fairly loose 'round here?"

"They'll tighten up before too long." Streicher jerked back the drapes, slid open a section of window and took a deep, satisfied breath. There were curses and mumblings from the pit. He ignored them and stepped out onto a wide patio. On the other side of the patio were a cluster of guest cottages that had all the ambiance of a motel. Streicher indicated that Vickers would be quartered in one of them and they started walking toward it. Vickers looked back at the house. It really was El Rancho Mars. There was even a strange steel pylon rising from the middle of it. In the first flush of the relentless desert dawn, it looked like the forgotten set for some B feature, raygun movie. It was set on a piece of high ground and sheltered by a few scrubby trees and coarse bushes. Beyond them, Vickers couldn't remember when he'd seen so much nothing. A scarcely defined dirt road ran from horizon to house. To the east, a line of low hills was still casting deep purple shadows.

Streicher pushed open the door to the guest cottage. It was dark inside, just two beds and lots of chaotic debris. There appeared to be two figures in one of the beds. Streicher threw Vickers' case on the spare bed and indicated that Vickers should do the same. One of the figures protested with a man's voice.

"What the fuck is going on?"

"You're getting a new roommate."

"I already got one."

"An official roommate."

"Is that the guy you kept unconscious all yesterday?"

"You shut your mouth, Fenton." He glanced at Vickers. "You can leave your stuff here and sort it out later. Let's go and eat."

They walked on around the house, past the empty heart-shaped pool. Its bottom was covered with leaves.

"When the sun gets hotter, you have to watch out for rattlesnakes. They bask."

Beyond the pool was a circle of fake Greek pillars. One had been smashed. Streicher noticed him looking at them.

"The cult put them up."

They went through an arch and into an open doorway. They were inside a long, low, tiled kitchen. A small, balding man in a chef's apron was loading an industrial-size coffee machine.

"This is Vickers, Albert."

"How d'you do, Vickers."

"Albert cooks for us." To Albert: "Vickers has been asleep for a day and a half. He's hungry."

"I heard about them bringing him in. There ain't nothing ready yet, though. You'll both have to wait."

"You can cook him up some eggs."

"Damned if I can. It's going to throw out my whole schedule. I've got twenty others to feed."

Vickers stored the tidbit of data. Streicher gave Albert a hard look.

"Just make some coffee and cook us up some eggs, Albert; don't fuck with me at this time of the morning." He turned to Vickers. "You want a drink or is it too early for you?"

Vickers took a seat at a long, scrubbed kitchen table.

"Sure, I'd like a drink."

Streicher had a bottle of Wild Turkey and two glasses.

"The others will be down in a while."

One by one they came down for breakfast. Streicher made the introductions. In each case Vickers was eyed with extreme suspicion. The first to arrive was Bronce. He was another body freak who'd already run seven miles that morning, a short brown bullet of a man with slit eyes and flat, East European cheekbones. He ignored Albert's handiwork and fixed himself a creation of carrots, celery and yogurt. As they shook hands, Vickers noticed a number of old but once serious scars on his chest and a look in his eye that suggested he wasn't quite sane. Vickers figured him for a cop who'd been busted for brutality and then found that he could live a whole lot better on the freelance violence market.

Vickers had met Parkwood before. The thin, fastidious corpse was withdrawn to the point of anonymity. They'd worked together on the Louisville business when Parkwood had been attached to DTL. Vickers wouldn't in a million years claim to know him, but he knew that he could be trusted. Vickers had also worked with Anna Treig. She'd been strikebreaking at the same time as he'd been there to take off the senior exec who'd started all the trouble in the first place. He'd seen her both at work and at play. She was a squat peasant woman who liked gin, stupid young boys and inflicting injury. Vickers suspected that he was probably frightened of her. Streicher seemed to notice something as he introduced them.

Sammy and Ralph were a two-man show, the classic combination of fast slender wit and linebacker power. Of course, Vickers had heard of them. Who hadn't? Two ghetto kids who'd taken a direct gutter meaness and sold it all the way to corporate hiring. The big debate was over whether they were also lovers. They appeared to deliberately distance themselves as far as possible from the rest.

The kitchen began to fill, both with people and the smell of bacon, waffles and coffee. Albert was now dishing out food and there started to be too many people for Vickers to absorb all the names and all the faces. The introductions became more perfunctory as people made increasing demands on Streicher's time and attenion. All Vickers could do was make a note of the ones who stood out from the crowd. Morse was a Dapper Dan dresser with a gold tooth who probably fancied himself as being in the tradition of the gunfighters of the Old West. Vickers couldn't imagine how he could have qualified for El Rancho Mars unless he was an amateur psycho with a private income. Eggy was subhuman, tatoos, chains, a shaved head and a look of desperate vacancy. Pointed at a target, he'd go off like a human buzz saw. There was no percentage in exchanging niceties with Eggy.

"Oh yeah, Vickers, meet our own chorus line. Zoe, Bobbie, Linda and Debbie."

The quartet was too hung over for Vickers to register with them but at least they didn't look at him as if he might be poisonous. What he couldn't fathom was what their role in the project might be, unless it was simple light relief. Even in their robes and in bad shape, they were so obviously Vegas that they looked undressed without feathers and spangles. Not just Vegas but *creme de* Vegas, they had to be either showgirls or hookers; Vickers didn't care which, he knew that within hours anything would be a relief from the gang of muscle and homicide that was otherwise assembled in the kitchen. Vickers started to make some calculations. Albert had said that he had to feed twenty other people. He assumed that the house held twenty-two including Streicher, twenty-three if Albert hadn't counted himself. There weren't twenty-two or twenty-three people in the kitchen. Maybe sixteen, seventeen tops. A half-dozen or so were still asleep or otherwise occupied. Those who were there could be divided into a number of distinct groups. Albert had developed an assistant who acted as busboy and dishwasher. Together they made up the domestic staff. Four men in various versions of military fatigues looked like simple ex-soldiers, maybe ex-marines. From the way they related to Streicher, he figured that they had to be his immediate staff. Subtracting the four showgirls and the nurses, it left a solid eight, nine or maybe more, all of whom were hired guns. Some were showboats like Morse or Sammy and Ralph. Others were cold calculators like Parkwood or meatgrinders like Eggy and Anna Treig. By far, the majority of them could command top dollar. Herbie Mossman had assembled himself about as ugly and dangerous a bunch as even a rich man could acquire.

A latecomer pushed his way through the crowded kitchen. He argued with Albert about whether breakfast was still being served, and then made straight for Vickers. There were people sitting on either side of him but it didn't seem to deter this young man. He tapped Bronce, who was on Vickers' right, on his shoulder.

"You want to move down one?"

"I'm through, I was just leaving anyway."

"Great."

He turned his attention to Vickers. He had something of a unique ability to shovel food into his mouth as fast as he could while talking at the same time.

"You're Vickers, right?"

"Right."

"You worked for Contec, right? Killed all those people in front of the Plaza and got fired, right?"

"In actual fact, someone was firing a 50 cal. frag gun at me. They did most of the killing, but otherwise you're just about right."

The young man looked like a pirate in his torn sweatsuit and red patterned do-rag. He had a large gold hoop in his left ear and one of his front teeth was missing. He put down his fork and extended a hand.

"I'm Eddie Fenton. We're sharing a room. I thought we ought to get acquainted."

"I'm pleased to meet you. It was you we woke up this morning?"

"Don't worry about it. Streicher's always pulling shit like that. It's the army in him. I ran into assholes like him in the Yemen."

"You were in the Yemen?"

"Sure was. All the fucking way."

"I was out there too."

"I know. I heard stories about you. I wasn't exactly in your league."

"What league?"

"You know what league. You were one cold motherfucker. I was only a grunt. My only claim to fame was when I shot two lieutenants and a captain in the middle of that mess at Shabwa."

Fenton was coming on strong, trying to build himself up to Vickers. Vickers smiled while he was wondering what he wanted.

"What had they done?"

"They wanted us to go up that hill in the middle of the town while a bunch of fuzzies were at the top with K10s and a T-launcher. We figured it was suicide and drew lots. I won. They were never able to pin it on me but it was a rodeo while they tried."

"So how did you get here?"

"Mossman got me out of Joliette."

Now Vickers was surprised. "Out of jail?"

"I didn't complain."

"What were you doing time for?"

Fenton put down his fork. "You really don't know who I am, do you? I thought you were just being cool."

"I don't have a clue."

"You must have been out of the country. Shit, we were famous."

"I'm sorry."

"You really never heard about the First National Security hijack?"

"You're that Eddie Fenton? The Mad Dog? The one who blew away . . ." Vickers hesitated. Fenton grinned.

"Twelve counts of murder in the first degree. I'm what they call a sociopath. Paradoxically, though, I also have an exceptional talent for team cooperation. I guess that's why Mossman had me pulled out. I was grateful."

"Do you have any idea what he wanted you for?"

Fenton had finished his food. He glanced around.

"Listen, why don't we go back to the room. We can talk there while we get things squared away. I've made a bit of a mess while I've been bunking on my own. I do it to hang up Streicher but you may not want to live in a pigsty."

"Don't call them the Chorus Line. Only Streicher calls them that. Nobody else likes it, particularly the girls themselves, and don't jump to the conclusion that they're just four long-legged bimbos put here for our entertainment. Debbie can shoot as well as I can and Linda could probably break you in half. The other two aren't far behind, either."

Vickers raised an eyebrow. "It gets stranger by the minute."

"Don't it just? You've only started. Wait until you've thought about it a bit."

Mad Dog Eddie Fenton sat down on his bed and opened a beer. He had clearly thought about it a good deal and was going to give Vickers at least some of the benefit. Vickers also sat down. Squaring away their belongings in the small guest cottage didn't take very long. Neither of them had very much. It was mainly a matter of throwing out the garbage that Eddie had accumulated while he'd had the place on his own. Inside of ten minutes he'd pulled out a six pack and the domestic effort was at an end.

"For a start, what would you say if I told you that this place was a high-tech fortress?"

"I wouldn't be that surprised. I suppose you could look on us as valuable property."

"Pretty damn valuable according to the stuff they've got strung out around this Hollywood nightmare. You want to see the red room."

"Red room?"

"Electronic defense control center. Red scopes, sound scoops, ground radar, heat sensors, tremblers, every bit of it is state of the art. They got some nasty stuff out on the perimeter too, remote Claymores, lasers, Bouncing Bettys, crossfire traps. This is no place to go taking an unscheduled stroll."

"Will I see this red room?"

Fenton nodded. "I'd imagine so. We all pull guard duty and all that means is that you sit in the red room and stare into the screens."

"They trust us with all that stuff!"

"We stand guard in threes. One of them and two of us."

"Who's them?"

Fenton treated Vickers to a look of scornful disbelief.

"You should have figured it for yourself by now or else you ain't as smart as I thought you were. You must have seen that Streicher's got four of his boys and the rest of us are recruits. Guess they think it's safe to put two of us to their one because, as of now, we don't have too much to be in cahoots about."

"It's a pretty weird bunch of recruits."

"You noticed that?"

"I've been wondering what you could expect from a bunch like that. We're a very odd combination for any kind of mission."

"And?"

Vickers smiled. He knew that he was expected to give out with something. Fenton seemed to be making a kind of overture. Vickers wasn't sure what he wanted. Was it just an offer of mutual back-watching or was something deeper going on? It would have been handy to note the sex of Fenton's earlier bed companion. He *was* fresh out of jail. Vickers decided to play along.

"I can't see how we could have been assembled for any specific missions. We don't fit any project that I could imagine. We're not a conceivable team. With the exception of you, everyone's either a loner or a couple. We're all general issue, all-purpose killers. There are no specialists. Only you, and possibly the four girls, have a record of being team players. There's just one function that fits us all like a glove."

It was Fenton's turn to smile. "Yeah?"

"We're intimidating. If you wanted to put the fear of God into someone you'd only have to walk in with the whole bunch of us. There's an old western movie called *The Magnificent Seven*."

"*The Magnificent Seven*? You got to be putting me on. I thought you were supposed to be one of the best."

"You know the movie?"

"Of course I know the movie. I was brought up on it, wasn't I."

"So think it through."

"Okay, listen up. You all look like shit. You've all got these big, inflated reputations but the truth is you're soft and lazy. You've been sitting here with your thumbs up your asses for too long. A lot of money's been spent on you and it's now time to start justifying it. It's time to go back to work."

It was eight thirty in the bright desert morning of Vickers' fourth day at El Rancho Mars. It seemed that, with the arrival of Vickers, Streicher had his full complement of recruits and he was now ready to start whipping them into some sort of shape. They had already been at it for two hours. They'd run five laps on a track that completely circled the house and had followed that with a strenuous bout of calisthenics. Some took the punishing exercise in their stride while others were a little green and sweaty behind it. Vickers stood halfway between the two extremes. The sudden exertion hadn't hurt him but he knew, as he fought for breath after fifty sit-ups, that he could have survived without it. After this first taste of what Streicher considered work, they were given fifteen minues for breakfast, fifteen minutes for a shower and then were expected to reassemble by the heart-shaped pool wearing combat clothes and with their weapons.

As they straggled back from their quarters, Streicher was there waiting, positioned so that he cast a dramatically long shadow. There were now only two of his boys flanking him. There had been all four of them around for the first workout phase. Vickers wondered what the other two were doing now. Fenton fell into step beside him.

"You think Streicher's going to give us any idea of what we're training for?"

Vickers grunted and hefted his Yasha. "I doubt it."

Streicher pointed out in the direction of the cult's abandoned ring of pillars.

"For a hundred meters, out to that last clump of trees, we've laid an electronic combat course. There are mines, traps and flip-ups of both good guys and bad guys. The idea is to get to the other side and back again as fast as you can without either being shot or blown up. There's nothing actually lethal in this system, but there is some stuff that can shake you up some. As the flip-ups and the holograms come at you, you'll find that some represent hostile opposition while others will be innocent bystanders. You are supposed to distinguish. You fucking psychopaths who can't tell one from the other, you'll do the course over until you can. Is all this clear to you?"

There were some growls among the general nodding. No professional ever wanted anything to do with combat simulators. Nobody actually protested, however, despite all the low grumbling. Streicher allowed himself a sardonic smile.

"One last thing, ladies and gentlemen, as you move into the combat run you'll find that the system has been tuned to the maximum degree of skill. Consider it a test of all these highly touted reputations."

Morse was the first one up. He was armed with a 12 guage Neilsen Autoshot with a police stock. As he loaded it, Streicher described the course.

"It's a two-way street. All the way to the end and back again. You'll find that we've laid out a complex of trenches, wire and sandbags. All real World War I. You can use them however you like. There's also a three-meter wall and a steel culvert. You go over the wall on the way in and through the culvert on the way out. That's mandatory. Move ahead, Mr. Morse."

Morse nodded and started toward the ring of pillars at a slow, careful walk. Streicher called after him.

"You're on the clock, Mr. Morse. If you don't complete the course in four minutes, you do it over."

Morse broke into a reluctant trot. The ground fell away quite steeply beyond the pillars and he was quickly lost from sight. There were a few seconds of silence and then all hell broke loose. There were explosions, the wump of sound shocks and the rapid-fire bark of Morse's shotgun. Multicolored smoke billowed up. Some of the recruits glanced at each other. There was a slight pause and then another eruption of noise.

"Two minutes. He's had half his time."

Streicher stopped his clock at 3:55 as Morse came trotting back through the ring of pillars. He looked out of breath and a little the worse for the wear.

"Just under the wire, Mr. Morse."

Morse flopped down onto the ground.

"Thank Christ; I wouldn't want to go through all that again."

Streicher grinned nastily. "Oh you will, Mr. Morse. You can count on that, but maybe not today. In the meantime, Miss Debbie, you're up next."

During the four days that Vickers had been at El Rancho Mars, he had learned to take Debbie and the three other girls a whole lot more seriously than first impressions had indicated. They were clearly hardened professionals and, since they were so exceptionally striking, he wondered how it was that he hadn't heard about them before. Debbie looked both practical and sexy in cut-off jungle greens. There was nothing frivolous about the lightweight M20 that she cradled on her left arm. One of Streicher's boys handed her a banana clip; she slapped it into the machine gun with the ease of long practice and then set off for the pillars at a purposeful lope.

Debbie was back in 3:12. She looked a good deal less ruffled than Morse.

"You're up next, Mr. Bronce."

Bronce flexed. A long-barrelled ultramag nestled in a brown leather shoulder holster next to his perfect pects. To Vickers it was a somewhat lightweight weapon for the kind of course it seemed to be. Bronce, on the other hand, was as struttingly confident as ever. He started down the course as if he were aiming to break a record. As soon as he was out of sight the firing started. When he was about a minute into the course, Streicher looked down sharply at a unit on his wrist. He tapped a button. The explosions stopped. Streicher signalled to his two boys.

"Curtis, Gomez. Something's happened to him and he's down. He probably walked into a beanbag. You'd better go in and fetch him out."

Curtis and Gomez hurried down the course. They came back lugging the limp body of Bronce. Fenton moved beside Vickers.

"He'll be madder than hell when he wakes up. The asshole likes to think he's Superman."

Streicher, Gomez and Curtis came back from the house where they'd left Bronce in the care of Hey Nurse.

"I hope that hasn't put you off, Mr. Vickers."

"I could think of better things to be doing, but what the hell."

"What the hell, indeed. You want to go ahead?"

"Whatever you say."

Gomez was in charge of handing out the ammunition.

"How many clips do you want?"

"Three."

He handed Vickers three clips for the Yasha. Vickers taped two together back to back and dropped the third into his pocket.

"Start the clock, Streicher."

Streicher had been right when he'd said that the course was "real World War I." The slope beyond the pillars was an untidy mess of trenches, razor wire, sandbagged parapets and flat representations of buildings like an unfinished movie set. He had no time, however, to stand and get his bearings. The computer that controlled the training course was programmed to play him like a rat in a maze, tracking his footfalls with sound sensors, following his body heat with thermals and all the time barraging him with an infinite variety of unpleasant surprises. An explosion of bright orange smoke went off uncomfortably close to him. He dived into the nearest trench, feeling that there was quite enough anxiety in his professional life without having to put himself through vicarious simulations. He hit the floor of the trench on all fours. A life-size cartoon samurai flipped. He let go a short blast from the Yasha and it went down again. There was an explosion behind him. This time the smoke was Prussian blue. A hail of rubber bullets slammed into the wall. He lay flat for a second and then scuttled, frogwise, up the trench. He really was a rat being goaded through a maze. Flip-up! A Nazi soldier on the edge of the trench. Burst! Gone! Red explosion! Green! Two trenches intersect. Flip-up! This time it's a little old lady. Don't fire! Magenta explosion and he's at the wall. The bad news is that it's made of vertical logs, Fort Apache style. The good news is there's a rope. Scrambling one handed and complaining how he's an assassin, not a fucking commando. Almost to the top there's a flip-up firing high velocity beanbags. Swing! Bean-bags miss but only just. Swing back, twist, bring up the Yasha. Burst, and the bad guy's gone. Straddle the top. The logs are sharpened to points. Drop. The clip in the Yasha is empty. Pull out, reverse, slam it. For an instant, he thinks about Debbie's legs, and then on again.

He's going across an open space and suddenly he doesn't feel so good. His own legs are heavy and his stomach's churning. That bastard Streicher! There's a Burroughs Tube in this set-up. He's being drenched with subsonics. He's surfing on solid ground and rubber bullets are snapping at his heels, but it's the end of the course. Hit the button and back. Flip-up, burst. Flip-up, burst. Flip-up good guy, hold your fire in the nick of time. Boom! Boom-boom! The smoke is lime green. Here's the culvert. Down on hands and knees. There's some-thing black blocking the pipe. Fire ahead blindly. He's almost deafened but it's gone. Out into the light again. YLO gunman. Z-i-i-ppp! Down into the trench. Crawl, crawl, crawl. There's gas and his eyes are tearing. And then he can see the tops of the pillars and he's through, doing his best to look nonchalant as he walks back to the group. The asshole likes to think of himself as Superman.

"3:51, Mr. Vickers. Only just adequate."

"I'd give a lot to see a TV."

"They've got us completely cut off."

"But no movies? No tapes, no card chips?"

"I guess they figured if they gave us monitors one of us at least would be able to rig them to pick up satellite signals." Debbie turned to Gomez. "Ain't that true, Gomez?"

"Believe me, I don't know any more than you do."

"I don't believe you. You're full of shit. You've got some idea of what's going on here, you just aren't telling."

Gomez shrugged. He was used to this sort of thing.

"Whatever you say."

Vickers, Debbie and Gomez had been teamed for guard duty. It was the midnight-to-dawn watch of Vickers' eleventh day at what he still thought of as El Rancho Mars.

"I know one thing, I'm getting fucking sick of that training. I can't see any point to it. It's not like we're training *for* anything. There's no pattern to it. It all seems to be make-work."

"No gain without pain."

"No gain period."

"What's the word, Gomez, is there any pattern to it?"
Gomez was starting to get a little irritable.

"What am I supposed to say?"

Debbie mimicked his flat, colorless accent. "I just do what
Streicher tells me."

"Will you lighten up?"

There were times when Debbie could ride someone beyond
any productive limit. Vickers was also getting tired of the way
she was beating her frustration into the ground.

"Yeah, knock it off. We've got to spend the whole night
together in here. It'd be better to get along."

Debbie slid deeper into her chair, at the same time crossing
her bare legs. The outburst of body language wasn't missed by
either Vickers or Gomez. The two men glanced briefly at each
other but held their silence. Debbie had a petulant streak.

There was something womblike about the red room. It was
dark, quiet and strangely oppressive. The deep-padded contour
chairs were just a little too comfortable. The air was just a little
too warm and a little too dry. The smell of rubber and electrons
could wrap itself around those on duty like a cocoon. The lines
and columns of LEDs glowed red, amber and green. They
could hypnotize anyone who stared at them for too long. There
was one, dim worklamp. All other light came from the sixteen
scopes that monitored the perimeter and approaches to the
house. The gray-green of the ground radar, the red ghosts on
the heat scopes and the patchwork multicolors of the thermals
were reflected in their watching faces. The dim, concentrated
quiet was like that of the cabin of a large aircraft, except it
slightly lacked the calm but watchful tension. The red room
quickly became boring. Vickers drank coffee from a styrofoam
cup. He wished that he had two or three Marvols, even a
greenie. He knew, very soon, the repetitive nothing on the
screens and scopes would put him to sleep.

"It's a pity we don't have a TV. I wanted to see what
happened with Tomoyo Nakamora and the gorilla. I wonder if
they ever got to fuck."

"The whole thing was disgusting."

"You don't believe in cross-species sex?"

"How would you like to fuck a dog?"

"Plenty of guys fuck sheep. At least, that's the legend."

"That's only . . ."

"Wait a minute!" Debbie was staring intently into the screen.

"What?"

"I thought I saw something."

"Where?"

"It was just a faint blip on the ground radar. It could have been a jack rabbit or nothing at all. It was right out on the edge."

"Let's take a look. You got a bearing?"

"Maybe oh one five."

"We'll go out on oh one five, on thermal."

Gomez tapped in instructions and, on the main screen, an image moved outward from the house in the rough direction that Debbie had indicated, segueing slowly from one clump of sensors to the next. The color patchwork of the thermal showed nothing but the blue groundheat of the rocks and sand.

"Looks like it was nothing."

"They ought to have robots out there. Then we could all go to bed."

"You can't use robots in this kind of country. Whatever they do, the sand always fucks 'em up."

"You sound pleased."

"I'm working."

The scan was now feeding from the outermost cluster of sensors. There was still nothing doing.

"We could go around the perimeter."

Debbie shrugged. "I don't know. It was probably nothing."

"Hold it."

There were four yellow smudges. Five, six, there were nine yellow smudges rapidly getting bigger.

"Faces. They give out more heat. Here come the bodies."

There were nine . . . no, ten of them, moving toward the house.

"Put up the audio."

Vickers pushed up a fader. The room was filled with the soft crunch of feet and the superamplified rustle of clothing. There was a quiet curse. Gomez picked up the phone.

"Streicher . . . yeah, right. Yeah, but listen, we've got a bunch of people out on the perimeter and moving this way; you'd better get down here."

He hung up. Debbie tapped the screen with a long, tangerine-flake fingernail. "What do we do about this?"

Gomez brought in the redscope. Ten figures were trudging across the desert. They appeared footsore.

"For the moment, we watch. Streicher's on his way down."

Vickers was thoughtful. He regarded the screen in front of him.

"If I were going to take a place like this, this is exactly the way I'd do it."

"Oh yeah?"

"The only other way would be to come in by air, but they'd have to figure that we've the capability to take out an unauthorized chopper."

Debbie was also staring into the screen.

"Why not just stand off and flatten the place with some kind of missile?"

"I don't see how it could be that kind of an emergency unless there's something that Streicher's *really* not telling us. You need a hell of a lot of justification before you start rocketing another corporation's real estate."

"They could just be lost. Massacring civilians is hardly encouraged."

Vickers grinned at Gomez. "That's why I'm glad I'm only offering advice and not making the decisions."

"And what advice would you offer, Mort?"

The three swivelled in their chairs as Streicher came in.

"If I was you, I'd play the odds and grease them right away but, then again, I'm not you."

Streicher scowled. "And that's a fact." He glanced at Gomez. "Try metal on them. See if they've got any weapons."

The presence of metal was indicated by a violet glow on the thermal screen.

"Three guys carrying frame packs that contain metal objects. I can't tell if they're cans of food or weapons. One other guy's got a pistol and the rest are clean."

"It all looks innocent."

"Or they could be trying to confuse you by loading all the weapons into three packs."

"Perhaps you should ease up on the advice, Vickers."

"*We should have hit a fucking road by now.*"

The muttered comment boomed and reverberated through the red room, blown out of proportion by the speakers.

"*We got to take a break.*"

First one figure and then another flopped to the ground. There was no mistaking their seeming exhaustion. Streicher was still undecided. One of the figures was rummaging in his pack. He continued poking through it for a full minute more. Gomez shook his head.

"This isn't right."

"Drop a flare on them."

The main screen changed to real image as the flare floated down and lit up the desert. The people on the ground were all dressed in identical black coveralls and stocking caps. Their faces were smeared with black makeup.

"They ain't the survivors of no plane crash."

Streicher nodded. "Hit them."

At that exact moment, the red room went haywire. The LEDs blinked frenziedly as though the system was in pain. Some screens blanked out, others froze and a couple exploded in abstract, psychedelic effects.

"They've hacked in."

"That's what that bastard was doing with the pack. He was tapping into one of our landlines."

"They're damned good."

Streicher nodded.

"Hit them with five minutes of everything in a random pattern. They've probably figured a way to neutralize the traps and weapons around them but it'll still shake them."

Gomez hit the weapon control keys. Streicher pressed the general alarm.

"You stay here, Gomez, and try and get control back. You other two, come with me."

The entire perimeter was lit up like the Fourth of July. Tracers, flares, magnesium, smoke, balls of red and green fire boiled into the sky. Swivelling miniguns made the earth smoke; starshells burst in flashes of blinding light. The noise blurred into a continuous booming shriek. Vickers, Fenton and Bronce watched the spectacle crouched in the shelter of the kitchen door, looking out across the patio.

"Pretty damn awesome."

"I'd hate to be down there even if I was hooked into the control system."

"The guy doing the hacking can always fuck up."

Bronce glanced at his watch. "It should stop at any moment."

"We move out after the firing stops."

Bronce nodded. He was still looking at his watch. It was like he could hardly wait to get going.

"Any second now."

The firing stopped like it had been switched off. The last two flares drifted to earth, the only things that now marked the perimeter were smoke and scattered pools of still burning, green liquid fire.

"They'll be coming in as fast as they can."

"So what are we waiting for?"

"Go ahead, we're right behind you."

Bronce took off like a hare out of the trap, crouching low and zigzagging across the patio. Fenton and Vickers found themselves staring at each other. Neither had made a move to follow him. For a moment there was a tense discomfort and then Fenton grinned.

"Let some other asshole get shot up."

"Right. He was begging for it."

Bronce was halfway across the patio and still running. There was a crackle of automatic fire from over on the right.

"Shit!"

Bronce was down and screaming. The screaming faded to sobs.

"Did you see where that came from?"

"No."

"This could turn into a mess. There are too many of us blundering about in the dark."

Almost in answer, a floodlight came on. There was a burst of multiple fire and the light was dead again. Bronce seemed to be trying to cry out something. Vickers ignored him. There were more bloodcurdling screams from another direction. These weren't the sound of mortal pain, though. It was shrieking, crazy rage. Eggy came round the corner of the house at a dead run, an old fashioined MT in one hand and a machete in the other. His teeth were bared in a howling grimace that was hardly human. He was stripped to the waist and his mass of neck chains flew and flailed behind him. He failed totally to see either Vickers or Fenton as he raced across the patio and back into the darkness. The howl turned into semi-articulate curses punctuated by bursts of wild firing.

"Unstable little fucker, isn't he."

"Maybe he just enjoys his vocation."

"Let's work our way around the outside of the house."

Fenton looked amused. "You want me to go first."

"You're nearest.'"

"If you're not behind me, I'll come back for you."

Fenton edged forward, keeping close to the cover of the wall. Vickers followed right behind. There was more firing and what sounded like the explosion of a grenade over by the heart-shaped pool. Vickers and Fenton paused and then hurried forward. They stopped again. Two figures came over the edge of the patio at a dead run on silent soles. Both Vickers and Fenton froze in the shadows. There was no mistake: black clothes, blacked-out faces. They were the opposition beyond a doubt. Vickers couldn't feel a thing about them. It was simply an exercise. They were no more human to him than the flip-ups on the training course. Both he and Fenton let the pair go right past them. They'd almost reached the living room windows before they cut them down. As soon as they'd fired, both men ran and finally hurled themselves down. Someone was shooting at them.

"What do we do now?"

"Crawl back to the cover of the house."

There was more firing, way to the left, beyond the curve of the window. An explosion followed four or five quick bursts. Vickers and Fenton eased themselves back into the shadows and waited tensely. Fenton nodded approvingly.

"You know? I like you, Vickers. You don't take any chances."

Vickers was watching the area of darkness from which the firing had come.

"When I haven't been told what I'm doing here I'm not about to stick my neck out."

Something was moving out there. Vickers braced himself and pointed his machine pistol, gripping it with both hands. There were figures coming around the front of the house. Fenton also took aim. The leading one waved its arm.

"Don't anybody shoot. It's me, Streicher."

Fenton didn't lower his gun. "We could pretend that we didn't hear and blow the sucker away."

"I don't think it's quite time for that, yet."

Vickers stepped forward and called out. "It's okay. It's just us, Vickers and Fenton. There's a couple of opposition bodies beside you there."

Streicher and the others halted.

"That accounts for all of them. Are you two okay?"

"Sure, we're okay."

Streicher sounded weary.

"We took some casualties."

Vickers flicked the Yasha onto safe and walked toward Streicher and the others. There were six of them, including Gomez, Garcia, Curtis and Linda. Parkwood was bending over one of the bodies. He rolled it onto its back.

"Does anyone have a flashlight?"

Gomez handed him one and he inspected the face of the body. Vickers joined him.

"Somebody should go take a look at Bronce. If he's not dead, he's hurt real bad."

Streicher looked at Linda.

"Go check."

She hurried to where Bronce was laying. Vickers watched her go. When the alarm had sounded she'd hardly bothered to dress. Someone inside the house was turning on the exterior lights. Linda called across the patio.

"Bronce is dead as far as I can tell."

"Shit." Streicher looked extremely unhappy. This was clearly the last thing that should have happened to his charges. "Who else got it?"

"Morse. It was his own fucking fault. He walked right into it."

"Who else?"

"Anna Teig. They blew her head clean off. One of them was tossing out whammies. Sammy was hit on the shoulder but he'll be okay. Ralph's looking after him. Zoe fell into a trench and broke her ankle."

"You'd better take a look at this." Parkwood was slowly straightening up from where he'd been examining the body. "You look too, Vickers. You're not going to like this."

Streicher and Vickers both peered down. Parkwood flashed the light on one of the faces. Vickers sighed.

"Oh Christ."

"You know her?"

"Sure he knows her, don't you, Mort?"

Parkwood seemed almost amused.

"Sure I know her."

Streicher looked angrily from Parkwood to Vickers.

"So who the hell is she?"

Vickers sighed. "Her name's Ilsa van Doren. She's a Contec corpse. She's had two tries at me already."

Streicher's eyes were cold and hard.

"So how did she get here?"

"That's what I was wondering."

Parkwood allowed himself a thin, cool smile.

"At least you've killed her."

Streicher scowled. "That could have been very convenient."

"What are you suggesting?"

Streicher was once again the closed-up professional.

"I'm not suggesting anything. Right now I want answers." He turned to Gomez, Garcia and Curtis. "We'll do it tonight, we can't wait until morning. Collect up the opposition dead. They can go in the cold store in the basement. We'll search them and find out what we can."

"All I know is that my partner here's been shot up and someone's going to pay for it."

For almost an hour, Ralph had moved backward and forward from the edge of hysteria. It had taken that long for Streicher's boys to bring in the bodies. The Contec connection had put Vickers on the receiving end of some hostile and suspicious stares. Three of their number had been killed and two more were wounded. Some of them needed an individual to hold responsible. Apparently Vickers might do until a more complete and satisfactory explanation came along. The search of the bodies had revealed little. Three had been recognized as Las Vegas freelancers, exactly the kind you'd hire if you were going to attempt an assault mission of this kind. Except for Ilsa, the others were mysteries. They had brand new and identical sets of clothes and a selection of brand new weapons.

Streicher seemed more shaken than he ought to be by the attack. This puzzled Vickers. He'd imagined the man was far more experienced. He had the jumpy preoccupation of someone who knows that hell will fall upon him the moment that he reports to his superiors. His authority seemed to be slipping and he had to openly restrain himself from leading the move to make a scapegoat out of Vickers.

"Somebody had to tell them where we are."

Vickers was calm and patient. It wasn't so much Streicher that worried him. With Streicher, discipline would always win out in the end. It was Ralph that bothered him the most. Ralph's lover, partner, companion or whatever, was wounded. Vickers couldn't trust that his alternate ranting and brooding might not explode into a full-scale flash of get even. Nobody had yet asked Vickers to hand over his weapon and he continued to hold onto it.

"How could I have told anyone where we are? I didn't know, and if they'd planted some gizmo on me, you would have found it. You ran tests on me for twenty-seven hours."

When the dead had been brought in, Streicher had insisted that everyone follow them down to the cold-room in the cellar. The thirteen bodies had been laid side by side on the concrete floor. They looked like wax figures under the harsh, white refrigerator neon, with as little relationship to life as the sides of beef and bacon that were hung along the wall on steel hooks. The Rancho was also prepared for a siege as well as an attack. There were a pair of plain wooden coffins stacked in a corner. These somehow disturbed Vickers more than the dead on display.

Streicher paced up and down the row of bodies. Everyone else waited, chilling down in the bone-cold, metallic air and listening to the ring of his boots. After the warm desert night the freeze came fast. Ralph was the first to crack.

"What I want to know is what are we going to do about this?"

The remark was thrown directly at Vickers. Ralph, however, wasn't the only one who was cold and angry. Debbie was squatting on the floor, massaging her legs.

"This is getting ridiculous, Streicher. We're professionals and we coped with the situation. Why are you keeping us down here freezing our collective ass off? We were just in genuine combat and we don't need this shit. If you think you're going to get Vickers to confess to something, you've got to be crazy."

Vickers gave her a half smile. Ralph immediately swung at one of the side of beef. There was a hollow thud. The meat swung backwards and forwards.

"Let me have a try at him. He'll tell everything he knows."

Streicher was glowering. Vickers was trying not to shiver

with the cold. He was getting tired of all this nonsense. When
people started punching meat, it was time to take the offensive.
His delivery was slow, fairly soft but very distinct.

"If you people didn't have shit for brains you'd realize that I
couldn't—in any way—have brought this team down on us."

Ralph was advancing on Vickers.

"Don't tell me I have shit for brains, motherfucker."

Vickers took a pace back and raised the Yasha.

"One more step and I'll cut your ass in half. I swear to
God."

For too many seconds it was a frozen tableau. Ralph
snarling, Vickers pointing the machine pistol at his stomach
while the onlookers tried not to think about what was going to
come next. Then Fenton, one hand in his pocket and the other
tapping his own gun against his shoulder, sauntered into the
picture.

"For so-called professionals, you really aren't thinking too
seriously. Vickers is right when he says you've got shit for
brains. Consider this . . ."

Debbie interrupted. "Could we consider it somewhere else?
I'm going to get sick if I stay down here any longer."

Vickers and Fenton both looked at Streicher.

"Well?"

Streicher nodded. He seemed to be more in control of
himself. Fenton turned to Ralph.

"How about you? Ready to discuss this upstairs?"

Ralph let go a little. Fenton put a hand on his shoulder.

"Let's go upstairs, shall we?"

There was collective relief as everyone filed out. Finally
there were only Vickers and Streicher left. Vickers took a final
look at the bodies and then motioned with his gun.

"I'd be happier if you went first."

Streicher continued to scowl.

"I'm not convinced of anything."

"Neither am I; that's why I don't want you behind me."

They reassembled in the living room. The curtains were
drawn back and it was like a glass box. There was a hint of
dawn in the eastern sky. Someone had helped himself to drinks
and most had put down their weapons. The mood was now one
of discussion rather than retaliatory kill. Vickers and Fenton
still clutched their guns. Vickers noted that, for a second time,
Fenton had slipped easily into the role of watching his back.

Again he wondered what it was that Fenton ultimately wanted. In the living room, he went even further. He seemed to be acting as Vickers' attorney.

"It's like he told you downstairs. If you think it through, you'd realize that neither he nor any of the rest of us could have guided that team in here."

Ralph was still clenching and unclenching his jaw and fists.

"Some motherfucker did."

"That's a fact, but it wasn't Vickers."

"Maybe you're just hot for his ass."

"Now you're really being stupid."

"I don't like to be called stupid."

Streicher was halfway out of his chair with a parade ground bellow.

"Just shut the fuck up, Ralph!" He turned to Fenton. "You go on, but you'd better make it good."

Fenton scanned the room, moving with scarcely concealed contempt.

"What everyone's forgetting is that we took those suckers with ease. If anyone in this room had managed to get out the location of this place and precise details of the defense set-up including the actual position of the landlines, they would also have reported on how many of us were staying here. How many are we?" He looked around questioningly. "Two dozen? Right? If they'd known that there were two dozen of us in here, would they have sent in a little bitty team of just ten?"

Vickers nodded. "They'd have either sent in a full-blown assault force of fifty or, much more likely, wouldn't have bothered in the first place."

Debbie reached for a bottle of Jack Daniels. "So who did tell Contec we were here?"

Fenton shrugged. "It must have been a leak on the outside."

"Why should an outside leak be any more likely to give out the wrong information?"

Fenton frowned; for the first time he looked uncertain.

"I don't know. Maybe they had bad information, maybe they had old information, maybe it was all part of some weird set-up. What can I tell you? Whatever the answer, it makes more sense than trying to work out an impossible theory so we can pin the blame on somebody here."

Neither Streicher nor Ralph appeared to be any closer to being convinced.

"It's all too easy to place the responsibility back in Las Vegas."

"How many people knew we were all out here, Streicher?"

"I can't tell you that."

"Do you even know?"

Debbie put down her bottle. "Tell me something, Streicher, why are you so all-fired keen to make one of us a traitor?"

Vickers noted the phrase "one of us." Debbie and maybe more had moved on from looking to hang Mort Vickers to searching for real answers. The suspicious glances were now directed at Streicher. Answers were something he didn't seem to have.

"I just have a feeling. I can't explain it. There's a great deal that I'm not permitted to talk about."

Vickers let the gun dangle by his side. He advanced on Streicher and nobody made a move to stop him.

"That's the trouble with guys like you. You're like trained dogs. You are fine just as long as someone's telling you what to do but if you ever start to lose faith in your master, everybody watch out, you go to pieces."

"I don't have to take your shit, Vickers."

Debbie made an impatient gesture. "Forget about Vickers, what we want to know is what *you* intend to do."

"I have to get instructions on this. Nothing I've been told covers what's happened here."

Parkwood yawned. Up to that point he'd kept out of the discussion.

"If that's the best you can do, Streicher, I think I'll go and get some sleep. You can wake me if there are developments."

There were noises of agreement and assent. Eggy stood up with a rattle of chrome chains.

"He's right. I've listened to enough of this garbage. I'm fucking off to bed."

Eggy had killed four of the intruders, apparently in a silent, berserk rage, but after they'd come back inside he'd become withdrawn and silent with a strange, heavy-lidded satiation that seemed to indicate that, for Eggy, bloodletting was a deep, profound, even awesome end in itself.

"I'm very disappointed in you, Streicher. Real disappointed. You know what I mean?"

Streicher's look was cold and hard but in the hardness there was a precise defeat. He'd lost control. Eggy looked him up and down and then stomped out. The lynching party rapidly disintegrated. Vickers glanced at Fenton, who was on his way to the door.

"I should thank you for backing me up tonight."

"You should, but later."

Vickers suddenly realized that Linda was waiting for Fenton. He grinned.

"Sure. Later."

The living room quickly emptied. Albert's helper had fallen asleep in the conversation pit. Streicher seemed about to say something to Vickers, then he thought better of it and left. Suddenly Vickers was alone to ask his own question as to why Ilsa van Doren should have been sent on what proved to be a suicide mission. At least he thought that he was alone. Then he saw Debbie. She was smiling wearily and holding out the bottle of Jack Daniels.

"It's been one long bastard of a night."

"That's true enough."

"You want to come back to my room for a nightcap?"

Vickers blinked. Debbie? It was the final twist in a very twisted day.

Once the passion had burned itself out, they slept together with the ill-fitting awkwardness of two people who are totally exhausted but also totally unfamiliar with each other. The sheets were bunched and bundled and Vickers drifted through fragmenting dreams of lights, explosions and tracer shells in the night. The knock on the door around two thirty in the afternoon came as something of a relief.

"What is it?"

The voice belonged to Gomez. "Streicher wants you down in the living room in twenty minutes. Both of you."

Vickers blinked. "How did you know I was in here?"

"Don't be ridiculous."

His boots moved away down the corridor. Debbie sat up. "Do I look as bad as you do?"

"Probably."

"That's not very complimentary after all I did for you."

"I didn't mean it that way. You ever been in a firefight before? It has its own unique hangover."

"I feel kind of numb."

"That's a part of it."

Debbie got out of bed and headed for the bathroom. Vickers was so numb that her legs caused no reaction. The hiss of the shower caused him to wonder about his own cleanliness. He was dirty and unshaven but what the hell. He rolled from the bed and started pulling on his pants.

"Are you going to shower?"

"No. I need some clean clothes out of my room. I'll see what Streicher wants first."

Before going to the living room, they stopped by the kitchen to see if Albert had any coffee. Fenton was already there with Linda.

"Streicher want to see you too?"

"Both of us."

Linda mock pouted. "He didn't ask for me."

"You might be the lucky one."

"That's always possible."

Parkwood was already in the living room as was Streicher, who was standing staring out of the picture window with his hands locked behind his back. He not only looked as though he hadn't slept but as if he'd been through a hard morning as well. Even so, Vickers didn't bother with courtesy.

"What do you want?"

"We'll wait until everyone's here."

Eggy crashed through the door. "What the fuck do you want, Streicher? I was spark out. You had your money's worth out of me last night."

"Close the door."

Parkwood looked slowly around with quizically raised eyebrows.

"Just the five of us?"

"I've been told to ship you out."

"Why us? What did we do?"

"Around here we just follow orders."

Parkwood pursed his lips. "Could it be anything to do with us having the highest scores on that ridiculous combat range of yours?"

"I don't know what you're talking about."

Streicher's face had already given him away, however. Parkwood smiled.

"You don't take enough care of your computer."

"You shouldn't have done that."

Streicher didn't sound as though he had anything to back up the threat. Parkwood continued to smile.

"What was it? Some kind of selection process? Somebody playing Darwin?"

Eggy glared at everyone in turn, finishing up with Streicher.

"So where the fuck are we going now? I've had a gutful of this place, I can tell you."

"You'll find out when you get there."

Vickers shook his head.

"Sweet Jesus Christ, this is ridiculous. This secrecy is obsessive."

Eggy snarled. "Can you manage to tell your asshole when to shit?"

"Transport is already here."

"What?"

"The transport is already here. You have fifteen minutes to gather up your stuff. I won't say it's been nice knowing you."

Debbie moved to protest. "Wait just a minute. What about the others? What's going to happen to them?"

"I don't have any instructions. I imagine they'll be transferred too. It seems that this place is going to be shut down."

"And we never filled the heart-shaped pool."

"Fuck you, Fenton."

Streicher stalked out of the room. Eggy spat after him.

"Fuck!" He again looked around. He still disliked the other four but he seemed to accept they were in the same circumstances and therefore had some common interests. "Shit!"

Vickers yawned and rubbed his eyes. He could have done with a couple more hours' sleep.

"That's the truth."

Debbie started for the door.

"I'm going to get my stuff together and say good-bye to the girls."

Apart from the wire mesh over the windows, the heavy duty, rough country tires and the lack of license plates, it was a regular, yellow school bus, the current year's model. The two men who came with it were less conventional. They were two of the most exquisitely turned out soldiers that Vickers had ever seen. The army-style steel helmets, the kind with the communicator in the side blister, were finished in polished chrome and the visors were mirrored to match. Their jump-boots were shined to a parade ground polish and their lightweight combat suits had knife-edge creases. Instead of the normal olive green they were a rather attractive mushroom gray. Of the five transportees, Eggy was the most disbelieving. He seemed to take their stylishness extremely personally. He bore down on them with a stiff-legged lurch.

"What the fuck are you supposed to be?"

The nearest of the pair raised his M90 and pointed uncompromisingly at Eggy's chest.

"Sir. You will surrender your weapon and board the bus." Eggy looked down at his worn MT and back to the soldier with a look of brute incomprehension.

"Run that by me again."

"Sir. You will surrender your weapon and board the bus. Your weapon will be stored in the luggage compartent and returned to you when we reach our destination."

The soldier had the robot voice of the hardcore corporate warrior. They might be prettied up but they were cold bastards who'd put a bullet through Eggy as easy as blinking. Debbie must have reached exactly that conclusion. She put down her bag and put a hand on Eggy's arm.

"Why don't you relax and go with the program until we get where we're going. He's got you cold anyway."

Eggy looked down at his gun again. He spun it on his finger and pushed it butt-end first toward the soldier.

"Here, cutie, stash it with the bags."

He climbed on board the bus. One by one the others followed him. Vickers paused before handing over his bag and his guns.

"I suppose it's no use in asking you where we're going."

"No sir."

"I thought not."

The bus was empty except for two more uniformed men. One was acting as a third guard, the other as driver. The five passengers spread out as far as possible, as though each one of them needed his or her privacy. Parkwood went all the way to the back and opened a dog-eared copy of Proust's *Remembrance of Things Past*. Debbie pulled her knees up to her chin and, almost immediately, appeared to go into a trance. Fenton flopped into a middle seat and stared out the window. Vickers did the same. Eggy, on the other hand, moved up to the front and stared through the windshield with the dumb rapt interest of a dog on a car ride. This rather discomfited the guard at the front. He'd positioned himself at the front of the bus with his back to the windshield. His M90 was slung across his chest. He tensed a little and his hand gripped the butt as Eggy lurched toward him. Eggy, however, simply looked him up and down and then ignored him. He took up position right beside him, only facing in the other direction. The other two guards boarded, the door closed with a hiss of air pressure, the air conditioner came on and the driver eased the bus into gear. They took up position in the back seat, one on each side of Parkwood. Parkwood apparently took exception to this as he immediately moved two seats forward and went back to his book.

The bus rolled and wallowed on the uneven desert road. The passengers hung onto the seats in front of them and, on a number of occasions, Eggy was jolted against the guard. On the third collision, he broke into a fiendishly vacant grin. Among the totems and geegaws festooned to his neck and chest was an old fashioned .45 caliber brass and lead bullet. It was clutched in an ornate silver eagle's claw that was in turn attached to a silver chain. Eggy dangled it in front of the guard's face.

"You know what's inside this?"

The guard was doing his best to keep his balance. For a brief instant he looked quite horrified. Beside Eggy he was just a callow boy. He swallowed and shook his head as the bus lurched again. Eggy laughed.

"Cyanide, cutie. Enough cyanide to kill four or five people. They ain't never going to touch me."

Fenton glanced at Vickers. He smiled ruefully and shook his head. Eggy was from some dangerous galaxy. Fenton seemed about to say something but, before he could, the bus was shaken by the boom of a not too distant explosion. The ground shook. Everyone in the bus hit the floor. They stayed down, counting the seconds. When there were no further explosions they gingerly moved to the back of the bus and looked out the window. Where El Rancho Mars had been there was now just a column of black smoke. The smoke from the first fireball was high in the air and starting to dissipate. A fresh black cloud was roiling up to replace it from what was obviously a raging inferno. Fenton looked at Vickers with narrowed eyes.

"They blew the house? Why in hell would they do that? It doesn't make any sense."

"Maybe it was another attack."

"Immediately after we left? It seems like too much of a coincidence."

Debbie was running down the bus, yelling at the driver.

"Stop, goddamn it! Stop the damn bus!"

She tried to grab him but, at the same time, the guard at the front grabbed her. She tried a hip throw on him but couldn't quite bring it off in the confined space. The guard managed to kick her feet out from under her and they both crashed into the first passenger seat. Eggy suddenly shrieked and charged down the bus to help out Debbie. He started pounding on the guard with his interlocked fists. The two guards in the rear had their guns up and, for a moment, it looked like carnage was going to spread all down the length of the bus. Vickers was on his feet and shouting, facing the rear guards and waving his arms.

"Hold it! For Christ's sakes hold it!"

Parkwood and Fenton hurried to the front and dragged the snarling Eggy off the guard and then helped the guard and Debbie disentangle themselves one from the other.

"Everyone just calm down now."

Eggy reluctantly relaxed but Debbie was still furious.

"I had friends in that place!"

The front guard had retrieved his gun and was wondering who to point it at. Fenton leaned toward the driver.

"It might be a good idea if you pulled over while we sort this thing out."

The driver had a voice like a robot.

"I have orders not to stop under any circumstance."

For a moment Fenton looked as though he was going to hit him. He clearly thought better of it and turned on the front guard.

"Do you know anything about this?"

"We were warned there might be an explosion. We were supposed to stop you becoming alarmed."

Vickers looked at the two rear guards.

"Is this what they told you?"

They both nodded. "We all had the same briefing."

Debbie continued to smoulder. "Why should they blow the place up? What happened to the people?"

One of the rear guards softened just the slightest fraction.

"They told us the others would be evacuated to another destination and then the place would be destroyed as a security precaution."

Neither Debbie nor Eggy seemed convinced. They both looked around belligerently.

"Does anyone believe this crap?"

The bus lurched, and Parkwood sat down.

"We may have been the cream of the crop, but the others who remained were valuable operatives and it would make no economic sense simply to destroy them. It goes against all corporate logic to wantonly waste money. On the other hand, though, the house itself was a moderately valuable installation and it also seems a great waste if they just blew it to cover our tracks. Of course, if we knew where our tracks were going, we'd have an idea how much they might be worth covering."

"But these bastards aren't going to tell us a fucking thing."

Eggy growled at the guards. They looked a little nervous but none of them volunteered any further information. Fenton and Vickers both sat down, but Debbie still stood, clutching the overhead rail with a white-knuckled hand.

"I think we should go back and find out exactly what happened. I want to know what became of Zoe, Bobbie and Linda."

Parkwood eyed the guards. "I don't think our friends are going to let us do that."

"Screw these assholes. We can take them."

Parkwood twitched his shoulder in the faintest of shrugs.

"Sure we could take them except we'd probably lose one, if not two of us in the process and the status of those of us left could become decidedly strange."

"You're a cold son of a bitch."

"Don't you think there's enough emotion flying around here?"

Eggy hulked over Parkwood.

"So what would you do, Iceman?"

"I'm going to stick with the program. Someone's gone to a lot of trouble to put us on this bus and I'm not about to get off it until I have a few more facts. Whatever happened at the house has happened and there's nothing we can do about it."

Debbie became stubborn. "You didn't have friends back there."

Parkwood's eyes froze. "If you were the professional you're supposed to be you wouldn't have had friends back there, either."

Vickers, who'd been watching intently, realized for the first time just how deadly Parkwood might be if pushed. He was what the Japanese had in mind when they made up the saying about the best killers being already dead. Eggy abruptly sat down.

"Yeah, go with the fucking program."

Debbie, now isolated, bit her lip. She pushed her way past the guards and went to the back of the bus. She sat down, staring out the rear window at the plume of smoke.

"You think I'm crazy, you should have seen my brother. He used to sit in the park and burn money until someone beat him up. Then he'd laugh in their faces. Somedays he'd go to the bank and he'd draw out a hundred in singles and then he'd go to this favorite bench that he had in the park and he'd take this big fucking radio that he had and he'd settle himself down and turn up the radio real loud so's people would notice him and then he'd start into setting fire to one bill after another. He'd do it real slow, holding each one up in the air until it was all burned up except for the last little corner that he was holding it by. He'd light them with this old fashioned Zippo that our uncle had given him. He claimed that he'd used it in Vietnam to burn gook huts."

"Your uncle was in Vietnam?"

Eggy shrugged. "I was never sure. He was my old man's oldest brother so I guess he could have been the right age. He claimed he was but I couldn't figure how he could have gone through all that and still stayed such an asshole."

Eggy's sudden burst of intimacy came out of nowhere. It was almost as much of a surprise as the blowing up of the house. They'd ridden in silence for a further two hours, bouncing and swaying along the unsurfaced desert trail when the outburst had begun without preamble or even a clearing of the throat. He talked at no one in particular, addressing the whole of the bus with the weird confidence of someone who lets go so rarely that he's certain everyone will be paying attention.

"Pretty soon, a crowd would start to gather. My brother would pretend not to notice them at first."

"What was your brother's name?"

"It don't matter." Eggy seemed to resent this second interuption. He glared around belligerently. "Anyone else got anything they want to ask?"

As one they shook their heads.

"Okay, like I was saying, first off a crowd would gather and my brother'd start by completely ignoring them. He'd just sit there burning his money, pretending it was the most normal thing in the world. Pretty soon some of the crowd would start mouthing off. They'd start making smart remarks to each other about how my brother was a mental case and ought to be locked up. If he wanted to get rid of his cash, he didn't have to burn it, he could give it to them. When my bro went on ignoring them, they got a bit bolder. They'd start coming onto him direct. 'Hey, fuck, what the fuck do you think you're doing? You insane or something? You gotta be fucking crazy.' You know what I mean? It was real slick, Oscar Wilde stuff. There was a pattern to it though, it always got physical in the end. They might make a grab for the money while it was actually burning but, usually, it would keep them mesmerized. Nine times out of ten, the violence would start when my bro reached into his pocket for a fresh bill. Some fool would grab for it, like he was rescuing the sacred dollar from the pyromaniac. My brother didn't actually resist, but he'd do his best not to let them get the bill and that always led to someone hitting him. Once the first punch had been thrown the dam was broken, all hell'd break loose. They'd be all over my brother and, because even then I wasn't going to stand by while a bunch of hysterical assholes beat on my bro, they be all over me too. Sometimes the cops would come and we'd get beat up all over again. When you're a kid and the cops beat on you, it can really hurt. They can do it without leaving marks, too . . . Jesus fucking Christ! Will you look at that!"

All heads turned to follow Eggy's open-mouthed gaze. The bus had crested a rise and in front of them, at the other side of a flat, dry valley, was a ridge of low, rocky hills. The side that faced the bus was a fairly steep escarpment. What had surprised Eggy was that someone had carved what, from a distance, looked like a giant mailslot right in the hillside. It was, however, a mailslot that could swallow a light cruiser, even if it was set sideways. The bottom edge of the vast, rectangular, manmade cave was level with the desert floor. All round the edge the living rock was reinforced with massive expanses of forbidding gray concrete. It was flanked by two enormous buttresses. Parkwood, who'd been standing up to get a better view, abruptly sat down.

"You all know what that is, don't you?"

Debbie's voice was awed. "It's a bunker, a nuclear survival bunker."

"I never realized they were so big."

"There's like as not a whole small city under those hills."

Vickers hoped that he looked as amazed as everyone else. Fortunately, no one seemed to be paying him any attention. Eggy was instantly suspicious but it was all directed at the distant bunker mouth.

"Why the fuck should they bring us to a survival bunker?"

Fenton grinned. "Maybe they think we're worth saving."

Vickers decided that it was time to ease naturally into the conversation.

"I doubt that."

"So?"

"Don't ask me. I gave up trying to make any sense out of all this when I left Las Vegas."

As the bus eased closer it became possible to make out more details of the approaches to the bunker entrance. A geometric system of roads and rail tracks fanned out from the giant cave. They ran through a complex, almost urban landscape of pillboxes, watchtowers, high wire fences and clumps of the squat pylons that enclosed electronic dragon's teeth. Vickers couldn't remember when he'd seen a place so heavily defended. He counted no less than twelve multiple launchers, each with its full complement of four Elisha surface-to-surface missiles. This wasn't to say that there weren't many more concealed in underground silos. Vickers didn't particularly want to think what might be lurking just below the surface. He knew it would, without a doubt, make the stuff that they had strung around El Rancho Mars look like a kid's Fourth of July fireworks show. He scanned along the top of the rocky escarpment. He could just about make out more structures that almost certainly housed SAM batteries. He covertly glanced around the bus. The others were taking similar stock of the formidable layout.

A number of heavy freightliners were moving along the road system, all heading for the bunker entrance. Squat, magnetic shunts were moving lines of boxcars in the same direction. A number of smaller, military-style vehicles rolled slowly along the roads as if on patrol. It was, though, like no other military installation that Vickers had ever seen. There was not a trace of either the all-pervading army green or even the dull tan favored by some desert forces. Everything here was the same mushroom gray as the uniforms of their guards.

The dirt trail along which the bus had been lurching wasn't in any way incorporated into the bunker's road and track system. In fact, by the time they reached the perimeter highway, it had been graded out of existence. The bus finally bounced onto the outer road in a less than graceful cloud of dust. It was clear that no volume of traffic had ever been planned between the bunker and El Rancho Mars.

The concrete under the bus's wheels was still a novelty when they were intercepted. Around this place, security apparently wasn't taken lightly. A jeep with a small rocket launcher, a Samurai armored car and a four-man motorcycle squad surrounded them and ran them to a halt with an air of accepting no argument. The driver was required to climb down from his cab and produce no fewer than four cards that were run through a data point on one of the bikes while a burly motorcyclist held the man's hand firmly down on the machine's sensor plate. All through the identification process the other three cyclists stood off with leveled M90s.

"They don't even trust their own 'round here, do they?"

The passengers had all moved to one side of the bus to watch the proceedings.

"I swear to God, they have the prettiest soldiers around this place."

"No shit."

Debbie was absolutely correct. As with the guards on the bus these new examples of the bunker's troops were turned out with an almost unnatural, parade-ground immaculacy. The motorcyclists were particularly flamboyant. In addition to the standard mushroom gray, they sported two-tone helmets, with opaque sun visors, flyaway wings on their epaulets, heavy black leather utility belts hung with a variety of offensive objects and mirror-finish black riding boots. Eggy seemed to find them particularly offensive.

"I hope nobody thinks they're going to get me into one of those monkey suits."

"No?"

"You better believe it. The one thing I don't do is uniforms. I hate uniforms."

Fenton glanced at him. "All those cops who beat you up as a kid when your brother was burning money?"

Eggy snarled. "Shut your mouth, Fenton."

"Anything you say."

The bus was allowed to move on. The patrol seemed to be satisfied that the driver wasn't a dangerous enemy infiltrator, but this single check wasn't the end of precautions. They were halted at two more static inspection points and also buzzed, and probably scanned, by a Dominator helicopter. Finally they pulled into a circular, walled area that might have been a rather odd parking lot, except there wasn't another vehicle in sight and there were armed guards pacing slowly along the top of the wall. The bus halted. The driver killed the engine and dismounted, as did the guard at the front. The guards in the rear moved forward, shepherding the passengers in front of them.

"Okay. This is as far as we go. Everyone off. Collect your luggage from the outside of the bus and then proceed through the red door in the wall in front of you."

"What about our weapons?"

"Those will be returned after the period of orientation."

"What the fuck is a period of orientation?"

"I can't answer any more questions."

Nobody said anything. There was no plausible fuss that could be caused in these fortifications. Nothing to do but go right on doing what they were told. Grudges, however, were being stored for later. The reception committee was waiting behind the red door. Its leader was possibly more exquisite than the motorcyclists they'd seen on the way in. From his polished boots to his gold-trimmed forage cap, he was the complete military dandy. As well as flyaway epaulets he also affected a considerable fall of red braided lanyard.

"I'm Deakin and I will be in charge of you during your period of orientation."

Deakin was short. Five four and he hated every inch of it. He attempted to inflate himself in compensation. He even strutted on his toes, a puffed up little bantam rooster who would play martinet to the point of mania if the air wasn't let out of his tires. Vickers made a note to do exactly that as soon as the opportunity presented itself.

"So where do we go from here, Deakin? We've been bouncing across a goddamn desert for too long and we need a drink and a place to stretch out."

Deakin indicated two much larger men in red coveralls with the word INDUCTION stenciled on the left breast pocket.

"You've been assigned to a temporary holding area; these gentlemen will take you down." He then fixed the group with a hard stare, which he probably believed was authoritative. "A point of information. I am Major Deakin. When you address me, you call me sir."

Vickers shook his head. "I don't think so. I'm a civilian and I don't call anybody sir. In fact, Major Deakin, I'm a contracted executive of Global Leisure and I don't even call Herbie Mossman sir."

Debbie giggled and clapped a hand to her mouth.

Deakin's eyes threatened to burst. As well as the two gorillas in red, he also had a four-man squad of regular soldiers. Three with M90s and one with a .50 cal. frag gun. For an instant, he looked as though he was going to turn them all loose on Vickers but then he wrestled himself under control and managed a strangled snarl.

"You have a lot to learn."

"Maybe we all have a lot to learn."

There was nothing now between them and the entrance to the bunker except a wide expanse of bare concrete that shimmered in the sun. The sheer size alone was enough to conjure a genuine awe. The bunker entrance had the same breathtaking scale of a major dam, the largest of bridges or maybe the pyramids of Egypt. Vickers couldn't be certain on the last count. Despite the time he'd spent in the Middle East, he'd never seen the pyramids. He was, however, aware that the common factor was a relentless permanency. All were built with no concession to artifice, simply to last forever. The huge slot in the hillside was, in fact, the head of an enormous elevator shaft. Six huge platforms, like the ones used to bring up planes on an aircraft carrier except many times the size, were arranged side by side. Each of them could accommodate six large tractor-trailer transports. The closer they came to the cavernous entrance, the more clearly they could hear the deep rumble that reverberated constantly from the multiple shafts. As the platforms moved they also released blasts of chill metallic air that cut through the hot desert afternoon like the breath of some cold alien.

The escort was moving the five new arrivals at a brisk pace

toward a single platform that was empty apart from a stack of multicolored plastic freight containers and a pair of Jeep Commanches still in their original crates. One of the Gorillas in Red coveralls stretched out a hand to help Debbie across the yards of rubber and steel seals that separated the platform from the loading dock. She coldly ignored him. Debbie also seemed to be establishing relative positions as fast as possible. For a few minutes the new arrivals and their escort stood around waiting as more freight and more people came aboard the platform. The wait considerably reduced the new arrivals' sense of importance that had been so inflated by the elaboration they'd come through to get to this place. They didn't even merit an instant elevator. They were just five more items to be ferried down into the bunker. Vickers passed the time looking at the only piece of visible decoration. Like everything else, it was big. Maybe fifty feet across, mounted on the rear wall of the elevator, a massive slab of symbolic bronze, a stylized bird, uncomfortably Nazi in its simplicity, with flames bursting out and around it. Vickers looked enquiringly at one of the Gorillas in Red.

"What's that thing?"

"That's our symbol, our logo if you like, the Phoenix." He indicated the same symbol on the shoulder of his coverall and on the soldiers' helmets.

Vickers nodded.

"I suppose that's apt but why isn't there a Contec logo up there? I thought this was a Contec bunker."

Parkwood's head turned slightly. A twinge in Vickers' stomach told him he'd made a really stupid slip. How the hell did he know it was a Contec bunker? Nobody had said a word about it. Fortunately only Parkwood seemed to have noticed. The Gorilla in Red just shrugged.

"I guess all bunkers have their own logo. It's a good for morale and stuff."

There was a muffled and somehow depressing sigh from somewhere far below and Vickers again felt a puff of the cold alien breath. The giant platform began to sink. As they descended slowly into the elevator shaft, Vickers experienced a moment of claustrophobic near panic. It was followed by an intense forboding. Debbie must have sensed something.

"What's wrong?"

"I was just wondering when I'd see the sky again."

FIVE

"AND I'M TELLING you I'm not fucking wearing that and it's going to take more than you two fucks to make me! Okay? Okay?"

Eggy was poising on the balls of his feet. His hands were flexing and clutching in the first feints of a particularly simian and probably bone-crushing martial art of his own devising. It wasn't enough, however, to faze the two Gorillas in Red. They stood their ground, rocklike and scowling. One held up the mellow yellow coverall with the phoenix on the shoulder and the word INDUCTEE stamped on the pocket that they seemed determined that Eggy should wear. The other laid back a pace with his hand resting protectively on his sidearm.

"It's the rules, pal. We don't make 'em, we just see that they're carried out. Every inductee gets color-coded yellow and that's it. So are we going to do it easy or does it have to be the hard way?"

"I told you, asshole, I'm nobody's fucking inductee. I'm a contract player and nobody color codes me."

Vickers took a slow step forward. He was glad that the four soldiers had been ditched along the way.

"He's got a point, you know."

"Are you refusing to wear a uniform too?"

Vickers nodded. "Uh-huh. Like he says, we're contract players. We may be on a covert assignment but there's certainly nothing in my contract that allows me to be automatically inducted into any uniformed force. I imagine it's the same for everyone else. If I've got to go back into the army, I get to keep my rank and I wind up a major."

In fact, Vickers was bluffing. He'd never had an opportunity to look at his Global Leisure contract and he didn't have a clue what they could make him do. Also, he'd never risen past captain but he was certain that the Gorillas would be ignorant on both points. They certainly seemed impressed enough to adopt a placating tone.

"Why don't you all go along with it for now and then sort it out later?"

"No way."

"So what do you want to do?"

"We get a bunch of lawyers down here and let them sort it out. Right now."

The Gorilla's lip curled. "Where do you expect to find a lawyer in a nuclear survival bunker?"

Parkwood laughed. "If there aren't fifty lawyers it's the only place this size in the Western Hemisphere where there aren't."

The second of the Red Gorillas began to look less than happy.

"We could be getting out of our depth here, Charlie. Why don't we punt this upstairs?"

The first Gorilla thought for a moment. On one hand, he wanted to see Eggy humbled but also didn't want to drop himself into official manure in the process. Finally he hung Eggy's coverall on the rack next to the four others. There had been coveralls for all.

"You keep an eye on this bunch, I'll go and get Deakin." He nodded toward Eggy. "If he tries anything, shoot him."

This descent into the bunker was something of an anti-climax. When the platform had reached the second level, the Gorillas had indicated that they should get off. The second level was far from impressive, a vast freight handling area with about the same air conditioned, white-light ambience as any mainline superfactory. Robot forklifts moved mountains of colored plastic containers and dumped them on wide, massive conveyors that carried them away and out of sight. As early as this, Vickers concluded that someone in the bunker's planning stage had suffered from an obsession with rank, insignia and color coding. The facers and handlers who moved in among the automated chaos as token human supervisors wore blue. By far the most overwhelming feature of the whole area was the newness of everything. Paint was new and slickly gleaming. Nothing was scraped or scuffed, the concrete floor was scarcely stained with oil leaks. The air was still full of the smell of packing grease and thinner. It was so new but so ordinary that it was almost unnerving. Vickers almost said as much to one of the Gorillas. The Gorilla sneered knowingly and gave a curt and cryptic answer.

"This is just the second level. Wait 'til they take you down to the bottoms."

The Gorilla whistled up a pair of yellow plastic golf carts and indicated that they should all climb in. It came as some relief as the escort of armed soldiers was dismissed. The two golf carts made their way across the freight area and turned into a wide main corridor where more blue uniformed facers hurried about their business like so many confident ants. From the wide corridor they turned into a narrower subsidiary. That, in its turn, opened onto a long, bare room not unlike the home team dressing room in a minor league stadium. It was here that the confrontation over uniforms had reached the point where Deakin had to be summoned. He arrived with predictable bluster.

"You know I have the authority to have you all shot."

"Bullshit. You're bluffing."

"I suggest you get into those uniforms while you still have the chance."

"Nobody's going to have us shot after all the trouble that's been taken to get us here."

There had been five uniforms waiting for them, each one name tagged and approximately the right size for its intended wearer.

"We think we ought to get some legal advice down here. We're all contract players and we don't need this plastic soldier routine."

Eggy nodded. "We real, Jack. Don't fuck with us."

Deakin cracked a sneer. "You don't know what real means any more. You're down here now. This isn't the upstairs world."

Vickers shook his head. "I don't think we're getting through to you, Deakin."

Eggy didn't wait to see if they were getting through or not. "There's only one way to settle this."

He took the coveralls intended for him back down from the rack and gave them a quick shake. He seemed about to try them on for size. For an unbelievable moment it looked as though Eggy had simply upped and quit. Then he got a firm grip on the shoulders and ripped outward. The fabric tore easily in his hands. As he dropped the separated halves, he grinned insanely.

"What uniform?"

Deakin moved sideways, ready for anything. One of the Gorillas had his sidearm halfway out. One more desperate time, Vickers tried to avoid a massacre.

"Are you seriously going to shoot an expensive professional assassin because he ripped up some lousy *overalls*?"

The voice boomed out of nowhere.

"My sentiments entirely, Mr. Vickers."

A red light in the ceiling was flashing on and off. The heads of the new arrivals whipped around in surprise, startled by the room's display of remote potential. Deakin stiffened and involuntarily gave a half salute. The two Gorillas relaxed and put up their sidearms. The voice boomed again.

"I think we can consider this first test concluded, Major Deakin."

The red light stopped flashing. A panel in the wall slid open. A tall Hispanic stepped through. His uniform was snappier and had twice as much decorative braid as Deakin's. If there was any logic in their dressing up, he had to be at least a colonel. Vickers was starting to wonder if he'd fallen into a road production of *The Student Prince*. The Hispanic even had a swagger cane tucked under his arm. His smile was brisk and affable.

"I'm Lamas. Welcome to Phoenix."

"What's going on here? Are you telling us this has been some kind of test?"

Lamas was inordinately pleased with himself.

"A whole battery of them to be precise. Why, do you object?"

"We're getting a little tired of the process. We feel we're entitled to some answers."

Lamas nodded amiably. "Indeed you are. Indeed you are, and very soon you'll be getting more than you really want."

"What were you testing for?"

"For? Oh, reaction to authority, evolution of group identity, group cooperation . . ." He glanced directly at Eggy. ". . . individual levels of aggression. Tours down here are not easy and you're going to need a great deal of preconditioning. You'll find we're full of surprises."

Vickers tried to locate the corridor down which they were walking on his whatbox. The pocket data terminal was his tourist guide for the bunker. He was trying to make sense of its labyrinth of tunnels and corridors but it was daunting. They were still at the stage of conducted tours. Nobody had yet managed to cut loose from the group. Off duty, they were confined to their quarters. Not that this was a particularly great hardship. Their quarters were cramped but that was only to be expected in a bunker where space, by necessity, would be at a premium. Beyond that every obvious effort seemed to have been made to ensure their comfort. The quarters could actually have been custom built for them. Five tiny bedrooms and two equally small bathrooms opened onto a central common room. The design had started Vickers thinking that they might be just one of a number of five-person cells. Maybe this was the way that Lutesinger and Lloyd-Ransom were organizing their killers.

While they attempted to adapt to their new surroundings and figure out the possible implications of what they were seeing, the group was provided with, if not everything they desired, at least everything they could expect from a middle range Holiday Inn. The common room was equiped with two built-in data terminals and four movable video monitors. There was access to what seemed to be an almost limitless choice of books, movies and music, both on direct dail and a chip service. It was also possible to make limited use of the main data banks to review what they'd so far been taught about the geography and function of the bunker. If, however, anyone tried to go further than the instructors had taken them, all access was blocked. On the second night Parkwood had tried to hack into the master computer and discovered to his chagrin that even the initial approaches were firmly blocked. The other thing that seemed to be blocked was any information from the outside world. The bunker had a piped-through sound system, the equivalent of an internal radio system, but that just played general purpose pop music and confined its nearly mindless news reports to work quotas and inter-level basketball games.

Other things were a good deal easier. The common room had a well stocked bar and a refrigerator filled with snack food. When meals were wanted or when the fridge needed restocking, all they had to do was to dial. Food and supplies were delivered by individuals whose brown coveralls identified them as domestic help. From their uniformly servile attitude, Vickers was led to assume that they were the lowest in what increasingly seemed to be a highly structured pecking order. Debbie had more than once voiced the tight-lipped comment that by far the majority of both handlers and domestics were women. As far as she could see, the bunker was reasserting some old and dubious values.

Back in the corridor, Vickers had finally located where they were on his whatbox. Unless he'd made an error, the five of them plus Deakin, who was acting as guide, mentor and instructor on this particular day, were walking north on corridor DD175 on the second level. The bunker was proving so complex that it took Vickers most of his time to keep up with the orientation lessons. So far, even with the help of the whatbox, he had only the haziest of outlines of the place's subterranean geography. His strongest general impression was that things got better as you went down. The ultra-privileged had their quarters on the seventh level—down in the bottoms. The group had yet to be taken down there but the rumors talked of almost offensive luxury. His mission to hit Lloyd-Ransom and Lutesinger was completely on hold. He didn't even know if they were actually in the Phoenix bunker. There had been no mention of either of them, which seemed a little strange if they had indeed taken over the bunker. Vickers' train of thought was cut short as Deakin halted and indicated that they should all make a turn to the right.

"We're going to make a small detour here to enable you to see a typical general living area."

They walked through an arch and into what might have been an open-plan prison or the crewdeck of an aircraft carrier. Tall, steel, four-tier combination bunk-and-locker units served as homes for maybe a hundred or more. This was the second

level. There was no luxury here, just a hard functionality. The
only semblance of privacy came from mesh screens that
sectioned the area into a series of twelve-person cubes. A
minimal softening of the cold metal was produced by a
scattering of photos and trinkets hung on the mesh. Not even
the long-bladed overhead fans could minimalize the unmistakable stench of too tightly packed humanity, the combination of
sweat, soiled clothing and boiled vegetables.

"Who lives here?"

"Handlers."

The five looked around, shocked both by the Spartan
wretchedness and also a little surprised at their own compara-
tive good fortune. Debbie noticed something and glanced at
Deakin.

"Is it all women in this area?"

Deakin nodded. "This is a female handlers' living area."

Vickers looked around with interest. Debbie was right. All
the off-duty people laying in their bunks or hanging out by the
vending machines on the far side of the area were women.

"Sexual segregation?"

"Pairing is frowned upon unless the bunker is actually
sealed, Heaven forbid."

"If the bunker was sealed they'd have to live this way for
months, maybe years."

Deakin seemed unconcerned.

"Nobody said survival was going to be easy."

This answer wasn't quite good enough for Eggy.

"How come we live so good?"

Deakin looked at him coldly.

"As you've told me so often, you're big-time security
operatives. You're supposed to be valuable."

Eggy shook his head. "It don't seem right."

"What are you, a communist or something?"

Vickers noticed that not only was everyone in the area a
woman, but also that everyone in the area was a passably
attractive woman. It was starting to look as though there were
no ugly people in the bunker. Vickers had been checking on
this. The few grotesques that he'd seen were, in some way, like
Eggy. They at least had something very particular going for
them, and they were in an extreme minority.

It was hot in the living area and many of the women wore
nothing more than skimpy, if very plain, underwear. Despite

the shadow of an idea that he was somehow intruding, Vickers felt something stir inside him. Sex was something else that had been put on hold since he'd arrived in the bunker. The affair with Debbie that had only just begun at El Rancho Mars hadn't exactly been terminated. They had agreed, when it became clear the five of them were to be thrown together in a closed group, that it would be a bad idea, in a situation of one woman and four men, for the one woman to be sleeping with one of the men. It would create unnecessary tensions within the group. After a week, though, he was having to cope with some unnecessary tensions of his own. It didn't help that a pretty, almost naked handler winked at him as Deakin hurried them on through. As they came out of the living area and turned into yet another corridor, Eggy still seemed disturbed by the conditions.

"All the handlers live like that?"

Deakin nodded. "And the facers and the domestics, the blue and the brown, they have it pretty minimal."

"No shit?" Eggy was thoughtful. "There ain't too much of all people being created equal, is there?"

Debbie had also been thinking.

"What's the ratio of women to men?"

"Five to one."

"Five women to every man?"

"Jesus Christ."

"Who thought that one up?"

"There'll be an entire planet to repopulate if this place is ever used."

"It does make a certain kind of sense."

"It's fucking insanity. I want out of this place."

Debbie was glaring angrily at Deakin. He, in turn, regarded her coldly.

"You're signed on to the end of your tour."

Debbie looked bitter.

"Don't I know it."

"So where are we off to now? I thought we got through with the tour of the air plant."

Although they hadn't seen the sun for ten days, the group of five maintained the solar day and even took their meals at the traditional times; the final one was a communal supper and it was unusual that Deakin should appear in their quarters after

the evening meal. It had come to be considered free time and
thus it was something of an unwelcome surprise when he came
into their quarters just as they were settling down to some after
dinner drinking. It was their tenth day quarantined in the
orientation process and tempers were beginning to fray a little.

"I thought I'd treat you to a night off."

By his own standards, Deakin was almost amiable. Fenton
scowled.

"There's got to be a catch in this."

"No catch. I thought you could use a trip out for a couple of
drinks and a chance to meet some of your colleagues."

"We're getting out of the bunker?"

"Of course not. Don't be ridiculous."

"So what about these drinks? Are you telling us there's a bar
in this place?"

"There's a security club room that you'll be able to use once
you're out of quarantine."

Eggy sucked on his beer.

"Do the handlers have a club room?"

"They have their own facilities."

"I'll bet they do."

"Who are these colleagues?"

Four other five-person groups like yourselves. Shall we
go?"

As bars went it was cramped, Spartan and drab. The lights
were too bright. The barroom decorations, the neon signs, the
helix machines, the risque holograms were totally absent. The
walls, ceiling and fittings were all made from some off-white
industrial plastic. It was like going to a party in the emergency
room. The whole place appeared to have been designed so it
could be hosed down after a rough night. By the standards of
the parts of the bunker they'd seen so far, it was close to idyllic
luxury. It was already fairly full. The other groups, each with
their own equivalent of Deakin, were already there. This
caused Eggy to wink at Vickers.

"At least we get to make an entrance."

Vickers was equally amused by the fact that, of the four
groups in the club room, two had been persuaded to wear the
yellow uniforms with INDUCTEE stenciled across the front.

"It looks like we're in the top ten around here."

Fenton was also glancing around. There was a good deal of
tension in the room.

"Top ten of what, I ask myself. Have you taken a look at that other bunch that refused uniforms?"

The rival five were nothing short of spectacular. There were three men and two women. The taller of the two women was a drama all on her own. From neck to toe, she was decked out in skintight black leather. She was a masochist's dream. She wore no less than three studded belts, matching wrist bands and a collar of long chromium spikes. Her head was shaved except for a long, cossack-style braided topknot.

"You can see why she turned down a set of coveralls."

"Maybe she'd make a companion for Eggy."

Eggy grimaced. "Too fucking freaky for me."

The second woman made up in breadth what she lacked in height. She was a muscle builder and had the muscle builder's preference for wearing next to nothing and letting definition speak for itself. She had arms like a lumberjack but, as though in compensation, she also had truly enormous breasts and a high-piled confection of white-blonde hair. Vickers suspected that a great deal of her development was steroid growth. If she ever stopped exercising, she'd balloon up to four hundred pounds. She wasn't the only one in the group who appeared to be using steroids. Yabu was built like a sumo wrestler. Vickers knew it had to be Yabu. Both his reputation and physical description were too totally unique. The legend of Yabu was repeated in every corporation across the Free World. He delighted in a particularly artistic and often Zen violence. It was claimed that he'd devised a stomach-turning method of crushing a man's skull between his two hands so the eyes first popped and then brainstuff hosed out from the empty sockets. The second man was the basic nonentity of the bunch. He was short, slight and beyond demonstrating that, in a certain conservative way, he was something of a snappy dresser. Nothing registered. Vickers wondered if he were another cold but deadly fish like Parkwood. The real *piece de resistance* in the group was the seven foot black man with the long ringletted hair who was, at that moment, baring his very white teeth at Eggy. Vickers glanced at Eggy with some alarm.

"You know him?"

"Big motherfucker. Calls himself Eight-Man."

The club room had fallen silent; Eight-Man actually started to growl. It was a sound that Vickers would have preferred to have missed. Eggy also let out a long animal snarl. He rushed at Eight-Man and punched him as hard as he could in the stomach. Eight-Man gasped, took a step back but recovered himself. He swung at Eggy, smashing him in the side of the head with a piledriver punch that should have felled a mule. Eggy stumbled, he staggered. For a moment it seemed as though he was going to fall into Yabu but Yabu stepped neatly out of the way. Eggy appeared poised to go down like a felled tree. Then he shook his head. It was a remarkable recovery. Everyone waited for the next escalating move. And then suddenly they were in each other's arms, slapping, pounding, hugging, shouting and heehooing. The room split between relief and revulsion. There was something disturbing about the fact that there was a deep bond between these two extreme individuals.

"I didn't know Eggy had friends."

The group moved forward to the bar as a mass and began demanding drinks from a rather agitated handler who seemed a little out of her depth as a bartender. A little of the tension in the room had eased and there was a more normal buzz of conversation, albeit punctuated by the occasional hollers and bellows from Eggy and Eight-Man. Vickers had only just started his first scotch when a young woman positioned herself very deliberately in front of him. She bore an uncomfortable similarity to Ilsa van Doren except that, where Ilsa gave the impression of even coming out of the shower with perfect makeup and hair, this woman wore no makeup and had her hair in a utilitarian bun.

"Welcome to Phoenix. The way they have things set up around here, a girl can't stand still and wait for an introduction."

Vickers looked across the room. This aspect of the situation hadn't occurred to him previously. Five women to each man could produce some very competitive women.

"There seem to be plenty of men here in security."

"There's still a thousand or more eager, predatory bimbos over in handler country."

Vickers nodded.

"It's got to be a weird situation."

"Weird isn't the word."

"Talking of weird, who are the leather goddess and the lady muscle builder?"

"Isn't it always the same? Everyone wants to know who

those two bitches are. The musclebound broad is Annie Flagg. She used to be the private bodyguard of Calley at Metropolitan until he choked on the canape. By all accounts it was so private that she had enough influence left over to get in here. I don't know much about Carmen Rainer except what you see. The rumor is that she ran something extremely nasty in London before the lefties took over. How do I get you to pay attention to me? Should I buy you a drink or not? By the way, my name's Singer. Abbie Singer.''

Vickers shook his head. ''No, thank you, I don't think I'm quite ready yet for another drink.''

It wasn't that he didn't find the attention flattering. Something had triggered his built-in protective instinct. He was convinced that a short, dark man, also in uniform, was staring at him intently. Abbie Singer was talking to him but he wasn't hearing her. He wasn't even sure that what she said was meant to be heard. It was possibly just a corraling maneuver.

''I'm sorry, what did you say?''

''You could at least look interested.''

He was right. The short, dark man, even though he was doing his best to appear random and casual, was definitely homing in on him. It was this kind of certain perception that had kept Vickers living as long as he had. The small, dark man seemed unsure of his method of approach. Abbie Singer was scarcely concealing her annoyance.

''Listen, if you don't want to talk to me, you only have to . . .''

''No, really, it's not that.''

The man made his move. ''Listen, Abbie, you don't mind if I take Mort away from you, do you? There's something I have to talk to him about.''

The small dark man had decided on the direct approach, an appeal to Vickers' curiosity. It worked. Vickers allowed himself to be drawn to one side. Abbie looked even more annoyed.

''I'll be waiting for you. I figure you owe me at least a drink.''

''Sure, sure, I'll be right back when I've taken care of this.'' He turned his attention to the small, dark man and his face hardened. ''Do I know you?''

''I thought you might have been sent to get me out.''

''I don't know what you're talking about.''

"I suppose you're going to tell me that you're not Victoria Morgenstern's favorite gun."

Was this one of the Contec intelligence spooks who'd gone in front of him? In this fool's case intelligence seemed to be a contradiction in terms.

"What's your name?"

"Hodding."

Vickers had already decided that Hodding was quite useless to him even in the event that he decided he'd go on with the Contec mission. His tone was one of patient contempt.

"Well, okay, Hodding, the first thing you need to know is that I was terminated by Contec and I'm now under exclusive contract to Global Leisure. You hear me?"

The piece of information seemed to shake Hodding. Vickers didn't give him the time to relax.

"And even if there might be some unfinished Contec business to concern me here, only a fucking idiot would try to buttonhole me about it in a place that's without a doubt under full eavesdrop!"

"You want to go somewhere?"

This sucker had a death wish.

"No, I don't want to go anywhere. I don't want to talk to you. I want you to get away from me and stay away from me. I don't want you to speak to me again unless it's in the course of your duties around the bunker. Are you understanding me?"

"Yes, but . . ."

"If you don't, I might be tempted to break your neck. Remember who I am, Hodding. You said it. I am Victoria Morgenstern's favorite hired gun."

For a few seconds, Hodding stood rooted and open mouthed. He had come to Vickers as a possible way out of a situation and he'd apparently turned up a monster. It took a final glare from Vickers to finally remind him what he should be doing. His mouth suddenly snapped shut and he moved away from Vickers as though he were infectious. Vickers also moved. He fought down the urge to look for cameras and microphones. Abbie Singer was back again. She gave him something on which to focus.

"Maybe I'll have that drink now."

She looked at him sharply. "Problem?"

Vickers took a deep breath and tried to look unconcerned.

"No, nothing. It was just some old business from before."

Abbie singer glanced at the ceiling.

"There are times when it seems a million miles away. It's all so locked in down here, it's another world."

"How long have you been down here?"

"Two months."

"When do you rotate out?"

"We don't know, nobody's been told."

"Nobody seems to be told anything in this place."

"They say it's security. You don't hear that you're getting out until literally a few hours before you go."

"Doesn't that make you crazy?"

As though to confirm that it did indeed make her crazy, she finished her drink in a single belt and moved to the bar for another.

"Sure it does, but you have to figure that it's going to be worth it in the long run."

Debbie was also at the bar. She eyed Vickers and Abbie and smiled nastily.

"Getting acquainted over there?"

Vickers spread his hands.

"Isn't this the get acquainted party?" He turned back to Abbie. "What do you mean you figure that it's got to be worth it in the long run? What's got to be worth it in the long run? Is this something else I don't know?"

Abbie looked at him as though he was an idiot who'd missed the obvious.

"We get to survive. If we're lucky enough to be down here when it happens."

"*When* it happens? I'd always hoped it was a matter of *if*."

"Not the way things are going lately. It's really starting to look grim."

Vickers was genuinely surprised. "You get news from outside?"

"Oh yeah, once you're out of quarantine, you get the internal news system piped in. These days, it's pretty much bad."

"I've been out of circulation for a while. What's been going on?"

"Basically the Soviets are finally and totally coming apart." She glanced around as though looking for some kind of confrontation. "I suppose it's all right to tell you. If we weren't supposed to talk they wouldn't have put us all here together."

"But the Soviets have been falling apart for decades."

"Yeah, but this seems to be it. It's really the last days. There's apparently been a whole string of military coups in Moscow and some of the regional centers. It's starting to look as though it's only a matter of time before bombs get loose one way or the other."

"Jesus Christ."

"The only consolation is that those of us who survive will inherit a new and cleansed world."

There was something in her eyes, a gleam that wasn't quite that of the brainwashed but was certainly some way down the road.

"Where are you recruited from?"

"The San Francisco Police Department; I was a Lieutenant of Detectives. Why do you ask?"

"No reason."

She put a hand on his arm. "Listen, I know this place can be confusing at first but you'll be thinking straighter tomorrow."

"Tomorrow? Why tomorrow?"

"They really don't tell you anything. I guess that's what happens when you pull Deakin. He's the kind of bastard who can turn a coffee break into a conspiracy. Believe me, I had to deal with plenty of his kind in the police force."

"What's going to happen tomorrow?"

"I'm sorry, I'm just running off at the mouth. Doctor Lutesinger is what's happening tomorrow. All four of us security squads are going down to the main lecture hall on the fifth level. He's coming up from the lowers to address us. It'll be the first time you'll have heard him speak. He's pretty impressive."

"Lutesinger is coming *here*? To speak to *us*?"

Again there was the slightest trace of fervor. "He's really something, you'll see. He's able to get things across so they make complete sense."

It was turning out to be a highly interesting evening. Vickers tried not to show the keenness of his interest.

"Lutesinger is in actual residence here? He *lives* in the bunker?"

"Sure he lives here. He rarely strays from the bottoms, though. That's why this lecture is quite an honor."

"Is Lloyd-Ransom here as well?"

Abbie Singer laughed. There was an edge of bitterness to it.

"Oh sure, Lloyd-Ransom's here. Once you get out of quarantine, you can't miss him, what with the smile and the gold braid and the pencil moustache. He's always parading around with his guards and his damn dogs." There was none of the same awe. That seemed to be reserved exclusively for Lutesinger. "They say he had a knack for turning up exactly where he's not wanted. He's also supposed to be the one behind all these Ruritanian uniforms."

"You sound like you don't like him."

"Yeah, but I know enough to be scared of him."

Vickers signalled for another drink. There was suddenly a hell of a lot to think about. He wasn't sure that he was ready to see Lutesinger in the morning. Suddenly he realized it was the usual trepidation he experienced when he was about to look over a target for the first time. He hadn't given up the mission. Deep inside, he was still a Contec corpse on a mission to kill Lutesinger and Lloyd-Ransom. He'd never known that he possessed such illogical reserves of loyalty. Over on the other side of the room, Eggy was imitating Marlon Brando.

"Charlie, I could have been a contender, Charlie."

"You all know the story of the ant and the grasshopper. How all summer the ant toiled ceaselessly storing up food for the winter while the grasshopper merely sang and sunned himself. You remember how, as the nights drew in and the winter turned cold, the grasshopper knew that he was going to starve. How, too late, he saw the error of his ways. Then he whipped out a gun, shot the ant stone dead and stole all his food."

There was a ripple of polite laughter from the small crowd. Doctor Lutesinger permitted himself a narrow acid smile and then returned to the business at hand.

"This poor fragment of humor in fact sums up the entire function of security in this complex. We have labored through a long summer to build this place and we must now guard that no grasshopper with a gun takes it away from us."

The term lecture hall was an extreme understatement. It was a spectacular multi-purpose theater down on the fifth level, where it seemed that few expenses were spared. It was a steep banking of some two hundred seats set into a high arching, acoustically perfect sound shell. The style was lavishly neo-deco complete with smoke mirrors and soft-light diffusion panels. Vickers found it more suited to a symphony concert than to an address by an elderly academic madman. Not that the elderly madman was doing all that badly. Just as the term

lecture hall had been a major understatement, so was the title
lecture. It was a full-scale theatrical production. White light
fell on Lutesinger like the approval of God. Behind him, in the
shadows at the rear of the stage was the forbidding, grim dark
line of his dozen-strong bodyguard. Even the dumbest of the
audience couldn't help but perceive that everything had been
done to invest Lutesinger with every last wringing of authority.
When Vickers and his companions had arrived, a hidden sound
system had been playing Mahler.

"Some of those among you are newcomers, and for your
benefit I shall first try to define the nature of this terrible winter
that is so close upon us."

Lutesinger paused, as if for dramatic effect. In contrast to
the pomp and circumstance of his surrounding, Lutesinger was
a stooped, spindly, fragile figure. He seemed to lean heavily on
the lucite column that served him as a lecturn. His long skeletal
hands clung to it and he only removed them long enough to
briefly emphasize a point. His suit was very plain and about
twenty years out of date, charcoal gray in a style favored by
conservative tax analysts. His voice was equally unimpressive.
It could have been of an elderly teutonic speech synthesiser.
There was, however, something hypnotic about the slow,
almost reptilian way that he swayed slightly as he spoke. The
overhead lights turned his eye sockets into black holes of
certainty. He was a paradox. He seemed so ancient and frail
and yet there was an energy and menace that was more than
just stage effects.

"The truth is that we don't know."

Again he paused. The house lights came down and the
audience vanished in the darkness. Lutesinger was all there
was.

"No matter how far our computers project, no matter how
long we sit and speculate, in the final analysis we always come
to the admission that we have no confident idea of what a
nuclear war is really like. We have a mass of data but it is
wholly the result of controlled tests. We have never seen the
nuclear fire blazing with the heat of anger and conflict. Our
only practical experience comes from the primitive bombs that
were dropped on Hiroshima and Nagasaki, that ludicrous
Pakistani explosion and the single airburst that destroyed Porto
Alegre and terminated the incident between Brazil and Argen-
tina. In every instance we were surprised by how little we

knew and how wrong our projections had been. It would seem that if there is a single constant rule that can be applied to the belligerent use of nuclear weapons it is that both the construction and the operation of this installation was planned according to the dictates of an almost infinite pessimism.''

Lutesinger's expression made it absolutely clear that the infinite pessimism had been all his. There was the smell of cigar smoke in the lecture hall. As far as Vickers could tell, it was drifting back from the front rows. It was not only expensive, it was also unusual in the largely nicotine free bunker. The front rows were taken up by the considerable entourage that had accompanied Lutesinger up from the bottoms. There was a sizeable clique of the overdone, comic opera uniforms in among them, and now he discovered that they smoked top-grade cigars. Vickers couldn't raise Eggy's quaintly socialist ire over the bunker's caste-like inequalities but the combination of blatant privilege and the stupid uniforms did disturb him more than a little, mainly regarding the insecurities of whoever designed the system. They not only verged on mania but were a direct throwback to a very Neanderthal, dress-up facism. It probably wasn't Lutesinger in the drably prim, dark suit. As Abbie Singer had told him, Lloyd-Ransom was a far more likely candidate, a career soldier with a delusion of Napoleonic grandeur. It was almost certain that he'd been one of a group of officers who'd been forced to resign their commissions in the SAS and flee London after an abortive but hastily hushed up military coup.

"In the early 1980s, a polymath group fronted by a Doctor Carl Sagan postulated the idea of a nuclear winter, a temporary ice age that might grip the earth in the aftermath of any major or prolonged nuclear exchange. The sun would be obscured by the clouds of dust that would be thrown up by so many monstrous explosions. Sagan and his group estimated that the nuclear winter might last for as long as two years. Here in Phoenix we could survive one that lasted five.

"Only science fiction has speculated on what we might ultimately find when the short-term horror abates and we finally emerge from this underground cocoon of ours. I suppose it's possible that we might find a monster-movie world of fused green sand that glows in the dark and hideous mutations. It is also possible, at the opposite extreme, that we will find we've inherited nothing, a severe, barren planet with continents that are endless desert surrounded by dead, poisoned oceans. One school of thought claims a world of grass and insects, another fantasizes about one that rapidly repopulates itself as if the atomic holocaust had never burned across the sky.

"These, however, are luxury predictions. They were framed in the luxury of pretending that the worst would never happen. These are the possibilities of 'what if' rather than 'what will be.' To the idle speculator the possible is limitless. For us, the probable is likely to be something that even outstrips from their imaginings."

There was something else bothering Vickers. He'd started to sweat slightly and there were tension pains growing at the base of his skull. There was little doubt that the symptoms indicated the room was in some way gimmicked. Vickers had an exceptionally high tolerance to subliminals. Instead of blindly accepting, he suffered something akin to allergy reactions, physical side effects, when anyone was beaming suggestion at him. Vickers was quite proud of this quirk of his DNA. The physical reactions were a discomfort; a really bad burst of motivation could break him out in hives, but it was infinitely preferable to being semi-brainwashed each time he walked into the supermarket. Whatever was being used to back up Lutesinger was fairly low key, probably just enough to lull the crowd into an uncritical acceptance of the flat Germanic delivery. The room was too big for anything really direct like sub-bass boomers, squarks or miniclicks. They'd probably floated a bunch of microdelics into the air conditioner. Not enough to make anyone weird, just sufficient to make the people passive. It occurred to Vickers that it was a pretty cavalier way of treating the bunker's self-contained atmosphere. If they kept on pumping out psychotropics each time they wanted to make a point, the air in the bunker would slowly be turned into a soup capable of sending half the population off to chase dinosaurs.

"From the time that nuclear weapons were developed during the final days of World War II, there was a human pretense that we could somehow control, even prevent, their spread and their ultimate use. It was a piece of supreme arrogance to believe that, once something so powerful and so devastating had been loosed on the earth, we could stop it fulfilling its eventual purpose, fulfilling its destructive destiny, if you like.

For a while it seemed as though our arrogance was justified. From the 1950s to the mid-90s, the Pax Atomica held. We had MAD, Mutually Assured Destruction—such an appropriate acronym—to steady the balance of power. There was one factor, however, for which no one had allowed. For the mutual assurance of destruction, there also had to be a degree of equality between the protagonists. The world expected matched superpowers to remain matched. When the Soviets began their slow descent into anarchy and chaos, the balance of terror was no longer a balance. It became clear to many of us that the coming of Red Armageddon, the ultimate failure of the communists' system and the panic unleashing of their nuclear arsenal was only a matter of time.''

Fenton leaned over to Vickers. "Maybe if we hadn't organized the Panic of '96, the Reds might still be okay.''

"I didn't know you were a communist.''

"I'm not. It's like I told you, I'm a sociopath. I'll take the opposite side at the slightest provocation.''

Somebody in front of them hissed. Fenton gave them the finger. It was almost like being back in school. The front rows were taken up by Lutesinger's flunkies. Behind them were the security in the yellow uniforms—the nice kids. The hood-lums—the one's who'd hung onto their own clothes—had made straight for the back row. Lutesinger was above them all, whispering in the darkness. He continued with his chill visions.

"With the financial support of the major corporations, the bunker scheme became active. For those of us directly involved, it was a daunting task. It was possibly the most awesome construction project since the building of the pyramids. This was more than a pharaoh's vanity. Our purpose was the continuation of the human race, the survival of mankind. With so much at stake we had no alternative but an absolute determination.''

Vickers thought about killing Lutesinger. Physically it'd be a breeze. He could snap the man's neck with one hand. The trick would be to get close to him. He wondered if there was any time when the man was on his own without the guards and the entourage.

"Here in Phoenix, and the other bunkers like this across the Free World, we will preserve the seeds of humanity. We will be buried here, safe while the firestorms rage and the nuclear winter closes its grip. It will be a dormant stage in the history of mankind. A waiting period until we can emerge to build once again upon the ashes. In doing this, we have become like insects going into the pupa stage. Indeed, as a species we could be seen to have mutated."

Lutesinger let everyone think about this.

"In this rebuilding, there is one great consolation. All we have to build on may be ashes but down here, in addition to the people, we have, in our storerooms, in our data banks and in our technology, the products of ten thousand years of the struggle toward civilization. We have the best that man has conceived and achieved. We have the good while the bad will have been swept away in the atomic fires. When we finally emerge it will be into a world that has been cleansed of man's superstition and folly. We will inherit a purified world."

"He talks as though it was all a foregone conclusion."

"He talks as though he couldn't wait for it to happen."

"A brand new, clean-slate world is some serious temptation."

Vickers had been unable to sleep. Huge, pink-fleshed steroid women stalked his dreams, reaching for him with their huge, slab-of-meat hands. Bent reptile men with black eyes advanced. They clutched bright chrome spears, like giant needles, in green arthritic hands. They lunged at the steroid women, who burst in explosions of blood and flesh. He fled through the darkness of a huge decaying building. His legs were heavy and his breathing labored. The building was coming apart and he was on a very high floor. The walls decomposed and ran down their steel supports like they were formed of some organic material that was suddenly putrefying. The ceilings also rotted and rained down on him while expanding gaps in the floor threatened to pitch him headlong into a hundred-story abyss. A steroid woman appeared from nowhere. She was all over him, smothering him. He couldn't breathe. He was going to suffocate. Then the floor gave way and they fell together. At that point, he decided that it was a very good time to wake up.

He found that he was sweating. It was probably the damn chemicals they'd pumped into the room while Lutesinger was doing his act. All the molecular persuaders had some kind of unpleasant after effect. God knows, he didn't need chemicals to kick off a cycle of bad dreams. In its own, there was enough in his subconscious just waiting to be dredged up to make him sweat. He decided that there were two possible antidotes. One was vitamin C and the other was alcohol. A series of screwdrivers might be an ideal solution. When, however, he stepped into the common room he found that he was not the only one who was awake and drinking. Parkwood sat in the deepest, most comfortable chair reading a novel by Celine and nursing a large scotch. He glanced up as Vickers came out of his cubicle.

"Sleepless night?"

"I hope a couple of drinks will put me out."

Vickers poured himself the first in the proposed series. Parkwood put down his book.

"It's probably whatever cloud they were floating us on for Lutesinger."

"You noticed that?"

"It could hardly be missed."

The two men sat in silence for a while, guarding their thoughts. This accidental moment so obviously lent itself to some sort of intimacy but neither seemed willing to be the first to drop his guard. It was hard to do without seeming less than professionally correct. Finally Parkwood sipped his scotch and smiled dryly.

"Doctor Lutesinger provided quite a spectacle."

"Didn't he just."

"He seemed particularly anxious to sell us the official philosophy."

"Anxious enough to dose us down the microdelics to help him get across."

Parkwood raised an eyebrow. "You thought microdelics?"

"Yeah, why?"

"I'd had much the same thought myself."

Again there was silence. Parkwood got up and poured himself another scotch. When he sat down again, he seemed to have made a decision. He fixed Vickers with a candidly even stare.

"You realize there's a madness down here."

"You realize that more than likely someone or something is listening into this conversation?"

Parkwood was surprisingly matter of fact.

"It doesn't really worry me very much. I've given this some

thought. If they're paranoid enough to have the whole place wired for surveillance—and they probably are—it would have to be hooked into an artificial intelligence that's programmed to hear a range of concepts, actions and direction of conversations that have been deemed by someone to be treasonous, subversive or whatever. I tried to hack toward it by that route but the whole subject is monkeyblocked every whichway, a fact that, in itself, proves they have something to hide. I figure they've probably given up on us ideologically. We're the hired guns. We've already proved we're subversive by going along with the programs only extremely grudgingly. We can cuss and spit on the sidewalk. Nobody's going to worry, we're a lost cause. If they come and cart Eggy away, I'll start to worry but until then . . . I'm not boring you, am I?"

Vickers blinked. It was the longest speech he had ever heard Parkwood make. He suspected that the cold, reserved corpse was fairly well advanced into the scotch.

"And what's this madness you started talking about?"

"Don't be coy with me, Mort. You've been aware that there's something weird about this whole setup since you had your first run-ins with Streicher. I've seen you looking at all those Ruritanian uniforms and the rest of the nonsense. You feel the same way I do."

"And how do you feel?"

"We're living in the middle of an adolescent fantasy. The huge surplus of women, all the fake pomp and circumstance. It's a wet dream, a teen-acne power trip. It's so bloody simpleminded. I presume you're familiar with the Charlie Manson story?"

"Everybody's familiar with the Charlie Manson story. They've made four movies about it."

"Remember when Charlie was at the peak of his megalomania and getting ready for Helter Skelter? According to Charlie there was this huge bottomless cave way out in the desert. When Armageddon came and the blacks start wiping out the whites, Charlie was going to take his people down into the cave where they could hole up until the devastation was complete and then come out and take over. The troglodytes inherit the earth."

"You think that's what's going on here?"

"The end of the world's a cheap shot in the mad prophet business."

"And you think Lutesinger a mad prophet?"

"Sure. He's so computerized that he may not know it yet, but yeah, he's one for sure. Plus, it's no secret that Lloyd-Ransom's been crazy as a loon for years."

"So what do you know about Lloyd-Ransom?"

Parkwood's eyes slitted.

"I'm a little drunk but I'm not going to stand still for this cross examination much longer."

"I know that."

"This conversation's supposed to be a two-way street, a mutual exchange of confidence."

"So tell me what you know about Lloyd-Ransom and then it'll be my turn."

"I doubt I know anything you don't know. Regular British Army, the kind of psychopath who can survive in the military as long as he keeps on heading out for the edge. Lloyd-Ransom eventually wound up in command of one of those SAS Twilight groups. The kind that they feed on raw meat and vodka and keep in cages when they're not on a mission. He notched up quite a body count during the withdrawal from Ulster and a bigger one in Namibia. He vanished for a while after the London coup crisis, resurfaced in Africa and freelanced for a couple of years before he came to the US via Singapore and hooked his way into corporate security. I haven't come across him in five years, but the last time I had dealings with him, he was a real teeth grinder."

"The more I learn about this place the more depressed I get."

"It's early days yet. Wait until we finally get shut in for real down here. That's when it's going to get hairy."

Vickers was surprised.

"Isn't that a little fatalistic?"

Parkwood looked a little shocked. "Did you hear what I just said?"

"Sure."

"All through that damned lecture I knew they were hosing us down with something. For no real reason I kept feeling this absolute gut certainty that the end was right at hand. Didn't you feel it?"

"All I felt was the sweats and a headache. I've got a really high tolerance to suggestion. I just get psychosomatic fever."

"You're lucky."

"Maybe."

"But why should they go to so much trouble to convince us that the end is at hand?"

Vickers stood up and went to get himself another drink.

"I would have thought that it was obvious. It's straight back to your mad prophet theory. Lutesinger and Lloyd-Ransom can't wait for Armageddon. It would make them kings of the world."

Parkwood pursed his lips.

"Of course. You're right. I was simply holding off from the ultimate."

"At least they're in no position to start a nuclear war themselves."

"Unless there's something we don't know."

Vickers raised his glass.

"That's always a risk."

Parkwood nodded. "Isn't it just."

The thought hung in the air. Vickers finished his screwdriver and decided he didn't need any more orange juice. He glanced at Parkwood.

"I'm going to switch to scotch, you want me to get you one?"

"Sure, why not."

As Vickers was pouring the whiskey, the main door to the group's quarters opened and Eggy walked in. His face was a picture of satisfaction.

"Still up?"

"Sure are."

"Drinking?"

"Uh-huh."

"Mind if I join you?"

"Go straight ahead."

Eggy poured himself a huge belt of Wild Turkey and dropped a couple of ice cubes into it. He turned and found that both Parkwood and Vickers were staring at him curiously.

"What do you guys want?"

"We want to know where you've been."

Eggy laughed, swallowed about half his drink and belched.

"I'll bet you do."

"Ah, come on, you can't come walking in here at this time of night and just grin at us like the cat that got the cream. Where's the cream, Eggy?"

"Yeah Eggy, what you got going?"

Eggy sat down.

"You want to know where I've been? You really want to know?"

"Sure we want to know. That's why we're sitting here staring at you."

Eggy leaned forward like a conspirator.

"I've been up in the women handlers' quarters. You wouldn't believe it. Some of those women take the five-to-one ratio very seriously."

"How long has this been going on?"

"A week. I ought to have thought of it earlier."

"You realize you're most likely under surveillance the whole time?"

Eggy shrugged.

"Fuck them. I hope they enjoy themselves. I'm not the only one. There's quite a few guys who drift up that way when they've got nothing to do."

Vickers and Parkwood glanced at each other. They both looked a little bemused. Eggy took another king-sized slug at his drink and looked around the room contentedly.

"You know something? I could almost get to like this place."

There was clearly something in the wind. Lamas and Deakin had arrived together. Both were immaculately turned out. Lamas with his height and his somewhat condescending casual sophistication, Deakin, ramrod stiff and more puffed up than usual. There was no doubt a major announcement was about to be handed down.

"What the fuck do you think Mutt and Jeff want?"

"I figure they'll be telling us pretty soon, the way Deakin's bouncing up and down."

The group gathered around the pair of uniformed officers with a single questioning expression. Lamas had obviously decided to let them sweat on the news for a few moments. He carefully fitted a cigarette into a black and silver holder.

"Gentlemen and lady . . ."

Debbie regarded him sourly but didn't say anything.

". . . you'll be pleased to hear that, as of tomorrow, you'll be fully operative Phoenix Bunker security personnel."

"What did we do to deserve that?"

Lamas exhaled cigarette smoke straight at Eggy.

"Sometimes I wonder."

Parkwood stepped in before the exchange could be extended.

"Will we be assigned to a regular set of duties?"

"Actually no. In many respects you're all spare parts until such a time as the bunker is sealed. You'll be given missions from time to time but otherwise you'll be able to continue your life of leisure. As it happens, though, your first mission is tomorrow."

Debbie still looked distrustful.

"What kind of mission?"

"Very routine. A major celeb will be coming down into the bottoms with an entire entourage. There'll be blanket security. You'll all get individual briefings."

Fenton raised an eyebrow.

"Individual briefings?"

"You'll all be fulfilling slightly different functions."

Parkwood wasn't quite satisfied.

"How is this group going to be organized? Is one of us going to be put in charge or what?"

"You'll all have equal status under my command for the time being."

Eggy spat on the floor.

"All for one, one for all?"

Lamas smiled coldly.

"Look at it this way. You'll get to see the bottoms for the first time. They really are very impressive."

SIX

THE BOTTOMS WEREN'T impressive, they were magnificent. For a full five minutes after the group stepped out of the passenger elevator, nobody said a word. They moved as though in a dream, craning their necks like awestruck tourists. It seemed impossible that such opulence could exist in a place that had survival as a basic function. The centerpiece of this lowest, most exclusive strata of the bunker was a wide soaring airshaft that, as far as Vickers could see, extended almost to the surface and was at least a hundred feet across at its base. The style went back to the futurism of the first half of the twentieth century. Flying sweeps of molded glass, scrolls of white concrete balconies and catwalks, expanses of stainless steel and towering pylons. Much was made of lights and mirrors. Red and yellow laser beams crisscrossed between the walls of shaft and fiber optics hung in gently waving cascades. It was a luxury condominium off on a billion dollar fantasy. At the same time as with so much of the rest of the bunker's house style, there were echoes of the grandiose dictatorships—no dictator, though, had ever managed to piss away the astronomical sums of money that must have been consumed by this place. Even Adolf Hitler and his tame architect Albert Speer had done little more than dream about raising cathedrals to themselves. Lutesinger hadn't been kidding when he'd compared the bunker to the building of the pyramids. They were equal in their transcendental waste.

The floor of the bottom level was an expanse of black and white marble, an open piazza liberally dotted with rocklike abstract statues with titles like Courage, Industry or Fortitude, elaborate fountains and indoor trees kept alive by banks of growlites. There were even animals. Squirrels clung to the trunks of the trees, parrots and other bright tropical birds roosted in the top branches. Peacocks stalked across the polished marble, fanning their tails and letting go with their ugly squawks. The animals surprised Vickers, possibly more than anything else. He knew the bunker had an extensive zoo backed up by vast sperm banks. He hadn't expected to see critters running around loose. Directly beneath the center of the shaft there was a tall black obelisk and an eternal flame. It was a final and not very pleasant resemblance to a tomb.

"It's like a temple to mankind."

Deakin was positively glowing. Fenton parked his gum in his cheek.

"It's something, that's for sure."

Eggy glanced around. He seemed wide-eyed with glazed horror. He clearly didn't approve of the bottoms. There was something in its luxury that he took very personally.

Both Eggy and Fenton were hefting big .60 caliber frag guns, as indeed were Debbie, Eight-Man and Carmen Rainer. In the latter case the weapon coordinated perfectly with today's outlandish leather sado-suit. The guns worried Vickers. They were so totally inappropriate for indoor escort work. In fact, coupled with Lamas's "individual briefing," they radically curtailed Vickers' gosh-wow rubbernecking. The "briefing" had been so short and concise that it was virtually non-existent. Lamas had come into Vickers' private cubicle while he was still dressing. He'd closed the door and sat down on the bed.

"I want you to listen extremely carefully. When you get down into the bottoms, Deakin will assign you a position. Once you've assumed that position you do nothing. Do you understand me? Absolutely *nothing*. You remain where you are and do nothing *no matter what is going on around you*. I won't answer any questions. All I want to know is have you got the instruction?"

Vickers had taken a deep breath and nodded.

"What will happen to me if I decide I'm not able to do nothing?"

"It wouldn't be a wise decision."

With that, Lamas had stood up and left the cubicle. Vickers had rejoined the others and had been issued a Yasha with two clips of ammunition. When he saw the frag guns being handed out, he realized that the individual briefings must have been fairly diverse.

There were two five-man security squads, the "hoodlums" who'd refused uniforms. They were led across the piazza to where a slight incline ran down to a huge pair of brass doors that clearly gave access to one of the main freight elevators. A ten-man squad of soldiers who looked like an honor party were lined up on either side of the doors. Deakin began positioning his people along the top of the incline in an open line. The ones with the frag guns were dispersed along the line. It only took a moment for Vickers to realize that the combination of the soldiers and themselves could be a very standard security layout for greeting a VIP but, as they were, facing down the ramp toward the doors, it was also an ideal layout for a slaughter. Anyone coming out of the elevator was completely at their mercy.

For maybe fifteen minutes they stood in silence. It was designed to be very restful down in the bottoms. Ambient sounds hummed and flauted from hidden speakers. The birds called and rustled in the trees. The fountains splashed and sparkled. For a bomb shelter it was close to idyllic. The sound of voices came from the other side of the piazza. Vickers turned his head. A small crowd was coming out from one of the main tunnels. They had to be the reception committee. They were a colorful bunch. The majority of the men were in the most flamboyant uniforms he'd seen so far. They ran to capes and plumes and the most absurd decorations. There was something almost medieval about the women with their long sweeping skirts and the high collars that framed their faces. Vickers muttered under his breath.

"Sweet Jesus, it's Camelot."

As they got closer he recognized two of the women, Thane Ride the TV star and Pagan Ouspenski the tireless socialite. They might be luxurious, but Vickers couldn't see why either of these luminaries should forsake their jet-set haunts unless someone had thoroughly convinced them that the end was nigh at any minute. More important, Vickers also recognized Lloyd-Ransom. He had an attractive Oriental woman on his arm and was preceded by a dog handler pulling back on the leashes of a trio of Dobermans. Two of the dogs were young with a decidedly crazed look in their yellow eyes. The third was an elderly bitch with a graying muzzle and half of her left hind leg missing. Vickers wondered if Lloyd-Ransom had had the dog all through his career. It hardly seemed possible that he'd acquired the animal in that condition. Lloyd-Ransom's immediate escort was completed by a pair of gray-uniformed soldiers with machine pistols at high port. Lloyd-Ransom himself cut an impressive figure in a spotless white uniform. He was slim and erect with the carriage of a professional soldier and the rather old fashioned, pencil-moustache good looks of a 1930s matinee idol.

The whole party halted at the start of the incline. The security teams became a part of the front row. Again everybody waited. There was a good deal of brittle conversation that Vickers did his best to ignore. Then a light came on beside the brass doors. An elevator was coming. There was a series of metallic clicks, a thump and a drawn-out hiss. The doors slowly slid open. The cavernous interior of the elevator was lit by a line of overhead spots. Some fifteen figures were crowded around a squat, dark object that seemed to be mounted on some kind of tracks or rollers.

A half-dozen men detached themselves from the main group. They came out of the elevator fast. They were dressed in the double-breasted suits and black shirts that were traditional among the inner circle of Global Leisure security. They carried snub-nosed Whooper machine guns. They quickly secured the area in front of the elevator. The waiting soldiers came to rigid attention and the security teams stiffened. The main party began to move forward. As soon as it came out into the brighter light, it was plain to see that the dark object on rollers was in fact not an object at all. It was a person. There was no mistaking the chrome tank treads.

"Herbie Mossman! What the fuck is Herbie Mossman doing here?"

Vickers glanced around to see if anyone had heard his quiet exclamation. Everyone else seemed to be intently watching the emergence from the elevator. Herbie Mossman appeared to

feel the need to go travelling in what looked like a bulletproof
spacesuit. His bulk was swathed in a tent of a glossy dark blue,
seemingly rubberized material that looked to be easily an inch
thick. It was gathered at a locking ring round his neck that in
turn sealed it to a plexiglass bubble helmet. The bulletproof
suit was obvious, but why the helmet? Was Mossman afraid of
a gas attack or did he suffer from a Howard Hughes germ
phobia? These, however, were the least of the questions that
buzzed across Vickers' mind as Mossman started slowly up the
long incline. He was flanked on each side by two lines of
young men in neat haircuts and dark ivy league suits, who were
most likely Mormons. The Utah/Nevada connection went back
to at least the 1960s. They were probably clones although the
Brigham Young Corporation denied that they had the technology. Mormon bodyguards were efficient to the point of suicide.
Assured of a place in the hereafter, they wouldn't hesitate to
take a bullet. When they hired out as mercenaries, they were
hotly sought after. Two top-class Vegas showgirls who, in their
own way, were probably equally sought after, walked demurely
behind Mossman's chair. Had he come for a protracted stay?

Vickers didn't have much time to ponder the problem. Four
of Lloyd-Ransom's officers moved forward to greet Mossman.
The soldiers beside the elevator doors snapped off a deft
present arms. Surprisingly, Lloyd-Ransom himself didn't
move. He simply stood his ground surrounded by his dogs,
guards and courtiers. It had to be a serious breach of protocol.
Herbie Mossman was, after all, the president of a major
corporation while Lloyd-Ransom, whatever his delusions, was
only the commander of a bunker. Mossman seemed to have the
same thought. His wheelchair stopped. He appeared to hesitate
as though unsure or even suspicious. If indeed he was
suspicious he was more than justified. Within five seconds all
hell had broken loose.

The soldiers dropped from parade ground to combat stance.
Their weapons came down and there was an explosion of
gunfire. Simultaneously, the security people at the top of the
incline who were armed with frag guns also opened up.
Mossman's people never had a chance. The attack was too fast
even for the Mormons. Two got their guns out but neither fired
a shot. One of the Global security men managed to loose off a
wild burst from his Whooper. It killed one soldier and set the
courtiers scattering, but then he too was cut down. After fifteen

seconds the firing stopped. The only survivors were a sobbing showgirl crouching behind Mossman's chair and Mossman himself, sitting helpless, saved by his suit but probably badly bruised. The four bunker officers were also dead. They'd been among the first to be hit. They'd obviously been designated as expendable. In the quiet aftermath of the massacre, a woman courtier went on screaming. Someone was throwing up.

Vickers got slowly to his feet. When the shooting had started he'd been too shocked to do anything but follow the order to do nothing. On immediate reflection, the best policy seemed to be to go on doing nothing. It was hardly the time to start picking sides. He didn't see how "do nothing" could mean stand around and get shot and he'd dropped to his knees. Beside him, Debbie jacked a fresh clip into her frag gun. She slowly walked forward toward Mossman's tracked wheelchair. Carmen Rainer, Eight-Man and Eggy all did the same. Mossman rolled backward toward the elevator. He'd only travelled a few feet though, before he stopped again as if realizing the futility. The killers were lazily converging on him. Eight-Man shot out the chair's power unit so he couldn't roll again if he wanted to. Inside the bubble his face was sweating. His fat pink lips were working but no sound could be heard. Eight-Man's shot had also taken out the speakers through which Mossman communicated with the outside world.

Carmen Rainer aimed a frag blast straight into Mossman's bloated, blue-swathed body. The effect was like a wave in a waterbed. The material stopped the slivers of metal but it couldn't absorb the close-up blast. Debbie and Eggy also fired. Mossman was being pulped inside his own, bulletproof suit. Blood spurted up into the helmet with each burst and then subsided again. The material simply wouldn't split.

Mossman was so plainly dead that the four assassins lowered their guns. For long seconds they stared at the grotesque corpse. Eight-Man shook his head, turned and started walking to where the living were waiting. The other three followed. The woman had stopped screaming, the ambient sound had been turned off, even the showgirl had stopped her sobbing. It was a terrible silence. Even the normal background groans and rumbles, the enclosed sounds of the bunker, seemed to have been stilled. Then a flock of birds erupted from a tree with a clatter of wings. Everyone flinched.

* * *

Vickers lay flat on his back and stared at the ceiling. Again he couldn't sleep. It was all becoming too dangerously confusing. What had always been thought of as impossible had been achieved. The president of Global Leisure had been slain and for the life of him he couldn't figure out why. Why had Mossman come to the bunker? What had induced him to change a ten-year habit and leave the stronghold of his Las Vegas penthouse domes? The thoughts went round and round in his head and kept coming back without acceptable answers, back to the same single imponderable. What the hell was going to happen next? How did Lloyd-Ransom expect to hold the bunker after this? They'd surely send in an army to get him. The corporations would forget their differences until they had his head on a spike. Unfortunately the entire security group, everyone who'd been there, would finish up with their heads on slightly lower poles. Even the bunker wasn't enough of a hiding place for the killers of Herbie Mossman. Vickers began to sweat. He wanted a drink. He wanted a cigarette but somehow he couldn't move. Most of all he wanted out. He couldn't believe that he'd walked into this mess of his own free will. He didn't even understand what was going on. What did Lloyd-Ransom, even dressed up like Hermann Goering, expect to gain by killing Herbie Mossman? Again he was asking why and getting no answers.

A thought occurred to him. There was one way that he might walk out of here. If he already had Lloyd-Ransom's head—and Lutesinger's as well—when the forces of retribution arrived, he'd be the automatic good guy. It might be his only chance. Now the question had become: how?

There was a commotion in the group's common room. Eggy was bellowing and there were other voices. Vickers sat bolt upright. What the hell was going on? A cold fear wrenched his gut. Had they come to cover their tracks? Was this the point of the whole charade? Had they been brought here only to finalize Mossman and now they were going to be greased themselves? The door of his cubicle was kicked open. A soldier with red and yellow tabs on his uniform and a Neanderthal expression on his face pointed a machine pistol at him.

"All right you! Out! Out! Move it!"

He had one of those hysterical, robot voices that are so favored by the military. Vickers hadn't seen the red and yellow

tabs before. What were they supposed to mean? The best thing
was to do what he was told. There really wasn't any viable
alternative. He couldn't quite believe that he'd come all this
way just to be concluded as a track-covering afterthought, but
he still had to fight down a gagging fear. There were guns all
over the common room, more of the mushroom uniforms with
the red and yellow tabs. Each brandished a machine pistol. The
others of the group had been herded to one end of the common
room. Eggy simply smouldered but Fenton, Debbie and
Parkwood all had a strained, wide-eyed look that seemed to
indicate they too had considered the possibility that this
unasked-for night visit might end in an execution. Vickers tried
a piece of token bravado.

"What about a drink?"

It didn't do him any good. It didn't even make him feel
better. The soldier who'd dragged him out of his cubicle
grabbed him by the shoulder and shoved.

"Over with the others."

The shove sent him stumbling into Fenton. Side by side, the
five of them eyed the soldiers and the guns that they were
pointing at them. Eggy's breathing was noisily audible. It
sounded like he was stewing from within. Fenton shook his
head.

"I really don't want to think about this."

There was a commotion of stamping boots outside the door
and a general stiffening of the soldiers in the room. The ones
nearest quickly backed away as a dog handler was pulled into
the room by three Dobermans. The sudden arrival of Lloyd-
Ransom's dogs put a different emphasis on what was happening. Was he coming here to watch the execution or had they
totally misread the situation? While they were still wondering,
Anthony Lloyd-Ransom himself strolled through the door of
their unit with one hand in the pocket of his immaculate
uniform jodphurs. He was a picture of studied casualness as he
paused to light a cigarette. He surveyed the five with a half
smile.

"My chaps seem to have scared you people shitless."

Vickers realized that he couldn't hear Eggy breathing any
more. He was quite surprised when Parkwood spoke up.

"It looked uncannily like an execution for a few moments
just now."

Vickers had to hand it to him. Parkwood's voice was calm

and even. He'd almost managed to sound unconcerned. Lloyd-Ransom seemed quite delighted.

"What on earth gave you the idea that I'd have you executed? I've put in a lot of time, trouble and expense to put this team together. It would hardly be rational."

It was Vickers' turn.

"Didn't things get a little irrational earlier?"

Lloyd-Ransom looked round at him with an expression of pleasant surprise. It was as though he was enjoying the spirit his hired guns were exhibiting.

"I'm sorry, what did you mean by that?"

Vickers began to get angry. It was as if Lloyd-Ransom placed them on the same level as his damned Dobermans.

"The murder of Herbie Mossman."

"You didn't find it rational?"

"The logic of it escapes me."

"Maybe you don't know all the facts."

"That's quite usual round here."

"In any case, you went along with it."

Vickers grimaced.

"That's all I did. I never fired a shot."

Lloyd-Ransom loosed a short, clipped laugh.

"That's just as well for you. The first round in your clip was an explosive charge. If you'd fired your gun, it would have cut you into two very messy halves."

Vickers was incredulous.

"What?"

"Just a little loyalty test. Technically, you're still under contract to Global."

"I take it I passed."

"You're still here, aren't you?"

"We were wondering about that a couple of moments ago."

A brisk gesture from Lloyd-Ransom dismissed all but two soldiers and the dog handler.

"You don't need to wonder any longer. The truth is that I'm really rather pleased with this team."

Eggy was still glaring.

"So why roust us in the middle of the night?"

"This wasn't a roust."

"You coulda fooled me."

"Those were my personal guard. I hand picked them but they tend to get carried away. They forget about diplomacy."

Parkwood raised an eyebrow.

"There could come a time when that might warrant some close watching."

"I don't think so."

"That's what Caligula said."

Lloyd-Ransom treated Parkwood to a long, cold look, then abruptly his expression changed. He looked at each of the five in turn as if making some final assessment.

"I think it's time a few things were explained to you."

"That'd make a change."

Eggy wasn't about to be placated. Lloyd-Ransom's eyes froze for a second time.

"I'd advise against any more interruptions."

There was a deviousness about Lloyd-Ransom. The facade he presented, the overdressed cynical fop tended to suck one in and lull one into forgetting how efficiently dangerous he could be. The man had spent two solid years in the bush making untrained and often unstable mercenaries do exactly what he wanted. Eggy was clearly just remembering this but he still needed a little room to save face.

"Would you advise against me having a drink?"

"Why don't you pour us all one?"

If anyone else had said that it would have provoked a probably obscene retort from Eggy. In this instance he said nothing. The five relaxed. Fenton and Debbie sat down. Lloyd-Ransom settled on the arm of a chair. Eggy handed him a drink and he removed his uniform cap.

"The first thing you need to know is that, on the outside, the situation is becoming extremely grave."

Lloyd-Ransom waited for a new mood of attention and anxiety to settle over the room.

"The Soviet civilian administration has completely collapsed. It's chaos. Next winter, millions will starve and there's absolutely nothing that can be done. The Red Army has split into no less than five identifiable groups and two of these are moving west, each followed by huge mobs of starving refugees. Some tank units of the leading army have already crossed the Kowalski line and are moving into West Poland. They may be hungry and disorganized and not directed by a central government, but they're still an invasion. If anything, it's worse. It's a ravenous mob spurred on by an absolute need to survive. If they aren't stopped they'll simply eat up Western Europe."

Fenton moved his hand in a gesture that wasn't quite a request for permission to speak.

"What about the Soviet missile system? Who's in control of that?"

Lloyd-Ransom spread his hands. "We don't know. If the rest of the story is anything to go by, it's probably as fragmented as anything else. Different groups in different parts of the country in charge of a couple hundred missiles each."

"And nobody has a clue if they're planning to fire them or not?"

Lloyd-Ransom looked from face to face.

"Sorry to say, but what the Russians may do is no longer the primary headache. Most people are now concerning themselves with what the Germans may do. If the Germans, backed up by the Poles, the British and the Dutch, can't hold the Russians on the ground with conventional weapons, and it's by no means certain that they can, the temptation will be to stop them in their tracks with a couple of low-yield airbursts." He paused. He glanced at Eggy. "I think I could use a refill."

Eggy got up and fetched the bottle but not without a noticeable demonstration of tried patience. Lloyd-Ransom sipped his drink and continued.

"If you think about it, it seems most unlikely that a jangled, disorganized and probably desperate Russian missile command is going to let the Red Army, whatever its condition, take nuclear hits without shooting back. Once the shooting back gets going, it's all the way in to the death. There's no power on earth that's going to stop it escalating. With Russia in the grip of total anarchy, even the communications aren't there. With no central government, there's no hotline. I hate to be the one to say it but it looks as though the world is staggering toward the end of this chapter."

There was a long and grim silence. It was Debbie who finally moved the conversation on to the other major puzzlement.

"Where does Mossman fit in to all this? Why did he have to be killed?"

It was a number of seconds before Lloyd-Ransom answered. Again his eyes were cold. He obviously wanted no argument.

"Mossman also decided that the end was at hand. In the past he assisted us and it was always agreed that, if the worst came, a place here was guaranteed for him and his immediate

entourage. This apparently was not enough for Herbie Mossman. Feeling that a crisis was at hand, he decided that he'd not
only move into the bunker but that he'd bring in his own people
and take over total control. His intention was to use his security
people and his Mormon guards to stage what would have
amounted to a coup here in the bunker."

The faces of the five indicated that they weren't rushing to
buy Lloyd-Ransom's explanation. It was Debbie who put it
into words.

"He only came in with a handful of people, how could they
have posed a threat?"

"His aim was to eliminate myself, Doctor Lutesinger and
most of the central command."

Lloyd-Ransom's face dissolved slightly, his determination to
convince took on a tinge of holy aura.

"He would have destroyed the vision. Working together
here over the last two years we have produced a vision of
survival and rebuilding that we are prepared to defend to the
death. We have to defend it; in the final analysis it may be the
only hope of mankind. I'm not about to entrust that vision to an
obese psychotic like Herbie Mossman."

Vickers experienced a chill. Lloyd-Ransom's madness went
beyond marble facades and Student Prince uniforms. He was
going on messianic. Eggy took a more practical approach.

"It seems that we're doing most of the defending."

"Why not? That's what you're being paid for."

Lloyd-Ransom may have found religion in the bunker but he
hadn't relinquished his grasp of reality. Parkwood nodded.

"That's true enough."

"In fact, there may well be a whole lot more for you to do
before this crisis is over. That's primarily why I've come down
here to talk to you. There may be a time when you come to
share the vision but, in the meantime, I expect all five of you to
go on doing your jobs. You're my hired guns and I expect you
to act accordingly. Does this cause anyone any problems?"

Nobody said a word. Lloyd-Ransom smiled. "That's good.
I've always liked to work with professionals."

"So what are we supposed to do from here on in?"

"You will be my enforcers, my troubleshooters. Like it or
not, you will become my ultimate goon squad. When the only
solution has to be simple but drastic, you will provide it. I'm
presuming that this doesn't cause any problems, either."

Again nobody spoke. Lloyd-Ransom nodded as if fairly satisfied that he had sufficient quantities of their loyalty.

"Depending on the extent of the crisis, there may be a very pressing need for drastic solutions. Apart from Mossman, it's almost certain that there are other groups and individuals who would like to take over this bunker. They are very likely to have infiltrated agents into the bunker already. As the crisis deepens, they are all going to be looking for the chance to make their moves. Our security here is the best possible, but no system can be perfect. A determined operative can always slip through the net."

Vickers did his best to keep his face expressionless. He could have sworn that Lloyd-Ransom had looked straight at him as he said the words "determined operative." Did he know or suspect something? If he did, he went on without giving any further sign.

"If we are forced to seal the bunker we will face a whole new set of problems and many of these have to be quickly, surgically eliminated. We have no idea how the various sections of the population will react when they realize that they are shut in and a nuclear holocaust is raging outside. Again it's the same as with the security system. Our psychological profiling is as comprehensive as it can be but nothing can be perfect. We also don't know what atomic war will mean. It will be a massive trauma but we have no idea as to how massive. There will be those who react antisocially; there will be those who react violently; some will become a danger to the bunker itself. Once again I will expect you to act swiftly and without question."

"We kill off the freakouts and the misfits?"

"That's a harsh way of putting it."

"But accurate?"

"It's going to be a very harsh world in the near future."

Lloyd-Ransom stood up. "If there are no questions I'll let you all get back to sleep."

"I've got one question."

"What's that?"

"Earlier, when you asked if any of us had any problems with the way you wanted things done, what would have happened if one of us had piped up that he or she didn't like the setup and wanted out?"

Lloyd-Ransom made a motion of his head in the direction of the remaining soldiers. His smile was cold.

"I would have had him or her shot out of hand."

"Harsh times."

"Remember that."

Lloyd-Ransom departed with his soldiers and his dogs. Everyone slumped slightly. Eggy shook his head.

"He's madder than I am."

"And he's our new bossman."

"I think I need a drink."

"You bastards never have to sleep with your fucking targets."

Debbie was standing, swaying badly. She had a large glass of straight vodka in her hand. After Lloyd-Ransom had left, nobody had bothered to go back to bed. The news had been too overwhelmingly dire. The whole group had started drinking. Uncharacteristically, Debbie had been the first to become emotional. Eggy was almost as drunk, but he was simply glum.

"I've fucked a target a couple of times. It wasn't no big thing."

"It was some casual weirdness, that's what it was. You didn't have to. They didn't give you a photograph and tell you 'Hey, get next to this one, flatter him, butter him up, suck his dick, lick his toes and only when the time is right can you turn around and zap him.' You know how that feels? You know how you get over that? You know how you keep it together when you've done it time after time, more times than you can remember?"

Fenton blearly shook his head. "Don't ask me. I'm just a thief."

"Nobody gives a damn, do they. Nobody cares a damn about how I feel."

Vickers looked at her blankly. If he hadn't been drunk he would have been surprised. He knew that there must have been all manner of strange, disturbing shit buried in Debbie's background but he'd never thought much about it. He hadn't expected that she'd start to fall apart after a few drinks. A few drinks, hell, he didn't think she'd fall apart after being told that a nuclear war was about to start. Something more than whiskey grabbed at his gut. He realized that he was refusing to believe it. He wasn't going to accept that it might be happening.

Debbie, meanwhile, was taking fast angry belts of her drink. She glared around belligerently.

"And another thing, I'm sick to my stomach of everybody calling me Debbie. 'Hey Debbie, Hi Debbie, How you doing Debbie, Smile Debbie, Show us your tits Debbie.' *I've had it. My name is Debbie Rafael*! You hear me? *Debbie Rafael*. That's what I want to be called. Fenton, Vickers, Parkwood and Rafael. *No more Debbie*."

"All they call me is Eggy."

"That's all the name you ever had. You don't have no more name than Eggy. *I do*. My name is Debbie Rafael and I want you bastards to start using it!" Abruptly she sagged, as though she'd finally run out of steam. She folded into a chair, her face creasing into self-pity. "I don't think I can handle any more of this."

Fenton tried to be drunkenly consoling.

"We all know it's going to be rough, but you can get through. We're all going to get through."

Debbie opened her mouth. At first no sound came but when it did it was a wail of pure, miserable anger.

"*You don't have to survive the fucking end of the world with five women to every man!*"

Debbie had such complete attention that nobody noticed Eggy grin and mutter to himself.

"Sure we do. Sure we do."

"I want to talk to you."

"You do?"

"I think we should take a little walk."

"Huh?"

Fenton took Vickers by the arm and steered him toward the door.

"Smile, make nice, nod your head real casual just in case someone's watching."

Vickers was beginning to feel the slightest bit alarmed. Fenton wasn't usually this elaborate and it indicated that there might be something major on his mind. Vickers allowed himself to be walked down to the nearest arterial corridor. They continued to walk with golf carts and freightlifts humming past them until they found an empty golf cart parked with its Vacant light on. Fenton slid behind the wheel and indicated that Vickers should get in. Vickers shrugged and did as he was asked. Fenton pulled out into the slow moving traffic.

"I expect you're wondering what this is all about."

"I'm curious."

"I just wanted to make sure that we had a little privacy."

"So what's wrong?"

"Not so much wrong, more interesting."

"So what's interesting?"

"There was another murder here last night."

"There was? Nobody tells me. I seem to be the forgotten man of profesional assassination."

"I did it."

"An official murder or a piece of your own moonlight?"

"Oh, it was quite official. A security officer called Hodding. They told me that he was a Red spy and he had to go."

"Hodding?"

"That's right."

Fenton was half grinning at Vickers. Vickers hoped his impassive expression was holding up.

"And Hodding was a Red spy?"

"That's what they said."

"Do the Reds have spies anymore?"

"He didn't look terribly Red. Looked more corporate to me. Also, he said the strangest thing before I shot him."

"Yeah, what?"

"When I got there, he was in the shower. A real *Psycho* job. Real Alfred Hitchcock. I ripped back the shower curtain and straight away he knew what I was at. He couldn't have missed, really, since I was holding this damn great automag in my fist at the time and pointing it straight at him." Fenton seemed to be enjoying himself. "He holds out his hands in front of him and says 'No, no, not me, it's Vickers that you want.'"

Despite Fenton's deadpan, almost humorous delivery, it was about as bad as it could get. Still, Vickers tried not to react.

"What did you do then?"

"I shot him. Then I walked away, pausing only to call the clean-up crew."

"What did you think he meant by 'it's Vickers you want'?"

Fenton grinned. "I thought you'd tell me."

"I spoke to him once."

"Yeah, I saw you."

"He seemed to think I was still working for Contec."

"And are you?"

"Does it look like it?"

"It could be hard to tell who you're working for."

"I'm working for Lloyd-Ransom except that I don't think he trusts me enough to give me anything to do."

Fenton didn't say anything. He went right on steering the golf cart, staring straight ahead. Vickers knew that he had to ask the question.

"Do you think anyone heard what he said? Apart from you, that is."

A slow smile spread over Fenton's face. He waited a few seconds before he answered. It occurred to Vickers that Fenton might be taking him somewhere to kill him. Fenton laughed as though he knew what Vickers was thinking.

"Worried?"

"I'm always worried."

"I don't think anyone heard him. The shower was running hard enough to confuse a microphone."

There was another pause. Again Fenton laughed.

"What's the matter? You trying to figure out a diplomatic way to ask me if I've told anyone?"

"Have you?"

"Not yet."

"Do you intend to?"

"I don't know. I don't think so."

"Why not? Fingering another Red agent would be automatic brownie points."

"That's if brownie points are all you're after. The way I see it, there's too much bullshit down here for me to put all of my eggs into one basket. You know what I mean?"

"I think so, but maybe you'd better go on so there's no room for a misunderstanding."

Fenton snorted and shook his head.

"I like you, Vickers, I really like you. None of us know what we're getting into down here and I reckon you'd be a useful man in a tight spot. Even more useful if you owed me a considerable debt of gratitude."

"And are you going to let me owe that debt of gratitude?"

"I figure it's my best bet. It's not only that I like you, I also don't trust Lloyd-Ransom."

"So what am I? Your ace in the hole?"

"Something like that."

"I suppose I should thank you."

"It wouldn't hurt."

Vickers knew that Fenton had him right in his pocket.

"I thought I had more class than this."

"Ain't nothing classy about sitting on your own each night, reading a book and swilling scotch until the words all blur. It also ain't classy to be horny and not do nothing about it. All it is, is stressful. You hear me?"

"He could have a point there."

The three of them stepped onto the escalator that led down into the bright, smokey, jostling clatter of the handlers' messhall.

"Jesus, it looks like a prison break. You'd expect them to start banging their tin cups on the tables."

"Some nights they do."

"Jesus."

"Survivors can't be choosers."

"That's the new saying, right?"

Eggy had persuaded Vickers and Parkwood to accompany him on one of his now almost nightly visits to the handlers' quarters. According to Eggy, Fenton was already up there. They had taken a little persuading, but after a while a certain boredom with the monotony of the bunker's routine had won out and they'd followed him to the elevators feeling like guilty schoolboys on their way to the wrong side of the tracks. When Debbie learned of the intended venture, she'd first of all come on disgusted and then shut herself in her cubicle. It had increased the feeling that they were acting cheap but, their minds being made up by then, her reaction didn't deter them.

Vickers wasn't quite ready for the noise, the brightness and the crowding. Although they complained about the smallness of their group quarters on the lower level, they were, in comparison, luxuriously spacious. The handlers' messhall did look like something out of a prison movie. There was the same stark institutional functionality even though, in this instance, the function was fun. The flourescent plates were too hard and bright. They made everyone look pale and tired. The roar of rowdy, alcohol conversation fought with the throb of loud pressure pop and was then thrown back by the flat metal walls and ceiling that added a harsh, unattractive ring. By far the worst, however, was the crowding. There was a claustrophobic desperation to the way that the people crushed in together,

laughing and shouting and drinking, teeth and smiles and eyes
that kept looking and searching, trying to find a getaway from
the knowledge that they were huddled in a hole in the ground
while the world above them tried to end itself. And so many
women, most of them extremely attractive. Women in uniforms, women in coveralls, women in bright civilian casuals,
women in little more than their underwear. Over on the far side
of the hall, three women were dancing on a table, bare
breasted, lewd and drunk, encouraged by a chorus of catcalls,
whistles and cheers. Vickers spotted Eight-Man shouting and
laughing at the dancers but there was no sign of Fenton.

"You're damn right, survivors can't be choosers."

Eggy led the way, elbowing through the crowd toward where
a line of women dispensed drinks across a stainless steel,
cafeteria style counter. Eggy had clearly cut a wide swath up
here in the handlers' section. A quite formidable number of
women smiled, giggled, greeted, kissed him or made obscene
suggestions. Eggy responded to it all as if it were no more than
his reasonable due. Vickers and Parkwood also came in for a
good deal of attention. The phrase "new meat" seemed to
precede them across the hall. There were appraising stares and
a few soft touches. Fingers briefly fondled their sleeves or
brushed their thighs. Someone stroked Vickers' hair and he
even felt a deft exploratory hand slide quickly between his
legs. With the odds stacked five to one against them, these
women didn't mess around. The crowd generated its own heat
and Vickers was starting to sweat. Cramming people in like
this was insane. If they ever did seal the bunker there was no
way that people could survive years of this and still be anything
like intact. Lloyd-Ransom couldn't seriously be thinking he
could solve all of his inmate psychological problems by fear
and assassination.

Eventually they reached the bar. Parkwood tried to order
Johnny Walker Black but was curtly informed that the best he
was going to get up here on Level Two was generic scotch,
along with generic bourbon, generic vodka, generic gin and
beer. Parkwood sighed and took what he could get. Eggy and
Vickers also equipped themselves with drinks then turned and
surveyed the crowd. They instantly provoked interest.

"Hi."

Half of the first pair was a petite redhead with green eyes,
large breasts and a slight lisp.

"My name's Yvonne and this is Johanna."

"Hi Yvonne. Hi Johanna."

Johanna was taller. One of the hundreds of leggy Vegas types that had been corralled in the bunker. Her hair was cropped short in a style that made her look a little like Louise Brooks. She had a very pretty smile that reminded Vickers exactly how long it'd been since he'd had his arms around a woman.

"Are you more of the hard men from down in security?"

"That's us."

"They say a hard man is good to find."

Johanna gave Yvonne a bleak look.

"Ignore her. She watches too many old movies."

"She'd be hard to ignore."

Yvonne grinned. "Charm, even. That's a rarity in these grim days. Most of the men down here think they've only got to crook their little finger and we'll come running."

"We do, let's face it."

"Like your friend here. He's never heard of charm."

She nodded toward Eggy. At that moment he was in deep leering conversation with a trio of blondes who, although obviously not triplets, had taken some pains to look that way. He seemed poised to take all three to some dark place where they could all become better acquainted. Without thinking, Vickers threw back about half his drink. He immediately regretted what he'd done. The stuff burned like only really cheap booze could. It was the kind of stuff they served in Skid Row wino taverns. Usually it took you one of two ways, either maudlin or fighting mad.

"Christ."

Both Yvonne and Johanna laughed at his gasping surprise.

"No brand name booze up here. They don't figure we're worth it. We're just the gene pool."

There was undisguised malice in their laughter. The two women might be coming on to them but they didn't feel obligated to make a pretense of liking them. When you were confined to the first and second levels it was easy to become bitter about how all the good stuff was reserved for those down below.

"The deeper you go the better it gets, only we don't get to go deeper."

"It'd be a nice thought when you boys come up here because

you're feeling horny, if you brought some of those down-below goodies with you. We're getting fucking sick of this crankcase gin.''

A big muscular woman with close-cropped hair was reeling through the crowd. Her eyes were rolled back in her head and she was at the far end of drunk and maybe more. Each of her lurches caused its own outbreak of confusion and curses and produced its own jostling ripples in the tightly packed mass of people. Yvonne was elbowed in one of the surges. Her drink spilled down the front of her coverall.

"Goddamn fucked up dyke. She's like that every night. She doesn't even try to hold her liquor." She handed her empty plastic cup to Parkwood. "Here, sweetie, get me another one."

"Sometimes I think we'll all be like her inside of six months."

"Drunks or dykes?"

"Either, probably both."

Vickers was beginning to suspect that after six months of this overcrowding they'd probably be climbing the walls and eating each other like rats in an experiment, but he kept the thought to himself. Johanna was making her move on him. She'd slipped in beside him and was leaning close enough for him to feel her breast against his arm. She finished her drink with a definite finality. Vickers pretended not to read the gesture and smiled.

"You want another?"

"I'd rather get out of here and go somewhere marginally quieter."

"I figure we should have one more each."

"You want to put a bit of distance between us?"

"I was thinking more about putting a bit of distance between us and the environment."

Johanna looked around at the raucous crowd. "You may be right at that."

They called up two more shots and finished them quickly. Vickers turned to see what was going on with his companions. Eggy had vanished and Parkwood was kissing Yvonne. As far as Vickers could remember, it was the first time that he had ever seen him make physical contact with another human. Clearly he had no more need of Vickers' moral support. Vickers glanced at Johanna and she nodded. They slipped through the crowd heading for the nearest exit. They emerged into a service corridor.

"You know where we are?"

"Sure. This is my neighborhood." She slipped her arm through his. "I know I should be grateful that I've got a place down here and I'm safe and everything but sometimes I think this living is going to drive me crazy."

"What did you do before?"

"I was doing public relations at the Global office in LA. I profiled out when they ran the first shortlist program. They offered me a place down here and I took it. Everything looked so bad. Of course, it was a hell of a wrench going from buying drinks for TV producers to riding a bunch of robots on the loading dock but anything has to be worth it to survive." She gave a slight shudder. "There are times when it gets to me, though."

"So you worked for Global?"

"Right. It seems like another life now."

"You heard what happened to Herbie Mossman?"

"It doesn't bother me. I used to hear stories from the girls in the Vegas tower. By all accounts he was a disgusting, fat freak." She tightened her grip on his arm. "I don't want to talk about it anymore. I just want to feel and not think. I don't even know your name."

"Mort Vickers."

"Are you really one of Lloyd-Ransom's top hired guns?"

"I guess so."

"Hmm." She snuggled up against him.

After walking for about three minutes, they turned into the entrance of a handlers' dormitory. The sign over the doorway read General Living Area 30.

"GLA 30. Home sweet home. You can believe me that the living here is pretty general."

The living area was a very different place, during the down period, from the bright, cramped regimentation that Vickers had seen previously. The main overhead lights had been turned off but, while the majority of bunk tiers were in complete darkness, here and there some of the women had rigged candles or small bulbs shaded by colored scarves inside their bunk spaces. The daytime effect of gray metal uniformity was softened and hidden, made feminine even. Brute reality was held at bay and there was an almost magical quality. Each lighted space was like a cell of muted color in some giant, shadowy honeycomb. There was a trace of musky scent in the air, a mingling of incense and perfume, and low murmured conversations combined with the normal background sounds of the bunker. A few tiers away, someone was quietly playing something Spanish on a guitar. Dark moving figures in some of the bunks made it clear that others had come back to the area with intentions similar to those of Vickers and Johanna.

Johanna squeezed his hand and led them between the tiers.

"It's lucky that I was assigned a bottom bunk. Any kind of athletics in an upper bunk can be quiet dangerous."

Johanna had strung Christmas tree lights throughout the steel mesh in back of her bunk. The bunk itself was covered in a black silk shawl with a red and gold dragon embroidered on it that was obviously not official issue. She sat down on the edge of the bunk and drew Vickers down beside her.

"I have really horrible wine if you want some. It even came in a plastic container; or some of that scotch from the messhall."

"You are . . . very . . . weird."

Her breath came in scarcely muffled, vocal gasps. Vickers was still conscious of the potential audience in the shadows but Johanna seemed to have shut it out.

"Very . . . weird . . . indeed."

Vickers grinned in the glow of the fairy lights.

"I'll . . . stop if you . . . don't . . . like it."

Johanna squirmed against him with an extra added thrust.

"I didn't . . . say I . . . didn't like it . . . quite the . . . reverse . . . I *like it very much*!"

Her breath came in a final shout, her back arched in a prolonged, teeth-clenching spasm. By then even Vickers had forgotten about the people all around them.

A little later she was kissing his shoulder. "You're a terrible pervert, Mort Vickers. You know that?"

"People have told me."

"Will you take these things off me now?"

"Why don't we wait a little bit."

He had to admit, she really did look magnificent. She formed her lips into a small pout.

"Please, if we do it again, I'd rather do it the usual way."

Vickers smiled. "Whatever you say."

As he fumbled with the fastening, she lay back with her eyes closed.

"Will you come and see me again, Mort Vickers?"

"Sure will."

He meant every word of it. Her eyes opened.

"You're a damned liar."

"Why do you say that?"

"You're too slick to be anything but a damned liar."

The single bunk was too narrow to allow them to lie comfortably side by side. Vickers swung his feet to the floor.

"You're wrong you know. I like you. I'll come and see you again. That's what you really want to know, isn't it? Whether I like you or not?"

Johanna laughed. "Don't flatter yourself. What I really want is to corral myself a nice reliable fuck so I can relax a bit in this rat race. I somehow don't think you're it. You've probably got something going with at least three women down where you live."

Vickers reached around for the wine.

"As a matter of fact, this is the first time I've got myself laid since I got here."

Johanna took the wine from him.

"I don't believe you."

"It's true, I swear."

"Then you're weirder than I thought you were."

Vickers leaned back against her body. There was something comforting in the feel of someone else's warmth. If the bunk had been a little wider he would have lain down and gone to sleep. He drank some more wine and let himself drift. He must have actually been slipping away. Johanna's voice startled him.

"You'd better think about going."

Vickers sat up. "Oh yeah?"

"They turn a blind eye to these visits as long as the visitors don't stay all night."

"Maybe next time you should come down to my quarters."

"That's not allowed. If anyone in a blue or brown uniform is caught below the second level without legitimate authority, they're arrested. You can be thrown out of the bunker or worse."

"Worse?"

"Worse is only implied. I've never really wanted to know the details."

Vickers wasn't quite convinced.

"There must be a way to swing it."

Johanna shook her head. "If there were, Eggy would have found it by now. He's using storerooms and machine pods for his twosomes and threesomes."

"It all sounds a bit un-American."

Johanna's voice was bitter. "This isn't America. It isn't any place but the bunker and we live by the bunker's rules. If you want the bunker's protection you have to go with the program. It's like the saying goes, survivors can't be choosers."

"I don't know about all this."

"I do. It's got to be worth it in the long run."

Vickers wondered what kind of persuasion was being used on them up here in the peon levels.

"I sure hope so. What the fuck is that?"

The overhead lights had come on at the far end of the living area. Row after row of the flourescent panels came to life, a regular measured progress across the ceiling. Vickers grabbed for his shirt.

"Maybe I had better get out of here."

"I don't think all this is on your account."

Speakers crackled in confirmation.

"Now hear this! Now hear this! This is a yellow alert. All personnel will go immediately to their designated emergency stations. I repeat. This is a yellow alert. *All* personnel will go *immediately* to their emergency stations. This is a general order. There will be no exceptions. This is not a drill. This is a full yellow alert. This is not a drill. This is not a drill. Now hear this . . ."

The speakers repeated the message over again. Vickers was struggling into his pants.

"I don't think they're messing around."

All over the area women, and a small smattering of visiting men, were hastily pulling on their clothes. Some were already running for the exits.

"This is a not a drill. This is a yellow alert. Hurry! Hurry! Hurry!"

The hectoring speakers refused to let up. Vickers slipped into his jacket. Johanna had everything on but her shoes. She looked up at Vickers.

"I'll see you again?"

"Sure."

"Kiss me."

They kissed briefly and then went their separate ways. Vickers jogged to the nearest elevator. In the event of a yellow alert, the security teams were supposed to assemble at a central point on the fourth level. There was a small crowd clustered around the elevators. Vickers saw the huge form of Yabu, head and shoulders above the handlers. While Vickers was still a dozen yards from the elevator bank a red light flashed and the doors opened on a down elevator. Yabu and a number of handlers stepped inside. Vickers called out.

"Hey Yabu, hold the lift!"

Yabu grabbed the closing door and pushed it back. Vickers slipped inside.

"It seems like some kind of shit is hitting the fan."

Yabu was impassive. "Maybe we'll see some action."

Vickers had absolutely no relationship with the giant Oriental. On a couple of occasions he had tried and failed to strike a conversation with him. After that he'd given up trying. It was thus that Vickers was more than a little surprised when he looked directly at him and smiled a Zen smile.

"You visit with the handler women?"

Vickers nodded. "Yeah, I guess so."

Yabu looked approving. "A man needs to get fucked now and again if he is to stay sane and healthy. I do the same myself."

He looked away; the conversation seemed to have been abruptly terminated. The handlers around them were having trouble stifling fits of giggles. Vickers shrugged. He was a little relieved when the doors slid open and he and Yabu were able to make their exit onto the fourth level.

The majority of four security groups were already assembled. The only one of his group who had yet to arrive was Eggy. As he joined the other three, they glanced at him briefly. Parkwood treated him to the slightest of conspiratorial smiles. Presumably it was supposed to indicate that he had had an entertaining time with Yvonne. It was the furthest he'd ever been in terms of camaraderie. After the swift, all round acknowledgement, the attention switched off. Everyone was too concerned with what was coming out of the speakers. The ones down on the fourth level were much more informative. They appeared to have been broadcasting situation details for some time.

". . . an exchange of tactical nuclear weapons is now being reported from the area to the west of Poznan where the forces of Greater Germany and West Poland have been engaged with a large splinter group of the Red Army. As of yet, there are no details of the exact circumstances or who fired first but a number of corporation satellites are relaying accounts of up to four detonations of a size consistent with atomic shells or neutron minisiles. Unconfirmed accounts from Berlin indicate, however, that the German and Polish front lines are being overrun by near-suicidal Russian attacks."

The elevator doors opened again and another anxious crowd rushed out. Eggy was among them. He hurried up to the rest of the group looking like he hadn't slept.

"Sounds like the ice has started to crack."

"That's one way of looking at it."

"Has anyone told us what we're supposed to be doing?"

"Not yet."

Mobs of people streamed past, all apparently possessed of both a purpose and a sense of urgency, while the security groups stood around feeling a little like forgotten spare parts as the speakers repeated the same bulletin over and over. Finally there was a news report. It did nothing to raise anyone's spirits.

"A report is now coming in from a Space Inc. observation satellite that a flight of intermediate-range surface-to-surface missiles, possibly SS 2000s or SS 2100s, are lifting from a complex of silos near Slutsk in White Russia, near the East Polish border. Although this launch hasn't been confirmed by any other satellite, it would appear to be a response to the battlefield exchange west of Poznan."

Still nobody had instructed them what to do. Then Fenton pointed.

"Here comes Deakin."

"About damn time."

Deakin wasn't just coming, he was coming at a run. He was out of breath and most of his normal bumptiousness had been sweated away. He waved quickly at the group.

"All of you, follow me. On the double."

Eggy fell into step beside him.

"What's going on?"

"All hell's breaking loose, that's what's going on."

The first stop was the armory where the group was given a choice of either pump shotguns or machine pistols. Vickers drew his customary Yasha. While he was taping three clips back to back for an ultrafast reload, another bulletin came over the public address.

"The launch of Russian intermediate range missiles is confirmed by four more satellites. A number of missiles have exploded in midair and more seem on course for nowhere but the open sea. This is only to be expected from the current chaos that is the Soviet Union. The remainder appear to be directly on target and are expected to reach their strikepoints in a little over eight minutes. Western Europe is under full nuclear attack. I will repeat that. Western Europe is under full nuclear attack."

It was only at the very end that the announcer's voice faltered. Bach's Toccata in D Minor welled up to fill the silence. Someone in what had come to be called the radio station couldn't resist a production. Then another voice took over.

"The bunker is now on Full Red Alert. All personnel, without exception, will stand to. The bunker is on Full Red Alert. This is not a drill. The Bunker is on Full Red Alert until further notice."

Bach was replaced by funereal electronics. There was no holding back the chill. The security group jogged to the nearest elevator. All over the bunker hooters were blowing, lights flashed and sirens wailed. People went on with their duties as though trying to drown the ballooning fear in routine. Everyone avoided everyone else's eyes and panic was, in some cases, only held at bay by inches. The handlers and facers who were clustered around the lift entrance backed away as Deakin and his charges ran up. As they rode the elevator, Deakin breathlessly issued their instructions.

"We're going up to the first level to reinforce discipline. Under a Red Alert the personnel on the surface are withdrawn into the first level. Any disturbance would be a disaster. You will be there to see that any potential disturbance is immediately stamped on."

"We're supposed to do this on our own?"

"Of course not. There are a hundred or more uniformed troops up there. You are simply back-up. You have a roving brief. You look for individuals who are about to become hysterical. You will shoot them out of hand. You understand

that? If there's a problem simply kill it. You do not have the
option of asking questions. Okay?''

Slowly and grimly all five nodded. There was a terrible
silence in the elevator. Deep inside Vickers' soul, something
was screaming that it wanted to be somewhere else, anywhere
else. He knew the voice well. He had heard it before in several
dozen firefights but he couldn't remember when he'd heard it
so insistent. He trusted that, when the action started, it would
be muffled by pumping adrenaline. The elevator stopped, the
doors sighed open and the silence was swallowed by the
echoing crash of marching feet. The huge freight elevators
were coming down loaded with men and materiel withdrawing
from the surface. Jeeps and armored cars were driven off the
platforms and parked in rows on the other side of the giant
manmade cavern. On previous visits, Vickers had wondered
about the first level. It had seemed so vast and bare and empty.
Now he realized that it was a parking lot for an army. Even
Parkwood seemed stunned.

"I can hardly believe this."

In some ways it was like a withdrawal. They were
unmistakably in retreat but hardly defeated. This was no
shattered army. It was clean and neat and orderly; it had fought
no battle but the air of depression was unmistakable. Lines of
gray-uniformed troops and blue-and-brown-uniformed workers
waited patiently for internal transport to take them further into
the bowels of the bunker. The fear was so intense that Vickers
could almost taste it but the discipline was holding. Every few
yards an armed soldier watched the slow processions that
snaked from the elevators, looking for any kind of irregularity
that might spark a panic. The five spread out, doing their best
to look as though they were reinforcing the uniformed guards
but secretly feeling a little redundant. Then, over on Vickers'
right, a man started screaming. At first it was completely
wordless but gradually it formed into words.

"No! No! No! No! I don't want to! I don't want to!"

Vickers knew exactly what he meant. A couple of soldiers
moved toward him. Abruptly, the man stopped shouting and
bolted. He was running directly toward Debbie. She didn't
hesitate. Her shotgun roared. The man spun and sprawled in a
bloody splatter. All over the area, guns were up. Would the
single moment of hysteria trigger a stampede? Three soldiers
ran up and threw a tarpaulan over the body. The lines started to

move again. Moments later, the speakers came on. The voice was carefully measured as if its owner was only just managing to maintain his control.

"For the last five minutes, communications have been lost with the entire continent of Europe. Satellite reports are still coming in but observers in the air report huge fountains of smoke and dust erupting not only from Germany but from France, Italy, Spain and the British Isles. Early estimates place the number of nuclear explosions somewhere in the region of two dozen."

Vickers found himself illogically wondering if it had been day or night over there. The lines of uniformed men and women kept on moving. It was as if everyone was in a trance. Fenton walked to where Vickers was standing.

"You think they'll seal the bunker now?"

Vickers blinked. Maybe he was the one in the trance.

"Say what?"

"You think they'll seal the bunker now?"

Vickers shook his head. "No, they'll wait a while yet. They'll get in as many bigwigs as possible. The Pope and the rest."

"And we'll wait too."

"That's always the way of it."

They waited for two hours and then for two hours more. The public address bulletins came fewer and further between. As a substitute someone began to pipe in music to the first level. Mainly it was more of the doom and gloom electronics that they'd been treated to on level four but at one point someone had slipped in Gene Kelly's "Singing in the Rain." It was yanked, however, after the first couple of verses and, for a full five minutes, sinister silence prevailed before the mood electronics returned. The flow of people and equipment coming down from the surface gradually diminished. In the fifth hour it came down to little more than a trickle. NCOs and officers started pulling out the uniformed guards but nobody made any attempt to relieve the security group. Also, nobody had bothered to send the clean-up crew for the man whom Debbie had shot. With nothing to do, the five gathered in a small, complaining group. Even in the face of global twilight it was still possible to complain. The body simply remained where it had fallen, covered by its makeshift shroud. By the end of the sixth hour, they were the only people left, apart from a couple of maintenance crews working on the parked vehicles.

"You think that we've been forgotten?"

An air of desolation was creeping across the hollow, echoing area. An elevator platform came to rest with a giant's cough. Its only passenger was a soldier in a jeep. Eggy beckoned and yelled at her.

"Hey you!"

The soldier spun the wheel and drove over to where they were standing.

"You want something?"

"What's going on on the surface?"

The woman pushed back her helmet and shrugged.

"Pretty much of nothing. There's only a skeleton missile crew out there. Everybody else is inside."

"And there's nothing happening? No explosions, no mushroom clouds or nothing?"

The soldier shook her head.

"Sun's going down peaceful as you like."

"You wouldn't see anything, Eggy. Not unless they'd nuked Las Vegas."

The soldier leaned on her steering wheel.

"You really think that this is it?"

The five all looked at her as though the question wasn't worth answering. She nodded, pulled down her helmet, put the jeep into gear and gunned it away to where the other vehicles were parked.

The music faded. The group looked at each other, the silent question "What now?" After a pause of some thirty seconds the speakers came to life again.

"A number of reports are coming in of further Soviet missile launches. The Trans-America space station has observed over eighty rockets lifting from sights to the south of the Zhigansk on the Arctic Circle in the Yakut region of Siberia. These firings are located too far to the east to be targeted on the European conflict. They can logically only be multi-warhead ICBMs targeted on North America."

"Jesus Christ."

Instinctively the group moved close together. The vehicle maintenance crews had stopped work. They were walking away from their vehicles out into the open, staring up at the speakers in the roof. There was a brief burst of music and then a new voice came on.

"This is Anthony Lloyd-Ransom and I'm talking to you directly because I see no way to minimize what I have to say. Unless we have been misinformed to a point that would scarcely seem possible, the world is advancing into global thermo-nuclear war and there is no way out. If we do not receive confirmation of some attempt at a cease-fire or strategic pullback in the next few minutes, I shall seal the bunker. I know it seems scarcely possible to believe but we now have to face the strong possibility that the future of mankind may, at any moment, be placed in our hands. If this is the case we are about to receive a truly awesome responsibility. We have to rise and accept it. I am well aware that it's impossible to divorce ourselves from the situation on the surface. I know that you are all afraid that, as I speak, we may be losing friends and loved ones, that cities we know and love are being consumed by firestorms."

Vickers sneezed. "I think there's tranquilizers being pumped into the air conditioning."

"Shut up, Vickers, don't you have no respect?"

Lloyd-Ransom's voice boomed on.

"The administration of this bunker expects, hard as it may be, that you set these considerations aside and rise to the monumental task that now confronts us. The thing that I ask will certainly tax us to the limits of our humanity. We are entering a valley of shadow the enormity of which no one has ever experienced. Our sole responsibility is to survive. The means to that survival will be our discipline and our sense of duty. The task will be long and arduous but I am confident that every one of you will find inside him or herself the strength to fight the sense of despair that will undoubtedly come upon us. We are going into a dark and terrible night and I pray that both God and our own strength will go with us."

"They all make the same speech."

"He didn't mention the flag."

The original voice came back over the speakers.

"Stand by for a message from the President of the United States."

Eggy scowled. "They're all in on the act."

There was the hiss and crackle of a long distance carrier

wave. The voice, when it came on, was distorted and scratchy
to the point of being hard to recognize.

"My fellow Americans. I am speaking to you from the
Orbital Command module some five hundred kilometers above
the earth . . ."

"The bastard got himself safely out of it."

"You think the donuts are safe?"

"The space stations?" Parkwood shook his head. "No,
there are too many hunter-killers up there. They'll go."

". . . this is one of the blackest moments in the history of
our nation. Indeed, this is the gravest situation our planet has
ever faced. Nuclear warheads have already been detonated
over Lawrence, Kansas, Chicago, West Los Angeles, Oakland
and New York City. More enemy missiles are right now in
flight. In the last few minutes, I have, after consultation with
the leaders of our major corporations, ordered a massive
retaliation against the Soviet Union. Even as I speak, our front
line of Peacemaker and Alamo missiles are being launched
from their silos. This is not a simple matter of revenge or
vindictiveness. The American people are neither vengeful nor
vindictive. In launching our first string of intercontinental
ballistic missiles, we are making it plain to the Soviet leaders
that this country will not sit idly by in the face of this barbaric
and unprovoked attack on our homeland, on our European
allies . . ."

"I didn't think there were any Soviet leaders."

"Sssh. Let him finish."

"I hope the bastard dies."

". . . or on any other parts of the Free World. Although
history will record this as our darkest hour and the name of
Soviet communism will live forever in infamy, I am confident
that there will be a history to recount the story. None of us can
predict the immediate future. All we can do is pray for the
strength, the courage and the fortitude to come through these
terrible times, to face the awful sacrifices that will have to be
made, and to undertake the mighty task of rebuilding that will
face us when these days of testing are over. My heart goes out
to you and my thoughts are constantly with you. God bless you
all."

The "Star Spangled Banner" boomed out, but halfway
through the first verse it was abruptly cut. The voice of
authority returned.

"The bunker is being sealed. I repeat, the bunker is being sealed."

The first sound was the screech of metal that wasn't accustomed to being moved. Enormous steel doors were closing across the entrances to the freight elevators. After they closed with a dull boom, there was a brief silence, then a series of deep muffled explosions came from somewhere beyond. These were followed by what, at first, was just a pattering, then a metallic hiss like hail on a tin roof. Quickly it grew to an all encompassing echoing roar. The method of sealing the bunker was comparatively simple. Sections of wall on the outside of the elevator shafts had been blown out and thousands of tons of dirt and sand poured into the empty space. The roar went on for a full five minutes before it finally subsided in a series of coughs and booms as the displaced material settled. On the first level, the soldiers and the security group stood as though stunned. Even after all they'd been through and after all the lectures, the conditioning and the brainwashing, they couldn't quite believe that it was really happening. They looked from one to the other as though waiting for someone to tell them it was only a drill or an elaborate joke. Nothing happened except that there was another grumble of settling dirt and rock.

Vickers tried to think of New York or Chicago in flames. He couldn't quite accept the idea. He still pictured them the way he'd seen them last, dirty, busy and bustling. He couldn't imagine there were giant craters where Central Park and the Loop had been. It wasn't possible that places that had been so teemingly alive could be burned to nothing: a single, terrible death. He knew in the end that he'd come to terms with it but right at that moment all he could do was try and protect himself by blanking it out. To his horror, he saw that Fenton was grinning at him like a gargoyle.

"You know what?"

Fenton's grin was actually like a rigor twitch. Vickers resisted backing away from him with some difficulty.

"What?"

"The Pope never made it."

Vickers blinked. "What the hell are you talking about?"

"Wasn't the Pope supposed to have a place down here when the war came?"

"Yeah, right. I heard that."

"So he didn't make it."

Vickers shook his head. On top of everything else, Fenton was the final straw.

"You're a sick man."

Fenton continued to grin.

"Maybe, but I ain't out frying cities."

SEVEN

EIGHTEEN MONTHS HAD PASSED.

The public address was playing "Frosty the Snowman" by the Ronettes. Fenton hacked at what was left of the Virginia ham with his hunting knife. Vickers poured himself a glass of port and wearily lowered himself into what had been Lloyd-Ransom's chair at the head of the long banquet table.

"They sure treat themselves well down here."

"We don't do so bad."

Fenton spoke through a mouthful of ham. Vickers scowled. The whole idea of Christmas in the bunker had put him in a particularly foul mood. The previous year had been bad enough, but this one was approaching obscene. All around them was the debris of the huge banquet that Lloyd-Ransom had thrown for his superpeople. The long main table had been set out on the piazza with the head of the table just in front of the black obelisk. The eternal flame hadn't worked in over a year. Five months in, something had gone wrong with the gas feed. The eternal flame was fueled with methane from the sewage plant, a feature that had proved far from successful. After it had flickered, abruptly died and stubbornly refused to

183

be rekindled, there had been a few days of superstitious fear until the butcher squads had gone to work on the second level and replaced the unfocused fear with a very definite mortal dread.

"We're eating their fucking leftovers."

Fenton was ladling dressing onto a plate. He covered it with cold gravy. Vickers picked up a bottle of Remy Martin that had been lying on its side. There was about three-quarters of an inch left in it. He rummaged for a clean glass.

"At least there's plenty of them."

"You're too much of a fucking pragmatist. Don't you ever get mad?"

"Now and again. I tell myself firmly that there's no percentage in it."

Vickers tried the brandy and was pleased to find that no one had flicked cigar ash into it. Sure he could get mad at the superpeople's psychotic consumption; sure it could make him crazy living in and off their garbage. On the other hand, he was drinking good brandy while most of the rest up on the other levels were numbing their minds on the bunker's rotgut gin.

"You'll get mad one day."

"Maybe."

"I'm going to be in the front row for that."

After this Christmas celebration, garbage was everywhere. The superpeople routinely partied like pigs but on this particular occassion they'd really excelled themselves. Crap was spread over half the piazza. There were cups and cartons, empty bottles and beer cans, forgotten plates and spilled food, there were even discarded pieces of clothing. A torn ballgown was draped over the statue titled Fidelity. When the drinking had reached a peak a few hours earlier, some of the celebrants had become extremely physical. A few were still scattered around, asleep, unconscious or maybe even dead. You never could tell and Vickers didn't particularly care. One of the fountains that was still working was making an unhappy, strained gurgle. It was undoubtedly clogged with party garbage. Vickers wondered if anyone would bother to fix it before it totally broke down. Water was already starting to spill out of its lower basin and run across the grimy black and white marble in a dirty brown river. In the middle of the mess was the incongruous, twelve-feet-high, silver fibreglass Christmas tree, lavishly garnished with red and green mirror balls. There was something a little disgusting about the tree. It was an insult to the real trees that had died so quickly after the sealing of the bunker but whose dead trunks still stood like black reminders. The peacocks and the other birds had also failed to survive the first year. Some said that the peacocks had been eaten at some superperson's banquet.

The music had changed. The PA was playing Roddy Reegan's "Christmas on Mars." There had to be a psycho loose in the booth. When the song was finished, the psycho identified himself. A deep, throaty voice purred through every level of the bunker like a combination of gravel and honey.

"Christmas night in the bunker, friends and babies, Christmas Two in the big hole. I guess there aren't too many of us asleep tonight. Maybe a lot of thinking going on, just laying there in your bunk and thinking. Thinking about the snow, the silent snow falling on white fields that go on and on, all the way to where the horizon meets the black starlit sky. Now isn't that a hell of a thing to think about on a night like this?" He let the thought sink in. "This is Bing Crosby with 'White Christmas.' If that don't get to you, nothing will."

"Wolfjohn is going to wake up one morning with an icepick in the back of his skull. He's pushing a whole lot too hard."

Vickers was looking at a bottle of Mouton Cadet. There was something unidentifiable floating in the wine.

"He's real popular with the women."

"Sure he's popular. He gets more pussy than Eggy but that won't save him if Lloyd-Ransom takes it into his head that he's dangerous. Disc jocks are infinitely expendable."

Vickers leaned back in his chair and propped his feet up on the table.

"He's just pleasing the customers. Shit, everybody dreams about outside. You'd be crazy if you didn't."

"There are days when he don't do nothing but Wantout propaganda. He's out to stir up trouble."

"Everybody's talking Wantout. Christ, you want to get out yourself."

"But I don't go around shouting about it."

Vickers was getting bored with the whole subject. That was all anyone talked about these days, what was going on outside.

"So Wolfjohn finds a butcher squad turned on him. That's his lookout, not mine."

Fenton tossed his hunting knife. It stuck in the table six feet in front of him, vibrating from side to side.

"I'll tell you one thing, if Lloyd-Ransom decides to grease Wolfjohn, it won't be a regular butcher squad, it'll be one of us."

"That won't do anything for our popularity level on Level Two."

"Maybe he'll get Debbie to do it. She won't mind. All she wants to do these days is snuff men."

The two men shook their heads in unison. In the year and a half since the bunker had been sealed, the position of the security execs had become stranger and stranger. As Vickers had always predicted, Lloyd-Ransom's regime had run on a combination of brutality and fear. The main problem that had to be tackled was that, beyond feeding and keeping themselves clean, there was really very little for the population of the bunker to do except sit and wait until the outside world was ready for them to emerge from their self-made caves. It was like Lutesinger had told them, they were seeds waiting for the moment to sprout, they were in a dormant period. Unfortunately the population wasn't dormant. They were alive and kicking, claustrophobic and subject to a stress-loaded sexual imbalance. They had plenty of time on their hands to become neurotic and hysterical, to gossip and complain, to plot and intrigue. There had been riots, and bizarre rumors had sparked equally bizarre days of panic. Crowd madness recurred like a cyclical epidemic, while other behavior defied all categorizing. There had been the weird secret society called the Convocation of Witches and their seemingly random stoning ceremonies. There had been the spontaneous blindness and the hunger sacrifices. An obscure group of women had sat in front of the doors on the first level, doused themselves with gasoline and burned to death. While the bunker waited, it also became an emotional powderkeg.

Lloyd-Ransom was neither a psychologist nor blessed with the common touch. He approached trouble like a surgeon. If, in his opinion, a cell or group of cells ceased to conform and so endangered the total being, the only answer was to cut it out. As soon as the bunker was sealed, he had started organizing the hard cases among his now largely idle military into viciously efficient execution groups, the "butcher squads" as they were dubbed. They became his first resort, his instrument of terror.

People, particularly people in the lower echelons, who talked or acted out of turn were likely to simply vanish or, if examples needed to be made, a changing shift might come across their horribly mutilated bodies. Surveillance and informing became endemic. Friends ratted on neighbors, jealous lovers turned in their rivals and all the time the computerized cameras watched everybody.

Lloyd-Ransom wasn't so stupid, however, as to just let his death squads run amok. Indeed, there had been a period when the butchers had actually started competing, squad against squad, in how sadistically grisly they could make their handiwork. At that point, there had had to be some judicious pruning. Seventeen of the more pathological butcher squad officers had been liquidated in a single evening. This was where Vickers' squad and the other ununiformed security execs were brought in. They were Lloyd-Ransom's ace in the hole. If he believed that one of the superpeople in the bottoms was working to seize power, or that a group of his officers were plotting a coup, Vickers or one or more of the others would be called upon to act. They performed the fine tuning on his machine. He trusted them in the same way that he trusted his dogs. They were his ultimate hired guns, totally amoral and owing their only basic allegiance to the man who had purchased their services and enabled them to survive the holocaust.

This position as Lloyd-Ransom's line of last resort also placed the two security groups in an odd relationship with the rest of the people. Where almost everyone, particularly the facers and handlers and the others who thought of themselves as rank and file, hated and feared the military and the uniformed security with a finely honed venom that was reinforced by every murder and atrocity, the ten without uniforms enjoyed a perverse popularity. They rarely did any harm to the rank and file and when they did kill, they did it quietly and cleanly and usually the victim was someone who the upper tiers regarded as deserving of what they got. On two occasions, when butcher squads had run wild among the women on the second level, the ten had been moved in to neutralize them. These incidents had made them celebrities, heroes even. They had been unable to resist the temptation to swagger. Already-fanciful clothing had become even more flamboyant. Eggy seemed to be doing his best to resemble a

big wheel among the in-crowd of Attila the Hun while even
Parkwood had affected a certain swashbuckling air with silk
scarves, a Panama hat and an automag hanging from his belt.

Although Lloyd-Ransom had quite obviously gone to considerable pains to cover all the details when designing the
machine that maintained his power, he also insisted on
supporting some very basic policies that seemed destined to
create division and unrest. A perfect example was the rigid
caste system that operated level to level. Set and unchanging,
with menial workers on the top levels and the privileged in the
bottoms, it was one of the absolutes on which the bunker was
built. When the bunker was first sealed most had been prepared
to rough it. They'd been spared nuclear destruction and they'd
tolerate anything within reason. As the months passed, though,
the stoic attitude weakened and reason gave way to resentment.
How come a certain few were having it so much better than the
many? Why were the favored few living in the marble halls of
the bottoms, dining on peacock and vintage wine while the
majority existed on concentrates and bad gin? It seemed to
Vickers that it was a set of circumstances tailor-made for
revolt. During an unguarded, supposedly informal moment,
Vickers had voiced this to Lloyd-Ransom. Lloyd-Ransom had
stared coldly at him.

"It's simply safety precaution. We must always look to the
future. When we finally emerge onto the surface, it will require
a strong hierarchical society to ensure that we survive. I didn't
go to all this trouble just to let loose the infection of socialism
all over again."

Vickers had accepted that there was a certain grotesque logic
to this. An area in which he could find no logic at all was in the
way that Lloyd-Ransom handled the matter of when exactly
they would unseal the bunker and start to investigate the
surface. For about the first nine months things had remained
fairly stable. The preoccupying paranoia had been with Red
spies and saboteurs. As it came up to the first year, things
began to change. All through the levels, people were getting
itchy. They wanted to know what was going on above their
heads. Officially, no one knew anything. The probes and
sensors that were supposed to measure temperature and
radiation, the satellite dishes that listened in to the world's
communication and the cameras that showed what was
happening in the immediate, surrounding desert had all gone
dead. Lutesinger had been wheeled out to explain how it was

likely that there'd been a surface burst almost on top of the
bunker. He hadn't explained why even the Russians should be
directing missiles to the middle of the Nevada desert.

As they moved into the second year, the itch turned into an
open demand. Why not at least send up an exploratory team to
check out surface conditions? Maybe things weren't as bad as
the predictions said. Maybe the worst of the radiation had
cooled off. Maybe the dust had settled and the nuclear winter
was over. Lloyd-Ransom flatly refused to entertain any of these
suggestions. As far as he was concerned, the only way out was
to fully unseal the bunker and unsealing the bunker was a
complicated process that involved tunneling up the blocked
elevator shafts. Questions were asked. Surely there must be
some other way out. Lloyd-Ransom said there wasn't and was
not widely believed. How could they have designed such a
complex structure as the bunker without some kind of bolt hole
exits? The strange behavior began. Graffiti appeared. The
Wantouts, as they were dubbed, became an active underground opposition and replaced the Reds as the primary targets
for both Lloyd-Ransom's paranoia and his death squads.

There was the ringing clacks of high heels from the entrance
to one of the tunnels that led away to the superpeople's private
quarters. The steps sounded halting and uneven. Vickers
glanced up. Almost unconsciously, his hand moved to the
Yasha that he now carried slung from one shoulder, Doc
Holliday style, by a leather strap. The woman was a tall,
attractive redhead. She was tottering and very drunk. The high
heels were a bright, flame red. She was dressed in a black, full-
length mink, which she hugged tightly to herself as though
uncertain as to whether it really belonged to her. Maybe it
didn't. Perhaps she'd stolen it. It was quite likely that she was
actually from one of the other levels, brought down as
partyfodder and now going back with an expensive souvenir.
She halted every few steps and stood, swaying. Vickers wasn't
sure if she was crying or giggling to herself. She saw him and
Fenton for the first time. She started and tightened her grip on
the coat. Fenton, who'd also been watching her, laughed.

"Don't be frightened. I'm not going to hurt you. Neither's
my good buddy here." He glanced at Vickers. "You're not
going to hurt her, are you?"

Vickers shook his head. "Not me."

The woman moved unsteadily toward the table.

"Is there anything to drink?"

"You're pretty far gone."

"I know that but I still want a drink."

"There's plenty left over but you're going to have to look for it."

The woman leaned heavily on the table and began to rummage through the mess. She found a bottle of champagne and put it to her mouth. Vickers noticed that she had green eyes.

"It's flat."

"What did you expect?"

As she drank, her coat fell open. She was naked beneath it. Her body was white and liberally freckled. There were a number of angry red welts across her torso as though she'd been recently flogged.

"What have they been doing to you?"

"Having their fun."

By the standards of the superpeople the ill treatment was comparatively mild. There had been rumors of snuff parties although Vickers had never seen any solid evidence. The woman had found a bottle of scotch with some left in it. She closed her coat, hugging the bottle to her like a baby.

"I've . . . got to be going. I think I've had enough for tonight."

She pushed herself away from the table. The clicks of her heels zigzagged across the black and white marble of the piazza in the direction of the elevators. Wolfjohn was playing "Oh Come All Ye Faithful" by the Mormon Tabernacle Choir. Vickers and Fenton lapsed into an almost-drunk silence. Even after eighteen months, it was all to easy to slip back into the trauma, back to thinking of all the people and all the places that had been wiped away like they had never been, all the faces and all the names and the locations that were gone forever. The more you tried to accept it, the more overwhelming the horror became. Vickers was quite relieved when he heard Eggy's voice booming from one of the tunnels.

"Hey, what's going on?"

Eggy had been drinking but he wasn't drunk. He was swaggering rather than staggering. His faced was covered in smeared, warrior-style red and purple war paint. War paint was a comparatively new addition to Eggy's repetoire and one that Vickers found a little disturbing. Eggy jerked his thumb back down the corridor.

"You want to see the horrorshow back there?"

Fenton looked up. "Horrowshow? That's a quaint, old fashioned word."

"It's pretty quaint and old fashioned back there. It's like something out of the Marquis de Sade."

"The superpeople are cutting up?"

Eggy dropped into a chair.

"Cutting up, slicing up, flogging and hogging it up. They've even got them chained by the feet from the ceiling. You've never seen so many people getting distorted at once. Eight-Man's going around boasting how he fucked Thane Ride in Lloyd-Ransom's four-poster."

"You're kidding."

"The hell I am. I believe him."

"I thought Thane Ride only fucked girls these days."

"According to Eight-Man she was so stoned she was past knowing."

"And where was Lloyd-Ransom at the time?"

"Who knows where he goes when he vanishes."

Vickers' eyes abruptly focused.

"Vanishes? Lloyd-Ransom vanishes?"

"That's what they're saying. Sometimes for as long as a couple of days. You two didn't hear about it?"

Both Fenton and Vickers shook their heads.

"Not a damn thing."

"Me neither."

Eggy shrugged. "There isn't really that much to tell. It's just that the word among the superpeople is that our glorious leader regularly disappears."

"So where does he go?"

"Who knows? There are some that say he goes outside."

"Outside?"

"That's what some of them are saying. It's probably just bullshit. I mean, how the hell would he get outside?"

The PA was playing Elvis Presley singing "Blue Christmas."

Alarms were suddenly howling.

"Shit!"

Vickers quickened his pace. He hurried down the corridor to the nearest wall phone. A handler was talking into it. When she saw Vickers coming toward her, her face took on a look of pure

terror. A hand flew to her mouth. She backed away to the full
length of the cord. She held out the phone to him.

"Please . . ."

Vickers neither had the time nor the disposition to be nice.
He simply took the handset and let the frightened woman
fluster away down the corridor. On the other end of the line,
someone was wanting to know what was going on.

"Hang up."

Vickers must have hit exactly the right note of authority
since the other end of the line did exactly what it was told.
Vickers punched in the code for Security Coordination.

"This is Vickers. What's going on?"

"There's a riot started on the second level. A bunch of
handlers refused to go on shift. Something about a cut in their
water allocation. A Code *D* squad went in but they must have
come on a bit too rough because fighting started and they were
driven out of the GLA."

"What GLA is it?"

"Twenty-six."

"Women's area, right?" Vickers was relieved. At least
Johanna, his on and off lover in GLA30, would not be directly
involved.

"Right."

"I'd better go up there, see if I can do anything. Are any
more of my group headed up there?"

"Parkwood and Debbie are on their way."

"I'll find them."

He hung up and jogged to the elevators. About the only
consolation in being a bunker corpse was that you were
virtually your own boss. As he stepped out onto the second
level, he found himself in the middle of a firefight. There was
smoke in the corridor and the acrid smell that comes with
gunfire. It was the kind of shock he could have done without.
The handlers had guns. They must have disarmed some of the
first Code *D* squad that went in. He threw himself back, but he
wasn't quite fast enough. The elevator doors closed behind
him. He pressed back against them, taking advantage of the
minimal cover provided by the entrance. A shotgun blast tore
up a piece of wall that was uncomfortably close. He slid down
into a crouch. The second level was a mess but this was
nothing new. At the best of times, its corridors were ugly with
garbage, graffiti and broken light panels. Even across the

elevator door, where Vickers crouched, someone had scrawled the angry but all too common slogan, "WE WANT OUT!"

Four security people in yellow uniforms were slowly moving up, pushing a golf cart in front of them, using it as cover. Further back a second squad was unreeling a steam hose. Further back still, Vickers spotted Parkwood and Debbie crouched behind another golf cart that had been overturned and thoroughly trashed. He looked in the other direction. The women had barricaded the entrance to the living area and were firing from behind an effective wall of stacked bunks and lockers. At least temporarily, they had the advantage. Another shotgun blast chewed up the wall beside him and Vickers decided that he'd be a great deal better off back with Parkwood and Debbie. The only problem was how to get there.

The group pushing the golf cart was almost level with him. It looked like the best chance that he was going to get. He tensed. He treated the barricade to a fast burst from his Yasha and jumped. As he rolled into cover behind the golf cart there was a burst of firing from the barricade. He estimated there were at least five weapons up there. Autoload shotguns and maybe one M90. It would be far from easy to get them out. He left the uniformed security to their slow progress and worked his way back to where the other two corpses were still crouched. It was with some relief that he ducked in beside them.

"Is it as much of a mess as it looks?"

"It's probably worse. The uniforms seem to have fucked things up about as bad as they could. That first Code *D* team that went in must have been a total bunch of clowns. They started manhandling the women. They even, by all accounts, put down their weapons. The women just grabbed their guns. They blew away two of them on the spot and they've got two more in there as hostages."

Parkwood sniffed. "I don't know what good they think hostages are going to do them. Lloyd-Ransom isn't going to deal. As far as he's concerned, everyone's expendable."

All three ducked as the M90 cut loose in a long, wild burst. Debris rained down from the ceiling.

"Have they made any demands? Do they want anything?"

"Not really. They're saying they want out but that's nothing new. I figure they've just been pushed too far."

"They must know that they'll be killed in the end. Nobody up here can have any illusions."

"That's less reason for them to give up easy."

There was another burst of firing. It was deafening in the closed space of the corridor. One of the uniforms trying to set up the steam hose was hit. He lay exposed, bleeding badly from a head wound. Parkwood turned so his back was against the upended golf cart.

"About the only piece of good luck in this whole mess is that it hasn't spread to the other living areas. It should be shift change right about now, but everyone's being held at their work stations. The other GLAs on this level are bottled up by the military. Lamas has taken charge and he seems to have some idea of what he's doing."

"What about Lloyd-Ransom?"

"Nobody's seen him."

"That's weird."

Parkwood's eyes were bleak.

"What isn't?"

Vickers glanced back. Behind them a mixed force of military grew and security yellow were moving up.

"I guess that's it for those women inside. It can only be a matter of time.

Debbie checked the clip on her machine pistol.

"It could be a lot of time and it may well cost dearly. It depends how much ammunition they have."

Vickers raised an eyebrow.

"You sound like you're on their side."

Debbie's head turned. She gave Vickers a long, cold stare.

"That's right. I probably am. At least they've got the courage to say *enough* after eighteen months in this stinking hole. Who wouldn't be on their side?"

"It might not be such a good idea to say so out loud!"

"Big Brother's still watching us?"

"Did it ever stop?"

"That, in itself, is reason to say enough."

Parkwood eased himself into a more comfortable position.

"Do you feel the remains of any collective sanity are right now slipping away?"

For some reason Debbie took this personally.

"I'm starting to dislike you."

"You're starting to dislike everybody. It's one of the symptoms."

Before the argument could escalate, there was another burst

of gunfire from the barricade and a flurry of movement behind them. Yabu and a captain in the military slid into their patch of cover. There wasn't quite room for five of them behind the golf cart and the captain had to scrunch up to avoid her left side being exposed. She seemed wild-eyed, as if the experience of being shot at was a little too much for her.

"Who's in charge up here?"

Parkwood regarded her with a perfectly straight face.

"I thought you were."

The captain's eyes widened as if she'd been slapped. Vickers looked away. He didn't want to see any more people come unhinged. Up ahead the squad with the steam hose had it in position and were looking back for some kind of instruction. Debbie glanced contemptuously at the captain.

"Don't you think you ought to give them some sort of order? You seem to be the highest rank around here."

The captain stood straight up, seemingly without stopping to think. Vickers reached to pull her down but he was too late. She opened her mouth and suddenly a section of her face, just above the left eye, was missing. She toppled backward.

"Oh Christ."

Vickers looked quickly over the top of the golf cart and yelled to the crew on the steam hose.

"Okay, goddammit, let them have it."

The valve opened with a roar. There were screams from the other side of the barricade. The crew let it run for about thirty seconds and then shut it off again. The steam drifted back past where the four corpses were crouched. Yabu ran a hand over his bald head.

"That probably wasn't too much of a good idea. We may have cooked a couple of them but the rest will pull back inside. They'll still have their weapons. Steam won't hurt them. They may even build a second barricade."

"I just wanted to stop them shooting at us."

Yabu's stone face cracked the faintest of smiles.

"Always a laudable motivation, but perhaps we should have tried to negotiate first."

"How in hell could anyone negotiate? Those women know they're all going to be killed."

"Some would have forced themselves to believe it. Individuals will become exceedingly credulous when the matter in hand is their own deaths. It might seem a cruel deception but it might have also saved a number of lives. As it is, they will fight with the knowledge that they are already doomed. You know the saying."

"The best killers have already died."

"Also the most frenzied have already died."

"Did the Japanese make that up?"

"I heard it was the Irish."

As Debbie had predicted, it did indeed take a good deal of time and a number of lives before the barricades were cleared and the uniforms fought their way into the living area. For almost two hours both security and military had held off from the final assault. Nobody in the corridor wanted to take the responsibility for giving the order. It was quite likely that, when all was said and done, Lloyd-Ransom would simply look at the casualty lists and, in a fit of pique, order the execution of whoever had assumed command. In the end, Lamas had arrived in the corridor with apparently enough authority to start something. Quite in character, he had decided that it would be done the hard way. More golf carts were moved up to provide a certain amount of cover. The barricades were hosed down with high pressure steam, pounded with ultrasonics and finished with frag grenades. One grim little major had suggested also using gas but this had been vetoed as far too likely to contaminate the air system of the whole bunker. Grappling hooks were shot into the tangle of metal and as much as possible was dragged away. Only then did the very reluctant troops move in.

The handlers fought like furies. When their ammunition at last ran out they used homemade fire bombs, they threw corrosive cleaning fluid into the faces of the attackers and they went for them with knives and steel bars. When the area had been all but secured, the butcher squads, who had effectively kept themselves out of the costly first assault, moved in to finish off the wounded and probably a number of women who had had no part in the fighting at all. The butchers swept through the living area killing everyone that so much as twitched. Their simplest technique was a fast bullet in the back of the head from a sidearm but others did fancier, more disgusting work with garroting wires and bayonets. Lamas made no effort to stop them. Apparently General Living Area 26 was to be used as a terrible example of the penalty for rebellion.

Vickers, Yabu, Debbie and Parkwood walked slowly into
the scene of carnage. Bunks had been overturned and the walls
were pitted with bullet holes and spattered with blood. A half-
dozen small fires were still smoking. There were bodies strewn
all over, both soldiers and handlers. A uniformed corporal had
a handler down on her knees. She was bleeding from a gash on
her forehead and the top of her uniform had been torn away. He
held a pistol but he seemed in no hurry to fire. He seemed to be
savoring her terror. Suddenly and inexplicably, Yabu erupted.

"Leave her alone!"

The corporal looked up and made a fatally stupid mistake.
He told Yabu to go fuck himself. Yabu was on the man before
anyone could stop him. The action was too fast for Vickers to
see exactly what he did. In one fluid movement, seemingly
impossible for one of Yabu's size and bulk, he ripped off the
corporal's helmet. He grasped the back of the man's head like a
basketball. His other hand came down, a clubbing fist. Blood
spurted out the man's eyes, ears and nose. Yabu let the body
drop to the ground. He looked defiantly around the room.

"I sleep with this woman. Nobody harms her."

He helped the woman to her feet with unexpected tenderness
and put a protective arm around her. The entire area froze.
Lloyd-Ransom, with his bodyguards and dog handler had
walked into the area at exactly the right moment to see the
whole incident. It was, however, a very different Lloyd-
Ransom. His white uniform was creased and dirty. His collar
was unbuttoned and he looked sallow and ill. His appearance
was something of a shock. Not as much of a shock, though, as
Yabu's next move. Yabu glared and walked slowly toward him,
still supporting the woman. His expression was one of
undisguised disgust.

"You've made a very bad mistake, Lloyd-Ransom. You
have left these people with no hope."

Yabu continued walking, right out of the area. Nobody, not
even Lloyd-Ransom, made an attempt to stop him.

There was a deep, uneasy silence in the security club room.
The people in there drank with a quiet determination. There
was far too much to blot out. It had been just about possible to
keep the butcher squad and the individual assassinations out of
sight and mind. The rationale was fairly easy. Life in the
bunker was lived at a fairly drastic level and, from time to

time, drastic solutions were required. The mass destruction of
an entire living area was something else entirely. It left no room
for moral maneuvering. A feeling hung in the air of the club
room, almost as the smell of fire and death still lingered on the
second level. The bunker was starting to tear itself apart. The
death toll was ninety-three and that was too much to be
dismissed as a "solution." It was a massacre. No omelette
could be worth that many eggs.

The public address didn't help lighten the weight of gloom.
Wolfjohn had taken it into his head to read the full list of names
in a slow, doleful rasp. Inside the club room, guilt was driving
a wedge between those who had taken part in the killing and
those who hadn't. Yabu's stand, even though it was a matter of
self-interest, had made it hard to use the excuse of blind
obedience. The whole bunker was wondering what would
happen next. For the moment, there seemed little danger that
Lloyd-Ransom would lose control of the bunker. The military
and its officers were still solidly behind him while security
seemed to be sullenly turning in on itself. Some of those
without uniforms were coming in for a good deal of hostility.
Yabu had been the one who'd actually made the protest but it
had also been noticed that Parkwood, Vickers, and Debbie had
virtually sat out the action well to the rear. Even some of their
own kind seemed about to turn against them. Annie Flagg,
Carmen Rainer and John Walker all appeared to side with the
uniforms. There had been some snide remarks but it had yet to go
any further.

The gloomy quiet that surrounded Wolfjohn's dirgelike
recitation of the names of the dead was broken by the ringing
of one of the wall phones. A uniform picked it up and looked
around.

"Rainer."

Carmen Rainer looked up from whispering quiet, deviant
suggestions to a petite, doe-eyed blonde.

"Yo."

"It's for you."

Rainer stood up. The day's creation of tight black vinyl and
leather straps were particularly bizarre. She took the handset,
listened for a few moments, nodded, hung up and sauntered
back to the blonde. She pinched her cheek.

"Got to go to work, sweetie."

Fenton overheard the remark and raised his head.

"Got someone to kill, dear?"

"I guess I have to do it all now nobody can count on you or Vickers or the rest of your little pacifist clique."

Vickers, who was already quite drunk, threw back the remainder of his shot.

"One of these day's I'm going to have to do something about that mouth of yours."

Carmen Rainer's lip curled.

"Are you capable? You were supposed to be a good corpse, but as far as I can see, you've lost it."

Vickers shrugged.

"Time will tell."

The sneer increased.

"Sure."

Rainer turned and walked to the door with an exaggerated sway. As the door hissed shut Fenton grunted.

"One of these days we really *are* going to do something about that bitch."

The doe-eyed blonde pouted. "I'm going to tell her you said that."

Wolfjohn finally finished the list of the dead. Mercifully, he didn't decide to go through it all again. Vickers hoped that he'd stop sticking his neck out and put on some music. Instead, he launched into a gravel-voiced monologue.

"It's a dark day in this hole in the ground, friends and babies, a dark, dark day. Ninety-three of us dead today at our own hands. This is madness, friends and babies. It's a black, black madness that's got a grip on us here. When you consider that we may be all of humanity there is left, you gotta know that we shouldn't be doing this to each other. We are the history of the new world down here. We shouldn't have to include this dreadful Black Thursday!!"

"I didn't know that it was Thursday."

"Honest?"

"I lost count months ago."

". . . in that history. We are down in this hole, friends and babies, and we are killing each other. Ninety-three of us died this afternoon and I, for one, don't see the reason for it. Ninety-fucking-three of us, friends and babies. Ninety-fucking-three of us when there's only a few thousand of us left."

"Is he drunk or what?"

The strain was starting to show in Wolfjohn's voice. The velvet of the rasp was starting to fray.

"What I want to know is why? Why did ninety-three of us have to die? Huh? I heard it was because they didn't want to go to work. Am I expected to believe that ninety-three people had to die because a bunch of women got pissed off and didn't want to go to work? So who decides that? Somebody want to explain that to me? Hey, Lloyd-Ransom, maybe you'd like to come on this mike up here and tell us all why those people had to . . ."

There was a pause. Something seemed to be going on in the background. Suddenly everyone in the club room was paying attention.

". . . What? What's the matter, honey? Lloyd-Ransom sent you up here to explain for him?" Wolfjohn's voice abruptly changed. "So it's my turn is it? Well fuck you! I'm not going to beg . . ."

There was a short, ugly sound of scarcely human pain and a booming thud as if the microphone had been knocked over. There was a long silence in the club room. Fenton slowly put down his drink.

"So they even greased Wolfjohn. The bitch Rainer was sent up there to finish him."

"He stuck it out too far."

"Jesus Christ, what harm did he do?"

Vickers stood up to get himself another scotch.

"He wanted to get the fuck out of this hole."

Eggy hurled a chair at the wall. One of the legs broke off. On the way down it knocked over a lamp that also smashed to the floor.

"They're calling it a fucking boycott! Me! Can you believe that? The women on the second level have decided they won't sleep with anyone in either security or the military. Even me!"

Debbie didn't seem impressed.

"It'll do you good not to have things your own way."

"After all I've done for them."

"What you've done for them is probably reason enough on its own for a boycott."

"There's going to be trouble."

"This *is* trouble. There's military all over the place, all of them looking for a chance to shoot someone."

"I've been damn good to those women on the second level. I figured there had to be a couple that'd weaken but they're all watching each other. If one breaks the rules the others'll shave her head. It's ridiculous."

"You'd probably enjoy that."

"I've been damn good to those women."

Vickers wondered if Johanna in GLA30 would be part of the boycott. She almost certainly would. He realized guiltily that it was the first time he'd thought of her since the start of the trouble.

On impulse, Vickers stepped off the elevator on level five. He had decided to go and see Lance Cattermole. Cattermole was the curator of the bunker's considerable archive. The archive was supposed to be the surviving record of human culture but, like so many things connected with the bunker, its planning was a little uneven. As Cattermole put it, "Too much of the damned Beatles and hardly anything on Pascal. The people who put this place together were obsessed with twentieth century junk culture." The attraction of Cattermole's dim, quiet, warren-like domain was that, down among the dark stacks that held the tapes and discs, the cards and books and artifacts, in the soft greenglow of the computer terminals, there was an illusion of peace and permanancy that was quite unlike anywhere else in the bunker. Cattermole's kingdom was a backwater, bypassed and largely untroubled by the madness that gripped most of the rest of the installation. It was a place where Vickers could hide for a few hours. There were a couple of additional attractions. One was that Cattermole kept a fine collection of vintage wines and was the kind of host who was more than willing to share a bottle or two with anyone who stopped by. The other was a tall, witty brunette called Yoko who had incredibly sensitive breasts and who was usually willing to treat Vickers to very skillful and inventive, standing sex back in the depths of the stacks. Yoko was one of the reasons he'd been neglecting Johanna.

Yoko smiled and winked as she let Vickers in through the outer door. Vickers smiled back.

"Where's the boss?"

"In his inner sanctum."

"Will he see me?"

"Sure."

The inner sanctum was an electronic cocoon of computer equipment. As Vickers ducked inside, Cattermole peered over the top of his rimless half-glasses.

"Have you come to kill me?"

Vickers laughed. "No, not this time."

"Well, that's a relief."

"Who'd want to kill you?"

"It gets hard to tell these days."

Yoko brushed against him carrying an armful of files and whispered something obscene in his ear. Vickers grinned.

"I've got to talk to your boss first."

Yoko flashed him a backward pout and vanished in among the stacks. Vickers turned his attention to Cattermole. There was something gnomelike about the curator of the archive. Given a green hat and pointed ears, he could have been one of Santa's little helpers. He was completely suited to his dim, cluttered environment from which he rarely emerged. On the few occasions when he did, he gave the impression of blinking at the light like a dazzled mole.

"Have you come down here with a specific purpose or do you just want to waste my time, drink my wine and maul my assistant?"

"I was thinking more of the latter."

Cattermole put down the whatbox he was using. He didn't seem particularly put out by the interruption. He smiled.

"I suppose I have to keep in with security. I have what ought be a rather fine Medoc; it should suit our purpose."

Cattermole disappeared into the confusion. He returned a couple of minutes later carrying a bottle, two glasses and a corkscrew.

"It'll need to breathe for a little while."

Nobody knew exactly where Cattermole kept his wine. It was one of the lesser of the bunker's mysteries. He let it stand uncorked for five minutes and then poured it. Vickers held his wine up to the light.

"You live pretty well down here."

"We do our best, but that's not to say that I won't be extremely glad to get out of here. I'm sure we've been down here long enough. If the surface hasn't returned to some approximation of normality by now, it probably never will."

He gave Vickers a sharp look. "Of course, I really shouldn't voice these things around you, should I? Isn't it some kind of official heresy?" He glanced up at an imaginary concealed microphone. "I hope you're getting all that."

Vickers sipped the Medoc appreciatively.

"You know you can say what you like around me. I don't give a damn. As it happens, I've been hearing stories that someone *has* been going outside."

Cattermole's eyes twinkled.

"The Lloyd-Ransom story. He doesn't know how to get out. I thought that at least you in security would know why Lloyd-Ransom regularly vanishes."

"I haven't heard a thing."

"My god, you people are impossible. You mean you really didn't know that our glorious leader has become an opium addict?"

"Say what?"

"Our leader has taken to hiding himself away and smoking considerable amounts of opium. It probably holds back the heart of his own particular darkness. He must have a considerable burden on his soul. He's not the only one, either. Opium has become quite a clandestine little trend among the superpersons."

"Where in hell are they getting opium from?"

"There's about a ton of it. Nuclear survival people were always very keen on stockpiling opium. It's a holdover from the twentieth century. They seemed to think it could provide a basis for some manner of ad hoc pharmacopeia. I've never been quite clear how that would be done but they kept on stashing it away."

"How do you know all this?"

"Me? I'm technically in charge of the ton of opium. It's supposed to be part of the medical archive. I have to tactfully look the other way when our leader comes down to cut himself off a slice."

Vickers grunted. Not only were a few thousand people being kept under the ground at one man's whim but now the one man turned out to be a dope fiend.

"What about Lutesinger? Is he going the same route?"

Cattermole took off his glasses.

"Now there's the real mystery. Nobody's seen him in

months. He's locked himself away in his quarters and refuses to see anyone. He has his food sent in but he never emerges."

"Goddamn it. It just gets weirder and weirder." Something occurred to Vickers. "Wait just a minute. When you said earlier that Lloyd-Ransom didn't know his way out of the bunker, you made it sound as though there are people who do."

Cattermole nodded. "Well, I do. I don't know about anyone else."

Vickers could hardly believe what he was hearing.

"Why are you doing this to me, Lance? Why in hell didn't you tell anybody?"

"Would you believe that nobody asked me?"

"No."

"How about the fact that I considered the information something of a liability."

"More like it. You want to tell me about it?"

Cattermole thoughtfully poured more Medoc.

"I don't know. What would you do with this information?" Vickers raised his eyes until they met Cattermole's.

"I'd try and get out, see what it's really like on the surface."

"Would you tell anyone else?"

"Maybe. I'd probably tell one or two others. People I can trust."

"I thought a few times I might try and get out but, when it came down to it, I didn't do anything." He patted his gnome's pot belly. "I decided I didn't have the figure for being intrepid."

There was a long pause. Finally Vickers put down his glass.

"So are you going to show me the way out?"

Cattermole thought. It took him almost a minute to decide.

"Yes. It's about time someone had a look at the surface." Cattermole hunted along the stacks until he found the card he was looking for. He dropped it into one of his computers. The monitor showed a detail of an architectural drawing. "These are the original drawings for the bunker. What many people don't realize is that parts of it were never properly finished. All over there are nooks and small corners where the heat or the lighting was never installed, the air conditioning was never piped through or the surveillance cameras were never put in. The largest of these is up on the first level way over in the back right away from the main elevators."

He spoke to the computer. "Level one, quadrant twelve . . . okay . . . left six . . . up seven . . . enlarge two hundred."

The screen filled with a honeycomb of small rooms against the outer wall of the first level. Cattermole tapped it with his finger.

"This was never built. It's like a cave. The support pillars are in and there's a floor but that's it. Nothing else was ever built. It was supposed to be some kind of store for vehicle spares but I guess they never got around to finishing it. There's no light in there but it's warm enough. There're a few oddities living in there. Now and again they send some soldiers up there to frighten them but for the most part they're left alone."

"Oddities?"

"Winos, crazies, maybe a couple of dozen of various individuals who crawled away because they couldn't stay afloat in the bunker population."

"And they live there?"

"Sure. They've got to live somewhere but they're not what we're concerned with. See this?"

Cattermole pointed to a pair of parallel lines that ran out from the complex of rooms, through the wall of the bunker and out for some distance beyond.

"You know what this is?"

"What?"

"It's a tunnel. It runs for about two hundred yards angling out and up until it comes out on the surface."

"It's a way out, damn it!"

Cattermole grinned. He was clearly warming to the conspiracy.

"That's right."

"But isn't it sealed or at least alarmed?"

"No, that's the beauty of it. Since the wiring was never put in, there are no cameras. It only appears on their scans as a dead area. The tunnel wouldn't appear at all. Surveillance runs the bunker and they never refer back to the original plans."

"How do we know that the tunnel was actually built? Maybe they never got around to that either."

Cattermole shook his head.

"No, it's there. It has to be. It goes through the bunker wall, it's an integral part. It stands to reason that it would have to be constructed at the same time as the wall."

"But how come it's the only one?"

"They must have thought that one was enough."

"And then it got lost in the shuffle?"

"You'd be surprised what got lost in the shuffle when this place was being put together."

"It's certainly worth checking out."

Vickers could feel an excitement. He could feel the breeze and see the open space and sky. The idea of being outside again was almost frightening. Cattermole poured out the last of the wine. He raised his glass in a toast.

"Out."

Vickers also raised his glass.

"Yeah, out."

"What will you do?"

"I need to think about this for a couple of days. I'll try and set up a situation where I won't be missed if I slip out for a while." He looked around the ceiling, again at imaginary microphones. "And talking of setups, I take it you have some way to neutralize the eavesdroppers."

"Sure. I've had the system patched in to my computers. When I think a conversation is going to get them excited, I have my computer send a nice relaxing simulation."

Vickers finished his wine.

"I'll let you know what I'm going to do before I do it."

Cattermole ushered him to the door of the inner sanctum.

"This should prove particularly interesting."

Yoko was waiting for him by the outer door to Cattermole's kingdom.

"I thought you'd forgotten about me."

"I must confess that I had."

The idea of there being a way out had put everything else to the back of his mind. Yoko, however, was enough to bring a few things hopping forward as she stood smouldering at him.

"That's not particularly flattering."

Vickers did his best to look contrite.

"If I stuck around and flattered you for a half hour or so would it make it up to you?"

"Just a half-hour?"

"An hour?"

Yoko glanced around. Cattermole had vanished back inside his nest of computers. She took hold of Vickers' hand.

"Let's see how flattering you can get."

It looked like they were heading into another confrontation with the military. Vickers and Fenton mingled with the crowd of workers going on shift. They were on the third level and moving toward the heavily guarded entrance to the power plant. Security around the plant was some of the tightest in the bunker. The power plant was, without a doubt, the most vulnerable spot in the underground installation. If the fusion reactor went out of control, it would vaporize the bunker and the land for miles around. Through its life it had specifically been guarded from saboteurs, Reds, anarchists and now Wantouts. Any second, Fenton and Vickers would discover how well it was defended against them. On the plus side, there was their reputation, on the minus side, there was the fact that they had absolutely no authority. The power plant was the only place that Vickers was going to get a radiation suit, though, and he didn't intend to venture outside without one. He wanted to see the sky again but he definitely didn't want to set himself up for cancer, radiation sickness or worse.

It had only been after a good deal of deliberation that Vickers had told Fenton about the tunnel. At first he had considered Parkwood. If anything, Parkwood was the more reliable of the two but Fenton had a streak of craziness that would be invaluable on such an extreme adventure. At first Fenton had wanted them to go out together, but after two hours and most of a bottle of whiskey, Vickers had persuaded him that the best idea was for one to go out first for a short exposure, nothing more than a two-hour look around. After faking the coin toss, the task fell to Vickers while Fenton would stay behind and cover for his absence. Vickers' only stipulation was that they should steal a radiation suit so he wasn't completely vulnerable to anything the outside might throw at him. When they'd sobered up, the idea of stealing a radiation suit from the power plant seemed a good deal more hazardous than it had in the light of the whiskey bottle. About the only thing they had on their side was that most people would have a hard time imagining why they would want to steal a radiation suit in the first place. It was the basis of their bluff.

The first test of this bluff was rapidly coming up. The regular power workers had to use a thumbprint check to pass through a combined bodyscan and ID gate. Each gate was manned by a human guard as a second line of security. There was no other way in. Vickers and Fenton joined the line that led up to one gate. They'd decided to go in together, claiming it was a line-of-duty visit. Their guard was blonde, cute apart from a pair of hard, calculating eyes. Vickers doubted that they could put anything over on her. As they approached, she coldly looked them up and down.

"What do you two want?"

"There's something we have to check out in the jumpers' locker room."

"You got passes?"

"We don't need passes."

The guard's face hardened. "I never heard that."

"You know who we are."

"Sure I know who you are but I still never heard that I should let you into the plant without passes."

Fenton glanced back at the line of plant workers who were backed up behind them.

"Why don't you let us just step inside and we'll talk about it. We're holding up the line here."

The woman put a hand on the strap of the M90 slung over her shoulder.

"I can't let you do that."

"Suppose you called the officer who can talk to us."

The guard thought about it.

"I suppose I could do that."

She pushed a button beside the thumbprint scanner. The officer, a rather vapid captain, appeared much more of a pushover than the guard. He was far more in awe of the two corpses than his subordinate.

"What seems to be going on here?"

The guard looked at the captain with scarcely veiled contempt.

"These two want to get in without passes."

"But you know who they are?"

"I don't have authority to let anyone through without a pass."

Fenton tried to take control of the situation.

"Listen, Captain, if we could just step through and explain the situation we'll stop holding up the line and I'm sure when you hear what we have to say you'll see it our way. And if you don't, we'll leave. Okay?"

The captain seemed uncertain. He looked like he wanted to ask someone what to do but was afraid of losing face. Fenton leaned in to his indecision.

"Well?"

The captain was tipped over.

"Yes, I suppose you'd better step inside."

Fenton and Vickers made to pass through but the guard didn't get out of the way. She looked enquiringly at the captain.

"Sir?"

The captain covered himself with impatient bluster.

"Yes, yes, let them through."

"On your authority sir?"

"Yes, damn it, on my authority. Now start this line moving." He waved Vickers and Fenton to where he was standing on the other side of the barrier. "So what is all this about?"

Fenton put an arm around the captain's shoulder and steered him away from the guards and the lines at the gates. Vickers followed them.

"It's like this, see. We think we might have a problem with one of your jumpers and all we wanted to do was to go down to the jumpers' locker room and discreetly go through his stuff."

The captain was looking nervous again.

"A jumper? One of the ones who actually go inside the reactor?"

"One of those. One of those exactly. That's why we have to be so very careful. I mean, those people don't have very long lifespans, do they?"

"It's not as bad as it was on the outside, we take better care . . ."

"Yeah, but what with contamination and their hair falling out and everything, they've still got plenty of room to get mean. Am I right?"

"I guess so."

"And if one of them went rogue they could do an untold amount of damage."

"That's right."

"We only had the faintest of whispers that one of these people might be up to something but there was no way that we could ignore it."

"What was this whisper?"

"That someone was stashing explosives inside the fusion loop."

The captain actually turned a little pale.

"You have to be joking. Do you know what even the smallest explosion in the fusion loop could do?"

"And that's why we have to go in and check things out."

The captain shook his head.

"If you want to go in and search why didn't you go through channels?"

Fenton removed his arm from around the captain's shoulder with a look of exasperation.

"Are you back on that again? You know what it's like around here. If we'd gone through channels everyone in the plant would have known about it inside half an hour. The whole point here is to keep it quiet. Quiet, you understand? If there's nothing to it we don't want to give the bastards any ideas, do we?"

"I guess not."

"So are you going to take us down there or do I have to get someone with some real clout?"

It was Vickers' moment to interrupt. "Do we have to fuck around with this jerk any longer? Let's just find his superior and explain how he's fucking us over."

Fenton became the calming influence.

"Hey, give him a break, will you? He wants to cooperate, he's just nervous. They go by the book down here, that's all." He turned to the captain. "You're going to help us out, aren't you?"

The captain caved in. "Okay, but I'm going to have to come down there with you.

Fenton beamed. "Sure. Let's go to it."

With the captain completely buffaloed, the rest was easy. They went through to the jumpers' locker room and opened the locker of one Jose Torres. The computer had selected him as being the same size as Vickers, so his radiation suit would fit. He was also off-shift so the suit would be hanging in his locker. While the captain watched, they searched every inch of the suit. Finally they delivered the verdict.

"There're no secret pockets or gimmicks in the suit that we can find. We're going to have to take it in for some lab tests."

Vickers had an apparent thought.

"We really ought to put another suit in its place so Torres

won't suspect anything." He looked at the captain. "Can you fix that for us? Can you get us another suit?"

The captain was now a hundred percent anxious to please. He practically skipped to the nearest wall phone. Inside of ten minutes, a mystified orderly had brought down a second orange radiation suit. Vickers folded Torres' original suit under his arm and let the increasingly relieved captain lead them back the way they'd come. As they walked out through the security check, Vickers couldn't resist a parting shot. He wagged a cautionary finger at the captain.

"Not a word now, right? Nothing to anyone?"

The captain was as eager as a terrier. "You can trust me."

"I sure hope we can."

Vickers and Fenton walked slowly between two lines of parked vehicles to the first level, doing their best to look like it was just a routine patrol. Over the past two days they'd conducted a lot of random, unauthorized patrols and no one had challenged them or even asked a question. This, however, was the big one. It was their first shot at the outside. Vickers had Jose Torres' radiation suit slung over his shoulder in a canvas tote bag and, in addition to the usual Yasha, he also carried a big 12 gauge Churchill autoload. As far as hardware went, Vickers was ready for the outside. Emotionally, he wasn't so sure. The dry metallic taste was in his mouth and the acid knot in his stomach. It was different, though, from preparing for combat. This was something completely unknown. He knew that he was scared of what he might find out there. All he could do was lean back on his nerves and carefully put one foot in front of the other.

They came to the end of the line of vehicles. They turned and walked up another. Without being too obvious about it, they were gradually working their way away from the sealed elevator door toward the far back of the level. After sauntering casually for another five minutes, they were between two rows of tall armored personnel carriers. As far as either of them could tell there were no cameras watching them in the darkness.

"This looks like as good a place as any."

Vickers dropped the tote bag on the ground. They stood still for a few seconds, waiting for any possible challenge. When

none came, Vickers bent down and dragged out the suit. He
unrolled it and laid it flat.

"You want to help me with this?"

"Sure."

Fenton held up the bulky orange suit while Vickers struggled
into it. Finally he pulled on the headpiece but left the faceplate
open.

"Christ, you could sweat to death in one of these."

They both glanced around at the black, silent lines of armor.
Nothing seemed to be moving. Vickers took a deep breath.

"I guess I'd better get going."

Fenton glanced at his watch. Vickers did the same. Fenton
had one more look round.

"You want to give me five minutes to get out of here?"

"Yeah, okay."

"Take it easy, right? Just two hours and then right back
inside."

Vickers nodded. "If I'm not back in three, you've never
heard of me."

Fenton briefly gripped Vickers' arm and then he walked
away. Vickers watched him go. His diminishing footsteps were
measured and even, as though he didn't have a care in the
world. The old familiar feeling of wanting to be somewhere
else crept over Vickers. He did his best to focus his attention on
the passage of time, staring at the digits on his watch, willing
them to change. He gave Fenton his full five minutes, then he
shouldered the Churchill and started determinedly into the
darkness.

It was like another world. At first the things that scuttled out of
the way of his flashlight beam were rats and lizards and small
desert rodents. As he got further in though, they sounded
bigger and a lot more timid. People? Mad enough to live out
here in the dark? No flooring had ever been put in and the
ground underfoot was covered with building debris. He had to
take care not to stumble on rocks, chunks of masonry and
discarded boards. Stacks of unused building material and heaps
of garbage gave the unfinished area a set of contours that
provided natural cover for whoever and whatever lurked. At
regular intervals there were small smokey fires with dark
figures crouched among them. Vickers didn't approach any. He
figured that those who had elected to live in this place had
sufficient troubles without the addition of being scared witless

by a monsterous, armed figure in an orange suit. At some
point, someone had clearly tried to marginally improve the
unfinished area. Loops of electrical cable hung down from the
ceiling like black jungle vines. Vickers had seen a handful of
jury-rigged lights off in the distance but they were quickly
extinguished when he threatened to come anywhere near them.
The oddities who hid out in the place were skittish and
extremely watchful.

It took Vickers over thirty-five minutes to locate the door.
He'd crossed the unfinished area by dead reckoning and then
worked his way along the wall. He'd missed the start of the
tunnel on the first pass. He hadn't been expecting it to be
concealed behind anything as mundane as a sheet of corrugated
tin. Vickers moved the tin to one side and shone his light into
the black space. The tunnel was nothing special. It was narrow
and the curved roof was just high enough to allow a man of
normal height to walk without stooping. Any group of people
coming down the tunnel would have to do it in single file. It
was clearly intended to be easily defensible. Instinctively,
Vickers ducked as he stepped inside.

Vickers saw something on the floor of the tunnel up ahead. It
looked as though someone had dumped some untidily coiled
electrical cable. He was sufficiently keyed up to stop and
regard it suspiciously before going forward. The mess seemed
harmless enough, an untidy confusion of cable ends, but
Vickers couldn't quite figure out why cable off-cuts should be
dumped some two hundred yards down a tunnel that had no
electric wiring. It wasn't anything to make him turn back,
though. Then one of the cables moved.

"Sweet Jesus Christ!"

The cables were snakes. Vickers detested snakes and knew
nothing about them. He could only assume that they were nasty
and probably poisonous. Vickers had no idea why they were
there but he only had the haziest idea of what snakes might be
capable. Presumably they had somehow gotten in from the
desert. His first impulse was to unhitch the Churchill and blow
the whole squirm of them away. He realized in time, though,
that if he started blazing away with an autoload in such a
confined space, he might, with luck, kill all the snakes and
avoid being hit by ricocheting pellets but the noise would
certainly destroy his hearing. His second impulse was to turn

back but that would totally destroy his self-respect. What was
he going to tell Fenton? There were snakes in the tunnel and
he'd chickened out? He walked gingerly forward. As far as he
could tell, the radiation suit was probably thick enough to stop
a snakebite but he didn't want to bank his life on it.

There were just enough foot-sized spaces in among the
snakes for him to walk through the living minefield without
actually treading directly on one of the reptiles. This wasn't to
say that one might not still take offense and sink its fangs into
his ankle. He tried his first step. One snake slithered lethargi-
cally but nothing threatened him. He paused on one foot. His
heart was pounding. He put his foot down for a second time.
At first it seemed okay, then a snake rattled at him. Vickers
wanted to jump, possibly to scream as well. Instead, he bit
down on his tongue. The snake coiled back but then, instead of
striking, it slipped harmlessly across his boot. One more step
and he'd be past the snakes. He wanted to shut his eyes but that
would hardly be very bright. He raised his foot and moved it
forward. Very slowly, he put it down. Three rattlers came up.
One snake struck at his boot. Its teeth sank in. Vickers felt
nothing but he still leapt. The snake's teeth were hooked into
the outer fabric of his boot. It jerked with him. It was only
shaken free when Vickers hit the ground. To his infinite relief,
it wriggled quickly away back to its companions. Vickers
leaned against the wall, sweating and gasping for breath. He
didn't move for a few moments, partly to let his heart stop
racing and partly to see that nothing had happened to his ankle.
When two minutes had passed and there was no sign of
swelling or anything else amiss, he straightened up and walked
on.

The tunnel ended in a steel, submarine-style bulkhead door
with a large locking wheel at its center. Vickers knew that this
was about as close to the moment of truth as he was going to
get. He closed the faceplate of his suit and turned on the air
supply. He gripped the wheel and twisted. Nothing happened.
Vickers bit his lip. He couldn't believe that he could have come
all this way to be stopped by a simple lock. He twisted again.
There was a little give. He threw all of his strength against the
wheel and grudgingly it started to turn. It was simply stiff from
lack of use. After three turns the wheel refused to turn any

further. Vickers pushed against the door. At first it resisted but, when Vickers put his shoulder to it, it slowly swung open.

As far as he could tell he was on the underside of a small bridge or large culvert. The door was built directly into the wall. Presumably the whole structure had been designed to conceal the secret exit. The light at either end of the tunnel was blinding. His first thought was how he wished he'd brought some dark glasses. Then something caught at his throat. It was eighteen months since he'd seen the sun. He looked at the radiation counter on his wrist. It still showed green. That meant, if the thing could be trusted, that the radiation level was negligible. He wasn't quite ready, however, to open his faceplate. His watch told him, what with the snakes and the other delays, he had already used up fifty minutes of his two hours. He checked the Yasha, slung the Churchill over his shoulder and started out into the world.

EIGHT

IT WAS HOT as hell inside the orange suit. The radiation counter still showed green and Vickers was almost but not quite tempted to take the damn thing off. The desert looked perfectly normal. A desert is hardly the liveliest of places but the scrub appeared to be growing and a small dun-colored lizard had scuttled from under a rock. The tunnel had come out on the shallow side of the escarpment under which the bunker was built. As far as he could figure it, he was on the opposite side of the hill from where the elevator entrances had been.

The secret exit had indeed been concealed by a small bridge that took an almost overgrown dirt road across a dry creekbed. He wondered if he should follow the road or simply head up to the top of the rise. The incline wasn't all that steep but it would still be an uncomfortable climb in the overheated suit. On the other hand, the road seemed to go nowhere and come from nowhere. He would learn a great deal more from the top of the escarpment. The condition of the roads and the other structures around the bunker entrance would indicate if there had indeed been a nuclear hit in the vicinity. With a good deal of reluctance, he began to trudge up the slope. Sweat was pouring down his body. In addition to dark glasses, something else he

should have brought with him was water. Inside the controlled
environment of the bunker it had been all too easy to forget
what it was like in the desert. Every few yards Vickers would
stop. Not only to catch his breath but also to look up at the
clear blue sky. After all the months in the bunker it was
breathtaking. The higher he climbed, the further he could see
across the immediate landscape. The drab scrub ran clear to the
low blue hills at the horizon. There were still no positive signs
of life but, equally, there also were no definite signs of death.
For Vickers there was something euphoric in just being able to
see so far after being shut in for so long. The combination of
the sense of space and the fact that his suit's system was
feeding something close to pure oxygen was making him
lightheaded. It was thus that the sudden and totally unexpected
voice hit him like a hammer blow.

"Hold it right there, buddy. Don't make a move or I'll blow
you clean away."

Vickers froze. Slowly and carefully, he raised his hands. The
suit had muffled his hearing and the faceplate only gave him a
very limited field of vision. Whoever now had the drop on him
had sneaked up on his considerable blind side. He felt like an
idiot.

"Let go the shotgun from your shoulder and step away from
it."

Vickers allowed the Churchill to drop and then took two
paces sideways. The voice came again.

"Okay, now the machine pistol. Same procedure, nice and
easy."

Vickers unhooked the shoulder strap and the Yasha also fell
to the ground. This time he took two paces back. Again he
raised his arms.

"Do you mind if I turn around and see who I'm talking to?"

"You can turn around but take it very slow. If you do the
slightest thing I don't like, I'm going to cut you in half."

Vickers very slowly turned. He wasn't sure what he
expected. Some desperate, ragged but armed survivor of the
holocaust? Nothing prepared him for what he saw. The
sergeant was short, a little overweight. The most apt description was regular army dapper. His olive-green fatigues were
spotless and had knife-edge creases. His helmet was polished,
completely unscarred by combat. A red scarf was stylishly
knotted at his throat and mirrored sunglasses reflected the deep

blue of the sky. The tag over his pocket read Slaughter K. His shoulder patch was that of the Eighty-Second Airborne. The M90 that was pointed at Vickers' stomach was maintained army style. It made no sense at all. Vickers spoke without thinking.

"What the hell are you supposed to be?"

The sergeant looked genuinely astonished.

"*You're* asking me that?"

"I guess I must look a little strange."

"You're not kidding, buddy boy. Where did you come from?" He raised his gun slightly. "You came from out of the bunker, didn't you?"

"I'm not sure I ought to be saying anything."

"Suit yourself. You just stay right where you are. I'm going to call this in."

Holding the M90 in one hand, he unclipped the radio from the front of his jacket. He pressed the send button and spoke into it.

"This is Slaughter. I'm on the back side of the hill. You better send a chopper over here on the double. There's something you just have to see."

While he talked, Vickers wondered if there might be a possibility of jumping him while he was distracted. To make sergeant in the Eighty-Second, you had to have plenty on the ball. Vickers figured that he might just make it without the radiation suit but in the bulky garment he didn't have a chance. He remained as he was with his hands in the air.

The chopper came fast. Inside of three minutes, Vickers heard the slap of its rotors. A Cobra light gunship skittered up over the crest of the hill and came at them at nothing feet, whipping up the sand and scrub with its bladewash. The implications in all this came at Vickers as hard and fast as the helicopter. Something in his grasp of recent history was seriously wrong. The Cobra settled. The machine seemed impatient. Its skids eased restlessly up and down, first touching and then not touching the ground. Three men came fast out of the side door while the door gunner covered Vickers with a multicannon. Two of the men were also from the Eighty-Second, a lieutenant and a captain. The third was in combat green but his shoulder patch was that of Contec security. All three carried M90s. They directed their first questions to Sergeant Slaughter.

"He came out of the bunker?"

"He's not saying anything but where else is there?"

"Did you see where he came from?"

Slaughter shook his head. "I first spotted him going up the slope. He was hard to miss. He was having such a time in that suit I was able to sneak up behind him and get the drop on him." He nodded to where Vickers' weapons were still laying in the dirt. "He was carrying those with him. It looked like he meant some kind of business."

The Contec security man nodded.

"The first thing is to get this faceplate open and see who we've got in here."

He reached for the helmet's release catch but Vickers took a hasty step back and clapped a protective hand over it.

"Just a goddamn minute."

Slaughter jerked his rifle. "Get that damn helmet off! Now!"

"What about the radiation?"

"What radiation?"

"The radiation from the bombs. You may be acclimated or something but . . ."

The Contec man's eyes narrowed.

"What the fuck have they been telling you in there?"

Vickers was cautious. He was so totally shocked and confused that he didn't want to make any mistake.

"There's no radiation?"

"None. There've been no bombs exploded around here since the 1960s."

"You're sure."

"There's no radiation. Damn it, man, even your own radiation counter's in the green."

Vickers closed his eyes for a moment. One step at a time was all he could manage. He popped the release on his helmet. The faceplate swung open. Despite his situation, the air tasted good. He took off the whole helmet. The Contec man's eyes widened.

"Well, shit."

The captain looked at him curiously.

"What?"

"He definitely came from inside the bunker."

"You know him?"

"I've seen pictures of him. His name is Vickers, Mort

Vickers. He was a Contec corpse who went in a while before the place was sealed."

Vickers looked at each of his captors in turn.

"I think I ought to talk to someone."

The captain nodded. "I think you'd better. You're coming with us."

He took Vickers by the arm and propelled him toward the helicopter. The lieutenant and the Contec man flanked them. Slaughter gathered up Vickers' weapons and brought up the rear. They ducked as they passed under the rotor blades. As they climbed into the Cobra, Vickers glanced at the captain.

"What's my status in all of this?"

"You're under arrest, Jack, until someone tells me different."

The chopper flipped up before they were even settled. The pilot was a gum-chewing Indian with crazy eyes. Vickers remembered the reputation of army chopper pilots. This sucker probably popped greenies all day. It was cramped inside the Cobra with two extra passengers and the door gunner sucked a toothpick and glared at them for the rest of the flight. The chopper crossed the top of the hill and Vickers was able to look down at what had been the approach system for the bunker entrance. The whole area was scarred by explosions. Sections of highway were nothing more than craters. Some of the blockhouses had been burned down to blackened stumps. Sometime since the bunker had been sealed, its surface installations had been the site of close and intense combat. The army, presumably the victors in the conflict, had established what, from its dugouts, camouflaged tents and parked helicopters, appeared to be a forward base in among the ruins.

"What happened here?"

"No questions, Vickers. You're under arrest."

Vickers scowled. "Suit yourself."

The Cobra dropped toward a white-marked landing area. A small crowd had gathered, apparently to stare at Vickers as he emerged from the gunship. No less than four video cameras were pointed at him. He couldn't imagine they were media and assumed that the army wanted a permanent record of the proceedings. The way everyone gawked was unnerving. They were treating him like a captured Martian. Someone had seemingly decided that he needed additional guarding. A half-dozen Military Police, in white helmets and toting Whoopers,

were gathered by the landing area. They surrounded Vickers as
he stumbled from the chopper and hustled him away to a tent
where more MPs stood with weapons at high port. Inside,
more army and more Contec security were waiting for him.
The feeling of being a captured Martian was tripled. There was
a single army folding cot in the middle of the tent. Vickers
stood beside it and looked slowly around. They really were
treating him like a specimen. The Contec officer from the
helicopter came in with a set of army fatigues over his arm. He
tossed them down on the cot.

"You can change out of that suit and into these."

"I can?"

"Right now, please."

"Now?"

"*Right* now."

Vickers stroked his chin. He needed a shave.

"You expect me to undress in front of all these people? I
don't get to retain *any* dignity?"

"You're in something of a unique situation."

Vickers' eyes were bleak.

"I am indeed."

Vickers put the cold Coke bottle against his forehead. He
couldn't remember when he'd last slept. He still hadn't shaved.
What they called the "debriefing" seemed to have been going
on for years, years of people asking him questions and shining
lights in his face. The current one was a major in Army
Intelligence. He varied the routine slightly. Others had bullied
or threatened, this one had a mildly amused smile and the
manner of a shrink. He wanted to know how Vickers had felt
about everything.

"Why don't you go through the basic story just once more."

The major also liked things repeated over and over. It was
starting to make Vickers belligerent.

"Do I have to? I'm exhausted."

"Just once more, please. I'd like to feel that I have it
straight."

A dull anger burned up inside Vickers.

"Straight? Nothing about this whole set-up is straight.
Eighteen months ago I'm down below, in the bunker. We're
told the Soviets have started World War III. Fucking President

himself tells us and we believe him. The bunker is sealed and for a year and a half we sit around going crazy thinking that we may be the only surviving remnant of humanity.''

The ordeal had started in the tent with the dozen or more officers gawking at him. That hadn't lasted, however; there'd been another quick chopper flight to a more permanent command post that had been set up in a run-down, presumably commandeered motel. A weathered neon sign beside a cracked and disused two-lane blacktop proclaimed it to be the Desert Inn. They rushed Vickers to Cabin 17 and surrounded him with guards. They seemed unwilling to let him linger as if he might contaminate something. Once he was installed in the cabin, the interrogators came and went without letup. Army, Contec, a couple of Federal agency types in dark suits, they came singly and in twos and threes. A stenobot watched every move. They wouldn't let him have a drink but a constant supply of ice cold Cokes was a novelty in itself. Everything in the bunker had tasted of metal for as long as he could remember.

"So after a year and a half, by combination of ingenuity, courage and idiot luck, I finally get out and I'm dragged in here and everyone's telling me that there never was a war and we've been squatting in a hole in the ground with our thumbs up our collective ass under the illusion it was Armageddon time.''

"It's very unfortunate but . . .''

"Unfortunate, shit!'' Vickers thought about hitting the major in the face with his Coke bottle. It was tempting but he was too tired. "Tell you what, why don't you go through it some of it again so *I* can get it straight?''

"What do you want to know?''

"What happened to our war?''

There was something very trying about the major's patience.

"It didn't happen. There was a marked deterioration in the international situation around the time that the bunker was sealed. For a week or so it really looked as though the Soviet Union was disintegrating. Then Podgorny and the revisionists staged their coup and took control of most of the Red Army in the west. Within days they were talking with the corporations and the Western governments. The grainlift was underway inside of two weeks and we were moving troops in to restore order while they cleared up the mess. Well, to be accurate, it wasn't strictly *us*; the troops were nominally neutral: Greeks, Cubans, Canadians, Swedes and what have you. Just so long as no one looked like either an American or a German. The Russians wouldn't have stood for that, too many long-standing prejudices."

Vickers finished the Coke and put the bottle down on the standard motel plastic coffee table. This one was a chipped but still garish metalflake blue.

"What about the President? We heard him giving the kiss-off speech. Too bad folks, the bombs are on their way but we are shooting back."

"Anyone can fake the President. Damn it, third-rate comics do him in their acts. You said yourself that he was supposed to be talking from a satellite donut and that it was extremely distorted."

Vickers pushed his hands through his hair. He wanted to take a hot shower and sleep for a week.

"And what about Herbie Mossman. Are you trying to tell me that he was a simulation too, or what?"

The major sighed.

"I've told you already. I can't comment about Mossman. You'll have to talk to your Contec people about that."

Vickers closed his eyes.

"I don't know."

"Why are you having such difficulty accepting all this?"

Vickers opened them angrily.

"Why? I've already told you why. If I accept what you're telling me, I have to admit that I've been taken for an incomparable fool. I've wasted eighteen months in a hole in the ground. Christ, man! I've been sitting there trying to come to terms with the idea that the whole world had been destroyed and now I find the world large as life and laughing in my face. People died in that bunker for fuck's sake, others went insane."

The Major stood up and turned on the motel room TV.

"How many times do I have to show you?"

He spun around the dail. There was porno, reruns, *Penal Colony*, *Wildest Dreams*, Jackie Gleason in *The Honeymooners*, soccer from Japan, jai alai from Los Angeles, an in-depth news show that was going on about some scandal inside Agrimex. A number of stations were off the air. It was exactly what you'd expect, considering that it was almost dawn. Vickers still wasn't quite prepared to lay down for it.

"You could have put this together to fool me. It wouldn't be hard to rig the TV and a bunch of tapes."

"Why would we do that?"

"Because there *was* a war and you're a well organized group of survivors who've been camped out here waiting for a crack to appear in the bunker's defenses. I'm the first crack and you want to use me to get inside."

The major was almost sympathetic.

"Isn't that a little farfetched? It flies in the face of all the available facts."

"All the available facts have come from your people."

"It's hardly plausible."

"Neither is the idea that I've been incarcerated in a fucking great hole in the ground because some lunatic decided that he wanted to fake the third world war. Why would anyone do that?"

The Major leaned back in his chair and regarded the ceiling.

"A lot of thought has been given to that question ever since the bunker was sealed."

And?"

"You said yourself that Lloyd-Ransom and Lutesinger were both crazy, that in the early days they seemed almost eager for a war to start. You told me that they had this destiny fixation and that they went to a great deal of trouble to convince all of you in the bunker to share it."

Vickers was grudging.

"Yes, but . . ."

"There was a crisis in Russia and it looked, for about a week, as though the Soviets might drag the rest of the world down in flames. I've already told you this."

"So?"

"So Lloyd-Ransom jumped the gun. To ensure his complete control of the bunker he sealed it before the crunch came. He had the special effects standing by to convince all of you that the war had actually started. When there was no crunch, Lloyd-Ransom must have been faced with the dilemma of his life. The loss of face obviously proved more than he could take. He let the bunker remain sealed and left all of you in less than blissful ignorance. He must have been sitting down there praying that the world would come to an end anyway and justify his actions. It's little wonder that he developed an opium habit."

Vickers didn't say anything. He just sat and stared. Later, a slow burning fury would start, but right at that moment there was nothing but confusion. Deep down he knew that the major was telling the truth. It was just so hard to let go of all the months that he'd spent below ground. The major seemed to sense this.

"If this was just an elaborate scheme to get you to reveal the bunker exit, don't you think we'd have tortured and drugged it out of you by now?"

Vickers looked down at the carpet. There were a number of small burns around the leg of his chair. He concentrated on the pattern they formed.

"I suppose so."

"So what else would it take to convince you and bring all this to an end?"

Vickers slowly raised his head.

"I want a newspaper. *The Los Angeles Tribune*, dated yesterday. If you're for real, you should be able to get me one in a couple hours."

"We could fake that too."

"Yeah, but it'd be hard."

"Is there anything else?"

Vickers nodded.

"Yes. If the newspaper pans out, I want to be put in touch with Victoria Morgenstern. I suppose that technically she's still my boss."

"I don't like the idea."

"There's really no other way."

Vickers compressed his lips.

"If that's the case, I'd like to know how much you intend paying me for all this. The way I see it, you owe me eighteen months' back pay, in addition to which I want interest and a damn great lump sum for going back into the bunker."

"You don't change, do you?"

Vickers nodded. He knew he had the absolute upper hand. One of the best antidotes to rage and shock had been the realization of just how valuable he was.

"I try not to."

When Vickers had asked to be put in touch with Victoria Morgenstern, he hadn't imagined that she would come all the way to the Desert Inn to talk to him in person. She was notorious for hating to ever leave New York, yet within twelve hours of his making the request, a black civilian helicopter had descended on the motel's makeshift landing pad. It had disgorged Victoria and a quartet of bodyguards. A little later, a motorcade of corporate and military brass had arrived. Vickers couldn't remember when he'd seen so much gold braid and so many dark Crynelle suits in the same place, all looking at him. If he had played his cards right he could probably have the world. He was their only hope of retaking the Phoenix Bunker. That was always provided that he survived the proposed return visit.

It had been decided that Vickers should go in on his own. He was to sneak back into the bunker and, as far as possible avoiding detection, he should contact as many people as possible, starting with his own security group, and spread the word about the true situation on the outside. It was hoped that this would start an uprising that would result in the overthrow of Lloyd-Ransom and Lutesinger and the opening of the bunker. It was a typical Morgenstern cost-effective first shot. The military had quickly realized from Vickers' description of the tunnel that to try and throw an armed force into the first level by that route would be bloody, costly and quite possibly doomed to initial failure. Vickers, on the other hand, was a different matter. If he could slip in past the cameras and stir up a mutiny, it wouldn't cost them anything. If something went wrong and Vickers was killed they would still have lost very little.

The preparations for the mission were made with considerable care. Vickers wasn't in any particular hurry and therefore exceedingly willing to take pains. After the arrival of Victoria Morgenstern, he'd been allowed alcohol for the first time and he'd been quite ready to lounge around for a couple of days, drinking, watching TV, reading the papers and generally reacclimating to the real world. In his desire to take it easy, though, Vickers was in a minority of one. Both the army brass and the Contec people were impatient for him to get going. The bunker fiasco had cost a total of billions and they wanted it at an end. Vickers naturally did his best to stall. His first ploy was to ask for a replica of a blue handler's uniform. Vickers' theory was that, if he went back in the common blue overall, it would help confuse surveillance systems. There was a good deal of logic in this. There was no way that Vickers' disappearance could have gone unnoticed inside the bunker. There would undoubtedly be some kind of lookout for him. A handler's uniform might help delay a positive identification. Vickers also hoped that it might well take the army two or three days to come up with the garment. Unfortunately, a whole stack of surplus bunker uniforms were located in a Las Vegas warehouse and they had one in his size, plus a couple of spares, at the Desert Inn within twelve hours. At this juncture, Vickers had made the last-ditch suggestion that maybe a full-scale assault squad could go in all disguised as bunker rank and file and let him off the hook. The suggestion was vetoed and cost effectiveness prevailed. Vickers would go in on his own.

The final briefing before he was choppered from the motel back to the concealed bunker exit became uncomfortably like the prelude to an execution. Vickers had showered, shaved and dressed in the blue coverall. A tracer was attached to his right thigh so his progress into the bunker and the fact of whether he was alive or not could be monitored from outside. He took advantage of the army's obsession for gadgetry and equipped himself with all the miniature killing or maiming devices they had in their stores. He had a gamut of weaponry taped to his body under the uniform that ranged from concussion pellets to gas caps.

When all his preparations were complete, he walked out of the motel room with his Yasha slung over his shoulder. Two military policemen accompanied him and this only heightened the effect that he was going to the lethal injection. The dusk was gathering and the floodlights were coming on all along the razor wire that ringed the Desert Inn compound. The brass had gathered in what had once been the motel's piano and topless go-go bar. They waited in a half circle, their crisp uniforms and decorations providing a strange contrast to dirty red plush and the pair of giant, chipped plaster nudes that supported either side of the small strippers' stage. Victoria Morgenstern seemed to have been affected by the proximity of so many uniforms. Instead of her usual, severely tailored success suit, she had changed into an equally severe, tan safari outfit with a slightly impractical pencil skirt. The ensemble was topped off with a too-cute leopardskin pillbox hat. If this was her idea of desert wear, Vickers could see why she didn't like to leave New York.

He tried to lighten the mood in the room with another demand for money but it didn't help. They seemed determined to treat him like the hero of a suicide mission. He looked around at the dusty drapes.

"Do I get a drink before I go?"

Nobody had thought of providing the hero with a final belt.

"What do you want?"

"One hell of a large scotch."

There was a minor flurry while an aide was dispatched for Vickers' drink. When he finally got it, he raised the glass in silent toast and downed it in two swift swallows. One by one, they shook his hand and wished him luck. Each time, he nodded.

"I'm going to need it."

The chopper crew were silent, anonymous in their visored helmets. He wasn't sure, but he had the impression that they were avoiding looking at him. It was as though they considered him some alien, unnatural thing from the bowels of the earth and, orders not withstanding, wanted no contact with him. The helicopter lifted up and away from the lights of the Desert Inn. For a few minutes they ran through dark and then they were over the sprawling forward base in front of the sealed bunker entrance. Vickers had the grim thought that the lights of the base might be his last glimpse of the outside world. They circled once then crested the escarpment and dropped into the blackness of the opposite slope. Finally the crew had to speak to him.

"Can you find the entrance tunnel in the dark?"

"I'll need some light."

The pilot nodded. There was something a little eerie about the green of the instruments reflected in the crew's redscope night goggles. Once again there was that similarity to an execution. The co-pilot cut in a sungun under the machine's nose. The surface of the desert was brightly illuminated but it still took them three passes before Vickers spotted the dry streambed and the small bridge. The chopper settled on skids and Vickers unbuckled his seatbelt.

"I suppose this is me."

The crew didn't say a word. Vickers looked back before he ducked out the door.

"I guess I should take it easy, right?"

The pilot finally raised a hand. Vickers dropped to the ground and backed away. He stood and watched as the chopper lifted, then he turned his back on the glow from the other side of the hill and walked slowly down the streambed. It was black as sin under the bridge and he pulled out his flashlight. He reached the door. Although he hadn't locked it, the door still refused to open. He'd half expected this and had equipped himself with a small crowbar. He set the flashlight on the ground and went to work. After he'd pried a handhold between the door and the frame, he threw his weight back and dragged it open. He paused for almost a minute, took a long backward look at the outside world and then, with considerable reluctance, stepped into the tunnel.

The snakes had gone. Vickers was some way into the tunnel, moving slowly and carefully. He was certain that he'd passed the point where he'd encountered them on the way out. He was relieved not to have to walk through the squirming, slithering mass of reptiles but he also couldn't imagine where they might have gone. The walls of the tunnel were solid concrete. There were no convenient holes through which snakes might exit. In his hyper state, it made him uneasy. He halted and slowly looked around. There didn't seem to be any changes in the tunnel and very cautiously he started forward.

He reached the end. The sheet of corrugated tin was still in place. It represented the start of the second stage of his return. He crouched down and dumped the crowbar and the flashlight. If he was going in posing as a handler, he supposed that he should also have ditched the Yasha as well. Handlers didn't carry guns. He couldn't, however, quite bring himself to do it. He wasn't going back into the bunker without protection of some kind. He slung the machine pistol over his back, moved the corrugated tin to one side and eased through the gap. It was hard moving through the unfinished area. He stumbled a number of times over piles of building debris but he didn't want to take any chances. A moving light or even an infrared scan on a level where no one was supposed to be could prove an instant give-away. He made it to the edge of the finished construction. He crouched in the dark among the parked vehicles. Here and there there was a dim inspection light but these were really only enough to give some form to the black shapes of the tanks and trucks. He peered into the gloom looking for the movement of a patrolling guard. Over by the elevator entrances, there were more lights burning but here in the back of the vehicle park, illumination was less than minimal.

Vickers felt his way along the flat, armored side of a personnel carrier. He halted, looked round and then moved up the length of another. He was starting to sweat. It was hot in the bunker and the air smelled lousy. It stank of oil and metal, industrial cleansers and decaying junk food. It was only since he'd been outside that he noticed how awful it was. He slid past another vehicle and another. So far so good. There was no alarm, no running feet; above all, no shots. He was beside a line of light Pacer tanks. He stopped again. His hands had started to shake and it was only with effort that he pulled his nerves under control. It was like waiting for some huge, cosmic other shoe to drop. Then he sneezed. That was something else that he'd grown too used to. The air was thick with all kinds of behavior modifiers, an accumulation of eighteen months' worth. God only knew how they'd combined and mutated in that time. This alone was sufficient reason for everyone down here to be crazy.

He started along another line of tanks, still going more by touch than by sight. He was continuing this blind man's progress when the light hit him. It was like a physical pain. Now he really was blind. Over his shrieking nerves, the voice of reason told him it was a sungun, probably similar to the one on the helicopter. It hardly seemed to matter. Everything else told him that he had been caught. The booming, amplified voice removed any doubts.

"Stand right where you are, Vickers. We've been waiting for you."

NINE

VICKERS WAS BLINDED. Sick to his stomach, he knew that he'd walked right into a trap. A feral instinct told him to run and keep on running. Reason, though, kept its grip. Run and they'll shoot you in the back for sure. Avoiding looking straight into the sungun, he slowly raised his arms.

"Been waiting for me?"

"For days. We have orders to shoot you on sight."

Although the voice was distorted by the booming amplification, Vickers was pretty sure that he recognized it. Carmen Rainer. She'd have been more than happy to shoot him on sight but presumably she just couldn't resist cat-and-mousing him before she put him out. He knew that he had only one card to play. It was a simple statement.

"I've been outside." Just to make sure there was no doubt: "I've been on the surface."

He held his arms straight out at his side. When your life's on the line, it's no disgrace to look like a crucifixion. There was no answer for almost a minute, then more lights came on and the sungun went out. Vickers tried to blink away the lingering afterimage. The sungun had been mounted on the turret of a light tank. Carmen Rainer was sitting in the turret, leaning on the fire control of the multicannon. She was smoking a cigar. Grouped around the base of the tank were four soldiers, Yabu and Parkwood.

"Lloyd-Ransom told us to ignore your bullshit and just blow you away."

"Perhaps he didn't want you to hear what I had to say."

Carmen Rainer flicked away her cigar butt.

"Orders are orders, Vickers."

Vickers knew why the hair-trigger Rainer had been put in charge. She glanced down at Yabu.

"Shoot him."

Yabu had a frag gun pointed at Vickers' stomach. For long seconds he did nothing then, finally, he shook his head.

"No, I want to hear what he has to say."

Parkwood nodded in agreement.

"I definitely want to hear what he has to say."

The soldiers looked confused but also made no move against Vickers. Carmen Rainer began to climb out of the tank turret. As always, she was sleek in black leather. Angrily, she jumped down to the ground.

"We've got our orders."

Yabu shifted position so his frag gun was pointed at Rainer.

"I want to know what he's seen on the outside."

"How do you know he's been outside? He's probably lying."

"Everyone's heard what was supposed to have happened when they tortured Fenton."

"That's only a rumor."

Vickers wanted to know about this.

"What do you mean 'when they tortured Fenton'?"

It was Parkwood who answered.

"When you came up missing Lloyd-Ransom became exceedingly agitated. He ordered a runback through the surveillance tapes and the story goes that you and Fenton were spotted doing something weird on the first level. Fenton was arrested. Carmen here was one of the ones who picked him up. The story goes that he finally confessed that you'd found a way out. He must have been a good friend; he stood up to the worst they could do for close to five hours."

"Did he survive?"

"No."

"Did Cattermole's name come up?"

"Cattermole was executed."

"Damn."

"You caused quite a ripple."

Yabu had had enough of the conversation.

"I want to know what is outside."

Even Carmen Rainer's attention was focused on Vickers. He took a deep breath. This was the difficult part. He remembered how stubbornly he'd resisted the truth. He knew their reaction might be violent but he pressed ahead.

"There never was a third world war."

Rainer closed her eyes and shook her head.

"No, no, he's lying for sure now. Shoot him like we were told to."

Oddly, she made no move to shoot him herself. Even Parkwood looked as though he didn't believe a word that Vickers was saying.

"What are you talking about?"

"I swear to God. Almost immediately after I got outside I was picked up by an army patrol. There's a whole base out there. They've been watching the place since the bunker was sealed."

Yabu's frown was like something out of an ancient Japanese print.

"There was no nuclear war?"

"It came close, but at the last moment the Russians were able to put the brakes on and ask for help. As far as anyone could figure it, Lloyd-Ranson jumped the gun and sealed the bunker early."

"Are you saying that he's been keeping up some kind of charade for eighteen months?"

"He'd made himself king of the hill. He'd decided that he was the saviour of mankind. He couldn't face the fact that mankind had managed to get by without him."

Parkwood's expression was both bleak and grave.

"That would be extremely psychotic behavior."

Vickers lowered his arms.

"Well?"

Carmen Rainer jerked.

"I don't have to listen to this garbage."

There was a chrome automag in her hand. She swung it straight-armed at Vickers. At the same time, Parkwood's weapon went off. He was also armed with a frag gun. Close up, it made a hideous mess. Blood, tissue and fragments of black leather were spattered all over the side of the nearest tank. There was little left of Carmen Rainer from the chest up. Vickers twisted his body and swung the Yasha round into his hand. At the same time, everyone else dropped into a crouch, weapons thrust forward and eyes darting to determine who was on whose side and who was going to shoot at who. By a complete miracle, nobody opened fire and continued the slaughter to a disastrous conclusion. Vickers slightly lowered his machine pistol and straightened up. Parkwood let the still smoking frag gun hang by his side.

"I didn't think she was acting quite rationally either."

There was a general easing of the immediate tension. The soldiers, for the time being, seemed ready to go along with the two corpses. Yabu was also going with the flow but he was far from happy.

"Have you any proof of what you say?"

"I've got the *LA Tribune* from three days ago."

"Show me."

Vickers unfastened the top of his blue overall. He pulled out a folded newspaper. It was the same *LA Tribune* that the major had sent for when he'd demanded proof. He handed it to Yabu, who read part of the front page, rapidly flipped through the rest of the paper and then handed it to Parkwood. Parkwood's examination was slower and more thorough. Finally he carefully refolded it and handed it back to Vickers.

"I think we should go and ask Lloyd-Ransom some questions. You'll go with us."

Vickers gave him a searching look.

"Am I a prisoner?"

"I don't see why."

"Then you believe me?"

"I don't want to believe you. I'd hate to think that I wasted eighteen months in this place but I want to know the truth."

Lamas and some of the worst scum of the butcher squads were waiting when they came out into the bottoms from the elevators. It was the same setup that had been used on Herbie Mossman. The three corpses were a little more prepared. They came out fast and Parkwood had Lamas covered with his frag gun before he could give any order to fire. He advanced briskly up the slope of black marble.

"You hesitated just a little too long, Lamas. It's that lack of combat tuning. Your men could take us out but I'll still drop you where you stand."

"Why hasn't Vickers been shot?"

"Vickers has been outside."

"That's impossible."

"You know damn well that's not true. You were *there* when they tortured Fenton."

Vickers and Yabu came up the slope at a slightly slower pace. Surprisingly, the soldiers were right behind them, backing them up. They seemed to have less trouble accepting the idea that Lloyd-Ransom was insane than anybody. Vickers reached the top of the slope just in time to catch the end of the conversation. He glanced abruptly at Parkwood. Had he also been there when they had tortured Fenton? He didn't have time to think about it. The scum from the butcher squads were only marginally in check. Even if they bought the idea that there was a real world outside they might be a little ambivalent about returning to it and maybe facing trial for mass murder. That was in the future, however. For the moment they were quiet, although they obviously knew that something unique was going on. They were watching, slit-eyed, to see which way Lamas would jump.

Parkwood, who seemed to have taken charge, beckoned to Vickers.

"Give him the newspaper."

Vickers again hauled out the rapidly becoming dogeared copy of the *Tribune*. He handed it to Lamas. Lamas read the headlines, read the date and then started to leaf through it.

"It could be a fake."

"Vickers brought it back from the outside. Even if they could fake something like that out there, it would mean that it's not a dead world."

"Maybe he faked it in here."

"Come on, Lamas, you know damn well that we don't have facilities down here to produce anything like this. This was printed on an old fashioned offset press. Do you know something we don't know?"

Lamas angrily folded the newspaper.

"I just don't believe this thing. It could rip the bunker apart."

"That's why we want to see Lloyd-Ransom."

Lamas's jaw clenched. He was plainly beset by some terrible doubts. He glanced back across the piazza to the tunnel entrances that led to the superpeoples' living quarters. In the end, he sighed.

"Yes. Something has to be very wrong. We'd better go talk to him."

They started across the piazza, Lamas and the three corpses. The soldiers and the butcher squad fell in behind them. They were halfway across, about level with the black obelisk, when Lamas motioned that they should all halt.

"There's a second line of defense."

Vickers glanced quickly at Parkwood and Yabu.

"You've got to admit that this is something of a paranoid reaction to the fact that someone may have gone outside."

Neither of them replied. Lamas walked slowly forward. After about ten paces he halted again and called out in the direction of the tunnels.

"This is Lamas. Vickers has come back and he claims that he's been outside. A number of us feel that we should talk to the Leader. We need to discuss the situation."

No answer came back. Lamas walked forward again. He seemed edgy and his hands were half raised.

"This is Lamas, I'm coming in. Don't shoot."

The words acted like a signal. There was a burst of rapid fire from one of the tunnels.

"Sweet Jesus."

The first burst hit Lamas, the second raked the piazza. Vickers hit the ground and rolled. A splinter of marble gashed his cheek but he made it into the shadow of the obelisk. Parkwood slid in beside him. Yabu was also safe behind the slablike statue called Industry. A number of soldiers and butcher squad were sprawled dead on the ground. Parkwood surveyed the scene with hard, angry eyes.

"It looks like we've started something."

"It could be the beginning of the end."

Parkwood eased over and looked intently at Vickers.

"*Are* you telling the truth about the outside?"

"Of course I'm telling the truth."

"Christ." Parkwood shook his head as though trying to settle his thoughts. "This is more of a mess than I care to cope with."

There was another flurry of fire from the tunnels. This time it was directed further down the piazza, toward the elevators. Vickers looked back. A number of figures were diving for cover along the top of the incline that ran down the elevator banks. He recognized Eggy's war paint. Lloyd-Ransom's guards were firing on their own. This had to be the final going to ground.

It had become a siege. Parkwood continued to take control of the situation and both the military and the security forces seemed content to go along with him. Not that there was that much to go along with; there were at least three miniguns and other heavy automatic weapons set up in the bottom tunnels and there was no way to get past them apart from an all-out and very costly frontal assault. They had tried twice and there were more bodies littering the marble of the piazza. There had been no third attempt. Attackers and defenders bided their time and stayed under cover. As a standoff, it was virtually complete.

Parkwood and Vickers used a lull in the initial firing to crawl back from the shadow of the obelisk to the elevators. It was there, under cover of the incline, that a motley crew were gathering; military, security, all manner of odd individuals, all had heard that Vickers had been outside. They'd come to find out the truth. The gunfire had badly confused them but also convinced everyone there that something was terribly wrong in the bunker. In that moment of confusion, Parkwood moved. Listening to no agruments, he separated the unarmed from the armed. He had no time or use for the unarmed and they were sent back, out of the way, to the upper levels. Those who had weapons were quickly marshalled into a firing line along the top of the incline. He kept a few back in a small reserve that also secured the elevator entrances and kept out any more sensation seekers.

Eggy led the first rush. A small group of a dozen security had managed to get into the largest of the tunnels. In the tunnel, however, there had been no more cover. Only Eggy and Eight-Man, who'd been last in, came back. The second attack was a larger, all military affair. Deakin led this bold frontal assault and nobody came back. After this, there were no more attempts to do it the hard way. They simply waited. Food was brought and Parkwood started a group of non-coms organizing replacements and duty rotations. Now and again there would be fire from the tunnels, minimal and ineffectual, as though they only wanted to remind the attackers that they were there and could keep them ducking and crouching. Lloyd-Ransom had created himself a bunker within a bunker. He had also, at the same time, created a strange revolution in his kingdom. In the bottoms, they'd been divided into attackers and defenders, the beleaguered elite and the insurgents. The rest of the population watched. Unknown to any of those in the bottoms, the security cameras on the piazza had been patched to the other levels' regular video system. Bunker life had come to a full stop while the entire population clustered around the public screens and watched and waited.

"Tanks."

"Tanks?"

"We could bring down tanks, light tanks from the first level. A Puma would fit in one of those tunnels. They're wide enough. We could use tanks to root them out."

"How could you bring them down here from the first level?"

"They'd fit in the passenger elevators."

"They're too heavy, they'd snap the cables. You can't put a Puma tank in a passenger elevator."

"Are you certain about that?"

"Absolutely."

"Shit."

The idea of outside help had been mooted.

"If they're out there like Vickers says, why don't we let them come on in and do the dying? We've been down here for eighteen months. You could say we did our tour."

Eggy was the first one to put it into words. There was immediate agreement.

"Hell, we could walk away and leave Lloyd-Ransom right where he is. We could start evacuating the bunker right now. If you're telling the truth, Vickers, I could be in Vegas tomorrow night, shooting craps and talking to women wearing perfume and real clothes. I could sleep in a bed as big as a fucking swimming pool. Has anyone figured how much back pay we've got coming? Let's leave Lloyd-Ransom to someone else."

Eight-Man shook his head. His eyes were bloodshot and angry.

"If he's had me in here for eighteen months for no reason, I want him."

Vickers hoisted his Yasha and stood up.

"I want him too. I want him for Fenton but I don't see why we shouldn't bring in fresh troops to spearhead the first assault. I sure as hell don't want to be the first into those tunnels."

Parkwood looked around at the group at the impromptu strategy brainstorm. He didn't seem totally convinced.

"So what should we do?"

Vickers realized that it was primarily Parkwood's caution to which everyone was looking.

"I'd suggest that two of us go outside and talk with the army. It's my guess that they'll pretty much do what we want so long as they get the bunker back."

Parkwood seemed to be trying to stare his way into Vickers' mind.

"Are you sure this isn't some terrible devious doublecross?"

Vickers met the gaze.

"What do I have to do to convince you? What possible doublecross could there be?"

"I don't know, but if there is, I swear I'll kill you."

Eight-Man leaned toward Parkwood.

"You send me with him to the outside and if there's the slightest thing wrong, I'll kill him."

Vickers was getting a little tired of being accused and threatened.

"Isn't this caution getting a little obsessive?"

"What would you do if you were in our position?"

Further argument was interrupted by a disturbance by the elevators. The troops that were supposed to be stopping people coming out of the elevator doors were having a hard job holding back a jostling crowd of handlers who had presumably ridden down from the second level. There was a good deal of pushing and yelling. Vickers thought that he recognized Johanna from GLA 30 doing her full share at the very front of the struggling mass. Was it her? If it was, she'd had most of her hair cropped off since he'd seen her last.

"Mort! Hey Mort!"

"Johanna!"

He moved quickly toward the nearest guard. There was a certain degree of guilt in his speed. Their affair was, at best, a sporadic business. He always promised to come back soon but frequently weeks would go by before he saw her again. With all the women in the bunker, it was all too easy to be sidetracked.

"Let her through."

The guard, who was doing his best to avoid being clawed by an angry redhead, shook his head.

"I can't do that."

"Just let her through, goddamn it!"

The guard shrugged. Johanna slipped quickly through the line. Immediately she threw her arms around Vickers' neck. Her breath smelled of gin and she was at least three-parts drunk. Suddenly he was in no mood for a romantic reunion. He held at her at arms' length.

"What the hell is this all about?"

"We're getting impatient up there. We want to know what's going on. Nobody would tell us anything so we came down here to find out."

"Getting drunk up there too?"

"So?"

"So you're in the way down here. There's people shooting at us and the last thing that we need is a bunch of drunk women who don't know what they're doing."

Behind them a mixture of soldiers and security were slowly herding the handlers back into the elevator car. Vickers jerked his thumb.

"Do you have any influence with these people?"

"You've been outside, haven't you?"

Vickers nodded.

"But I don't have time to tell you about it right now."

"What was out there?"

There was a desperate look in her eyes. Vickers sighed.

"There's people out there. The world is a lot less dead than we were led to believe."

Johanna suddenly relaxed. Her shoulders dropped.

"Thank God for that."

Vickers took her by the arm and propelled her quickly toward the elevator.

"Tell them what I told you. Tell them that someone will be going on the air as soon as the situation down here is under control. You've got to spread the word and stop people panicking. It's very important."

The line parted and Johanna was eased through and on into the elevator. She turned and held a hand out to Vickers.

"Mort, will I see you when this is all over?"

Vickers nodded and did his best to smile. "Sure sweetheart, you'll see me."

"There really is no need for you to go out armed, is there Vickers? I mean, you're supposed to be real good friends with these guys on the surface."

"I'm getting very tired of all this."

"You've got nothing to worry about if you're telling the truth."

It had been decided that Eight-Man would indeed go out to the surface with Vickers as the bunker's insurance policy. The single rule was very simple. If it turned out that Vickers had been lying in any major respect, Eight-Man should feel completely free to shoot him out of hand. Vickers handed over his Yasha. Once again he was a virtual prisoner.

They walked down the tunnel in silence. Eight-Man had insisted that Vickers walk ahead. Vickers kept his flashlight pointed at the ground. He watched for the snakes but for a second time there was no sign of them. Again it puzzled him. Where could they have gone or, alternatively, where had they come from in the first place? They reached the door. Vickers turned and faced Eight-Man.

"You remember the outside of the bunker?"

"Kinda."

"This comes out on the underside of the bridge. It's partway up the shallow side of the hill, the opposite side from the main entrance. There may be a reception committee. They have a tracer on me and they've probably been alerted that I'm coming out."

"And you're warning me not to overreact?"

"Something like that."

Eight-Man smiled but his eyes were frozen.

"Vickers, you don't have to worry about me."

Vickers refused to be intimidated.

"I worry about everything, my friend. There's been altogether too much shooting first and asking questions afterward."

Eight-Man's distrust seemed to melt a fraction.

"I'll hold it together."

Vickers nodded.

"Help me with this door."

Behind the pressure of both their shoulders, the door swung open. They stepped out under the bridge. Vickers realized that, since he'd been back in the bunker, he'd lost all track of time. It was early morning, maybe an hour or so after dawn. There was the slightest of chills in the air. Vickers could practically feel the shudder run through Eight-Man as they stepped out from the shadows under the bridge and he looked up at the sky. He remembered his own first speechless shock when he'd first emerged from the bunker.

"Take a deep breath. The first thing you realize is that the air in the bunker's so lousy it's enough to make you insane all on its own."

Eight-Man turned a full three hundred and sixty degrees, just gazing up at the sky. When he looked back at Vickers, much of the dislike and distrust had gone out of his eyes.

"I've been hurting for this."

Unfortunately his euphoria didn't have a chance to last. There was a reception committee. Slaughter was waiting with a brace of MPs and a Cobra gunship. Once again the door gunner was on full, white-knuckle alert. This time, however, the guns were pointing at Eight-Man rather than Vickers. Slaughter, behind his mirrored shades, was particularly hostile.

"What the hell is this, Vickers?"

Vickers made no attempt to stop for Slaughter or the military policemen.

"What's the matter Slaughter? You been out here all night?"

Slaughter barred his way.

"I don't have orders to cover this guy."

Vickers came to an angry standstill.

"For your information, Slaughter, 'this guy' is a big wheel in bunker security and that's about all you need to know. Now . . ." He glanced back at Eight-Man, who was clearly starting to see him in a different light, and then again glared at Slaughter. ". . . if you don't have any really serious objections, that Cobra is going to fly us directly to the Desert Inn where I can talk to some people who won't waste time telling me what their orders cover."

Although Slaughter didn't say another word, it was plain that he was having a major culture conflict between his own spotless gung ho and Eight-Man's earrings and ringlets. The door gunner, on the other hand, kept slipping Eight-Man covert and awestruck glances. He was a skinny black kid who looked as though he came from some frost belt inner city and probably made it into the army on a redundancy break. Eight-Man didn't notice either of them. He was too busy looking out of the door. As they passed over the destruction in front of the bunker entrance, Eight-Man's eyes widened. He turned accusingly to Vickers.

"I thought you said there hadn't been a war."

"This was just a local action. The troops who were left outside when the bunker was sealed remembered the Alamo. By all accounts they kept a couple of divisions of regular army rapid deployment troops at bay for ten days before they went down."

"Didn't they realize who they were fighting?"

"I guess they'd bought the package."

Eight-Man scowled. "I guess we bought the package too."

"I don't see how either Contec or the army could commit combat troops to this situation. We only have the sketchiest idea of the internal situation in the bunker. We couldn't take sides."

Victoria Morgenstern was behaving true to type and Vickers was running increasingly low on patience.

"Take sides? You already took sides. I went back into the bunker and did exactly what you wanted in a matter of hours. Nobody will resist your people coming in, in fact you'll be welcomed. All I need is fresh troops to get Lloyd-Ransom out of his bunker within a bunker. The people down there are just about shot."

Morgenstern didn't seem impressed. Neither did Getz, the colonel who was in charge of the Desert Inn operation. They were back in Cabin 17 and Vickers was far from having it his way. Morgenstern, Getz and the aides who surrounded them felt they had both right and reason on their side.

"You have to look at it from the practical point of view. By your own admission, there are close to four thousand people down there loaded to the gills on all manner of mind alterers. It's going to take months to reorient all of them to the real world. What's the point of throwing a lot of fresh, expensively trained people into that environment? You know the principle as well as anyone. You don't request additional manpower when the problem can be solved with the resources at hand."

"I'm afraid of the toll it's going to take of the resources at hand."

"That's not really our concern."

Eight-Man, who hadn't been much help thus far, suddenly glared.

"What you're saying is that you wouldn't be sorry to see these misfit bunker freaks thinned out a bit. It'd cut down on the bill for the rehab and psych we're all going to need when we get out of there."

Morgenstern avoided his eyes.

"I didn't say that."

"But you've thought about it." He rounded on Vickers. "And what about you, man? You sound like you're working for them. Whose side are you on and what are you trying to pull?"

"I'm trying to get us out of the bunker without any more losses."

Eight-Man jerked his head toward Getz and Morgenstern.

"These fucks don't give a damn. They'd be quite happy if we all stayed down there and rotted."

"They want their bunker back."

"But they're not in any particular hurry. If they were, they'd lend us the help."

Vickers cradled his head in his hands. The situation was rapidly approaching the impossible. He'd expected intractable self-interest from Morgenstern but not to this extent. He didn't want to go back to the bunker empty-handed. In fact, he wasn't sure if Eight-Man would let him go back to the bunker empty-handed.

"I need a drink."

"Somebody get Vickers a drink."

Three minutes later a scotch and ice arrived. They seemed to have his number. While he sipped it and cast around for a solution he was acutely aware that everyone was watching him. Suddenly he had an idea. Numbers weren't the only answer.

"If I can't have men, will you give me equipment?"

Morgenstern blinked.

"I don't see why not, within reason." She looked toward Getz, clearly tossing him the ball. Getz hadn't been expecting this.

"I don't know. I can't make any guarantees."

Eight-Man's lip curled.

"What can you do?"

Vickers ignored the exchange. He was warming to his idea.

"If we could blast our way into Lloyd-Ransom's redoubt, we could probably flush him out with only minimal loss."

Getz was guarded.

"What did you have in mind?"

"I was thinking of a Marriot rocket."

Even Eight-Man looked at him as though he were insane.

"A Marriot rocket?"

"Sure, why not? Shoot a Marriot down one of these tunnels and you won't see much more resistance."

"But a *Marriot*? That ain't no ordinary anti-tank missile. Those suckers can cream a Calvin-class landcruiser. If you let one off in the bottoms you're liable to bring the roof down."

Vickers shook his head.

"Hell no. That bunker's supposed to stand up to a nuclear war."

"The only other alternative is a full frontal assault that could well cost us hundreds of lives. I swear it would be worth the gamble."

Getz interrupted.

"I'm afraid the discussion is academic, gentlemen. I have no intention of giving you people a Marriot rocket."

"What's with you?"

"This business is edging toward madness and I for one don't want to be responsible."

Victoria Morgenstern abruptly demonstrated who was really in command.

"Give him the damn rocket; I'll be responsible."

Getz actually went white and only just avoided sputtering with indignation.

"You can't order me to do something like this."

"Of course I can and you know it. Who do you think's picking up the tab for this affair? You didn't imagine it was the Federal Government, did you? As long as you're here, you're out on loan to Contec."

"It's not just a matter of money, it's a matter of authority."

"Everything's a matter of money, Colonel. Now, are you going to give the appropriate orders or am I going to call the Pentagon?"

The colonel's voice went robot as he damped down his fury.

"I'll see to it."

He stood up but Vickers held out a restraining hand.

"Hold it, I haven't quite finished."

Morgenstern looked sideways at Vickers.

"Don't push your luck."

"Why should it stop now?"

"What more do you want?"

"I want two Marriots, one as a back-up, and I want an army crew to fire them. I also think it'd be a very good idea if you sent in an extra twenty or thirty of your people, not as combat troops, just observers, mainly to get everyone used to people from the outside. It's going to be a shock."

"Is that all?"

"You've got to admit that it's only reasonable."

Victoria Morgenstern also stood up. "Eminently reasonable." She looked coldly at Getz. "You have any problems with that?"

Getz all but clicked his heels. His voice was still robot. "No problem at all."

Deep in back of his eyes, though, was the look of a man who, if he ever got the chance to walk all over Victoria Morgenstern, would gleefully stomp with both feet. Victoria appeared not to notice. She actually smiled.

"If everyone's satisfied maybe we can get this thing finished."

A squad from the surface manhandled the number-one Marriot from the elevator. It was twelve feet long and eighteen inches thick, painted black with an orange stripe around the warhead. For ease of handling it was mounted on the most abbreviated version of its launch cradle. The presence of the outsiders had a bizarre effect on the bunker inmates with whom they came into contact. They were afflicted by a diffidence that Vickers would never have expected. They treated them as if they were from another planet. He had actually watched hardened bunker military back away from the first outsiders to enter the bottoms. He realized that the whole bunker was about to go into its second traumatic shock. Losing the world had been bad enough, finding it again might prove to be altogether too much. Vickers began to realize what Eight-Man had meant by rehab and psych. He also realized that it would be a pure arrogance to think that he'd be immune to it. The best he could do was to shelve the worst symptoms until after the bunker was secure. All he wanted to do was to fire the missile and get it over with.

The second rocket was coming out of another elevator. For their part, the outsiders did their best to accentuate the difference between themselves and the people in the bunker. They kept their faces covered with visors and breathing masks as though they considered the air in the bunker tainted and unfit to breathe. Inside the tunnels of the other side of the piazza, the defenders seemed to sense that something was going on. They kept up a sporadic sniping that forced everyone to keep their heads down while the missiles were readied. Their gun crews had developed the knack of being able to lay fire exactly along the top of the incline that led down to the elevators. It meant that there was not only the danger of being hit by a bullet but also the constant irritant of flying splinters of marble. The defenders had one other trick. Now and again a suicide volunteer would sprint out of one of the tunnels clutching a grenade launcher. He or she would try to drop a grenade onto the area by the elevators before one of the attackers dropped him. Parkwood had lost no less than ten men to these random attacks. Vickers' chief worry was that a grenade might ignite one of the rockets before it could be fired. Fortunately the suicide attacks had become markedly fewer. Vickers could only conclude with some relief that Lloyd-Ransom was running short of volunteers.

The pair of Marriots was set up just below the edge of the incline. The fire control box had been placed behind a wall of sandbags. With the exception of a handful of troops who remained to keep up a token fire, everyone was evacuated to the upper levels. Those who stayed were issued with heavy duty ear protectors. When a Marriot went off in an enclosed space, the noise would be quite literally deafening. Once the preparations were complete, Vickers and Parkwood crawled up the incline and lay beside the missiles for a final look around. Parkwood still held onto his doubts.

"Are you sure this isn't going to bring down the roof?"

Vickers patted the Marriot. He was starting to enjoy the recklessness of overkill.

"I'm not sure but I'm pretty certain that the odds are in our favor. The way I see it, the missile should punch a hole in the outer wall but not detonate until it's right in the middle of Lloyd-Ransom's apartment complex. There should be enough substructure in there to soak up the blast before it does any real harm.''

"I wish I had your optimism."

"Can you think of a better way?"

"No."

"So let's get to it."

On a sudden impulse, Vickers raised himself up and sprayed the tunnel entrances with his Yasha. The action was so out of character that he surprised himself as well as Parkwood.

"What's the matter with you?"

"I guess I'm getting light-headed."

Parkwood waved back the last handful of troops, then he and Vickers scrambled down the slope themselves. They all took shelter in another sandbagged elevator. This final withdrawal was the signal to the rocket crew to start the brief countdown. Parkwood hit the elevator control panel and the doors slid shut. After that there was nothing left to do but wait. The first noise was the roar of the chemical rocket. Vickers clamped his hands over his ear protectors. There was a brief moment of silence and then it seemed as though the whole world had exploded. The entire bunker shuddered. The elevator car bounced on its cables. For a moment it felt as though the cables were going to snap. There was a small window in the elevator door. Its glass blew inward. A terrible rumbling went on and on. Parkwood opened the door and peered out. Glass and masonry were cascading down from the outside of the wide central airshaft. Parkwood looked back in horror.

"Damn it Vickers, it looks like you've caved in the roof."

"It's okay! It's okay!" The last large section of masonry crashed down to the piazza and then there was quiet. Rolling billows of dust filled the air, obscuring everything like a dense fog, but no more of the structure collapsed. The roof was intact. Vickers and Parkwood emerged from the elevator with handkerchiefs pressed to their faces.

"You think there's anyone left alive in there?"

"We'll soon see."

Another set of elevator doors opened and the evacuated bunker troops streamed back into the bottoms. It wasn't only soldiers and security. A full cross section of the bunker population was crowded in with them, a spectrum of colored coveralls and uniforms. Ignoring the choking dust, the heaps of jagged rubble and the possibility of further collapses, they surged across the ruined piazza, angry running figures in the dust and smoke.

"Should we try and stop them?"

"Just try it. They're mad as hell. I doubt a bomb would stop them."

While Vickers and Eight-Man had been out on the surface, word had run through the bunker that their long and unpleasant confinement had been without the slightest of valid reasons. In the end, the multiplying welter of conflicting stories forced Parkwood to go on the air and give a condensed version of the true situation. The varied panic instantly changed to a single, common fury. When the outsiders were first seen on the public video screens, the terrible news was absolutely confirmed. Parkwood was compelled to split his force and send more than half of his people to hold back the mobs who were massing in from the elevators on all levels. The mood had rapidly escalated to one of bloody revenge. Everyone wanted to get down to the bottoms and carve a piece of Lloyd-Ransom or one of his last-stand followers.

More elevator doors hissed open and another crowd from the upper levels swarmed out to add to the chaos. The major in charge of the outsiders fought his way to where Vickers and Parkwood were standing, letting it all swirl around them.

"Shouldn't we do something about this? If there's anyone left alive in that mess they're going to be slaughtered. This is a lynch mob."

Parkwood nodded.

"That's what it is."

"And you're going to do nothing?"

"If you want to save those bastards with your own people, feel free. Frankly, I don't give a damn."

Vickers had found himself a breathing mask.

"I'm going in there. I want to get to Lloyd-Ransom and Lutesinger before the mob does."

Parkwood looked around for a mask of his own.

"I'm coming with you."

Eggy and Yabu were still standing nearby. Parkwood beckoned to them.

"We're going inside, you want to come with us?"

Both indicated grim agreement. The outside major was still agitating.

"Something has to be done."

"Then do it!"

As they spoke, there was an eruption of yelling and howling from the other side of the piazza. A number of dazed and blackened figures had stumbled out of the ruins. The mob immediately set upon them. The major was gathering up his troops. He led them toward the center of the disturbance. Vickers, Parkwood, Yabu and Eggy followed behind, letting them clear a path through the angry mob. There was ugliness in the shattered tunnels and there were fires burning deep in the complex. Figures reeled from the smoke, but no sooner did they come into sight than they were seized by the crowd that was pouring in from the elevators. There were very few gunshots; the first people into the tunnels were mainly handlers and facers armed with clubs, knives or razors. The lack of gunfire was more than compensated for by a non-stop chorus of truly horrible screams. It was a scene from hell that the outside major and his men only served to confuse with their largely ineffectual efforts to save the lives of Lloyd-Ransom's surrendering followers. There was a frenzy about the attackers that went beyond even the most deep-rooted anger. It was like they were, at the same time, working out their own guilt for all that had happened in the bunker and all the bizarre dreams that had been dreamed there.

Vickers and his companions eased their way through the carnage, side-stepping the sudden knots of violence as best they could and trying hard to blot out the worst of the bloody vignettes. And then they were past the violence. Four armed intruders moving quickly up the tunnel with their flashlights and breathing masks. The dazed offenders shied away from them. They reached the end of the tunnel and realized they had to decide on a new direction. Vickers looked to Parkwood.

"Do you have that map?"

"Right here."

While Parkwood studied the map, Vickers turned his flash on the interior of the complex. The Marriot had literally torn it apart. Walls were missing and ceilings sagged. Smoke was everywhere and there was no guarantee that more of the structure would not collapse any minute. Vickers found it hard to equate this ruin with the luxury inner sanctum that had been the scene of such decadence and excess.

"Both Lloyd-Ransom's and Lutesinger's quarters are on the

same radial corridor. They're about as far in as you can go and three stories up within the complex. We'll have to hope that there are some stairs left intact, there's no chance of a lift."

"I'd sure hate for that bastard to escape."

Parkwood led the way and the others followed in single file, heading deeper into the ruins. They were moving along a corridor that led past what had once been a row of luxury suites. Now the mirrors were smashed and the drapes were burning. A woman in ripped, charred purple silk and an advanced state of hysteria suddenly staggered through one of the broken doorways. She tried to grab hold of Eggy.

"Help me! For God's sake help me!"

Eggy recoiled.

"Get the fuck away from me!"

The woman spun off him at a tangent and then lurched away frantically, looking for someone else to save her. The four watched her go and then moved on in the other direction.

By a miracle, one stairwell was intact. The four climbed cautiously, watching the streams of plaster dust that poured down with each step and listening to the ominous creaks. Finally they were in the last corridor. The area had hardly been touched by the explosion. Even the doors along the corridor hadn't been blown open. It was quite possible that, behind them, there were people who were alive and maybe armed. A new kind of caution gripped the four of them. With weapons raised they moved slowly and silently down the final stretch. Parkwood signalled to Vickers by tapping the map. When he had his attention, he pulled off his breathing mask and whispered urgently.

"The two suites, Lloyd-Ransom's and Lutesinger's, are side by side." He pointed with his gun. "Those two at the end there."

Eggy and Yabu were also listening attentively as Parkwood went on.

"Two of us will go one way and two the other. Vickers, you and Yabu take the lefthand door. That's Lloyd-Ransom's; I'll give you that. Eggy and I will take the other. That's Lutesinger's."

For a moment, Eggy looked as though he was going to protest, then he changed his mind and grinned.

"Save a piece of him for me."

They positioned themselves beside the doors. Vickers and Parkwood hung back with machine pistols clutched at high port. Yabu and Eggy were poised to kick in the doors.

"Go!"

The two doors crashed in at the same time. Vickers and Parkwood went through first, Yabu and Eggy followed.

"Sweet Jesus."

Lloyd-Ransom's outer reception room was deserted. It had come through the explosion completely unscathed. There was even a dim light burning, enough to show that it had been decorated in a strange, funereal Art Deco, all smoked mirrors and black glass. Only one of the mirrors had smashed.

"It's like Dracula's living room."

"You think he's escaped?"

Vickers put a finger to his lips. A brighter light was shining from the half-open door of the master bedroom. Again the guns were leveled. Again they moved with a tense, trained stealth. This time they went through the door together. The room wasn't exactly deserted but everyone in there was stone dead. The Dobermans were stretched out on the thick pile of the carpet. They'd been poisoned. They lay at the foot of the bed like the dogs on a medieval tomb. Thane Ride, the one-time TV idol, had also taken poison; the flecks of blood on her lips indicated something old fashioned like cyanide. She lay flat on her back on the huge circular bed, staring with dead eyes at her reflection in the mirrored ceiling. She had dressed and arranged herself for death. She wore a black nightgown, her hair was combed out and her makeup was perfect. In the final moments, she'd crossed her feet at the ankles, folded her arms across her chest and prepared to die. Lloyd-Ransom had also tried to make a beautiful corpse but it had gone wrong for him. As far as Vickers could reconstruct, he must have dressed up in his best dress uniform, sat down beside the already deceased woman and placed the barrel of his revolver in his mouth. He probably expected that he'd sprawl back romantically. Unfortunately, the blast that blew away the back of his head had also knocked him clear off the bed and into an ungainly heap on the floor.

Yabu nudged the body with his toe. "You notice that he did it exactly like Adolf Hitler?"

"He'd have to, wouldn't he?"

"I don't understand why Thane Ride felt it necessary to play the Eva Braun part. Such an absolute gesture would hardly seem in character."

"Maybe she felt she wouldn't have much of a career left when she got out of here."

"I've never known even the most extreme notoriety to hurt anyone's TV career. Where I come from an actress hoped to make millions by fucking a gorilla."

"Tomoyo Nakamora, how could I ever forget her?"

"Even in a place like this."

"Did she ever do it in the end?"

"I don't know. The last I heard was that the gorilla was trying to back out of the deal."

The two men made a slow inspection of the bedroom.

"It's an appropriate place in which to die."

The somber color scheme of the reception room was carried through, only instead of Art Deco, the bedroom was dark chinoise. A red dragon chased its coiling tail around all four of the black walls. An ornate but obviously well used opium pipe was at hand on an antique bedside table. Vickers and Yabu were about to start going through drawers and cupboards when they heard Parkwood's voice from outside in the corridor.

"Are you all secure in there?"

"Yeah, all secure."

Parkwood came through the reception room and into the bedroom.

"Jesus Christ!"

"I guess it's the end of the story."

"Not quite. You'd better come and look in the other suite."

There was no way of telling how long Lutesinger had been dead. The shrunken, mummified figure was still hanging from the ceiling of the austere, sparsely furnished room.

"He could have been like this for months."

"I checked the environment controls. He set the suite for complete dehumidity before he hung himself or, at least, somebody did. It's like he wanted to turn into a mummy."

"They must have known down here that something was wrong. Why didn't anyone break in and find out?"

"I don't want to think about what went on down here."

Vickers looked away from the wrinkled, dehydrated face. He felt a little sick. The only mercy was that the eyes were closed. He hitched the Yasha over his shoulder.

"I've had enough of this."

Eggy, with a sudden demonstration of unexpected friendship, put a hand on his shoulder.

"I'm with you, bro. Let's get the fuck out of here and let someone else clean up the mess."

Behind them the body slowly started to turn. The break-in had disturbed the previously still air. Coming hard on the heels of the exploding rocket, the motion was too much for the dried-out neck tendons. They parted. The head jerked back and the body fell to the floor with a leathery clatter. The head bounced. Out in the corridor Vickers really fought not to throw up. He managed it but only with great difficulty.

TEN

THERE WERE STEAKS and beer at the Desert Inn. On the way
out of the inner sanctum, Vickers had sworn that he'd never eat
again but when he actually smelled frying from the motel
coffee shop that served as the officers' mess, he realized that
he was starving. He'd been living on coffee, pills and scotch
for close to three days. By the time he'd loaded a mess tray
with two sizable steaks, a double order of fries, two eggs and
four slices of wheat toast, his mouth was actually watering.
The only snag was that he didn't get to eat the meal in
peace. Halfway through, Victoria Morgenstern sat down at his
table.

"So you're out."

"I didn't know it was going to be so difficult. I thought once
things were squared away you'd start evacuating those
people."

"You can't hurry these things. Those people have a lot of
adjusting to do."

"Hurry things? It took four hours of screaming bloody
murder before they'd let *me* out."

"That was a mistake. You were absolutely exempted from
the containment order."

Although both Contec and the army had refused to enter the bunker in a combat role, neither showed any hesitation in taking control and acting as virtual jailers once the situation was under control. Suddenly Victoria was making up the rules and Getz was enforcing them. Specially flown in admin teams set up shop on the first level and, backed up by armed troops, they started opening files and handing out ID cards. It had suddenly been decided that the evacuation of the bunker would take place on an individual basis and only after each individual had been thoroughly screened. The key points were "stability, adaptability and attitude" and the process threatened to take months.

"What is this containment order shit, Victoria?"

"What are you complaining about? You and your friends are all out and free, aren't you?"

Indeed, when Vickers had talked his way out he'd managed to bring Parkwood, Yabu and Eggy out with him. They were at another table eating without interruption. Vickers jabbed angrily at his steak.

"That's not the point."

"Isn't it? That's strange coming from you. I thought all you cared about was number one."

"I spent a long time in that place. For most of the people in there it's been a nightmare. They've been through enough. The last thing they need is being hung up in a whole lot of bullshit bureaucracy."

"I have every compassion for the people in the bunker but . . ."

"That's a lot of crap. You never had compassion for anyone. You don't do compassion."

"We can't just let those people loose. A lot of them are crazy. They need all the help they can get."

"Sure, and you're going to keep them penned up in the bunker while you help them."

"You're not thinking. I'm telling you we can't just turn them loose. The problem of who actually employs them and who owes them back pay is almost insurmountable."

"I knew it would all come down to money in the end."

"You've been taken care of. Contec's picking up your tab without question."

"They damn well better."

Victoria did her best to look placating. It hardly suited her.

"Try and look at it from our point of view. There's no way we can just dump nearly four thousand badly fucked up individuals back into the world without credit lines, jobs or anything. The first stop would be Las Vegas. Can you imagine how the Vegas authorities would react if we did that?"

Vickers very carefully put down his fork.

"And who are the Las Vegas authorities these days?"

Victoria looked at him sharply.

"What?"

"I was wondering who was minding the shop now that Herbie Mossman's dead."

For a moment she avoided his eyes.

"As a matter of fact, we are."

"Contec?"

"Without Mossman and the personal loyalty he commanded from his staff, Global Leisure started to come unglued. There was a merger."

"How convenient."

"What do you mean by that?"

"I was never too happy about the Mossman assassination. I was also struck by the fact that when I came out the first time, nobody was particularly interested in what had happened."

Victoria's answer came a little too quickly and neatly.

"It was old news by then."

"I got the impression that everyone knew about it. When I asked about it, the army told me to go see Contec and Contec just got close-mouthed."

Victoria Morgenstern looked as though she was sucking on a lemon.

"You know the story. Herbie Mossman got into the bunker at the start of the crisis. You know what he was like. He was so pathological about preserving himself that he wouldn't even breathe the air. Lloyd-Ransom thought that he'd try and take over and had him killed."

"That's what Lloyd-Ransom told me. I didn't believe him, either."

Morgenstern's face became properly impassive.

"So what outrageous theory do you have, Mort?"

"I figure Lloyd-Ransom was doing his last job for the old firm. It's my guess that Contec, probably you, either stampeded or lured Herbie into the bunker and Lloyd-Ransom had instructions to kill him, thus opening the way for the takeover. Of course, Lloyd-Ransom had his own plans but that's history. Nobody knew what he had in mind when the original orders were given. Even as things turned out, it must have worked quite well. Sure you lost a bunker for eighteen months, but you got Global."

Victoria's mouth curled into a tight little smile.

"That's quite fantastic."

"Isn't it just?"

"And complete nonsense."

"Maybe."

"You don't have any bright ideas of circulating this wild tale, do you? Like giving it to the media or anything?"

Vicker grinned.

"Who? Me? You know I wouldn't do a thing like that. I'm a good Contec corpse; I know how to keep my mouth shut."

"I'm very glad of that." Victoria stood up. "I'll leave you to finish your meal in peace."

Vickers looked down at his plate. His appetite wasn't what it had been when he'd started. "Yeah."

"You're taking some time off?"

"I figure I deserve it."

"You'll find that your credit's been taken care of."

"That's nice of you."

"It's the least I could do."

"Right."

"I'll expect you back in New York in a month. I hope you can manage not to get into trouble."

Vickers sat in the cocktail bar in the Las Vegas airport. He was working on his fourth large scotch. For the first time in as long as he could remember he had absolutely nothing to do. He felt lost. He was very aware that he was pouring booze into himself to fill a yawning psychological emptiness. He couldn't quite grasp the fact that it was all over. The idea of time off was meaningless. He had homed in on the airport almost by instinct, but beyond that he didn't have a clue where he wanted to go. His only solid idea was, after all that had happened, he absolutely didn't want to stay in Las Vegas. There was something horrifying about the moving crowd in the Hawaiian shirts and leisure clothes. They were so dumbly, obliviously alive.

Not that he'd made any real effort to get out of town. He hadn't booked a ticket, he hadn't even looked at schedules. His first impulse had been to head back to New York. New York, however, meant work, maybe another contract, the possibility of more deaths. For the moment that was out of the question. He'd considered staying with Joe Stalin, except that Joe Stalin probably thought that he was dead. He couldn't face the prospect of explaining all that had happened since they'd last seen each other. At the same time, the idea of a holiday was totally absurd. A week earlier, he firmly believed that the world had been burned to a nuclear crisp. It was nearly impossible to accept the idea of laying on a beach somewhere sipping some misbegotten drink that came with a baby umbrella in it while looking at women in tans and bikinis. He felt hollow and the only available solution seemed to be to fill the hollowness with whiskey.

"Give me another, will you?"

The bartender looked doubtful.

"Are you sure about that, pilgrim?"

Vickers' eyes became don't-mess-with-me slits.

"Sure I'm sure."

"Suit yourself."

The bartender poured him another double shot and ran Vickers' credit card through the machine for the fifth time. The Las Vegas airport dressed their bartenders like parodies of Mississippi gamblers, string ties and brocade vests. Vickers wasn't prepared to take flack from anyone in a string tie. As he filled the hollowness with more scotch, it was replaced by hostility. He had a suspicion that as well as being in some kind of delayed shock, he was probably also suffering a multiple comedown from all the mind alterers he'd been fed in the bunker. Why else would the bartender sound like John Wayne? John Wayne hovered protectively.

"Don't care to fly, huh?"

"I don't even have a ticket."

"Think maybe you ought to go home or something?"

Home? For Vickers the concept was weird. The hollowness

expanded as he realized that the bunker was the only place that he could think of as home. He was like an ex-con, just out of the penitentiary. Somehow he had to get a grip on himself. His first task was to deal with Big John.

"Listen, I'm just sitting here in your bar getting drunk as a skunk. If you don't like it just tell me and I'll go someplace else, otherwise just keep pouring and if I get out of line, call the cops."

The bartender seemed to be weighing Vickers in the balance. Finally he made up his mind. John Wayne ran out and he was nothing but cold.

"I'm sorry, sir. I really don't think I can serve you any more."

Vickers had a compact .32 auto in a shoulder holster under the jacket of his brand new suit. For a moment he was tempted to shoot the bartender. In an instant of clarity he realized that there was a certain logic in not turning the entire bunker population loose en masse. They were all at least as crazy as he was. He resisted the urge to homicide and instead swallowed what was left of his drink in one burning gulp.

"If that's the case, fuck you."

"You have a nice day too, sir."

He slid off the barstool and started a little unsteadily in the direction of the check-in machines. The Intercontinental Pyramid dominated the skyline beyond the nearest expanse of panoramic glass. He remembered how he'd rappeled down from the fifty-fifth floor and the urge to get the hell out of Las Vegas became overwhelming. Then the voice came from behind.

"Hey Mort, wait up!"

Vickers twitched. He had to fight down a reckless impulse to go for his gun. He slowly turned. A woman in a red dress was hurrying after him. Her outfit had the kind of wide shoulders and narrow skirt that were fashionable before he'd gone into the bunker. A tiny matching hat with a veil was perched on the top of her short dark hair. What was this all about? Then he recognized the face.

"Johanna?"

He'd never seen her in makeup and real clothes. She was really quite stunning.

"What the fuck are you doing here? How did you get out of the bunker?"

"I've had more gracious receptions."

"I'm sorry; I'm drunk. The bartender just refused to serve me any more booze. I'm not sure I'm quite ready to be back in the world. How are you doing?"

"I think it's fabulous."

"Fabulous?"

"Yeah, fabulous. I can wear clothes again, makeup. I had my hair done and a facial. I've had about a hundred showers. Unrationed water is quite a novelty. You can't believe what a relief it is to be out of that blue uniform and have space to move around."

"How did you get out? I thought they were only letting people out in ones and twos."

"I got myself to the head of the line."

"How did you do that?"

"I told them that I was your girl friend. I figured that after carrying a torch for so long I ought to make some use of you. You'll be flattered to hear that your name actually cut some ice."

"I'm a fucking hero."

"You're a fucking bastard."

"Really?"

"I spent more than one night pining for you."

"It was an impossible situation."

"Not for you men it wasn't. Sexually you were in hog heaven."

"Jesus Christ."

Vickers turned and started to stagger away. Johanna put a hand on his arm.

"Wait, Mort. I'm sorry. Don't go off this way."

Vickers halted. His legs suddenly felt weak. A wave of self-pity threatened to engulf him.

"I'm sorry too."

Johanna raised an eyebrow.

"Do you actually have anywhere to go?"

Vickers stared at her blearily.

"Go?"

"Or are you just planning to hang around the airport drinking yourself unconscious?"

Vickers squinted belligerently at her.

"I've got a thousand places to go."

"You really don't know what to do, do you, now this adventure's at an end. You look like a little boy lost."

"I don't need this."

Her expression abruptly softened.

"Do you even have the approximation of a home?"

Vickers swayed, his smile was lopsided.

"I've got some new clothes and an awful lot of money. That's all I need.

"Why don't you come to Los Angeles with me. Contec is putting me in the Beverly Wiltshire while they figure out what to do with me. It could be fun. You can relax, work out some of the knots."

Vickers was very tempted but he wasn't quite ready to admit it.

"I don't want to go to Los Angeles. There are too many people who don't like me in LA to make it very relaxing.'

"That's a pity. I don't like to see you drunk, wandering around on your own like this."

The only word was vulnerable. He didn't want to be drunk and wandering around like this either.

"I . . . why don't you come with me."

"You don't know where you're going."

Details of a flight to Rio came up on the Faxcast.

"Rio. Come to Rio with me. We can lay on the beach and look at the sky."

"Rio?"

"The plane leaves in forty-five minutes."

"What about Contec? I'm supposed to go to LA."

"I can square anything with Contec. Contec loves me."

"You're sure."

Now Vickers was becoming expansive.

"Sure I'm sure."

He held out his arm. Johanna hesitated just long enough and then she sighed and took it. Arm in arm they walked toward the Amjet check-in.

"Do you really have a great deal of money?"

"A great deal."

"That's nice."

"Isn't it."

"Maybe we could even make love in the toilet of the plane."

Vickers shook his head.

"It's going to be a long time before I do anything in an enclosed space."

BESTSELLING
Science Fiction
and
Fantasy